Marsali T\_\_\_\_\_ \_\_\_\_ \_\_ \_\_\_\_ _____, _____ Her family

En\_\_\_\_\_ a\_ \_\_ _____, \_\_\_\_ a year o\_ _____ training and took up \_\_\_\_ \_\_\_ \_\_\_\_, teaching English and French to secondary-school children in Aith, Shetland. Gradually her role expanded to doing drama too, and both primary- and secondary-school pupils have won prizes performing her plays at the local Drama Festival. Some of these plays were in Shetlandic, the local dialect.

*Death from a Shetland Cliff* is the eighth novel in her much-loved Shetland Sailing Mysteries series.

# DEATH FROM A SHETLAND CLIFF

## MARSALI TAYLOR

ACCENT

First published in 2020 by Headline Accent
An imprint of HEADLINE PUBLISHING GROUP

1

Cataloguing in Publication Data is available from the British Library

ISBN 978 1 4722 7593 6

Typeset in 10.5/13pt Bembo Std by Jouve (UK), Milton Keynes

Printed and bound in Great Britain by Clays Ltd, Elcograf S.p.A.

Headline's policy is to use papers that are natural, renewable and recyclable
products and made from wood grown in well-managed forests and other
controlled sources. The logging and manufacturing processes are expected
to conform to the environmental regulations of the country of origin.

HEADLINE PUBLISHING GROUP
An Hachette UK Company
Carmelite House
50 Victoria Embankment
London
EC4Y 0DZ

www.headline.co.uk
www.hachette.co.uk

To Mr Craig Parnaby,
Consultant Colorectal Surgeon MBChB MSc FRCS
with my heartfelt gratitude for his skill in operating on a serious
pelvic infection, and his dedication to every aspect of my aftercare.
Now I'm determined to be well again!

After cancer problems while I was writing *The Trowie Mound Murders*,
I'd hoped for peace, healthwise, but eight years on a simmering
pelvic infection blew out of control. Thank you to Miss Weber for
her emergency operation in Lerwick, and thank you to Mr Macfar-
lane, Leona, Sue and all the staff of Ward 1 for their care of me here
in Shetland until I could be flown down for the ten-hour operation
by Mr Parnaby and his team at the Aberdeen Royal Infirmary.
Thank you to Mr Parnaby, his anaesthetist Dr Alastair Hunter, and
his ward round team, led by Dr Duncan Scrimgeour; thank you to
Dr Marzoug who performed the second draining of Collection 1
using CT scanning.

I was in the Aberdeen Royal Infirmary for three weeks, and at a
strange time: spring 2020. When I went in the world was normal.
There was no wifi in the ARI, but my daughter, who flew up from
London for the op, told me of closed schools and empty supermarket
shelves; later phone calls added working from home and lockdown in
the house; my husband, who stayed at CLAN Aberdeen throughout
my time in hospital, described marked shop floors, social distancing
and restrictions on going out. Alas for our plans for him to bring me
juice, fruit and a supply of books from the Oxfam bookshop; it was
the first shop to close, and halfway through my time, hospital visitors
were banned (thank goodness for the complete works of Jane Austen
on Kindle). Wifi was set up then, and the news, FB and emails gave
me my first encounter with a changed world.

During this time the care and support of the ward staff was particularly important. Thank you to the stoma nurses, Christine, Effie and Emma. Thank you to Ailsa, Amy, Becca, Bethany, Carla, Carys, Dean, Debbie, Donna, Fiona, Grace, Katie and Katy, Lindsay, the two Lorraines, Lynne, Martin, Sandra and all the other staff of the big Ward 206, and the individual wards on the other side (naturally I had a shot at getting Covid symptoms, and had to be isolated in case). Thank you for your expertise, your kindness, your warm friendliness; thank you for pressing me with juice and snacks when I had no appetite; thank you for your smiles and encouraging comments as I tottered round the ward, first on a zimmer frame then on my own two feet. You made all the difference to my time at the ARI.

Thank you all.

# I

# The Starting Line

In a sailing race, the start is across an imaginary line on the water between two buoys. The line is at right angles to the wind. The committee boat will hoist a flag at five minutes to go, a second flag at four minutes, one flag will be lowered at one minute, and the second at go. A gun will be fired, or a hooter sounded, with each flag movement.

# Chapter One

Wednesday 20th August

*HW 00.17 (1.5); LW 06.33 (0.5); HW 15.54 (1.4); LW 18.39 (0.5)*

*Sunrise 04.32, sunset 19.44; moonrise 15.21, moonset 22.18.*

*Gibbous moon.*

**ben-end:** the bedroom of a two-roomed cottage, or the 'best' room, if there are bedrooms upstairs [Scandinavian, *ben*, the inner or better room of a house]

'I was wondering,' my friend Magnie said, 'if you'd mebbe come and check oot me cousin Tamar's hoose wi' me.'

It was a bonny late summer afternoon at the marina. We'd checked over the red-sailed Mirrors for the bairns' next practice for the Junior Interclub, which was to be held here at Brae a week on Saturday, run simultaneously (just to keep things interesting) with our own Pico regatta. Now we were sitting on the slatted-wood benches in the cockpit of my *Khalida*, having a three-o'clock cup of tea.

It was good to be home in Shetland, and back aboard my own boat. *Sørlandet*, the Norwegian tall ship I worked aboard, was based in Kristiansand, but since we were sailing all over the place I'd decided it was easiet just to keep *Khalida* in Brae, where Magnie could keep an eye on her for me. She was the smallest yacht in the marina, and the most old-fashioned, but I looked with satisfaction at the neatly folded mainsail above us, and the gleaming wood and brushed navy cushions in her cabin after this morning's clean-out.

Cat was up on the foredeck, washing his white paws after a foray along the ebb, and the marina seal was sculling along the sterns of the yachts opposite us. It was all beautifully peaceful after four months of being second mate aboard a ship filled with up to seventy trainees.

I wriggled my back into a more comfortable position against the wire guard rails, and put my feet up on the opposite bench. 'Do I ken your cousin Tamar?'

'She's the lady o' the Ladie,' Magnie said, and chuckled to himself at the joke.

I nodded southwards towards the narrow channel between Brae and the 'White City' of Aith. 'The Ladie down at Houbansetter? The crofthouse looking over the sound?'

Magnie nodded, and settled into yarn mode. 'My cousin Tamar, she's the last o' the older generation o' the Irvines o' the Ladie. Her mother's mother was first cousin to me grandmother, but she's a piece older as me.'

Given that Magnie was now in his seventies, although you'd never have guessed it from the spryness of him, that made her a good age. Magnie's pause suggested he was working it out. 'Yea, she'll be into her nineties.' He waved that away with one hand. 'Sharp as a tack, though. There was never any doiting in the Irvine side. Anyway, she had a fall twartree weeks ago, getting up in the night, and broke her hip. She's in Wastview, but she's champing to get oot o' there.'

'Wastview?'

'The Care Centre over at Walls. The hospital threw her out two days after the accident, but they said she couldna come straight back to the house on her own, so it had to be Wastview until they had the Occupational Therapy and Physio set up, coming to visit her, and that takes a bit longer, apparently, for folk "outwith central areas".' He went momentarily from Shetland dialect into English as he quoted some doctor. 'But they need the bed now, and one of the lasses that works there said she had the dentist in Brae, and she'd put her home on the way. Tomorrow. I said I'd go over and check everything was ready for her.' He gave me a sideways look out of his pebble-green eyes. 'I thought maybe you might come alang. A woman's eye, all that.'

4

Given that I'd lived on a series of boats for the last fifteen years, since I was sixteen, I didn't see why just being female qualified me for the post of Chief Inspector of Housework, especially since Magnie's crofthouse was kept as spick and span as it ever had been when his mother was alive. 'When were you thinking of going over?'

'No time like now, if you're no' busy.'

'Nothing happening here until the bairns in the evening,' I agreed, and rose to rinse the mugs. Ten minutes later, I was jolting along in Magnie's mustard-yellow Fiat, around the head of the voe, along the broad road south to Voe, and onto the single track towards Aith. We drove past the loch where we'd met the njuggle last winter, past the little cluster of houses at Gonfirth, turned right onto the South Voxter road, and stopped to open the gate to a road going into the hills, rich with royal purple heather. We squeezed past a red hire car belonging to some tourist walker who didn't quite understand about passing places, and round a double corner to the view over the Sound o' Houbansetter.

It was a stretch of water I knew well. It looked wider from up here than it felt sailing through it. Before us was the sound itself, the narrow passage between Busta voe to the north and Aith voe to the south. From the opposite shore, the Blade of Papa Little beckoned, a long, crooked sandbank waiting to catch the keels of unwary yachts. The tide was three-quarters out; the shore glistened with dark orange weed. The Hippopotami, a jagged pair of isolated rocks on the other side of the sound, stood out dark against the grey-blue water. It looked a lovely spot, with the Ward of Papa Little green against the blue sky, but the wind funnelling through the sound flecked the dancing waves with white. It would be a cold, exposed place in a flying northerly gale.

Magnie parked the car behind a scarlet runabout that I took to be Tamar's. I got out and looked around. There had once been a community in these few acres of land, with three families scraping a living from the croft and the sea. There was green pasture below the houses, and rough grazing above; the heather moor, studded with great boulders, began at the hill dyke. Only the Ladie was still intact.

The other two had regressed to bare walls, with gaping doorways and gables stretching to the sky, and the remains of stone dykes enclosing them. A flock of Shetland sheep grazed around them, black, grey, rust-brown. Quiensetter, that was the house on the other side of the jetty, and Houbansetter was beyond Tamar's, all three fine and handy for the Eid or Voe shop in the days when everything was done by water, but left stranded at the end of a rough track when the world turned to wheels.

The substantial stone-built jetty was recent, and still in use. The tarmac road stopped level with Tamar's house, but a wide gravel track ran on down to the pier area. There had been several salmon cages in the voe through my childhood; they were gone now, but there were three lines of mussels on this side of the sound, and another five opposite, at the opening to Eid voe. The jetty area had been tidied up to just one Portakabin and two metal containers, several boats in different stages of repair, salmon feed bins of mussel ropes, and a workhorse aluminium motorboat tied to the pier. A tawny cat disappeared quickly under the hut as we approached.

There was a trodden path to Tamar's door, leading across a stone-slab bridge over the burn that trickled down beside the gate into the garden. A brown Shetland wren landed on the drystone dyke that enclosed it, bobbed at us, chittered indignantly, then flew into a cranny between two grey-lichened stones.

Tamar's house had been refurbished within an inch of its life. It still had the bones of a traditional crofthouse, with house, barn and byre all in one long line, but there was an extension on the back, dormer windows looking out over the sound, and a glass sit-ootery running along the front. It was whitewashed so thickly you could have steered by it on a moonless night – Magnie's doing, I'd have betted, for his own, just visible diagonally across the voe, was equally eye-blinding. A wheelbarrow sat by the front door, ready to be pushed back and forward to the road.

'Does your cousin really manage to barrow her shopping back from the car?'

'Oh yea.' Magnie put the key in the back extension door, turned it, and pushed the door open. 'She's kept herself spry. She'll be itching to be walking along the banks again. She has a niece and a nephew an' all, the bairns o' her late brothers, and twa sets o' great-nieces and nephews to do the heavy fetching and carrying for her. There now.'

He snicked on the light, and we came into the back porch. This bit of the house had the usual refurbished crofthouse arrangement, a toilet and utilities room tacked on to the back of the house below, a bathroom above. There were shelves of tins and jam jars above the washing machine worktop, an upright fridge-freezer, and a row of coat hooks on the wooden v-lining.

Magnie led me through into the kitchen/living area – the *but-end*, you'd call it in Shetlan. Tamar had resisted change here. The cream-coloured Rayburn still squatted in the middle of one wall, with a china sink beside it. There was a dresser with rose and white plates and a pine table and two chairs by the window, with the usual on-land clutter at one end of the table: opened letters, a mug of pens, a china pillbox, a whistle on a lanyard. One chair was pushed in under, as if it was never used; the other stood aslant. There was no sign of tidying up needed: the worksurfaces were clear, the clean dishes stacked in the draining rack by the sink, and the pans in a tripod rack, lids upturned on each one.

'Twartree weeks?' I said. 'We'd likely need to check the fridge and the breadbin.'

'I suppose,' Magnie said, without enthusiasm. 'There'll be black bags under the sink.'

I dug a bin bag out, and opened the fridge door. It said a lot about the way modern food was filled with preservatives; even after three weeks, there was very little that would have been condemned on board a boat. The pack of mince had to go, there was a touch of mould on the opened cheese, and I didn't even try opening the milk, but the red and orange peppers were still remarkably firm, and the yoghurt was within its sell-by date.

Magnie rustled a carrier bag at me. 'I'm brung milk and fresh bread.' He handed it to me to be put away, then gestured slantways through the door into the house. 'Her bedroom's upstairs. Her folk were at her to move down, make a new bedroom in the sitting room, but she said she'd slept in a right bedroom all her days, and she was over old to change. Go you, lass, and see if you can find clean sheets and a nightie for her, while I get the Rayburn lit.'

'She's never still working with peats!' I said.

'Na, na, oil, though the Highland Fuel lorry's no' exactly enthusiastic about coming over this road.'

I could imagine it wouldn't be. I went out into the passage between the two sides of the house, and saw straight away why Tamar's family were worried about her upstairs bedroom. The stairs were best grade traditional crofthouse, with a gradient similar to a ladder's, going straight up between wooden walls. Someone had added a sturdy bannister opposite the usual hand-rope. The stairs ended in a two metres by one landing. The middle door was the upstairs bathroom over the extension, and the bedroom on the left was obviously a guest room, neat and bare, with twin beds covered with camberwick bedspreads. I went into the one on the right, Tamar's room, feeling like an intruder. I didn't even know her – but I suspected Magnie felt it wasn't proper that he should be making her bed, or handling her nightie.

It was a bonny room, painted white, with the ceiling sloping down to a metre from the floor. That last metre was lined on this first wall with three long shelves of older paperbacks. Above them was a traditional skylight, with an iron rod sticking out from it. I pushed it open for some air, and looked around. There was a bareness about the room that pleased me; the mantelpiece had only two scaddiman's heids on it, with a little metal tripod between them, and the room's one painting above it, an unfinished drawing of a horse. My policeman lover Gavin would like it, I thought, going over to look. His family farm in the remote Highlands included two Highland ponies, gentle enough beasts, he'd assured me, but I was still wary of large animals that had a bite at one end and a kick at the other. The picture was about thirty centimetres square, red chalk on yellowed paper, a fiery, impatient charger with a strong, arched neck and flared nostrils, like the warhorses in medieval paintings. The muscles were so beautifully shaded you felt you could run your hand over the satin skin, but the legs were only sketched. One front hoof pawed the air.

Otherwise, there was the bed and a chest of drawers beside it, with a jug and basin and a businesslike reading lamp on top. A pot-bellied stove crouched in the fireplace, and a pile of clothes waited on the chair in the far corner. The dormer window had a padded seat, with a seriously expensive long-lens camera set at one side, and spyglasses on the sill. Tamar could sit there to watch the stars, or the northern lights, or the sun dipping down behind Papa Little and rising again half an hour later at midsummer.

It looked all as she must have left it: a book tumbled from the bedside table, the bedcovers pushed sideways, the mattress hauled to a slant, as if she'd caught at it as she fell. The medics must have had an awkward job manoeuvring their stretcher down those stairs. I found a clean downie cover with matching pillowcases in the bottom drawer of the chest, and a pair of warm pyjamas in cheerful colours. I was just coaxing the last downie corner in when I heard Magnie give an exclamation, followed by, 'Lass, come you here and look at this!'

I abandoned the downie, and went downstairs. Magnie was in the sitting room below the guest room, the ben end. It was obviously the 'good room' where Tamar brought the minister, should there still be one for this area, should he or she come to call, with an armchair on each side of the open fireplace, a mahogany desk with brass handles, and an old-fashioned china cabinet set in one corner of the room. Magnie had pulled down the lid of the desk, and opened both drawers, as if he was looking for something.

'What're you lost?' I asked.

He shook his head. 'I'm lost nothing.' He spread a hand round. 'This is how I found it.'

I looked around and saw what he was seeing: the two desk drawers pulled right out, and the door of the china cabinet swinging open. The woman who'd scoured her kitchen before going to bed wouldn't have left it like this.

We stared at each other. I felt sick with rage at the idea of someone taking advantage of an old lady's accident to raid her house, and Magnie's face mirrored my feelings. 'Someone's been in here,' he said. He turned on his heel, looking around. 'But how . . . ?'

He went out into the glass porch which ran along the front of the house. I watched through the sitting-room window as he rattled the door and checked the windows. He returned, shaking his head. 'It's all locked up tight. They'd have done that, the ambulance folk. She had her keys in the hospital with her.'

'The bedroom window was locked,' I said. 'I opened it for air. And what were they looking for? Money?'

'I suppose,' Magnie said dubiously. 'It's kinda out o' the way for an opportunist thief.' We looked at the neat piles of papers in the desk drawers, the letters docketed into pigeonholes above. In the china cabinet, there was a selection of ornaments that looked to have been brought back by a seaman ancestor, Chinese plates, a coloured pheasant, an irridescent shell, and a wooden box, with the lid ajar. 'They looked in the box too.' He picked it up in his gnarled hands, shook his head, and gave another look around. 'The TV's still there, and the DVD player. Her laptop's in the sit-ootery.'

'It's not how I'd imagine an opportunist burglary to look,' I said slowly. 'It's all very tidy, as if someone was frightened of making a mess. Frightened of making a noise. Searching silently. For loose cash?' My eyes returned to the desk, then to the wooden box. 'Papers?'

'Let's make a cup o' tea,' Magnie said, 'and think about it.'

We took the mugs out into the sit-ootery. It ran the length of the house, with the afternoon sun streaming full in on the pots of geraniums and vine with its bunches of grapes. I tried one; it was surprisingly sweet. There was a couch along the wall, where we sat down. Just thirty metres away, the sun glistened on the crinkled leaves of oarweed revealed as the tide ebbed. Three herring gulls stood on patrol on the Blade.

'I didn't ask Tamar how she'd come to fall,' Magnie said. 'I just took it that she'd got up to pee and tripped. But she'd never a locked the back door during the night. None o' us old folk do that.'

I gave him a questioning look.

'In case o' you taking ill or dying in the night,' he explained, with hard-headed realism. 'So that folk could get in without breaking the door.' He nodded over to our right, up towards Brae. 'Since we were both living alone, we kinda kept an eye on each other.'

I looked across the water at his house. 'Lights on and off, that kind of thing?'

He nodded. 'Easy enough to just give a phone call if there's no sign o' life when there should be.'

'So, maybe,' I said, 'she heard someone in the house, and got up, and then fell, and the noise of that scared them away.'

Magnie was silent for a moment, staring out across the glinting water. 'I dinna like it. It's no' what we're used to.'

I agreed with that. Burglars coming in at dark of night to ransack an old lady's papers . . . it didn't happen in Shetland. Oh, yes, in Lerwick, there was a bit of opportunistic petty thieving, usually with drugs involved, but not here in the country. Not in a remote cottage like this. I thought about being a burglar. You could open drawers more quietly than you could close them. You'd open each one, check it, and then, just before you left, you'd close them with silent care, and leave – with what you came for? Without it? And if he, she, hadn't found what they wanted, would they be back, once the house was open again?

'I don't suppose . . .' Magnie and I both began together. I gestured him to continue. 'I don't suppose you'd think about maybe bringing your *Khalida* over to the jetty here for a start? Just to keep an eye on things?'

'That's what I was thinking too. Is there nobody else who could stay for a bit? Family?'

'She won't have them. She says they worry her quite enough on visits, and Loretta cleaning, and to have them in the house wi' radios playing and the TV blaring non-stop, would fret her into a decline.' He gave me a sideways look from his pebble-green eyes. 'But she might have you, if you'd consider it. She's aye interested in what you're up to. She was never a conventional one herself.'

'Oh?'

He didn't need encouragement. 'Yea, yea, you ask her all about it. She left Shetland at fifteen, and worked to a big hoose south for a bit, then drave a taxi in London. After that she travelled all over, taking photographs for the newspapers. She came back to London in the Swinging Sixties, got taken on by the BBC, worked wi' David Attenborough for a start, then she did a wildlife book travelling through Canada. She musta been well over seventy when she came back here. Now she's settled down watching otters.'

It all sounded very interesting, but not a life that would lead to incriminating papers. I glanced over my shoulder at the opened drawers. 'If they'd got what they came for, wouldn't they have closed the drawers again, so that nobody knew they'd been?'

'Unless she disturbed them just after they'd found it.'

I made a face. 'I dinna like it. What's the depth at that jetty?'

'Deep enough for you, I'm pretty sure, though you'll need a fender-board, to keep you off the stones.'

'I have one.' I looked at the jetty for a moment, assessing; rough built of stones, but with several workmanlike bollards, for the salmon boats to moor to. It looked like I could lie there comfortably, with a gangplank. 'You ask her if she'll have me. If she thinks I'll be useful, I'll sail over tomorrow.'

# Chapter Two

**ness:** a headland [Old Norse, *nes*]

It would be dark quickly this evening. The light clouds on the horizon had gathered in until the sky was overcast with large, black cumulus. We got the bairns out as soon as we could, three pairs in Mirrors, and another four in the neon-pink sailed Picos. As racing practice it was a failure; they seemed not to have a watch between them, and buoys were rounded leaving a gap you could drive a yacht through. We had several shots at starting, until they all managed to get over the line within twenty seconds of the hooter, then a bit of mark work, setting the skippers to go close enough for their crews to pat the buoy as they rounded it.

By quarter past seven the light was already thickening, the water darkening. The four white lights of the astroturf pitch blazed out; the sun lit the windows of the houses facing the water and made a pale gold path across our triangular course. Below the houses, there was a cropped field, the short new grass vivid green.

We did two more triangles to get spinnaker practice in, nagging those who couldn't be bothered to fly their little balloons of green, orange, and blue. It was an uphill struggle. Still, they'd get competitive (too late) when they saw their fellow sailors at the Interclub. Next week we'd need to put Magnie out in a Mirror, to give them something to race against. He'd been my sailing teacher twenty years ago, and a mean competitive skipper in his day. Even single-handed he'd have been round that course and over the line before the first of them had finished the triangle.

We got them ashore just after eight, and left them washing the boats while Magnie and I retrieved the buoys. The gold flush along the bottom of the eastern cumulus faded to grey, and the clouds jostled over the sun, leaving only a chink of bright sky. The wind was soft, the water warm as I reached over to catch the nylon stem of the neon mooring buoys. Then it was time for drinking chocolate, and a bit of rope work, and signing off log books. It was black dark by 9, though the sky still showed chinks of duck-egg blue, and the water gleamed between the hills. I gathered up the books and pieces of rope, poured the last of the chocolate into a mug for myself, and headed for the bar. 'They're going to have to wake up next Saturday, against Sandwick and Walls and Lerwick. I thought the modern bairn was supposed to be keen and competitive.'

'Na, na,' Magnie said, 'no' these days. It warps their psyches, or something. It must be very discouraging for their teachers, especially the sports ones. Kinda hard to be non-competitive in hockey or on sports day.'

'They can give everyone prizes, like *Alice in Wonderland*.'

'Well, we're going to do that wi' the Picos,' Magnie said. 'I printed out the list dastreen. Skipper prize, crew prize, hat-trick prize, standing start prize, they'll surely all get one of the medals by the end o' it.'

'Do our best,' I agreed, mindful of modern thought. 'But the Junior Interclub is old-style one prize only for the best club.' I set my mug down, and was just about to go and wash it, then head for *Khalida*, when the club door opened, and a stranger came in.

One look at him said 'crofter'. He was in his fifties, wearing jeans and a gansey in brown stripes of Fair Isle pattern on a white ground, but he gave the impression of just having taken his boiler suit and yellow rubber boots off. His cheeks were pinkly scrubbed, his thinning hair brushed back, and his fair brows were drawn together in a worried frown, which cleared when he saw us. It wasn't done to launch straight into what he'd come for, so he commented on the weather and bought a pint, and Magnie introduced him as Joanie o' Cole.

14

Cole was even further off the beaten track than the Ladie. The road we'd turned off to get to Tamar's house continued northwards to Cole, a crofthouse set looking out across Cole Deep, the round pool of deep sea that was cradled between Papa Little, Muckle Roe and Linga. From a sea point of view, there was the headland on the Brae side of the Ladie, there were steep banks, and beyond that, just round the curve, was Cole. I betted the Highland Fuels lorry didn't like going there either.

Joanie settled himself with an elbow on the bar. 'I'm blyde to find the two o' you here. I was wanting a word wi' you.' He shuffled slightly on the bar. 'I'm no' wanting to make a total fool o' myself, if it turns out to be nothing.' He took a gulp from his pint, and settled into his story. 'I was out walking over the hill, checking on where the sheep were, before we drive the hill to get the lambs off.'

The sheep sales started in mid-September, and involved every crofter for that area walking through with their dogs, rounding up all the sheep on that bit of scattald, separating them out into who owned what, taking the lambs off their mothers, and driving the ewes back onto the hill again.

'I got up to the top o' Cole Ness, and sat me down a start, just looking oot over. It was that clear a day I could make out the houses on Papa Stour, and even see the clefts on the hills o' Foula. Well, I had me dog wi' me, and he sat at me feet, then got bored and snuffled about a bit, and then he lifted his nose and gave this queer, mournful howl, then he began sniffing along and following some trail straight towards the Skro.' He looked at Magnie, who nodded, then round to me. 'You maybe dinna ken it by that name, Cass. It's the deep geo just around the corner from the point o' the Ladie, facing towards Linga. There's the cleft in the hill, wi' a bit o' a burn running down from above, and then the peerie beach at the bottom. I thought maybe there'd been a sheep gone over the banks, though I widna expect him to behave like that for that, so I followed him.' He took another swallow of his pint. 'And when I came to the head o' the geo, and looked down over, then there was something black lying down there. I had me spyglasses wi' me, and I tried to get a

15

closer look, but I couldna see right, it was lying partly under an overhang o' the bank, in a shadow. But I'm faerd—' He lifted his head and looked at us. 'I'm faerd it might be a body.'

There was a long silence.

'So,' he finished, 'I thought I'd come and see, Magnie, if we could maybe go over there in your boat tomorrow. I'd a taken me own one but it's laid up, with the engine in pieces all over the floor of her.' He paused, looked sideways at us, then finished in a rush. 'An' I didna fancy going on me own, but I didna want to phone the police either, in case it was a dead seal, half-rotted, so that the flippers looked like fingers, or a stuffed boilersuit scarecrow that had blown away in a gale. I thought I'd better have a closer look first. If it was someen, a fisherman lost at sea maybe, though he wisna clad in oilskins, then a day's delay'll no hurt him. I could see that.' He lifted his glass again and tipped the last of the pint down his throat, then set the empty glass on the bar with fingers that trembled slightly.

'Yea, yea,' Magnie said, 'that'll be no bother. When would you like to go? The morn's morn?'

Joanie nodded. 'I suppose. I set a flag, wi' a bit of heather stem and me handkie, on the hill above it, so that it'll be easy to find again.'

'Leave here at ten o'clock?' Magnie turned to me. 'Will that suit you, Cass?'

I jerked my head up. 'You're no' needing me!' In these last two years I'd seen far more dead bodies than I'd ever wanted to. The idea of going to look at one voluntarily didn't appeal. 'I'd need to go and moor up at the Ladie, ready for Tamar coming home.'

'You canna do that mid-morning,' Magnie said. 'Low water's at seven.'

I glanced over my shoulder at the water just beginning to lap its way up the dinghy slip, and conceded that one. 'I want low water to see what I'm doing.'

'There you are, then, right on the spot. Tell you what,' Magnie conceded, 'you don't need to go on the beach. We'll gather the poor soul up, and you can phone the police. You'll ken the right things to say.'

Joanie nodded in agreement. I could see I wasn't going to get out of it. 'About half past ten, then,' I said, added a goodnight, and headed for *Khalida*.

Outside, the wind had fallen to a cold breath on my bare arm. The sky was not yet dark; there was a band of lavender along the horizon, shading up to creamy-blue that gradually deepened to indigo. Three stars glittered. Even as I watched, the lavender darkened to heather purple.

It was dark inside *Khalida*, with the marina pontoon lights casting a slanted silver beam through the long windows. I brushed my teeth out in the cockpit, teased my dark curls out of their daytime plait, then lit the oil lamp and set the kettle on to boil. It wasn't cold yet, but I would take a day or two to acclimatise to being back on board my small, unheated boat, with the forehatch open to let Cat come and go as he pleased, instead of in the warmth of *Sørlandet*, with a radiator in every cabin. The plus side of her size, of course, was that by the time the kettle had boiled, the gas had also warmed up the whole cabin. I put my hot-water bottle in my berth, with my nightshirt wrapped round it, then focused on what I'd need for the morning. I'd moor bow to the prevailing wind, which was southerly for the moment, so I tied extra fenders along my port guard rail, ready to flip over when we got to the jetty. The fender board was buried under oars and light-airs sails up in the forepeak, so I dug it out, and laid it on deck. Cat watched with interest from the cabin roof, whiskers twitching; he knew all about preparing for sea. I got my mooring ropes out from the cockpit locker, and fastened them to the cleats, under the ropes holding me in the pontoon. The boathook was all ready on the cabin roof. That should do for preparation. I went back below, and sat down at the prop-leg table. Cat clambered into my lap and treadled for a bit before curling around.

'It's all very well being a good citizen,' I told him. 'Of course we need to let this poor man's family know he's been found. I just wish they'd picked someone else to do the phoning.'

Gavin, on our goodnight phone call, was inclined to be sceptical. 'What do you mean, he's found a dead body and not reported it yet?'

'He isn't sure it is one. He doesn't want to be lampooned in every squad at the Brae Up Helly A next year as the man who reported a scarecrow to the police.'

His voice teased. 'And they thought you'd know a dead body if you saw one.'

'Experience tells. But we've agreed I'll guard the boat while they inspect. How's your day been?'

His sigh travelled through the miles between us. 'Paperwork. More paperwork. Well, computer work. HOLMES, you know, the big Home Office computer that links every crime in the country. If this is promotion, give me the old-fashioned beat any day. At least you get to talk to people in between filling in forms about what they said, and what you did, and who you handed it on to, and what they reported back, and what action you authorised on their report, and who you detailed to carry out that action, and the computer reminding you if they haven't done it by then . . .' He ran out of breath. 'I wish I was joking.'

I knew he wasn't. 'Life at sea's getting like that too. Did you know I have to have a passage plan for every time I leave the marina? It can be as simple as a scrawled "Heading towards Houbansetter" in the log, but I'm supposed to have it, in case HM Coastguard stop me and check. Then there's the new e-border as it applies to yachts.'

'Oh yes?'

'We have to fill in a detailed passage plan before leaving the UK, including port of destination and time of arrival. No allowance for a wind shift en route which means you have to go somewhere else, and arrive at a totally different time.' I brooded darkly over that for a moment or two. 'I thought all these upper-class men that run the country were supposed to have a yacht at Cowes.'

'With the actual sailing done by a crew.'

'That would explain it.'

'But if they'd had HOLMES up and running when they were chasing Peter Sutcliffe they'd have caught him sooner and saved several lives.' He paused to think about that for a moment, then spoke more cheerfully. 'On the plus side, it looks like I can get off to join you next weekend. Wednesday to Sunday. My reward for spending a whole week in Newcastle.'

My world brightened instantly. 'Oh, that'll be good. I'll probably be back at Brae by then, not with Magnie's cousin. How d'you fancy helping out with a bairns' regatta?'

'I'll bring my oilskins.' He gave a huge yawn. 'Goodnight, *mo chridhe*. I'll see you soon. Good luck with your body tomorrow.'

# Chapter Three

*HW 00.53 (1.5); LW 07:11 (0.5); HW 13:31 (1.4); LW 19:18 (0.6)*

*Sunrise 04.34, sunset 19.41; moonrise 16.20, moonset 22.59.*

*Moon waning gibbous.*

**geo** or **gyo:** a V-shaped cleft in a coast edge [Old Norse, *gja*]

It would take me half an hour to motor to the jetty. I got up at six, and set off at half past.

Brae was sleeping as I left. There was a long streak of pink between the eastern clouds that gradually faded to ivory. White mist lay over the hills, with tendrils creeping down the gullies gouged out by burns. The green grass was wet with dew, and hexagons of spider-web hung suspended like tent canopies between clumps of grass. A pair of swans sculled along the outer rim of the marina, wings curved upwards, followed by three cygnets. It was very still, with only the wash of a long-passed salmon boat still lapping against the shore. I didn't bother hoisting the sails, but set off under motor, and chugged down the voe to the sound of Houbansetter.

The main pier, at the point between the bays of Houbansetter and Quiensetter, was a substantial jetty, a squared U of great stones filled in with aggregate. From above, I'd seen how the sides sloped outwards below the surface of the water, with waves sucking round the barnacle-whitened rocks. It wouldn't have been my pier of choice – I'd have preferred to anchor off – but if Tamar needed me in the night, I couldn't be a dinghy ride away.

I throttled back to ticking over a hundred yards from the jetty, then went forward, flipped the fenders down, and tied the fender board over them – it was simply a plank that went between them and the rough jetty, much cheaper to replace than a burst fender. My depth right now was five metres. I dropped my anchor over board and edged in: four metres below the keel, three and a half. It levelled off at that. I went past the jetty and reversed to it, then flung a loop of line around the aft bollard, fastened it loosely, and nipped forrard to loop another round the forrard one. Then, with two ends fastened, I spent the next half hour adjusting everything until I was satisfied that she'd stay comfortably at that, with no extra weight on any one cleat, and enough slack to allow for the metre of tide that would be coming in later. That done, I took the anchor line back to the jib winch, tightened it off, and surveyed my arrangements with satisfaction.

Cat had come up into the cockpit to watch proceedings as soon as I'd got the lines on. He knew all about keeping out of the way while I got things organised, but didn't wait for me to rig the gangplank across to the jetty. As soon as I'd stopped going from one end of the boat to the other, pulling in here, letting out there, he leapt lightly ashore, and sat down, giving the place a long look round.

It was worth looking at. My heart swelled with the bonniness of it. *Home.* I hadn't realised how much I'd missed it: these low, green hills all around me, the soft, rich green of sheep-cropped grass, and the light glistening on the olive curves of the kelp at the water's edge, and the rich purple of the heather on Linga. I knew every inch of these waters; I'd spent a good bit of my childhood and teenage years sailing over them in my own Mirror, *Osprey.* Just opposite me were the twin rocks we'd christened the Hippopotami, hidden at high water. After the dinghy races were over, at the Brae and Aith regattas, I'd joined the keel-boat sailors going around Papa Little, and discussed just how close to the Blade we could go at this state of tide. It was fully exposed now, a long spit of sand-brown shingle running out towards the jetty, but the catch was the bend ending it, underwater even now, but only covered by a foot or so, and visible in the line of calm water over it. There were two seagulls standing on it, some thirty metres from the shore, looking as if they were walking on water.

On shore, the Portakabin was clear of my view of Tamar's cottage, and the road down to it. I'd hear any car arriving. Satisfied, I headed below to put the kettle on and have some breakfast. I was just buttering my toast when a caterwauling erupted from shore. I jumped up to look, and saw Cat nose to nose with a large stripey cat. They were both swollen out as far as they could go, with Cat's long grey fur giving him an edge in the size stakes; both sets of ears were back, both tails lashing. I was tempted to interfere by chasing the stripey, but if he was the resident tom there'd be a showdown sooner or later. I looked around, and saw they'd got an audience: there were seven, eight, eleven other cats sitting watching, three stretched along the sun-warmed lengths of salmon cage piping, one peering down from the top of the cabin, several sitting bolt upright on rocks or boats. Salmon farms tended to attract a population of feral cats. These were all colours: the lead stripey, two black, several with patches of stripes on a white ground, a couple of tortoiseshells. Even as I watched, there was a mewing sound from the Portakabin, and a pair of ketlings crawled out from underneath it, one black, one tortoiseshell, and began to chase each other.

I brought my toast up into the cockpit, ready to interfere if Cat looked like getting the worst of any battle. The yowling and tail-lashing had subsided into sitting and staring at each other by the time I heard the brrr of Magnie's engine in the distance. I rinsed out my cup, tipped my toast crumbs overboard, and gave my shore lines a check over. All well.

Magnie curved his boat in beside *Khalida*, with Joanie holding her off as I clambered aboard. She was a traditional double-ended clinker boat, with a small cabin. The engine was underneath a comfortably warm box in the middle of the cockpit. If what Joanie had seen was a body, there would be just enough room to lay it between the engine box and the boat's sides, and he'd already stowed a blue tarpaulin aboard, in case. I settled myself on the engine box.

Joanie looked more worried this morning, as if a night's brooding had made him less convinced that he'd seen anything at all. His hair was hidden under a knitted toorie cap, and he'd reverted to his boilersuit, with a glimpse of grey working gansey at the neck. A well-worn parka was flung down on the cabin seat. Neither he nor Magnie was wearing lifejackets, since there were no bairns to be set a good example to. I gave Magnie a look. 'Could you no' find the lifejackets?'

He sighed, and fished two out from the cabin. 'Here, Joanie, boy, it'll keep Cass happy if we put een o' these on.'

It was quite obvious from the way he fumbled that Joanie wasn't used to wearing one. I looked away as he tangled it behind his back, gazing out at the banks we were approaching. It was a precipitous, treacherous corner, with a toothed bite out of the smooth, green hill as if some sea giant had risen and taken the land in one great gulp that made a curved cliff geo going back thirty metres into the hill. *Skro* was old Norse for a landslide; as we came closer, the tumbles of rock and exposed red earth down its face became clear, ribbed with green grass like textured knitting. The beach at its foot was a curve of pale grey stones heaped above rock-studded sand, with the seaweed line littered with bright plastic: a red fuel container, a yellow buoy, a tangle of green rope.

'It's there,' Joanie said. He pointed with his left hand. 'On the east side o' the geo, under the overhang.'

I looked where he was pointing. The sea had nibbled away at the foot of the cliffs, so that there was a curved space the height of a bent-over child notched into the bank at each side of the beach. There was something long and dark, the length of a log, a bit wider, lying in the shadow. The light gleamed on something white among it.

'Aye aye,' Magnie said. He nosed the boat onto the beach with a gentle scrunch, and I jumped out and held her for the men to follow. They looked, exchanged mouth-pulled-down glances, and set off

23

up the beach, taking it at a steady pace. Pebbles slithered under their rubber boots, then there was the scrunch of seaweed, followed by the clack of the larger stones at the top of the beach. Whoever he was, he was above the high-tide mark. I tensed at the thought. That meant that he wasn't a drowned seaman. He'd fallen down the Skro from the headland above. Reluctantly, I turned my head around to look.

Joanie was standing back while Magnie crouched down beside what was unmistakably a body. I could see the long line of legs in the dark trousers, ending in shoes. One arm was flung out over the beach, the other under him. I didn't try to make out details of the head or hands; if he'd been there a while, the seagulls and ravens would have eaten their fill. There was a slight, sickening smell on the air.

'Hey,' I called. Their heads turned. I hauled the boat up a bit, wound her painter round a handy rock, and set off up the beach. They came a couple of steps towards me, and waited.

'He's above the high-water mark,' I said. I looked then and saw him clearly, a long, dark shape, dressed in black from head to foot, with some of the clothing torn away from the stomach, and a gleam of white bones where one hand had been. 'Isn't he? I mean, is he where the sea couldn't have put him?'

The men exchanged a wary glance, then Magnie nodded. 'Yea, he's well above the black seaweed.'

'That means he fell,' I said. I squinted upwards against the sun, to where the top of the geo was outlined black against the sky. 'Or came here in a boat . . . something else. I don't think we should touch him. I think mebbe it's a matter for the police.'

Magnie still had the starting flags we'd been using with the bairns in his boat. We took one out and I set it at the tide-mark while the men laid the tarpaulin over the body and weighed it down with stones. It wouldn't make any difference now, but it was the only mark of respect we could make towards what had once been a human being, living and moving like us.

I kept a good hold of the prow as the men returned from their work. Magnie was expressionless; Joanie's face had a green tinge under his tan. He fumbled in his boiler-suit pocket and produced a half-bottle of whisky. 'Would you take a dram, boy?'

Magnie shook his head. 'Cass, lass, how about you make us a cup o' tea while we head for somewhere you'll get a phone signal?'

I clambered aboard, and went forward into the little cabin, glad to be moving away from that still thing on the beach. By the time the kettle had boiled, we were bobbing gently off Linga, and the men had recovered enough to get into speculation.

'Two weeks, three at the most,' Magnie was saying. 'You ken yourself, boy, how fast the birds can turn a dead sheep to a skeleton. There was more o' him than that.'

'Above the water line, though, and clad,' Joanie said. 'Below it, the crabs would have been at him, and the peerie fish. And the clothes would have stopped the birds from having a right go at him.'

'They can get through sheep's wool easy enough,' Magnie said.

I passed the tea round, and Joanie grabbed his as if it was a life-saver. He opened his bottle one-handed and poured a generous dram in, then took a long drink. 'Him?' I asked.

Both men nodded. 'He was wearing men's clothes and shoes,' Magnie said.

'And that's another thing,' Joanie said. 'Why was he rigged all in black like that?' He drank the second half of his mugful, and turned to me. 'Black breeks, black shoes, a black jumper, a black toorie-cap. Would you no' say he was up to no good?'

Up to no good? I remembered the opened drawers in Tamar's best room. 'Two or three weeks, you think?'

Magnie's eyes met mine. He gave a little shake of his head, and I fell silent, but I could see he was thinking as I was. Someone had been up to no good in Tamar's house 'twartree weeks ago'. If this was her burglar, what was he doing dead in this geo just around the corner from the house?

I pulled my phone out of my pocket. I had a signal now. It wasn't quite an emergency, so I went for 101, which should give me the local station.

'Hello, Police Scotland, Shetland North, Brae Station.' It sounded like the young officer with the sticky-out ears. 'PC Buchanan speaking.'

'Hello there. It's Cass Lynch here.' I gave him a second to remember who I was. 'I want to report finding a body.'

'A body.' His voice was commendably steady. 'Can you give me more details, Cass?'

'He was spotted from above on the beach of the Skro by Joanie o' Cole.' I suddenly realised I didn't know his other name, and looked across at him enquiringly.

'Irvine,' he said. His voice was slightly too loud. 'John Irvine.'

'John Irvine,' I repeated to the policeman. 'We've marked the place with a white flag on the beach, and we covered the body with a tarpaulin. It's just around the point from the Ladie, on the Linga side.'

'Okay.' I could hear the sound of him scribbling. 'Yes, I ken where you are. What's the easiest way for us to get to the body? Do we need to call the coastguard?'

'From the water,' I said. 'You can take a boat into the beach, easy enough.'

'I can bring them back,' Magnie said, beside me. I repeated that to PC Buchanan, and passed the phone over, then sat back and drank my tea while they arranged where and when. I hadn't touched the body, but it felt like that sweet, decaying smell still clung to my fingers. I shuddered, tipped the rest of my tea into the water and leaned over the boat's side to rinse the mug out and immerse my hands in the salt-clean water.

Magnie handed me my phone back. 'So, they're coming over now, and I'll put them over.'

'They're no' needing me,' I said firmly. 'If you put me back to the Ladie, I can make sure everything's ready for Tamar coming home.'

'We're done that.'

'Someone needs to be there to open the door for her, and make a cup of tea.'

'He'll be wanting to take statements.'

'He can want. He just needs Joanie, about how he came to see the body.'

Joanie grunted gloomily. Magnie shook his head at my stubbornness, but turned his boat around and charged towards Houbansetter, parking the boat alongside *Khalida*. I clambered over into her. 'See you later. Let me know how you get on with the police.'

# Chapter Four

**but-end:** the living room of a two-roomed cottage [Middle English, *bute*, the outer part of a house]

Some sort of truce must have been declared, for Cat was sitting in a patch of sun on the pier, while the stripey was curled up on the step of the Portakabin. It was only quarter to eleven. Around half past twelve, Magnie had said, for the care home wife to put her home. I made another cup of tea, and sat down in the cockpit, feet up on the opposite bench.

It was good to have time to myself like this. I was still enjoying life on board *Sørlandet* of course, but my former lover, Alain, was making me restless. Our relationhip was ten years over, but he'd had a go at resurrecting it when he'd joined *Sørlandet* as third mate at the start of the summer. He wasn't trying to chat me up any more, but he kept including me in his planning for his next voyage on his own yacht, a long-keeled Vancouver which he reckoned would take him round the world. I'd be out on deck, and he'd come up to me with speculation about a great circle route, or the hurricane season in the Caribbean. I could see through him; it was all stuff he knew about already, he was just drawing me in, and the annoying thing was that I could feel myself being drawn as he talked of the long waves of the Atlantic and the warm nights in Santa Lucia, of the song of a hump-backed whale reverberating through the boat's hull and flying fish like birds skimming alongside. I'd done with the life of a wanderer. I was going to have two years aboard *Sørlandet*, sailing those warm seas on the east coast of America, and then I'd come home with her, back to grey northern seas and the simmer dims, the all-night light in summer. If Gavin asked me, I'd become a policeman's wife. We'd have children. If I wanted the wild Atlantic, I'd sail *Khalida* out to the western isles, to St Kilda, to Rockhall.

I shoved myself up, away from the speculation. If I started now, I could make some soup for lunch. The sun dodged out and in of the clouds as I worked, so that one moment the cabin was bathed in sunlight reflected up from the water onto my white ceiling, the next the sea was pewter-grey, and my hands were casting dark shadows over the knife as I chopped the leek and carrots. I'd got it all boiling and turned the gas to simmer when I heard Magnie's engine chugging back towards us. A quick scoit through the companionway showed him passing the nearest end of Linga, with several people on board. I got the spyglasses out. Yes, they'd brought the local doctor as well as PC Buchanan and another uniformed officer. At the back of the boat, not a blonde hair out of place, was Sergeant Peterson, who'd been Gavin's sidekick on his Shetland cases. I might have known she'd be about. Still, I consoled myself, this one was nothing to do with me; at least, I hoped not. A man, all dressed in black, like a burglar, come to grief about the same time as someone had been snooping around Tamar's house . . .

I kept watching. The sun dazzled on the water again. A rainbow arched across the south west, with a fainter shadow below it, which shone in front of the clouds for only a moment, brightening the hill behind it with hazed colours, then evaporated as quickly as it had appeared. Five minutes later I felt the first drops of rain on my face. Cat abandoned his post of vantage over the stripey, strolled across the gangplank, then leapt for cover as soon as he was out of sight, into the cabin and onto the settee berth, shaking his white paws fastidiously.

My soup was almost ready by the time the boat reappeared, with the same load of people, and no sign of the blue tarpaulin. No doubt the poor soul, whoever he was, whatever he'd done, would need to be left in situ until they got a forensics expert up from the mainland.

That would be this evening, at the very quickest. I shrugged it all away, ladled two helpings of my soup into a pan, and headed up to the house to be ready for Tamar coming home. It was only a three-minute walk from the jetty: along the pier and up the gravel track between the salmon feed tubs of mussel lines, over a hurdle tied by the Portakabin and across the green field, with thistle rosettes in the grass, and the bright yellow heads of coltsfoot. The sky had cleared to summer blue to welcome her, the sea lightened to pale green, flecked with white horses.

I heard the car before I saw it, winding up the road; then it appeared at last, bumping down the last piece of track, garish yellow against the green hills. I put the kettle on, then went along the path to meet them.

Tamar was standing by the passenger door by the time I reached them, taller than me, slim in trousers and a moss-green yoke jumper. I looked at her face, and couldn't look away. There was something about it that reminded me of a raven: the strong features, the alert eyes under still-dark brows. Her hair was iron-grey, brushed up in a plume over her brow and coiled in a spiral at the back. There was a mass of wrinkles across her brow and at her jaw, but she wore them like war-scars. The elbow-crutches the care-centre woman fished out of the back seat seemed irrelevant to someone so fiercely alive; you believed she could walk without them on will-power alone. We daandered one on each side of her down the grass track to the house, and into the living room. She gave a long look around, settled herself down in the chair by the Rayburn, and thanked her driver. Her voice, which I'd expected to be as harsh as a raven's croak, was unexpectedly musical, low as a cat's purr, but it was still the voice of the witch inviting Handsel and Gretel into her gingerbread house. 'A cup of tea?'

The woman shook her head. 'I'd need to get on.' She added to me, 'I have a dentist appointment in Brae, and I'm later than I meant to be, with having to negotiate that car left parked half across the road.'

'The tourist one?' I said, remembering the red car Magnie and I had passed yesterday.

'Some walker,' she said, 'who doesn't quite understand about passing places.'

I frowned. 'It was there yesterday too. A camper?'

'Didn't see a tent. Well, you take care, Tamar, and remember we'll be pleased to see you over at Wastview any time you feel you need a bit of company.'

I saw her out and came back to the living room, to find Tamar's dark eyes summing me up.

'Well,' she said, 'so you're the sailor who's willing to take a berth ashore, looking after a cantankerous old woman.'

There was no point in soft-soaping that face. I looked straight into her fierce eyes. 'Unless you really need me in the house at night, I'll sleep on board, and if you're cantankerous enough to forget the rules of civil behaviour, I'll sail away again.'

She looked startled, then a thin smile curved her lips. 'A helper, not a servant. Agreed.' She held out one hand, and I shook it, feeling the brittle bones under the linen-fine skin, then stepped back.

'What do you want me to do first?'

She gave that thin smile again. 'Let's test your intelligence. Left to yourself, where would you start?'

It was half past one. 'I'd check whether you had lunch before they brought you over, and give you the soup I've made if you hadn't. I'd get the kettle on, to make you a cup of tea. I'd ask what you want to do this afternoon. I'd find out what time you wanted dinner, and what you'd like for it.'

'No, they didn't, and yes to your soup. Coffee, not tea.' She was tack-sharp. 'Rest this afternoon, and be glad to be home. Dinner at six thirty. Is there bread in the house, and can you do scrambled eggs?' I nodded. Her fierce gaze went around the room and returned to me. 'Magnie said you need to learn to run a house and look after a man.'

Oh, he did, did he? 'I can run a boat. I don't see why a house should be any different. My cooking's based on how little gas it uses up.'

'Fry-ups, a pressure cooker, or an old-fashioned haybox?'

'Stir-fries and vacuum flasks.' It was amazing what could keep cooking in a flask. Rice, of course, but I'd also made soup and stews, putting them in the flask first thing, and leaving them all day.

She nodded. 'You'll soon learn. I was half your age when I got my first job down south. "In service", they called it. A lot of Shetland lasses went off south to be maids in a big house. I was under-cook in the main home of the laird over at Sand. A mansion in Perthshire. I started just at this time of year, and the first thing I saw was a great pile of dead pheasants on the kitchen table. Never seen one in my life, of course.' The thin mouth crooked downwards. 'That was the tail end of the war. What I don't know about pickling and preserving every last thing that grows isn't worth knowing.' Her eyes shot up to mine again. 'Magnie said you haven't got a driving licence. How are you going to do the shopping?'

'Eid Community Co-op or Brae Co-op. They both have a handy marina.'

She laughed out loud at that, a harsh rasp. 'Resourceful within your self-imposed difficulties. If you can drive at all, we'll shop together. I'll sit passed-driver.' She gave me another of her sharp glances. 'I went to London at sixteen. Drove a taxi there for a bit.' Her voice went mock-Cockney. '"Ad that Winston Churchill in the back of me cab several times over, guvnor." Get that kettle on, and I'll tell you about it.'

The in-out sun had warmed the conservatory to a summer-day feel. I served us the soup with a slice of bread, then made the coffee and sat down beside Tamar, with the little table between us. She didn't launch straight into reminiscences though; she was still assessing me. 'Haven't settled down yet, have you? I can see it in your eyes.' She lifted her coffee, took a sip, and nodded to herself. 'Sailor's eyes, like my father's, always looking at the horizon. He was in the Navy, died just before I went to Monikie House.' She set her mug down again. 'What do you know about otters?'

The change of subject startled me. 'Not much. Shore creatures sometimes seen at sea, harmless if left alone.'

'Most things are.' She nodded shorewards, where the first glistening seaweed was beginning to appear above the water. 'That's one down there. That's what I do nowadays, after photographing polar bears and orangutangs. I enjoy the horizon I can have.' She passed me the spyglasses, and I focused them to my eyes, then scanned along the shore. I passed him twice before I saw him, the same brown as the seaweed, grooming his coat exactly as Cat did, and paying particular attention to his webbed paws.

'That's the dog otter,' Tamar said. 'Full grown, a real beauty. Look at the shine on that coat. They spend hours grooming – their coat is really important, for warmth and for waterproofing. You'll see the rest of the family while you're here. A week's leave you've got, haven't you, while your boat's in dry dock?'

I nodded. 'Just over. I have a lift back to Norway a week on Sunday, but I'll need to put my boat back to Brae marina before then.'

'Plenty of time to learn how to make jam. I just hope the blackbirds haven't taken all the rasps. I'll get you to go out and pick all you can, later. For now, I'll doze a bit, in my own chair, just glad to be home.' She glanced around her, then over her shoulder into the but-end. 'Did you notice where those men put my hospital bag?'

'In the kitchen.' I got up, fetched it, and laid it on the chair beside hers. 'Shall I put everything away?'

She nodded. 'There'll be dirty washing up in the bedroom too, so you can put a load on. Once it's dried, it can go back in here.' She shot a glance up at me. 'Everyone my age has their hospital case packed and ready. My sponge bag can go in the downstairs bathroom for now. Just lay the items out on the shelf.' She fished inside it, and brought out a round object wrapped in a handkie. 'This can go up in the bedroom. It lives on the mantelpiece.'

I took it from her, and was surprised at the weight. The handkie fell open to disclose one of those decorated eggs in polished brass, with blobs of dark red stones on it, a circle of diamanté around it, and a flourish of embossing. Tamar laughed at me.

'Garish, isn't it? But useful.' Her face softened. 'It was given to me by someone I loved. Open it.'

I gripped the diamanté circle and unscrewed the thing. There was a little pair of scissors, a nail file, a knife, a perfume bottle and several other implements I couldn't identify stuck in a nest of scarlet velvet. 'Handy,' I agreed, and headed up to plonk it on its little tripod below the prancing horse sketch, and bring down the laundry basket.

The phone rang as I was halfway down the stairs. I stumbled down the last steps, and charged into the living room, looking around for it. The table would be the obvious place, and there it was, one of those cordless handsets on a little charging stand. I picked it up. 'Hello, Tamar Irvine's house?'

It was an elderly man who spoke. 'Good afternoon.' His voice was educated Scots, with a faint trace of Shetland lingering in the vowel sounds, *efternoon*. 'This is Tamar's brother, Archie. Is she home now?'

'She's not long arrived. I'll pass the phone over.' I took it into the conservatory, and held it out to Tamar. 'Your brother Archie.'

She took it, smiling. 'Archie! How are you?'

I left them to it and went back to the kitchen to load the washing machine, and get it going. Luckily it was a straightforward one, with a handy guide to what number meant what on the front. I put the laundry basket back upstairs. I washed up the tea-mugs and assessed the supplies of egg and cheese. I was just running out of things to do, when I heard Tamar say a very firm, 'No.' She repeated it: 'No, I'm not going to. I'm leaving the choice to you.'

I headed into the toilet, to avoid listening to a family conversation, and when I came out she'd put the phone down, and was staring out over the grey water with eyes that didn't see it. She turned her head as I came in. 'Have you made a will, Cass?'

I shook my head. 'Nothing to leave . . . well, my *Khalida* now, I suppose.'

'No baggage.' Tamar sighed. 'I used to be like that . . . all I owned could go in a rucksack. Now I've spent twenty years getting comfortable.' She waved a hand in the air. 'Joanie's has a few sheep on my hill apportionment, and he'd like the croft land too, but he doesn't need the house.'

'Joanie o' Cole?'

'Yes, my nephew.' A quick, sharp look. 'Do you know him?'

I nodded. 'I hadn't connected him with you.'

'His boy Gary'll inherit Cole, but he's got a daughter, Kayleigh too. She'd be your age, near enough.'

That rang a bell. Of course, Kayleigh Irvine. 'She was in the year below me. A real crofter lass.'

Tamar looked around her. 'If she had children they'd have their father's surname, not that there's any sign of her taking an interest in men, or them taking any in her. I'd like to think there'd still be Irvines at the Ladie after I'm gone.' Another sharp look. 'Do you think that's foolish? To pass over the women just for the name?'

'She could keep the Irvine name. Her husband could change.'

We looked at each other, and thought of a Shetland man changing his name, and laughed. 'Pigs would fly,' Tamar said. Her head tilted. 'Is that a car on the road?'

A pause, and I heard it too, rolling slowly downwards. I went to the window and craned my neck. 'A red hire car. Are you expecting anyone?'

'I was hoping for peace and quiet, after the hospital,' Tamar said.

I kept looking. 'A woman – town clothes – in her forties, I'd say – mid-brown hair streaked blonde.'

Tamar frowned, and shook her head. I moved hastily back from the window, as she turned towards the house. 'Better put the kettle on again.'

I was just filling it, and waiting for the door to be pushed open, when a sudden bang like a shot reverberating through the house made me jump. It was the knocker on the kitchen door, and the first rap was followed by another, with a touch of impatience. I went to the door, and opened it.

The woman from the car was standing there. 'Hello,' she said, in a voice that was pure London. 'I'm Felicity, Tamar's niece. I've come to look after her.'

# II

# The First Beat

The first 'leg' of a sailing race is into the wind, meaning the yachts have to zig-zag towards the first buoy. An experienced skipper will judge the angles so that he sails the leg as the two sides of a right-angled triangle, with the start line to the first buoy as the hypotenuse.

# Chapter Five

**laird's haa:** the larger house belonging to the laird, or landlord. In Shetland these ranged up from simple two-storey houses to substantial mansions like the Auld Haa in Scalloway [Scots, *ha*, the main house on a farm; English *hall*, a manor house]

Felicity was in her forties, on the tall side of medium, and slim enough to wear that summer's cut-off jeans and boxy crop tops. No, not slim; she had that scrawny look of someone too driven to eat proper meals. The clothes were expensive casual: the jeans were navy cloth, the top nautical stripes, and she carried a large scarlet handbag. No doubt I ought to have recognised the gold logo. A pair of jewelled butterflies danced from her ears, and another glittered in her belly-button. Her hair was cut in a bob, smoothed with mousse to give that just-ran-a-comb-through-it look. The original colour seemed to be mid-brown, overlaid with fair strands. The short fringe emphasised her high brow and darkened eyebrows. Her eyes seemed too big, green searchlights seeking out other people's frailties. They swept round the hall behind me, pricing each item of furniture, and came to rest on my face, dismissing me as the help. *Second mate of the Sørlandet*, I reminded myself, and stuck my chin up.

'Tamar's resting right now.' I stood back and gestured her into the back porch. 'Come in. I'll go and tell her you're here.'

Tamar was levering herself into a sitting up position. 'Felicity?' Her face was harsh, unreadable. 'It must be five years since I last heard from her. The vultures are gathering.' She placed her legs on the floor. 'Well, bring her through.'

I ushered Felicity in, and Tamar looked up at me with the flicker of a wink. Her voice was clear and imperious: 'Afternoon tea in the conservatory, please, Cass.'

I wasn't sure what game she was playing, but I didn't mind going along with it. Once I was back in the living room I hauled off my jumper to show the black t-shirt underneath, and put on the frilled pinnie I'd noticed in the table drawer. A flash of amusement crossed Tamar's face as I came in. 'Sandwiches, Cass, and cake.'

I went for my best Jeeves manner. 'Yes, madam.'

Sandwiches. I left the kitchen door open and listened to them exchanging small-talk as I buttered slices of white loaf and plastered them with tuna mayonnaise, then set out the cups and saucers. The silver teapot from the dresser, I presumed. Matching plates. There were ivory-handled knives in the cutlery drawer. Crusts off the sandwiches. Cake was off, but Magnie's groceries had included best Jamaica ginger cake, so I buttered some of that too. By that time the kettle was boiling. I warmed the pot, added the tea leaves, re-boiled the water and poured it on, still bubbling.

'. . . commissioned an exciting series of articles by a former Royal servant,' Felicity was saying.

Tamar's brows rose. 'Really? Which royal?'

'It's a tremendous scoop.' She gave me a quick glance. I kept my face maidservantly-impassive. Felicity leaned forward, and whispered a name.

I thought Tamar overdid the widened eyes. 'Really? But my dear, that's marvellous.'

'Our circulation will treble.'

'Well, yes, indeed. Everyone will want to read about *them*.' Tamar caught my glance, and said smoothly, 'Felicity is the proprietor of a London glossy, Cass. *Latest!*, it's called. Bring over the small table. I'll pour.'

I organised the tray, then handed cups and plates around. 'Tuna mayonnaise, madam.'

'This is marvellous,' Felicity said. I thought she meant the view, where the alternating sunshine and showers was creating rainbows which suddenly glowed out against the clouds, purple, navy, blue, green, yellow, orange, red, then faded again. Then I realised she was looking at me. 'A real maid! Where did you find her?'

'Oh, a friend of mine recommended her.' Tamar waved that away. 'So, what brings you up here to Shetland?'

'Well, you, of course, Aunt Tamar. Daddy said you'd had that fall, and were back at home now, and refusing all medical help. I thought you'd be happy to have a member of the family living with you for a bit. Just until you're able to manage on your own.'

'I am managing on my own,' Tamar said. 'Cass is doing the leg-work, I do the thinking. How's your father?'

'Oh, Daddy's fine. Busy, as always.'

'No sign of him retiring then.'

Felicity shook her head so vigorously that her short hair stood out. 'Goodness, no! The law lets them go on till they drop in harness.' She laughed. 'The more out of touch they are, the better for us. A judge needing the modern world explained to him is always a good headline.'

'I'm sure Archie's managing to keep in touch with the latest news,' Tamar said drily. She turned her head to me. 'We're talking about my youngest brother, Cass, the one who phoned earlier. He went in for law, ended up Solicitor General and is rumoured to be on the next honours list.'

'How did Daddy manage to do that?' Felicity said. Her words fell abruptly into the sunny room. She realised that, and smiled, the interviewer wooing a witness. 'I mean, how could your parents possibly afford it?' She glanced out of the window at the ruins of Houbansetter. 'A crofter's boy from here?'

Tamar raised her brows. 'Being a crofter's boy never stopped a lad o' pairts in Scotland.'

'But it was before grants, and all that. And he went to school in Edinburgh – there's an old photo of him in school uniform. Fettes, he said.' She was leaning forward now, hands spread in front of her, as if she wanted to tug the information out of Tamar. 'That wouldn't have been cheap.'

Tamar shrugged her away with a casual wave of the hands, but her shoulders were tense. 'I was the oldest of the family, remember, and Archie was the tail-end Charlie. I'd left home before he was born, and by the time he was growing up I was in London, learning to work my first camera.' There was a flash of malice in her eyes. 'It wasn't like now, where people can just jump on a plane, hire a car and arrive on my doorstep. To get home, I had to take the train to Edinburgh, the tram to Leith, get on a ship for Aith, then ask someone to put me home by boat from there, or get a lift with the shop van, or walk the five miles of track.'

Felicity ignored that. 'It seems strange though. Maybe someone sponsored him?'

'If they did, your father would be the one to ask.'

Felicity shook her head. 'He just dismisses it when I ask. Old history.'

'Well then.' Tamar poured herself another cup of tea. 'Another sandwich?'

I passed the plate round. I was wondering about it myself. Of course, nowadays a child from Shetland could go as far as any rich man's son or daughter. Tuition was free at Scottish universities, and there were still some grants and bursaries. Sullom Voe Terminal had been good at sponsoring Shetland children – but that was now, and Tamar's brother must have grown up in the forties or fifties.

His job explained Felicity – that cut-glass voice, that city confidence. She hadn't gone to the local school either. 'What about papers?' she asked.

'I don't have any papers relating to your father.' Tamar's voice was cool. Her eyes flicked towards the sitting room and back. I remembered the drawers that had been pulled open. 'Why should I have? He'd have all his own documents.'

The two pairs of green eyes met, like swords crossing. It was Felicity who looked away first. 'I just thought you might have all the family papers here, since it's the family home.'

42

Tamar shook her head. There was something triumphant about her twisted smile, like a card player laying down a winning hand. 'Only documents relating to my parents and grandparents. Birth certificates, death certificates – the letter from the Admiralty about my father's death. There's nothing of my generation.' She set down her cup with a hard chink that signalled the end of the conversation. 'Except my own.'

Felicity considered this for a moment, eyes narrowed, then abandoned the attack. 'I wasn't sure how you'd be off for food, so I brought some Waitrose frozen meals in my suitcase, and some fruit. Where would you like me to sleep?'

The Waitrose food turned out to be exotics: Amy's Kitchen Broccoli and Cheese Bake, Rice and Bean Burrito, and two Mini-chicken Dinners. The fruit was a bag of Essential Royal Gala Apples, a tray of Perfectly Ripe Conference Pears, and a sachet of Essential Dark Sweet Pitted Cherries. I stowed the meals in the fridge alongside Magnie's leg of lamb from his own hill-reared sheep and his two boxes of home-laid eggs, and put the fruit beside the apples and bananas I'd picked up at Brae's splendid new Co-op, then headed upstairs to find bedding for the guest bedroom.

Felicity's face, when she came to see what I was doing, suggested that this simple, wood-lined room wasn't what she was used to. She registered the lack of en-suite, tested the skylight fastening, then turned to watch me putting the downie into its cover. *Ocean Yachtmaster*, I reminded myself, as I spread it over the fitted sheet I'd just coaxed on, and turned my attention to the pillows. That outranked a purveyor of royal gossip any day. Her green eyes considered me. 'Are you from round here, Cass?'

I didn't mind calling Tamar madam, but I wasn't truckling to Felicity. I put on my best stupid face, and jerked my chin at the window. 'I grew up on Muckle Roe, over there.'

'Do your parents have a croft?'

'No,' I said. I longed to add that my father was a company director and my mother an internationally-known opera singer, just to wipe the condescending look from her face. I clamped my lips against the temptation, and concentrated on wriggling the inner fold of the pillowcase around the plump pillow end. Tamar wanted me to be part of the furniture.

It didn't stop her. 'What's your usual work?'

I thought back to only two years ago. 'A bit of this and that. Waitressing, mostly. Baby-sitting. Summer temping.' There was no need to explain that baby-sitting summer temping had been teaching dinghy sailing in the Med. I put the camberwick bedspread back and stood upright. 'Will that be everything?'

Her glance dropped to my ringless fingers, then came back up to my make-up free face. It lingered on the scar along my right cheek, then moved away. 'You aren't married, then.'

I laid the second pillow down on the first. 'There you are. Is that everything you'll need?'

'I should think so. Thank you.' There was no actual gratitude in her voice, just a cool dismissal. I was at the door before she thought of her next question.

'Where are you sleeping?'

'At home,' I said, and got myself down the stairs at double speed. Tamar greeted me with a raised eyebrow. 'Twenty questions,' I said softly.

She nodded. 'There would be.'

I could see as clearly as she did that Felicity's visit wasn't prompted by a sudden rush of affection for her great-aunt. *The vultures are gathering.* 'Those fancy meals won't keep – will I do the scrambled eggs for you, and one of them for your niece?'

'Do the eggs for us. You'll eat with us.'

I grinned at her. 'It's not in role.'

'You can't get the staff these days. I don't trust her.' She gave a long sigh. 'I'm old, and I'm tired, and I don't want anyone saying I've said something I didn't. You stick with us.'

'Okay,' I agreed.

I hung the washing out from the line outside the back door. Now the clouds had spread to heavy skeins of dark fleece, and the sea had darkened to slate purple, slashed with white as the wind rose. A good drying day. Cat spotted me from the pier, and came bounding up towards me, a grey shape against the green grass. He greeted me with his soundless meow, and swarmed before me into the house. I didn't think Tamar would mind; if ever there was a woman who should be accompanied by a witch's cat, that was her.

I was just about to start scrambling eggs when there was a put-put sound from the voe. Magnie's boat came out from behind the point and headed for the pier. I hurried down to catch his bow. 'Aye, aye. How's it going?'

'I brought you up a fry of mackerel for your denner.' He reached up a carrier bag heavy with fish. 'If there's too much for you I've nae doot that Cat'll manage some.'

'He fairly will.' He was at my heels already, sniffing up towards the bag. I lifted it higher, and gestured up to the house. 'Are you coming up to eat them with us?'

Magnie gave Felicity's car a doubtful look. 'You hae visitors.'

'Tamar's niece, Felicity. From London.'

'Aye, aye.' He scratched his chin, thinking. 'She'll be one o' Archie's bairns. I mind them as peerie tings, coming up to visit their grandmidder. They both came for a start, and then once the lass got older, that'll be this lass, then it was just the boy that came.'

'She doesn't look like she was ever a child who liked beachcombing and running wild round hills,' I agreed.

Magnie shook his head. 'I'll leave you for this night. Tell Tamar I was asking for her, and I'll give her a phone later.'

He made as if to start his engine again, and I put out a hand to stop him. 'What about the police?'

'Oh, they came, and they lookit, and then they went home.' He gave me a sideways look. 'Your blonde pal was in charge of them.'

'I saw her.'

'Well, maybe they'll send your man up to investigate.'

'Not for someone falling off a cliff.'

'Likely no.' Magnie put his hand on the key of the boat and paused. 'Did you mention what we found in the sitting room to Tamar yet?'

45

'I wasn't sure if I should. I was thinking it might make her nervous, an old lady living alone, to know somebody'd been in the house.'

Magnie snorted.

'Now I've met her, I think it's the snooper who might need protecting if he comes back.'

'I'll tell her about it when I phone,' Magnie said. 'Have a good night, now.'

I shoved him off and headed back up to the house, dangling the carrier bag out of Cat's reach. 'Mackerel,' I said to Felicity, and wasn't surprised to see her make a fastidiously distasteful face, like Cat offered cheap catfood.

'I'll have a frozen meal, thanks.'

I put tatties on to boil, sprinkled the fish with oatmeal, and heated up the Waitrose meal as per the instructions. Cat made himself at home in the sit-ootery. Felicity put herself out to be entertaining, and I was able to sit back and eat while she and Tamar talked about places in London.

'And you'll never guess who I met the other day, coming out of Zédel's,' she said. The casual tone put me straight on alert. 'Eddie Ryland.'

Tamar took another mouthful of mackerel, then lifted her head, brows raised. 'Should I know him?' She paused. 'Oh, *Ryland*. One of the Sand family.'

'The Laird, isn't that what you call them up here?' Felicity asked.

'Not our laird, exactly. My mother, your grandmother, was from Sand, and we'd go over to our grandparents in the holidays, when we were children. They had the haa there, the big house. You'd see the laird o' Sand about, from time to time.'

'They had a place in Scotland too, didn't they?' Felicity persisted.

Tamar nodded, and turned to me. 'That's the place I was telling you about, Cass, where I began work. Monikie House, just ten miles north of Dundee. The laird then was Edward Ryland too, though he mostly got called after the estate, Monikie. His wife was a battleaxe.' Her voice hardened. 'Madam Monikie. I couldn't get away fast enough. He'll be long gone now.'

'It's his grandson who runs the place now,' Felicity said. 'He's Edward too, of course. Do you know his father, old Edward?'

Tamar frowned. 'He's never still living?'

'Just,' Felicity said. 'He's very frail, Eddie was saying, not expected to last long. He had a stroke. They managed to get him into a nursing home. Now they're sorting through a hundred years' worth of papers.'

'Hardly a hundred years,' Tamar said. 'He'll just be into his nineties.'

Felicity waved an impatient hand. 'You know what I mean. Drawerfuls of old bills, and letters and lawyer reports.'

Tamar was silent for a moment, eyes on the dimming water. 'Well,' she said at last, 'it comes to us all. So this Eddie is his grandson. He'll be in his twenties, maybe?'

'The really funny thing was,' Felicity said, 'that when I first saw Eddie's father, it was from behind, and I thought he was my brother Lachlan. He looks just like him.'

'Really?' Tamar said. Her voice challenged. 'Do you have some theory about that?'

'I wondered if that was why my father was given an expensive education. If it was the laird who paid for it.'

Tamar said drily, 'I have no reason to believe that my mother was unfaithful to my father, if that's what you're thinking. Here in the country, it would certainly have been remarked on.' She set her knife and fork down, and looked straight at Felicity. 'You'll have to suspect your own mother.'

That silenced her. Tamar rose. 'Cass, we'll have our fruit and coffee in the conservatory, and then after that, I think I'll go to bed. It's been a long day.'

The conversation didn't return to the Rylands until she was sitting at her dressing table, brushing her hair, and plaiting it for the night. Her eyes in the mirror were softer, reminiscent. 'So Edward's not long for this world. I mind him from my time at Monikie House. We were the same age, but you'd never have thought it. He had that public school confidence, you know. He was handsome too, with

47

brown eyes, and a lock of hair that kept falling over his forehead.'
She sighed, and shook her head. 'Well, maybe it's just as well I can't
see him now, as old and wrinkled as I am. I'll remember him as that
high-couraged boy, who thought the world was his for the taking.'
Her face twisted. 'Until his mother taught him better.' She laid the
brush down, and used her zimmer frame to steady her as she rose.
'Go down and get the radio for me, Cass, from the sit-ootery. I saw
Magnie had brought me a *Radio Times*. Bring that as well. I'm weary,
but not sleepy yet.'

I went downstairs. Cat had gone from the sit-ootery, but Felicity
had made herself at home, with another cup of coffee beside her, and
her tablet in her lap. There was a ping as another email came in. 'Is
she okay?' she asked, without raising her head.

'Just tired.' I followed the radio flex to the socket, unplugged it,
and picked it up. The *Radio Times* was on the sofa. I took them both
up, and installed the radio on Tamar's bedside table, turning the aer-
ial until there was a decent signal. 'Radio 4?'

'Of course.' She leaned back on her pillows. 'You go to your boat
now, Cass, save yourself any more cross-questioning tonight. What
time do you want to come and get me up?'

'Whatever time suits you – I don't mind.'

'Well then, shall we say a cup of tea at eight, and then I'll shower
and dress at my own speed. You can help me down the stairs when
I'm done.'

'Are you okay about being left with—' I jerked my chin towards
the other bedroom.

Tamar gave a harsh crack of laughter. 'If she's up before ten, I'll
be very surprised. If she is, I'll be lying quietly on my bed, reading
the papers online.'

'Okay,' I said, and slipped out of the house.

It was only quarter past eight, but already the land had darkened.
The night air was cool, fresh after the rain of the day, and smelling
of damp earth and flowering currant leaves. Cat was waiting for me
aboard, a grey shadow curled up against the white curve of fibreglass. I walked across my gangplank and dropped down into the

cockpit. There was an unpleasant smell in the cabin, which it took me a moment or two to identify as Cat's litter tray. His innards were playing up, it seemed; maybe he'd found something dodgy on the shore, though he was usually fussy about that sort of thing. Maybe he'd stolen a dead fish from the resident stripey, and felt duty-bound to eat it. I tipped the litter tray contents into a black bag, refilled it with sawdust pellets and put the bag into the cockpit. Gas on; kettle on for a bedtime mug of drinking chocolate; candle lit in the lantern, to cast a gold glow over my varnished wood. It wasn't bedtime, of course, but I felt in the mood for wriggling into my berth and reading.

It had been a long day, with far too much crammed into it. There had been the dead man of this morning, that Magnie had thought had been there twartree weeks, and the attempt to rifle Tamar's papers. I wondered if Magnie had phoned her yet. Then there were Felicity's hints and questions about her father. The laird's son, that's what she seemed to be saying, but I couldn't see what that had to do with the price of fish, as my Irish granny used to say. The laird of Tamar's youth was long dead, and Tamar's mother too. It could be proved with DNA, but could you put in a retrospective claim for your share of the inheritance? The Haa at Sand wasn't anything exciting, but the Perthshire mansion sounded worth a few bob. I wondered what the law on bastards inheriting was. Equal shares with legitimate children, I thought, in Scotland.

Gavin would know; or if he didn't, he'd have the internet. I stretched across to take my phone from the table, and called him. 'Hi! How's the course going?'

'Let's talk about something interesting.'

'Isn't it, even at all?'

'It's interesting,' he conceded, 'and if I had forty-eight hours in every working day, with sleeping time extra, it would be practicable. All I can do with it is pick out two or three ideas and try to introduce them into my practice.'

'Is that possible, or would they like you to totally overhaul what you're doing?'

'They can like,' he said. 'How's your day been? Freya told me about your body.'

Freya. Sergeant Peterson. 'Not mine. Joanie o' Cole's. All I did was point out that it was above the high-water mark, and stop them bringing the poor soul aboard.'

'They've identified him already, she said. He'd hired a car, which Bolt's have been trying to get back for the last fortnight. They knew all about him, of course, from his driving licence. Derek Luncarty, from Dundee.'

*Monikie House, ten miles north of Dundee.* 'Actually in Dundee?'

There was a moment's silence. 'Oh,' he said, voice alert. 'Is that ringing a bell?'

'It might. Does he bide anywhere near a place called Monikie House?'

'Let me get my computer on.'

I heard a ping as he started it up, and while we waited for it to warm up, I explained about Felicity and her questions.

'So,' he said, when I'd finished, 'on the basis of a family resemblance to her brother, she thinks her father might be a son of the late laird.' I could hear his fingers tapping on the keys. 'Inheritance . . . yes, illegitimate children inherit equally with legitimate.'

'I thought that.'

There was another short silence as he read on. 'And you can put in a claim for inheritance up to twenty years later.'

'Tamar said her brother would have his own papers, but someone was searching in her desk drawers.'

'Interesting. Freya did say the name of where he came from, but I didn't take a note of it. I think you should tell her all this.'

I made a three-year-old face at Cat, but kept my voice equable. 'Okay.'

'I'll get her to give you a call.' His voice changed gear. 'So, what else is new with you? How's Cat taking to life back on his own ship?'

# Chapter Six

*HW 01.33 (1.5); LW 07.53 (0.5); HW 14.15 (1.3); LW 20.04 (0.6)*

*Sunrise 04.37, sunset 19.38; moonrise 17.06, moonset 23.00.*

*Third quarter moon.*

**houll:** rounded top of a hill or hillock

I was woken by rain drumming on my roof. I raised myself up to look out, and saw the world was muffled in white mist, with Papa Little only a hundred yards away barely visible, and rain tin-tacking the still water. Another midgy day; I could maybe spend part of the morning fitting that catflap.

The rain stopped as suddenly as it had started. I got the last drip down my neck as I opened the hatch to look out. The air was warm, the voe mirror still, and the midges dived in for the kill, whirring like fighter pilots. I ducked back in and had a mug of chocolate in bed while Cat ate the last of the mackerel. After he'd eaten, I let him out, then had a basin wash in the cabin before dressing, sprayed myself generously with midge-repellent and headed out.

The grass to the house was grey with dew. Water lay on the cropped grass in the parks, already growing green again, and filled the tractor tyre gouges. The burn rushed through its channel in a foaming brown stream. There was no sound of life above me when I went in, but as the kettle boiled I heard Tamar rise and go to the toilet, moving slowly with her stick. I waited until she was back in bed, then took her up a cup of tea. 'Sure you don't want breakfast in bed?'

'Good morning, Cass. I'd rather get up, after I've had this. Thank you.'

'You're welcome. How did you sleep?'

'Very well.' Tamar tilted her head in the direction of the spare room. 'A bit of wandering in the night. Rummaging about downstairs.' She was surprisingly unfazed by it, but I didn't like it; someone else rummaging about. 'I didn't bother to get up. There are no papers about her father or the Rylands in my desk, so she can look all she likes.' She gave her malicious smile and changed the subject. 'Have you a plan for meals today?'

'Soup for lunch again, if you don't mind, then for dinner, I'll stick Magnie's lamb in the oven, boil potatoes, and see what greens are in your garden.'

'That sounds good. There are apples, aren't there? If you pick me a bowl of blackcurrants or gooseberries as well, I'll show you how to make a crumble.'

'Deal.'

I left Tamar drinking her tea and checking the news on her tablet, and headed out for a walk up through the toun and over the hill, to shake the fidgets out of my legs, and to see what was going on down in the Skro. The grass up to the hill dyke was soft to walk on. I swung over the fence dividing it from the hill proper, and strode on through the heather, the stems crunching under my boots and releasing a honey scent. It wasn't as far as it looked; in less than ten minutes I was up on the top of the hill, looking out over my childhood sailing territory: Brae, the Røna, the circle of Cole Deep, with a major set of salmon cages now, surmounted with a red wooden shed for the salmon boys. Rumour said it had beds and a 40" colour TV, so that the boys tended to be stuck there during major football matches. I grinned at the memory of one of my sailing friends winding up a rather stuffy official from south; the official had been keen to know the story of the house in the water, and John had shaken his head and stalled until the official had gone to the toilet after their meal. When he'd returned, it was to John saying solemnly, 'And that was the story of the house on the lake,' and then refusing to say any more.

Brae was north of me, just visible above the purple curve of Linga. To the west, the Guns o' Vementry guarded the opening to the wide Atlantic. Another week and I'd be sailing there, on *Sørlandet*. My heart leapt at the prospect of nothing but sea and sky for a fortnight; another part of me, the part that was rejoicing in this windswept silence, recoiled from being back among the brightly–jacketed gabble of trainees again, the formal meals at the captain's table, the bells ringing off every move. I shook the disloyalty away, and concentrated on rubber-necking.

Forensics must have arrived yesterday by plane, or been first off this morning's ferry. Two boats were by the Skro, and there was a swarm of dark figures and a white tent further up the beach. One of the boat's was Magnie's, and the other was a large motorboat that tourists could hire for fishing trips. Magnie was sitting in his boat, under cover of the small wheelhouse, peacefully reading what was pretty certain to be today's *Shetland Times*. I wondered if there was a capitals 'body found' headline, or just a dignified paragraph in one corner. The motorboat was anchored slightly back from the beach, and there was a rubber dinghy pulled up on the shore. The tent was dancing even in this light breeze, and I could see white-suited officials moving around inside it. There was a uniform at each corner, holding it down, and a knot of people in the doorway. I spotted Sergeant Peterson's blonde head among them. *Monikie House, just north of Dundee . . .* a goodly inheritance. *There are no papers about her father or the Rylands in my desk*, Tamar had said. It was an odd way of putting it.

It wasn't any of my business. I turned away and headed down the hill at the same moment as a black car came around the corner above Tamar's house and headed straight for the pier. A man got out, and marched down to *Khalida*. A shout drifted up on the wind. He stood by her for a moment, then shook his head and turned round, scanning the hill. I raised a hand and continued downwards. He was likely whichever of Tamar's relatives was working from the pier, wondering what I was doing there.

I saw him clock me, then he went over to his car. My eyes were on the rough going, heather, boulders and uneven peat, until a shot made me jerk my eyes upwards. My eye caught something black falling from the top of the net poles. A flock of starlings flew upwards, chacking in alarm. There was a second bang, a third, and two more fell, one dropping like a stone, the other's spread wings catching the air so that it swirled downwards, then lay still, a black huddle on the red gravel path. I quickened my pace towards the road, and came down it at a swift march. I wasn't having some shooting idiot firing at random with Cat around.

He was much younger than he'd looked from a distance: sixteen, seventeen, a young Viking, with a burnished fair head, a summer tan and the bluest of eyes. He was dressed in jeans and a grey fleece. He had a rifle in one hand, and three dead starlings in the other, wings trailing. He turned as I approached and gave me an unfriendly stare. 'This your yacht? You canna park here. This is a private jetty.' He was scowling now, and hefting the gun in one hand, barrel in my direction. 'So just go elsewhere.'

A cold finger went down my spine at that muzzle pointing towards me, and the bullet scar on my cheek tingled, but I wasn't going to be intimidated by a teenager. I looked him straight in the face. 'Lower that gun, please.'

I kept staring at him until he complied. 'I'm looking after Tamar,' I said. 'I'm Cass, from Brae.'

'Harald,' he said. 'Tamar's me great-aunt.' The scowl hadn't quite gone yet. 'Me mam's Tamar's home help. Nobody told us she had another one coming.' Then he frowned and glanced behind him at Felicity's red car parked beside Tamar's. He jerked his head round to stare at the cottage. 'Are you saying Tamar's home?'

'She came back yesterday.'

He didn't like it. He glanced over at the cottage again, biting his lip, then turned back to me, face still wary.

'I'm just giving a hand, these few days,' I said. 'Magnie o' Strom sent me.'

'Oh, Magnie!' He abandoned suspicion, and turned on the charm. 'That's different.' He bent down to lay his rifle on the ground, and when he came up he was flashing a practised this-gets-me-my-own-way smile. 'Pleased to meet you, Cass. Sorry no' to be more welcoming. We're no' had tourists parking their yachts here yet, but we dinna want them to start. Before you know where you're at they're talking insurance and liability.'

He sounded like he was quoting someone else, but maybe he was just an old head on young shoulders. Fifteen, sixteen, I'd say, bright, maybe of older parents; he had a bit more poise than was usual at that age. The golden boy, who was used to everything he did being right. I looked at the broad smile, and imagined girls falling into his lap, then remembered the surly sound of his voice when he'd first spoken. I wondered how he behaved when crossed.

He brandished the starlings at me, as if he was trying to distract my attention from the gun. 'Bloody pests these. I was just feeding the cats, up in the shed. I'll leave you to get sorted, then.' He went up to the Portakabin and undid the padlock. The mewing noise intensified as he went in, and was cut off as he shut the door. I noted cat-feeding as a point in his favour, though I wasn't convinced Cat would thank me for a pre-killed stirling instead of a tin of best Whiskas. All the same, I added an extra rope around my lines, tied with my most fiendish knot, in case he decided to cast *Khalida* adrift while my back was turned, called Cat, and headed up to the Ladie.

I'd expected one of Harald's parents to be in the house, but there was no sign of visitors. When I went upstairs, Tamar was alone, listening to the start of *Woman's Hour*. She was dressed in loose trousers and a green jumper, and looked as if a night in her own bed had done her good: her eyes were brighter, her skin less drawn. She glanced up as I came in. 'Was that shots?'

'Your nephew, Harald, shooting stirlings.'

'Great-nephew. Loretta's golden boy. You'll meet her this afternoon, when she comes to do my housework.' She snorted. 'No, don't think she's doing it out of the goodness of her heart. She's my home help. The Social Work pay her to come and put up with my tongue. That, and the hope that I'll leave the croft to Harald.'

'I got the impression he was a golden boy,' I agreed. 'Is he old enough to drive?'

Tamar snorted, and went into quoting mode. 'The rules o' this country are that stupid, they're no good for country folk. How is poor Harald supposed to get to his work if he's no' allowed to drive?'

'So that's his parents' car?'

'Oh, no, his. Bought for his sixteenth birthday.'

I was throwing stones in a glass house here; in the longship summer, I'd driven without a licence. At the end of the investigation, Gavin had presented me with a Provisional Application form, and on my next leave I planned to get an intensive course of lessons and try for my test. But, I mollified my conscience, I hadn't been sixteen, or a boy racer inclined to brandish rifles at strangers.

'No insurance, of course,' Tamar said. 'But it's no use telling Loretta anything. What the bairns want, they get. Too much money all her life. She was born just after the oil came, when grants were flowing like water. Luckily her husband's a fisherman, so they're not short of a bob or two. And as for her Lady Di nonsense – well, you'll see her.' She stretched out a hand to the radio, and switched it off. 'I'll get you to give me a hand down the stairs.' She paused, and tilted her head towards the guest bedroom. 'No sign of life from there. Probably doesn't know there is a morning.'

I wasn't really a lot of help. Tamar had had her weeks in Wastview to get back on her feet, so all I had to do was go slowly in front of her, to be grabbed at if she felt off-balance. We reached ground-level in good order, and headed to the kitchen, where we had a boiled egg each, with buttered toast. After we'd eaten I fished in the fridge and brought out Magnie's leg of lamb. 'Hot for fifteen minutes, he said, and then turn it right down and leave it all afternoon.'

'You could roast potatoes with it,' Tamar said.

I'd never done roast tatties, except wrapped in foil, in the embers of a bonfire. I supposed the principle was the same, without the charring. 'From the garden?'

'There's a tin basin in the porch. Do you know a tattie show if you see one?'

I tried to dredge up twenty-year-old memories of helping Magnie's mother take up the tatties. 'Probably.'

'The spade's in the shed there, made out of the old cludgie.'

'Okay,' I said, and headed out. Above my head, there was a step, and the sound of running water. I glanced at my watch. 10.30. The morning was practically gone already.

Cat came out with me, and trotted ahead, with the occasional glance back to check I was really coming this way. The walled yaird, the former kale-growing area, had been planted around with sycamores. Inside, there were fruit bushes round the walls, gooseberry, redcurrant, blackcurrant, all hanging with fruit, enough to make a dozen crumbles. Maybe they would freeze? Or no, I could see my jam lesson coming soon. Cat bounded into the nearest thicket. A blackbird flew up, chuck-chucking in alarm, and scolded him from the safety of a branch outside the walls. There was a stand of raspberries at the far end, and a jaggedy bramble thrust long stems up one corner, covered with tight green berries. Magnie had one similar, a prickly horror that had caused us problems as children when we were trying to ransack his garden at kale-casting time. There were even strawberries in an earth-filled fishbox, gleaming red under their broad serrated leaves. The sheltered air swarmed with midges. I went back into the porch for another skoosh of midge-repellent, and rubbed my face, hands, ears and neck with it.

Potatoes. In the middle there were four raised beds, in a cross-shape, with a wheelbarrow width of path between them. Here were the vegetables. I hefted my tin basin under one arm, and went forward to test my raw veg recognition skills. Those feathery tops would be carrots, and the broader leaves beside them could be parsnips? I dug a finger down into the earth beside one. Yes, parsnips. These fat pale-yellow balls breaking the surface were obviously turnips. I could do carrots and neeps boiled together, then mashed, with butter. The next frame had cauliflowers, brussels sprouts, and an odd triangulary sort of broccoli. Crossing over, there was a tangle of low peas. I took a pod and tried it. Mange tout. Finally, I came to the potatoes, knobbled shows that were starting to wither. The spade was in the shed that had been the cludgie.

That was easy enough to spot too: a block-built square with a wooden door, gapped at top and bottom, so that you could see if it was occupied. It had been an actual toilet, with the burn diverted into a pipe which was converted now to a tap. The pedestal marks were still on the floor, and the blocked wastepipe projected out. An ancient piece of twine still dangled newspaper squares from a rusty nail. I thought of coming out here in the cold of winter, and shuddered. There were times when I was grateful for civilisation. Otherwise, there were shelves of dusty boxes, a Windolene spray bottle labelled 'Rhubarb' in black felt-tip letters, plant pots, string, metal biscuit tins (one labelled 'Documents'), a high stack of ice-cream tubs, a couple of bags of compost, and a hanging board for the tools, white-painted, with black marker outlines of what should live there. I turned around, looking, and a patch of bright colour caught my eye: a scarlet box labelled 'Marksman' 500. .22 pellets for Harald's gun. There was a pair of pegs sticking out from above the door, obviously where he kept the thing. I supposed it was safe enough out here, though I suspected the law said it should be securely locked up.

I took the spade from its nail, and returned to the potatoes. The earth broke as the spade went into it, exposing the beige curves of potatoes among it. *Pommes de terre*, earth apples. The soil was soft under my fingers as I teased them free. One show-full would be plenty. I filled the basin with them, and stood up, hesitating over whether I should haul Cat back into the house with me. It seemed a pity, when he was having fun skulking in the bushes. Then I heard the Portakabin door slam, crunching steps on the gravel, and Harald loomed into view. He was still carrying the rifle.

He stopped dead when he saw me, looking from me to the open door of the shed. I could see him considering, then, with a grunt, he turned on his heel and took himself and the rifle off. He flung it into the boot of his car, and slammed himself into the drivers' seat. A few moments, then the car started, and headed up the track in a spurt of gravel.

I watched him go, gunning the engine bad-temperedly at every small rise.

Felicity was up when I arrived back in the kitchen, and simultaneously making herself a cup of coffee and talking on the phone. Her thin brows were drawn together and her green eyes snapped. Her voice was sharp with tension. 'Look, I have it under control. You just need to get us more time.'

She registered me coming in, and cut off abruptly. 'Have to go. I'll speak later.' When she turned back to me, she was all smiles. 'Lunch?' she said, looking at my potatoes.

'Dinner,' I said, and took them through to Tamar, who was in the sit-ootery, spyglasses to her eyes.

'One of the youngsters,' she said, 'the boy. At the point.' She passed the glasses to me, and I caught a glimpse of a brown back and slim tail slipping into the water. I gave her the glasses back, and proffered the basin.

'A good haul,' Tamar said. She lifted one up. 'Nice size. How do you plan to cook them?'

'Boiled?' I said. 'They're too small to roast, surely?'

'They are,' Tamar agreed, her dark eyes watching me like a teacher waiting to see if the pupil would get it right. I stifled a squirm of annoyance. 'What about vegetables?'

'There's plenty of everything.' There was no shame in admitting to ignorance. Boats didn't have vegetable patches. 'There's a lot of stuff that looks ready. I don't know what should be eaten first.'

'Have a look at the cauliflower, and see if the head's beginning to spread out, like broccoli. If it is, we'll have that. Can you make a cheese sauce?'

'Yes.'

She laughed. 'Don't be mutinous. How should I know what you can and can't cook? I've never lived on board a small yacht.'

'Who lives on a yacht?' Felicity said, coming through at that point. She'd made Tamar a coffee, I noticed, but didn't offer me one.

'Cass,' Tamar said. 'At the jetty there.'

She gave me a startled look. 'Is this the Shetland equivalent of living in the back of a van?'

'No,' I said. 'It's my home.'

'Keeps the bills down, I suppose,' she said vaguely. She set Tamar's coffee down in front of her, and sat down on the sofa. 'So, what do people do here in the morning, when they're on holiday?' She gave a dismissive glance out at the bonny day, the sweep of green hills, the grey sea.

'What do you do in London?' Tamar took the thought from my head.

'Oh, well, like on a public holiday? I'd get the papers, meet friends for brunch . . . a bit of shopping, maybe.'

'The Brae Co-op's open,' I said helpfully.

Felicity ignored me. 'Theatres . . . museums . . . exhibitions . . .'

'Do you actually go to them?' Tamar asked.

Felicity waved a hand dismissively. 'Well, of course, I'm generally too busy, but they're there.'

Tamar gave her witch's grin. 'I never went to them when I lived there either. We do have a very nice museum, if you want to drive into Lerwick, and you could probably get brunch there too.'

Her fair hair flew out as she shook her head. 'Oh, no, I'm here to keep you company!'

Tamar lifted her glasses again. 'Well, what I'm doing is watching otters. You're welcome to join me.'

Felicity's mouth turned down. 'Do you have the morning papers? If not, I could go and get them.'

'That could take you a while,' Tamar said, deadpan. 'They haven't left Aberdeen yet.'

I suppressed a smile at Felicity's face, and escaped outside again. The cauliflower was a nice, tight, white head, so I left it, and turned my attention to the mangetout. I was just picking away, with my bowl half-full, when there was an engine roar from around the point, and the big motorboat backed out, spun round on itself and headed back for Brae in a plume of white wash. I couldn't see inside it, of course, but there looked to be a good number of people aboard, as if they'd finished what they were doing there. There was something long and black in the back that might just have been a body bag. Five minutes later, Magnie's boat followed it, at a more sedate pace, with Sergeant Peterson's blonde head visible among the others sitting round the engine cover. I nipped down to *Khalida*, and got my own spyglasses out. Yes, I thought it was a body bag. I supposed the poor soul had been long enough out in the wind and weather that there was nothing to be learned from leaving him there.

I watched them into the marina. The big motorboat stayed there, but Magnie dropped his passengers off, then curved around and came out again, heading back – for forensics folk, maybe, examining the ground the body had lain on?

I was just about to go back to picking peas when my phone rang. 'Cass?' It was Sergeant Peterson, brisk as usual. I didn't see why she needed to have my phone number.

'Speaking.'

'Gavin suggested I tell you a bit more about your body, if you're interested.'

My inner three-year-old was longing to say that it wasn't my body, and I wasn't interested in the least. My mature self squashed the toddler. 'Well, yes.'

'Obviously these are just preliminary findings. Definite results will come from the forensic reports.' Her voice relaxed slightly. 'As definite as forensics is willing to be, that is.'

'Scientific probabilities,' I agreed. I put my bowl down and settled myself on the cockpit seat. Cat appeared from the shore and jumped up on my lap, purring. 'So, what are you allowed to tell me?'

'Well, we've got a tentative identification, from the hire car. His name was Derek Luncarty, and he came from near Dundee. There's a Shetland connection – he worked on the estate of the Rylands, who are the lairds of Sand.'

What was it Hamlet said, *O, my prophetic soul*? That feeling I'd had in my waters, that we hadn't heard the last of this.

'The old lady I'm helping,' I said, 'she worked there when she was young. Her mother was from Sand, so that's how she came to get the job.'

'So I've heard.'

Of course. This was Shetland. What else did Gavin say I had to tell her? 'She has a niece staying, Felicity, from London. She arrived yesterday. She was asking questions about the Ryland connection – saying that her father, no, her brother, looked just like some scion of the Rylands. She seemed to be implying that Tamar's mother had had an affair with one of them.' I smiled. 'Tamar turned the tables on her by suggesting she ask her own mother.'

'Hang on. I'm writing this down.'

'Felicity wanted to look at papers, but Tamar said she didn't have anything. Someone had been searching, though, I think.' I explained what Magnie and I had found, when we'd come to the house. 'And Felicity was rummaging about in the night, but Tamar said,' I made it clear I was quoting, 'There are no papers about her father or the Rylands in my desk.'

'Interestingly precise. When you and Magnie went to the house, there was no sign of a forced entry?'

'None.'

'What sort of locks are there?'

I shook my head, trying to visualise them, then remembered opening the sit-ootery door to let the air in. 'None on the front door, just a bolt inside. The back door, into the kitchen, that's a normal mortice lock.' I hadn't had to fiddle with a Yale while I was going in and out to get vegetables.

'No burglar alarms.'

'At the Ladie?'

'Some old people are nervous, living alone.'

'I think it would be the burglar who'd need to be protected from Tamar. She takes no prisoners.'

'Okay. I'll come and talk to your old lady, see if she has any idea what he was doing there. If he visited her. She's alert, then? I'm told she's over ninety.'

'Sharp as a tack.'

'I believe she fell and broke her hip on the 2nd of August.'

'It would be about then,' I agreed.

'Luncarty came up to Shetland on the 1st, and hired a car from the airport. He stayed one night in a B&B in Lerwick. We don't know where he spent the other nights. The hire car was due back on the 4th, but he never turned up with it. From his mileage, he went from the airport to Lerwick, then went another thirty miles – that fits with where the car was found.'

'On the road to Tamar's house?' The one that Magnie and I had seen on our way over, the one the care-centre woman had complained about. *Left by some tourist who doesn't realise there's a house here . . .* or by some shady character who didn't want anyone to know he was visiting the house.

'On the road to the Ladie, or to Cole – the home of the man who reported the body.'

'It was past the Cole turn-off, and a fair distance from the Ladie still.'

'Just short of the brow of the hill. Stopped just before anyone in the house would see it. Would half an hour from now be a convenient time for me to talk to Ms Irvine?'

'Fine,' I agreed. 'But if he was coming here, what was he doing falling over the Skro? It's well out of the way between here and where his car was.'

'Ah,' she said, sounding like the cat who'd been at the cream. 'That's one of the most interesting parts of the very tentative forensic comments. He did die of falling from the cliff, unless the PM finds some other cause, like poison, but it's what happened before that. His back was peppered with shotgun pellets.'

I felt as though the air had been sucked from my lungs. 'Someone shot him?'

'From a good distance. I'm working on the hypothesis that the pain of it made him lose the direction of his car. John Irvine mentioned that his dog seemed to be following a trail – blood, perhaps.' She paused, and then asked, very gently, 'Do you know if there's a shotgun at the Ladie?'

# Chapter Seven

**baa:** an isolated rock, wholly or partially submerged (Scots, *ball* or *baw*)

I went back to the house and into the sit-ootery to tell Tamar and Felicity of the treat in store. 'I just had a phone call from Sergeant Peterson. She wants to come and talk to you, Tamar.'

Tamar's brows rose. 'It's a crime now to fall over and break a hip?'

I shook my head. 'It's a tourist whose car was found on this road. I've to let her explain herself.'

'The red car half blocking the road?' Felicity said.

I nodded.

Tamar frowned. 'I can't think why I should know about some tourist who can't park properly, but I suppose she has her job to do. How did you get on with the cauliflower, Cass?'

I displayed the peas, and went off to get more, keeping an eye on the road for a police car rumbling down. It arrived exactly twenty-eight minutes from the phone call, and Sergeant Peterson got out of it, showing no sign of having spent her morning grubbing around a dead body on a beach. Her fair hair was sleeked back into its pony tail, her brows immaculate, her pink lipstick followed the thin curve of her mouth. We greeted each other with polite lack of enthusiasm, and I brought her into the sit-ootery.

'Tamar, this is Sergeant Peterson.'

'Detective Sergeant Peterson,' she corrected me.

Tamar's brows rose. 'Really?' She set her spyglasses down. 'And how can I help you, Detective Sergeant?' There was just the hint of an emphasis on the 'Detective'.

DS Peterson gestured at a chair. 'May I?'

Tamar gave a royal wave, and waited. Felicity was showing no signs of moving, so I sat down too, ignoring a sharp look from DS Peterson. *Peterson*, I was tempted to call her, as if she'd been a less-than-favourite teacher at the school.

She settled herself down in the chair, and took a police notebook out of her pocket. 'How are you doing, Ms Irvine? I hope this visit is at a convenient time.'

Tamar gave her a dry look. 'I'm doing fine, thank you, but not planning to go out for my usual pre-lunch walk right now.'

'I'm trying to trace the movements of a visitor to Shetland, a Derek Luncarty, from near Dundee.'

Tamar shrugged, then shook her head. 'I don't recognise the name.'

DS Peterson fished in her black bag for a photograph, and passed it across. Tamar studied it for a moment, then handed it back. 'No.'

All the same, I thought for a moment that there had been a flash of recognition; not at the face, at the name perhaps? If he'd been an estate worker at Monikie, his father might have been there before him, his grandfather. I kept my face neutral.

'He didn't call on you just before your accident?'

Tamar shook her head. 'Why do you think he would have?'

DS Peterson dodged that one. 'Do you keep a gun in the house?'

Tamar gave a short laugh. 'To repel callers with?'

'This is a country household, Ms Irvine. You might well have a gun to scare birds away from lambing sheep, or keep down the rabbits.'

Tamar looked her straight in the eye. 'Wouldn't you know whether I had a permit?'

'You don't have one.'

'That's your answer, then.'

Neatly evaded, I thought, remembering Harald's shooting of the morning. Tamar took the thought from my head. 'However, my great-nephew, Harald, has a .22 air-rifle, which he uses to pot at wild birds. You have my full permission to confiscate it from him.'

66

'Harald Irvine?'

'No, Harald Williamson. My niece's son. They live at Solvarg, Brae, one of those big new-builds.'

DS Peterson noted it in her book. I hoped she'd give him a hard time; even if he fed semi-wild ketlings, I hadn't taken to scowls-one-minute, smiles-the-next Harald.

'So who is the man?' Felicity asked.

DS Peterson raised her immaculate brows. 'And you are, madam?'

'Felicity Irvine. Tamar's niece. I'm visiting from London, to help Aunt Tamar out until she's properly on her feet.'

DS Peterson flicked a glance at me, and let her claws show. 'I thought Cass was doing that.'

'Cass is the hired help. I'm family.'

You had to be pretty posh, I reflected, to have such delightful manners. I kept working on the neutral face, and wondered what Tamar would be having for lunch if it had been left to Felicity.

DS Peterson flourished her photograph again. 'Derek Luncarty, from Monikie, near Dundee.' She flicked a glance at Tamar from her green eyes. 'He's an employee of the Ryland family.'

Tamar raised her head at that. 'The Rylands of Sand Haa?'

DS Peterson nodded, and waited. Tamar kept quiet, but I thought I saw surprise in her eyes, quickly followed by relief. It was Felicity who rushed into speech.

'But I know the Rylands. Eddie's a good friend of mine, we often meet up in the City. What's one of their staff doing up here?'

'They have an estate out to the west.'

'So you think he was calling on Tamar?'

I could see DS Peterson wasn't wanting to let slip a grain of information that she didn't have to. 'His car was found some way along this road, just over the hill there.'

Tamar's brows drew together. 'Why is it still there?'

DS Peterson turned to her. 'Ms Irvine?'

'A visitor, you said, and you expected him to have visited me over two weeks ago.' Tamar's voice was incisive. 'What's happened to the driver, that the car's still there?'

DS Peterson flicked a quick glance at me, acknowledging the *sharp as a tack* that I'd warned her about. 'You're quick on the uptake, Ms Irvine. The driver's in police custody.' Tamar wasn't the only one who could use economy in telling the exact truth. 'We're trying to find out what he was doing along this road. Your accident was on the 2nd, I believe?'

'I believe so.'

'So it's possible he took advantage of you being away to come here.'

'Why would he do that?'

'Why would he call on you at all? Have you any connection with the Rylands?'

'Not now.' Tamar's sardonic look would have stripped varnish. 'People like the Rylands don't normally send one of their flunkeys to ask after the broken hip of an ex-maid from over seventy years ago.'

DS Peterson scribbled a few notes in her jotter, then looked up again. 'I gather you only came out of Wastview yesterday. Have you had a chance yet to look around your home?'

Tamar's brows rose. 'Are you holding him on suspicion of burglary?'

'If he didn't come to visit you, then that's a possibility, isn't it? He'd heard you were away, and came to see what he could find.'

Felicity jerked forward in her chair, like one of our dinghies suddenly hitting Gibbie's Baa, the underwater rock just outside the marina. Her hands clenched on the arm as if she was about to thrust herself upright, then, as DS Peterson's head turned to her, she relaxed them again, and made an elaborate parade of uncrossing her legs. 'I'm forgetting my manners, Detective. Would you like a coffee?'

'No, thank you, madam.' DS Peterson turned back to Tamar. 'Which of course raises the question, what might he expect to find?'

Tamar swept a hand round the shabby furniture of the sit-ootery. Her eyes sparked, as if she was suddenly enjoying herself. 'You think he might be after the Chippendale?'

'He wasn't an opportunist thief, after your TV and computer. Not out here. You don't have any genuine valuables that you keep quiet about, to save insuring them?'

68

'A Leonardo or Ming vase that I picked up for pennies in Europe in the chaos after the war?' Tamar gave her short laugh.

If Felicity hadn't been keeping such a hold over herself, she'd have been leaning forward. 'Did you leave the house unlocked, Aunt Tamar? When you fell?'

'No. The ambulance men took my keys and made sure everything was secure.'

'There was no sign of any disturbance when you left?'

'I didn't ask them to carry the stretcher round so that I could inspect the house.'

It was time I shoved my oar in. 'Well, actually . . .'

DS Peterson turned courteously towards me, as if she'd never heard this bit of evidence. 'Yes, Ms Lynch?'

'I didn't want to worry you with it yet,' I said to Tamar, 'but when Magnie and I got here to get things ready for you, the drawers in your desk were both open, and the little box in the china cabinet, its lid was ajar, and the door of the cabinet was swinging open.'

Felicity didn't move, but a slow colour spread up her throat and burned in her cheeks. Tamar sat up straighter in her chair. She gave a quick glance towards Felicity, and a smile that made me glad I was on the side of the angels. 'Yes, Magnie told me about that last night. I'm sorry you were worried about it. I was going through papers a few days before my fall, and fancied there was a damp feel about them. That's why I left the drawers open.'

I didn't believe a word of it, and nor did Felicity. Tamar smiled again. 'I presume there was no sign, Cass, of anyone having broken into the house?'

'None.'

'Well, Detective Sergeant, that's your mystery cleared up for you.' Tamar set her hands on the arms of her chair, and levered herself upwards. 'Let me show you out.'

We had soup for lunch, with bread and an apple to follow. Tamar ate it with a good appetite, and gave me a nod of approval; Felicity picked at it, with constant sidelong glances at Tamar, as if she was restraining herself from asking questions. After it, I went back out into the garden and picked blackcurrants while Tamar strolled to the road and back, then she showed me how to make the crumble topping, and Felicity watched us with an air of disbelief; in her world, I supposed, crumble came ready-made from Waitrose. It was surprisingly easy. I shoved the roast in as per Magnie's instructions, and the crumble went on the bottom shelf. Sorted. I'd just washed up the mixing bowls and was wiping down the work surfaces when a car scrunched down the road. The woman who got out of it had to be Harald's mother. She was tall and fair, but not the older parent I'd imagined; she was in her late thirties, with the trimness of someone who kept herself busy. She was wearing jeans and a blue yoke jumper. For a moment I had that sense of familiarity, then I remembered Tamar's Lady Di comment and almost laughed out loud. Yes, there was already a resemblance in the regular features, the English-rose skin, but Loretta had copied the short, flicked-back haircut, and walked as if she expected people to bring her flowers as she passed.

She was almost at the kitchen door when the far side car door opened, and out came a twenty-years younger edition in the latest teenage gear: low slung crop trousers, a short top, a stone glinting in her navel and a yard of perfectly manicured hair flowing down her back.

Once they came into the kitchen I could see their expressions. The mother had something of Tamar's determination; she was likely simultaneously the backbone of the local hall committee, and the reason nobody volunteered for anything. The daughter just looked spoiled, with eyes that expected to get their own way over a sulky mouth. They looked out of place against Tamar's crofthouse. I betted their own house was a shining new-build where the kitchen units were changed at the first scratch. Loretta's hands were perfectly manicured, I noticed, and blue stone earrings ringed with diamanté enhanced the improbable blue of her eyes. She carried a basket with rubber gloves and a pinnie. Her daughter clutched a candy-pink folder scrawled with curlicue drawings.

'Hi,' I said. 'I'm Cass.'

Loretta nodded. 'Yea, Magnie said he'd got you to come and give Tamar a hand for a start.'

'I'd've come, o' course,' the girl said, 'but there's me schoolwork to consider.'

'Yea,' I agreed, and reflected that if I'd been Tamar, I'd have been dubious about being looked after by the daughter. She didn't look as if she'd ever had to boil a kettle for herself, let alone an egg. 'Tamar's just in by. I'll put the kettle on.'

I dug out mugs this time, added the milk carton and sugar packet, and took them all through on a tray. Tamar looked up as I came in. 'Cass, have you met my niece, Loretta? And this is Leeza. She's come to let me do her homework for her.'

It was a moment before the sarcasm got through to Leeza. She flushed red, and said, 'You're going to help me with it. I'll actually do it.'

Loretta had sat herself down on the sofa beside Felicity. I could feel the prickling between them like that electric spark in the air before a thunderstorm, town mouse and country mouse viewing each other with equal contempt. I set out the mugs to the accompaniment of Felicity telling Tamar all about an exhibition of Elizabethan jewellery in London, pointedly excluding her country cousin, and Tamar, a flash of malice in her eyes, was encouraging her with reminiscences of Cheapside. Loretta didn't like it, that was obvious; her eyes flicked from Felicity's dancing butterfly earrings over to Leeza, taking out coloured pens from her schoolbag, then to the beads Tamar had round her neck – they looked like red glass to me, but I supposed they might be valuable. I wondered if Loretta was worried Felicity was going to cut her out with Tamar.

'Tea?' I asked her.

She jumped, and brought her eyes back round to me. 'I'll just have a cup,' she said, 'and then I'll redd up a bit, seeing as how I didn't get while you were away, Tamar.'

'Didn't you?' Tamar said. Her voice was bland. 'I thought the Social Services paid you to come every week, whatever.'

'Yea, well, there didn't seem any point since you weren't here.'

71

'You could maybe do some extra cupboard-turning out, then,' Tamar said, 'over this week. There's always something to be done in a house.' She turned her head to me. 'Not that I would do it, of course, any more than you would, Cass, but I'm assured housework never ends, if you're willing to waste time on it.'

I was tempted to retort in defence of the cleanliness of my bilges, but the spark in her eye saved me the bother.

Tamar turned back to Loretta. 'Especially if you're being paid for it, of course.'

'My time sheet'll agree with the hours I'm put in, never fear,' Loretta said. She shifted in her seat and prepared to let the cat out of the bag. 'This is an awful thing this. The dead man in the geo, poor soul.'

Tamar's head jerked up. 'He's dead?' Her face smoothed over, but not before I'd seen the shock in it. 'The policewoman didn't say that.'

'Dead for twartree weeks,' Loretta said, 'and just lying there in the geo all that time, until Joanie happened to pass by and see him. So the police were here then?'

'Asking if there'd been any sign of disturbance in the house. He was an employee of the Rylands, apparently.'

Felicity's colour didn't change, but her hands gripped in her lap, and she shot Loretta a sharp glance.

Tamar added smoothly, 'Harald would know him, if he came up to Shetland for the Rylands.' She added to me, 'Harald works for them over at Sand, back and fore.'

Loretta stiffened. 'No reason why he should,' she retorted. 'He doesna ken everybody that comes back and fore.'

'Derek Luncarty,' Tamar said.

Loretta shrugged. 'I don't know anyone o' that name. Did they think he was trying to burgle from you, while you were in the hospital?'

'That seemed to be their idea.' Tamar frowned. 'So what did he die of?'

'Fallen over the banks, that's what they seemed to be saying.'

Tamar's expression didn't change, but I thought I saw relief in her eyes. I supposed that she was glad that even as irritating a

72

great-nephew as Harald hadn't actually shot someone, even a nefarious someone snooping round her house while she was in hospital.

'The policewoman was asking about guns,' Felicity said.

That was a new idea to Loretta. I could see her considering it, ready to pass on round her cronies. 'Do you think he was shot, then?'

'Harald has a licence for his air rifle, of course?' Tamar said.

Loretta bristled, like a bull who'd seen a red rag. 'It's no his gun. It belongs to Brian. Harald's no' age to own a gun.'

'He'd need a licence to shoot one.'

'A few stirlings, on our own land, miles from anyone? What for is he needing a piece o' paper for that?'

Tamar raised her brows. 'Our own land?'

Loretta had the grace to blush. 'Weel, Irvine land. You're no' objected to him shooting on it afore.'

'That,' Tamar retorted, 'was before someone apparently took to shooting at people.'

# Chapter Eight

**croft:** a small area of farm land, generally rented from the laird under crofting tenure, though the house on it belongs to the crofter (Scots, *croft*, a small farm).

Tamar turned her attention to Leeza. 'So what's this homework you have, then?'

Leeza brightened at that. 'It's for history. We're to do a family tree.'

'What, everyone in your class? That could raise a few awkward skeletons. I'm surprised your teacher is allowed to ask you to do it.'

'Skeletons?' Leeza asked.

'Things people would prefer were forgotten.'

Leeza tilted her head in a sly look. 'Do we have skeletons?'

'Not more than half your class, I'm sure.' Tamar settled herself more upright in her chair and pulled the table towards her. 'Well, let's get going then. Loretta, why don't you start with the hoovering?'

Loretta turned out to be one of those people who keep talking as they work. I heard her as I dealt with roasting trays and the leg of lamb in the kitchen. Her voice carried through from the living room in a running commentary on the people that Leeza was putting into her family tree, a thin trickle of spite: 'She never did a hand's turn in her life, just looked for a well-off man to marry.' 'And don't forget that Gary. Sleekit. If he offers to do you a good turn, you look and see how he'll profit from it before you say yes.'

There was merciful silence while she went into the sitting room, apart from the drone of the hoover, then she came back into the kitchen, gave the floor a thorough going over, propped up the hoover just where it would be most in the way, got a bucket and mop out, and started on me. 'Did you see that latest photos o' the Royal bairns, now?'

I could truthfully say that I hadn't.

'They are the cute, and aye that bonny rigged. Old-fashioned, like. I always tried to dress my bairns that same way, bonny frocks for Leeza, instead o' the leggings they all wear now.'

Maman had tried to dress me like a pretty girl too. It hadn't taken.

'And I'm no wearing it right now, but me engagement ring was the exact same as the one Prince Charles gave Lady Diana. I was only a peerie lass then, o' course, but I promised myself that when my time came I'd have one like that.' Loretta disappeared into the downstairs bathroom, and snatches of sentences came back to me over the sound of running water; something about a most awful interesting radio programme she'd listened to – the last king and queen o' Russia, before the revolution – the bonny jewellery they gave each other – decorated Easter eggs –

'And do you know this?' she said, popping her head out again. 'They found one in America somewhere, in a car boot sale, and it sold for sixteen million pounds. What do you say to that?'

'Sounds a lot for an Easter egg.'

She disappeared again. 'Ah, but they were special ones. Did you hear that programme, Tamar?' She didn't wait for a reply, but headed into the back toilet. The details of the extravagances of the Romanovs were mercifully obscured by scrubbing, then the toilet being flushed. All their riches hadn't done them any good; the main thing I remembered about them was a photo of a bearded man and an elegant woman, surrounded by white-frocked lasses, and the horrible way that they'd died, shot down in a cellar.

Loretta took herself and the hoover upstairs, and I went through to see how the family tree was getting on.

'What was all that about the Romanovs?' Tamar said.

'Some radio programme she'd listened to.'

'Last night. The jewels of the Romanovs. She has a thing about

75

royal jewellery.' She glanced at Leeza's bent head and shut her thin lips on a further comment.

'So she was saying. How's the family tree going?'

Leeza turned her book around. 'Here, see.'

She had that ornate teenage-girl handwriting, with flourishes on the tails of the g and y, and a circle instead of a dot over every i. The tree itself was straightforward enough so far.

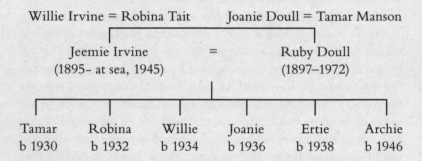

'Our teacher said we weren't to put dates for living people,' Leeza said, 'but Tamar says she doesn't mind.'

'My brothers and sister,' Tamar said. 'Robina was a nurse, and she married a Scottish man, Jim Baxter, and moved to Fife. She's been dead, oh, twenty years. They had a boy, James. He died just recently. Oh, and a girl. Now, what was she called? Her daughter visited here, redding up kin.' She paused, frowning. 'Grace, that was it, the mother, and the daughter was . . . was . . . She sent me a Christmas card. It'll come back to me.'

Leeza added 'm Jim Baxter' and 'James + Grace' under Robina's name, added a line going down from Grace, wrote 'daughter' and put her pen down again.

'Willie, my oldest brother, he married a Walls lass, Ellie, and they emigrated to New Zealand in the late fifties. He's dead now too. They had children and grandchildren. I suppose the children would still be living.' She frowned again. 'You can see that I was a very bad aunt. Will was the first one, and then they stopped using family names. Bruce and Jenny, I think. One of Bruce's children was a boy, Bob.'

Leeza wrote it down. 'Then Joanie. I know about him. Joanie o' Cole's father. What was his wife called?'

'Mary. Mary Tait, from Eshaness.'

The pen paused. 'And Joanie's children are Kayleigh and Gary. Neither of them is married.' She noted them, and looked up. 'What was Joanie's wife called?'

Tamar's lips thinned. 'I don't remember. I was away in London.'

That, I presumed, was the skeleton. Magnie would know all about it.

'Then Ertie was my grandfather. I remember him fine. And Granny Joyce, in Lerwick. Joyce Anderson.'

From Tamar's expression, I gathered that she and her sister-in-law weren't bosom buddies.

Leeza added 'Brian Williamson' beside her mother, and herself and Harald below, then looked up at Felicity. 'Now your family. Archie's children.'

'Our tail-end Archie,' Tamar said. I looked at the dates. Yes, he'd been eight years younger than Leeza's grandfather and born the year after Tamar's father's death. Felicity was leaning forward too; I saw her eyes flick up to her grandfather's dates, and back to her own father's. A posthumous child, I thought, and wondered if there was any truth in her speculation about the laird.

'My mother is Georgia Cavendish,' she said. 'There's my older brother, Lachlan, and me.'

Leeza noted it. 'All done.' She closed the book and shoved it back into her school sack, then added, as an afterthought, 'Thanks, Tamar.'

Upstairs, there was silence from the hoover. Loretta's footsteps moved across the bedroom, towards the fireplace. There was a long pause. Tamar's eyes flicked upwards. She frowned, then turned to me. 'Cass, why don't you put the kettle on, then call Loretta down for a cup of tea?'

★

The family was out in force. No sooner had we got Loretta, Leeza and Felicity settled round the sit-ootery than a Land Rover came scrunching its way down the track. Loretta rose immediately and went to the window. 'It's Kayleigh.' Her immaculately lipsticked mouth turned downwards. 'Well, we're pretty well finished here, if you've got all you need, Leeza.' She picked up her cup, drank the rest of her tea in a gulp, then seemed to have second thoughts. She shot a glance at Tamar, frowned, and relaxed into her chair again. 'Oh, we're in no hurry. I'll maybe manage another cup of tea. How about you, Leeza?'

'But you dinna like Kayleigh, Mam,' Leeza protested. 'You always say she smells o' sheep.'

Loretta's smile just managed to stay pinned on. 'That's no reason to be bad neighbours wi' family.' She refilled her cup. 'Besides, she can help you with your family tree. She was in New Zealand last summer. She'd have redded them up.'

Tamar had her witch's smile again. I rose and headed for the door. The gate chinked, the back door opened. A robust voice called, 'Aye, aye, Tamar, it's me.'

I recognised Kayleigh straight away. She'd always been a crofter lass: not tall, but broad-shouldered and sturdy, with arm muscles toned over years of wrestling cows, sheep and ponies. Her skin was tanned, her black hair cut short, and her teeth shone white as she smiled. 'Aye, aye, Cass, we're no' seen each other for long, but I'd a known it was you even if I'd no' seen the boat at the pier. Is Tamar in by?'

Something on the mantelpiece jingled as she crossed the living room. 'Now, then, Tamar, how are you doing?' Her tone cooled. 'Now then, Loretta. Leeza.' Her gaze moved to Felicity. 'And you'll be me cousin Felicity, from London? I don't think we're ever actually met.' She held out her hand and gave Felicity's languid one a vigorous shake. 'Fine to meet you.'

'The kettle's just boiled,' I said. 'Tea or coffee?'

'I never say no to a cup o' tea.'

I went off to get it. Kayleigh's voice boomed after me: 'I was just passing, to have a look at the sheep, so I thought I'd stop off and see how you were getting on. What are the doctors saying?'

Tamar grimaced. 'On my feet and use it all I can.'

'Comfrey, that's what you want,' Kayleigh said briskly. 'Bone-knit. I shoulda thought to bring some. You can apply it as a poultice, or make tea out of it.'

'There's plenty in the garden,' Tamar said. 'I'll get Cass to make me a cup after tea.'

'And one at bedtime too.'

'It'll have me up and down in the night. First thing in the morning will be fine.'

Loretta sniffed. 'Old wives' potions. I wouldn't touch it if I were you, Tamar.'

'Lady Di called it natural remedies,' Kayleigh retorted.

There was a charged silence with the pair of them glaring at each other. Felicity watched them, her eyes calculating, flicking from one to the other, as if she was wondering how to add fuel to this fire. Tamar broke the silence. 'You're just in time to help Leeza with her homework. Her teacher's got them all doing family trees.' Kayleigh's cheeks reddened, and she shot a dark glance at Tamar, but Leeza plunged in, oblivious to the undercurrents.

'Yes, I need the New Zealand side of the family. You visited them, didn't you?'

Kayleigh's angry flush changed to wariness. She shot a quick look at Tamar. 'Yea. Yea, I did, last summer. They're in the Taranaki region, on North Island. They've got a nice herd of Kiwi-cross kye.' Now she looked at Tamar, and spoke more naturally. 'It's a Fresian-Holstein/Jersey cross breed, bonny beasts. Their herd's black. Mid-sized. They reminded me a bit o' Shetland kye.'

Loretta yawned, and covered her mouth daintily with rose-tipped fingers. 'I presume we're no' related to the kye.'

Kayleigh glared at her. 'Will was the farmer. Willie's oldest boy. He's into his sixties now, and his son Allan is working the farm with him.'

'Hold on,' Leeza said. She'd got her notebook out again. 'Allan.' She gave Tamar an accusing look. 'You said Bruce and Jenny.'

Kayleigh frowned. 'No, he was definitely Allan.' The couch

creaked as she dropped down into it. 'Let me think. They invited the whole clan round to meet me. Bruce and Jenny, that sounds right, and then a mird o' cousins around my age.' She squinted down at Leeza's jotter, and her tone softened. She smiled. 'Yea, Bob, I mind him. He was interested in farming but of course their own farm would go down through Allan's family. Allan had a boy, canna remember his name, and he was keen. He had a peerie flock o' Texels that he was right proud o'. Bruce, and his wife was Cynnie —' She spelt it out. 'There was Bob and two sisters — em, em, Sylvie, that was it, and Emma. They all took me for a day out up Mount Taranaki. Amazing scenery. Jenny, she had a husband and two lasses o' primary-school age, but I canna mind their names. I only met them at the dinner. They lived in Auckland.'

Leeza wrote it all in, and began to shut her book, then opened it again. 'I don't have your mother's name. Tamar couldna mind it.'

Black fury filled Kayleigh's face for a moment. She swallowed it down, and spoke normally, though her neck muscles were rigid. 'Angela Crossland.'

'From Newcastle,' Loretta added. 'She didna stay here long.'

The silence was dangerous. It stretched out for what seemed like a minute, then Kayleigh snorted and looked back at Tamar. 'Are you going to be well enough for the morn? I'd like you to see my young dog.'

'I may not be able to stay the whole afternoon.' Tamar looked at me. 'It's the Westside Sheepdog Trials, Cass, held over at Stump. It's part of the Scottish National series. I was almost the only woman entrant for, oh, a number of years when I first came back to Shetland. Kayleigh's taken over from me.'

Loretta folded her lips tight on a sharp comment.

'This dog's the one I brought over a while ago, to let you see her. The brown one, Moss's granddaughter.'

Tamar nodded.

'She was rounding up the hens at four weeks old. I've been working her with Moss, and she's going to be good.'

'What do you say, Cass? Shall we drive over?'

I nodded. It was always interesting watching dogs herding sheep; sometimes for the skill of the dog and handler, and sometimes for the orneriness of the sheep, going every way but the one the dog wanted.

'Good,' Kayleigh said. Her chair creaked as she leaned back. 'Also . . . well, you ken me, Tamar. I'm no' one to beat around the bush or come fjaarmin round to get in your good books. Geordie o' Greenbank approached me the other day. You ken, he's the secretary o' the Grazings Committee at the moment.'

'I know him.' Tamar left the silence for Kayleigh to fill.

'He was wondering if you were thinking o' reassigning your croft. I ken you still have your sheep running on it, but you're no' really fit for working the land. If you would consider it, I'd be blyde to take it over from you.'

Loretta gave an outraged squeal, and Kayleigh ploughed over her. 'You know I'm always been keen on the land, and wanted a place o' me own. This croft has been in our family for generations. It's a good size wi' Quiensetter as well, big enough to be worth working. I'd keep up your flock o' sheep, and I could have cows, and maybe a couple of ponies. It could be a right traditional croft, with a mixture of everything.' She leaned forward. 'Would you no' like to see that growing around you?'

Loretta rose to her feet. 'You think you can just ask and have?'

Kayleigh glared at her. 'This is our land.'

'Our land, aye, right. So why you? What about my Harald? He's as much right to it as you have – more! He's a boy!'

'He's no' an Irvine.'

Loretta's eyes narrowed. 'No more are you. And at least he'll have bairns to pass it on to.' Loretta gave a contemptuous look down Kayeligh's jumper and jeans, and Kayleigh flushed and took a step forward, raising her hand. There was a ringing slap and Loretta reeled back, her cheek scarlet, then came forward, hands crooked like claws, snatching towards Kayleigh's eyes.

'*Enough*,' Tamar said. She didn't raise her voice, but her tone cut through both their voices. 'Sit down, both of you.' Reluctantly, they

81

obeyed. 'I'm well aware that the land could be better used.' Hope sprang up in Kayleigh's face. 'I'll think about it.' Her glance cut across both faces. 'And when I've decided, I'll let you know.' She rose. 'Now, I think it's time for my afternoon rest. Don't forget your homework, Leeza.'

She sat in her chair, upright as a queen on her throne, while they made their goodbyes and left, Loretta with one last, suspicious look at Felicity.

Felicity's searchlight eyes were bright with malicious interest, but she didn't speak.

'Cass, a hand upstairs, if you please,' Tamar said.

I went behind her as she made her way upwards, and flung the top cover back so that she could lie down on the bed. 'Thanks,' she said. She paused, then slanted a sideways look at me. 'Well, what do you make of them?'

'Not my job to make anything of them.' That violence had shocked me though, it was so un-Shetland. Maybe Tamar's accident had brought the unspoken tensions over inheritance to the surface; and Loretta hadn't liked being the imitation sophisticate to Felicity's real thing, with all her talk of London. 'Did you really need to encourage the town mouse to show up the wannabe country one?'

A flash in her eyes showed she'd taken my meaning. 'Loretta and Felicity are both as self-centred as they come. At least Kayleigh has a bit of gumption about her. She'd make a better job of the croft than Harald, and a more interesting one than her brother Gary. He'd just put more muckle-nosed sheep on it – but he's an Irvine.'

'She's only my age,' I pointed out. 'She's got plenty of time yet to marry.'

Tamar humphed at that. 'Late marriages are harder. People have got into their own ways.'

'Thirty isn't late!'

Tamar gave me a dry look. 'Have I touched a nerve there? Maybe if you don't make up your mind soon your policeman will go off with someone like that blonde Detective Sergeant. The bird in the hand.'

I took a long breath. 'If she doesn't marry, well, you're a long-lived bunch. The croft'll be Irvine for another sixty years.'

'You heard Loretta. She's not an Irvine. Her mother came up here and bade with Joanie o' Cole long enough to have the two children, then did a moonlight.'

That rang a bell. Kayleigh had only ever had a father, no mother at Sports Day or Prizegiving. 'He raised them. He called them his name. Are you going to let the lack of a piece of paper count over that?'

'Hmmm.'

'Besides,' I finished up, drawing the cover over her, 'you're an independent woman yourself. You made a life, and an interesting one, doing what you wanted. If she'd make a better job of the croft, she should have it.'

'Gary, Kayleigh, Harald. Maybe someone else altogether.' I looked sharply at her. There was a spark in her eyes that meant mischief. 'I'll think about it.'

I headed down the path to *Khalida*. I had the impression, as I opened the washboards, of a scuffling inside, but Cat was curled up on my berth, raising his head to greet me with his silent meow. I stroked his head, and dealt with his litter tray once more. Maybe he'd got out of the way of British cat food, though I couldn't see why the Norwegian stuff should be any different, and he'd never had bother with mackerel before. I'd have to get him some whitefish, and see if that would settle his innards. In the meantime, I dug a tin of tuna in oil out of the bilges, and refilled his plate, which he'd licked clean. He stretched and came down to sniff at it, arching his back and raising his tail, then tucked in.

I had work to do. I renewed the midge-repellent, then headed ashore and set up a couple of fishboxes as a sawing-horse. I'd got a piece of ply the size of my lower washboard, so I drew the present one as a template, cut around it, then used the catflap template to draw and cut another hole. It was for shore use only, so it didn't need to withstand a storm at sea. I was busy adding a layer of woodstain when a black pick-up came over the hill, scrunched down the gravel to the pier and stopped. There was a blare of rock music as the door opened, and a man got out, dressed in working overalls and boots. He gave a look around, then came over to me, and greeted me as if he knew me. 'Aye, aye, Cass. Long time no see.'

I gave him a blank look.

'Gary,' he said. 'We were at the school together, though you were two years above me. You'll maybe no remember me.'

'Kayleigh's wee brother,' I said, placing him. Joanie o' Cole's son, Kayleigh's rival heir for the croft. What was it Loretta had said about him, voice grumbling over the rattle of the hoover? *Sleekit. If he offers to do you a good turn, you look and see how he'll profit from it afore you say yes.* He'd been one to watch in the playground too, I remembered now; you didn't swap anything with him, however much he tried to wheedle you.

He'd turned out good-looking enough, with broad shoulders and the family beak nose giving him a Clint Eastwood look, though there was a pinched look about his eyes, and a tight curl to his mouth. I'd no doubt he could ladle on the charm when he wanted. Some foolish lass would fall for it and regret it, if one hadn't already. I glanced at his left hand, but there was no ring there, not that that meant anything. A ring was a dangerous thing aboard a boat, and he spent a good deal of time with mussels and creels, if the accumulation by the pier was anything to go by.

'You're busy,' he said.

'A washboard with a catflap.' I waved a couple of midgies away. 'It's not the time of year to be leaving the forehatch open.'

'You're staying with Tamar for a start, me Dad was saying.'

I nodded, and balanced my washboard on the fishboxes to dry. It would likely get covered with stuck midgies, but I'd sand them off later.

Gary leaned against a salmon feed container and gave me a smile. 'Just if the subject comes up, you could maybe have a word wi' her, casual-like, about what she's thinking to do wi' the croft. Just running a few Shetland ewes on it's no' working it properly. Now you know yourself if you're to make a living out o' a croft you need as much land as you can get.'

He paused, still training that 500-watt smile on me. I nodded.

'Well, then, if she should be talking about it, you just put in a word for me, will you do that?'

He'd been a bad one to cross, and *Khalida* was just too vulnerable at the pier here, beside his workboat. An accidental scrape of its metal bows along her side could do considerable damage to the gleaming white fibreglass of her hull. All the same, even with *Khalida* as a hostage, I wasn't going to let him intimidate me into promising to help him. 'She has been speaking about it, but it's no' my business. It's up to the family to sort out between them.' I smiled back at him, a smile as false as his. 'Besides, if Tamar'll no listen to you —' I put a slight emphasis on the you — 'why should she take any notice o' me?'

He made a face, mouth turned down. 'That's true enough. Well, I'll no' keep you. I'll likely see you around.'

He clattered across the stone beach, thumped himself into his workboat, got the engine going with a jerk and a roar, and set off towards Brae.

# III

## The weather mark and the two reaching legs

The first leg of a sailing race ends with the weather mark, the most up-wind buoy. Once the yacht has gone around it, she's on a reach, her fastest point of sail, heading straight for the next buoy, the gybe mark, where the sail crashes over from full out on one side to full out on the other. The second reaching leg takes her back to the starting line.

# Chapter Nine

**trow's hadd:** the den of a *trow*, the Shetland race of little people [Old Norse, *troll*, Scots, *hauld*, a dwelling)

Just in case Gary was bearing a grudge, I found a plank on shore, made a second fender board with it, for *Khalida*'s seaward side, and rigged it so that it hung at the height of his workboat's metal gunwale. After that I got out my measuring tape. Now my post on *Sørlandet* gave me a steady wage coming in, my *Khalida* was going to get new sails. I'd printed out the measurement form, but it would take time to fill it in. I spent the next hour messing about with lengths of rope hauled up the mast and stretched from bow to genoa cars, measuring everything at least three times and only writing each set of figures on the form once two measurements from opposite ends matched. It was after five before I'd got most of it done. By that time the woodstain had dried, so I added another coat. Quarter past. The roast would be getting near ready by now, and Tamar had probably had enough of lying down. I left the papers on my chart table to look over again later, and headed back up to the house. Cat decided to come too this time, then, as we reached the gate, suddenly changed his mind and bounded back to the boat. Odd; I watched him go, frowning, and thought I could make out a movement on the sand-grey gravel of the pier as he came to the gangplank, a shadow behind him as he went over it. He missed his pal Rat, I knew; maybe he'd made friends with one of the shore cats. It would explain the cleaned plate, and maybe the disordered innards too, since there was no sign otherwise of anything being wrong with him.

The kitchen was filled with the smell of the roast, best Shetland hill-grazed lamb. My mouth watered in anticipation. I was just about to open the oven and see how it was doing when the phone rang. I gave it a moment to let Tamar take the call if she wanted to, then picked the but-end extension up. A man's voice came straight out at me, sharp and angry: 'Tamar, what the devil . . . ?'

I cut in quickly. 'Tamar Irvine's house, Cass speaking.'

There was a startled pause, then he spoke again, in a voice smooth as a good Scotch whisky, with a lingering peatiness about it. 'Cass. Delighted to speak to you again. It's Tamar's brother, Archie – we spoke yesterday.'

That placed him. I glanced across at his photo on the mantel-piece, and tried to remember exactly how high up the law ladder he'd climbed. Had Tamar said Solicitor General, depute to the Lord Advocate himself? The white and gold Adam background of the photo suggested it had been taken at Bute House, the First Minister's residence. There was no hint of a Shetland accent now; his voice was best public-school Scots.

'I can see how much of a help you're being to Tamar.' I imagined him leaning over a jury, charming them to his point of view, and felt my thrawn nature kicking in. I'd never liked being charmed.

'Doing me best,' I said. I let my accent broaden. 'She's having a lie-down. Will I get her to call you back when she's risen?'

'Let me check my diary.' A page rustled. 'Yes, I'm in all evening, if she wants to phone me then.'

'Yea, I'll make sure she knows.'

He cut in quickly. 'I'm glad to get a chance to speak to you, Cass. Tell me, how is she really?'

'She's doing braawly well,' I said. 'She's moving about the house. She feels the hip after a couple o' hours o' moving, and then she lays her down for a bit. But she's making a good recovery.'

'Mmmphm.' He paused for a moment. 'And mentally, how's she doing?'

'Oh, there's no sign o' her doiting yet.'

'Not taken to imagining things, or dragging up old grievances?'

I could hear in his voice that it was important. I wondered what old grievance he was thinking of. Surely Tamar must have been away in London as he was growing up. Maybe she'd been aggrieved that he'd had a University education while she'd been sent off to be a servant? Bearing old grudges didn't seem like Tamar.

The whisky-smooth voice persisted, with a laugh making a joke of it. 'Or threatening to write her memoirs, scandal and all?'

So that was what he was worried about. 'No' that she's told me. Naa, she's no' been speaking o' that.' I added some reassurance. 'She's speaking about going over to the Sheepdog Trials at Skeld the morn.'

Now his laugh held relief. 'That's good. You keep her thinking about that, Cass, and I'll speak to her later.'

'You don't want to speak to Felicity?'

There was silence for a moment, then he covered, smoothly, 'Yes, if she's about. Thank you again for looking after Tamar.'

'You're welcome,' I said, and laid the phone on the worktop. Felicity was still in the sit-ootery, flicking through pages on her tablet now. 'Hi,' I said, 'it's your father on the phone.'

A startled flush rose up her cheeks under the smoothing make-up. Her mouth set in an angry line. She rose with an abrupt movement, picked up the phone and headed for the sitting room without a word.

I headed upstairs, thoughtful. Old scandals . . . I supposed in his position you didn't want an illegitimate birth from seventy years ago and four hundred miles away to suddenly surface, especially if your own daughter seemed to want to bring it to light to help the circulation of her magazine.

'Who was that?' Tamar asked.

'Your brother Archie. He said he'd be in this evening, if you wanted to phone back. He's talking to Felicity now.'

An angry voice floated upwards, too muffled to hear the words. Tamar cocked her head sideways. 'Did he know she was here?'

'Maybe . . . I'm not sure. No, I got the impression he knew she was here, but not from her telling him.' I wondered how he'd meant to finish that opening sentence: *What the devil is Felicity doing up there?*

'Interesting.' She pulled herself up in the bed. 'Cass, can I give you something to keep on your boat?'

'So long as it's not inflammable substances or dangerous chemicals. Or firearms.'

Her eyes flicked up to mine, then dropped to the bullet-straight line across my cheek. 'I'd forgotten. No, I won't give you a gun to have on board. Can you hide me a box of papers? Down in, what do you call down in the keel of a boat, the bilges?'

'The bilges can be wet,' I said, 'but I can find a dry place. How big?'

'Shoe box, or biscuit tin. If you look in the shed by the vegetables you'll find something. One that won't look too out of place aboard.'

'You think someone might look?'

She answered obliquely. 'Do you lock the boat up, when you're not in it?'

I shook my head. 'Cat likes to come and go. When I'm not here at all, yes. Magnie has the key.'

'Well then. A corner people wouldn't find easily, shoved under obvious boat stuff. Do you have somewhere like that?'

I looked her straight in the eye. 'These papers, would they be important enough to destroy my boat for, if they couldn't be found?'

That gave her pause. Her gaze went downwards, towards the sound of voices from below, then up again. She looked, unseeing, at the mantelpiece, face still as she considered it. 'No. No.' She turned back to me, expression alive again. 'On the contrary. If there's any chance they're aboard, the loss of your boat would be the last thing she'd—' She corrected herself quickly. '—they'd want.'

I made a face, but took her word for it. 'Okay. So you need a small box or biscuit tin sneaked in to you, and sneaked out again.'

'Thanks, Cass. If you could bring it to me now, I can give it back to you at bedtime.'

The shed was well supplied with old boxes; it was a right trow's hadd in there, with all sorts of gear stowed in a jumble. If there was a pot of gold, it was well hidden. I chose a large ice-cream tub, on the grounds that that was what I stowed my own gear in, managed to get it out from under the pile of assorted containers stowed on top without bringing the lot down on me, rinsed and dried it in the kitchen, found newspaper and parcel tape, and took them all up to Tamar. She nodded in satisfaction at my haul. 'Give me ten minutes, then come up and give me a hand downstairs, I'll sit in the conservatory until dinner's ready. It smells good.'

I checked the roast and set the plates to warm, then headed up again. The ice-cream tub was on the bed, taped within an inch of its life. 'Put it in the bottom drawer,' Tamar said, 'with a blanket over it.' She tilted her head downwards towards where we could still hear Felicity's voice, arguing. 'In case she comes snooping.'

It was heavier than I'd have expected, with maybe a book as well as papers. *They're not there to find* . . . because they'd been kept up here? The horse painting above the mantelpiece was slightly askew. I shut my imaginings of a safe behind it down, and put the box into the drawer.

'Good,' Tamar said. 'That's that sorted.'

I went down the stairs before her, and had just settled her into her chair when Felicity came back into the sit-ootery, eyes sparking, a spot of scarlet on each cheek, and her mouth set in a sullen line. I'd seen that face in my mirror after each of my teenage rows with my father over him going to the Gulf and me going to Maman in France.

'Your father annoying you?' Tamar asked.

Felicity scowled, and didn't answer. I headed for the living room, and my roast. It turned out as good as it smelled, with the skin crisped above tenderly pink flesh, although my carving was more like hacking – still, everyone got enough, and Tamar's and my joint blackcurrant crumble was a masterpiece. I wouldn't be able to make it aboard *Khalida*, but I could definitely do it in a Rayburn oven.

It was a quiet evening. I did the dishes, then nipped down to screw the catflap into its hole and set the new washboard in the cabin opening. Cat was initially reluctant, but after a couple of goes with me half-shoving him through, I thought he'd got the idea, and closed the forepeak hatch. I went back up to the cottage to find Felicity flicking at her tablet. Tamar got me to bring the radio down again, and Felicity brightened up at *Front Row* and *Any Questions?*, while Tamar flicked through a catalogue labelled *Skeld Hairst Show and Sheepdog Trials*. Tomorrow's excitement, I presumed. She saw me looking at it.

'I'm just reminding myself what I entered, by way of flowers and vegetables. We'll have a busy morning tomorrow.'

I dredged up memories of the Voe show. 'Best three of the same kind, that sort of thing?'

'And an arrangement or two. We'll need to pick the flowers, and take them over for one o'clock.'

'Okay,' I said, and got on with reading *Bleak House*, a charity shop find in hardback with print that had seemed fine under the shop's strip lighting, but had turned out to be too small to read aboard *Khalida* after dark. One benefit of a fixed abode, I decided, was that you could have a decent reading light without running your batteries down. At nine, I helped Tamar upwards, waited on the landing till she'd got her pyjamas on, then went in and retrieved the ice-cream tub. 'Goodnight. Same time again tomorrow?'

She nodded. 'Goodnight, Cass. Thanks.' She smiled, a real smile, not her witch's grin. 'Your policeman's onto a good thing. Maybe he'll resist the blonde.'

'I'll woo him with crumble,' I said.

Felicity was on her mobile again as I passed through, sending more urgent financial stuff to her long-suffering PA. All was not well, I gathered, in the world of *Latest!* magazine. I wondered if that was what had sparked off this sudden devotion to her great-aunt.

I called goodnight, slid out of the back door and headed down the path to *Khalida*. It had seemed black dark from inside the house, but now I was outside there was still a flush of duck-egg blue above the Aith hills, and a last gleam of gold lying along the hilltop. On the other side of the sky Venus shone out, bright and steady. Cat was waiting for me on the cabin roof, a dark silhouette against the curve of white fibreglass. I greeted him, and headed below.

Hide Tamar's tub first. The best place for anything to go unnoticed was among other similar things, and my bilges were full of labelled ice-cream tubs. I'd have called them a trow's hadd too, except that I knew there was no pot of gold among them. I taped a bit of white plastic bag on the lid and wrote *Spare Fuses 5 amp / 7 amp / 10 amp / Oil – Fuel – Air Filters – Impellers* in big letters with a marker pen, then put it at the bottom of the locker full of engine spares and assorted tools that I didn't use often. It wouldn't escape a serious search that opened everything, but I hoped nobody would come looking.

It was too early to sleep. Cat's bowl was empty again. I put down the rest of the tuna, brushed my teeth on deck, then lit the oil lamp below, and sat down in the corner behind the table. Gavin should be finished his day's form-filling procedure lectures. If he was in the pub with the rest of the squad, he could phone me later.

He answered on the second ring. '*Halo*, Cass. How're you doing?'

'I cooked a roast today, and made a crumble. Both good, too. How were the forms?'

He groaned. 'We moved on from forms to procedure with witnesses, as a finisher, then one of those question and answer sessions. I'd kill for a decent crumble. The hotel we were in only did trendy catering – you know, the sort of presentation that involves squiggle lines of sauce across the meat, and part of the meal served in a separate little dish. Oh, and slates.'

'I don't know,' I said. 'I've never done trendy catering. What do you mean, slates?'

'The food comes on them.'

'Slates? You mean, you have to eat off them?'

A sigh came across the ether. 'Yesterday, I had my pudding served in a jam jar as well.'

I thought about that for a moment. 'Why?'

'It's fashionable. Even Inverness restaurants are doing it now. I was hoping the fad might be past down south.'

I envisaged eating a steak off a slate, and sticky toffee pudding out of a jam jar, and decided it wouldn't work. 'How do they wash the slates?'

'Dishwasher, I suppose. Anyway, I'm on my way home now. I decided I couldn't be bothered with the old–boys–network and bonding in the pub, and took the first train to Inverness. We're almost at Newtonmore. Shall I phone you properly when I get to the flat? It'll be another hour or so.'

'Yes, do that. Nothing much to report here.'

I struggled on with *Bleak House* using my head torch for a bit, then lit the lantern and pottered gently bedwards. I'd just wriggled into my berth when there was a miaow outside, repeated with that ominous note of 'I've got something to show you.' I leapt up and had just shoved my feet into my seaboots when Cat came in and dumped a small, terrified mouse on the cabin floor. He watched it for a moment, but when it didn't move, he headed back out again, leaving me to pick it up in a dishtowel and return it to the pier. It seemed unharmed.

It was, I supposed, mouse time of year. I was back in bed, hoping Cat wouldn't just bring it, or another one, straight back in, by the time Gavin phoned. My hot-water bottle was cosy at my feet, and my candle flickered on the engine box. The gold gleams reminded me.

'I forgot to tell you,' I said, 'that Tamar gave me a mysterious package to hide in the bilges.'

'Hide from whom?'

'She didn't say.' *She* quickly corrected to *they.* 'I think it's Felicity. She was dead keen on finding papers about the Ryland connection, you know, the Sand laird. Tamar said . . .' I paused trying to think. 'Yes, she said that Archie, that's her brother, had his own papers, but she repeated that she didn't have anything about the Rylands in her desk. She said it twice, and whatever this is, it was in her bedroom. It's heavy too, more like a book than papers, but papers was what she said it was. Anyway,' I finished, getting back to essentials, 'she promised nobody would ransack the boat for them.'

'You're supposed to be innocently helping out an old lady, not getting involved in mysterious papers and inheritance skulduggery. The sooner I get up there the better.'

We'd just said goodnight properly when Cat returned, mouse-free, and curled into my neck. I blew out the candle and lay enjoying the waves lapping at *Khalida*'s hull, the complete darkness. On board *Sørlandet* there was always somebody on duty, and the deck lights shining, and the generator rumbling. This was better, this stillness. I sighed, and let it soothe me to sleep.

# Chapter Ten

Saturday 23rd August

*HW 02.21 (1.4); LW 08.41 (0.6); HW 15.07 (1.3); LW 20.59 (0.6)*

*Sunrise 04.39, sunset 19.35; moonrise 17.43, moonset 23.52.*

*Third quarter moon.*

**toun:** the cultivated or grazed area associated with a crofthouse [Old Norse, *tun*, a fenced plot or home field]

I woke just after six to the noise of Cat washing. He was slurping more noisily than usual, bumping into the top of my head with the effort he was putting into it, and purring loudly at the same time. I opened my eyes. The sun was glowing through the long window, making the condensation translucent, and casting a soft glow of gold onto the couch. Cat had moved along from his usual place in the crook of my neck into the patch of sunlight. I could hear the rasp of his tongue, mixed with purring and the occasional protesting squeak. I woke up properly at that, and lifted my head. My independent Cat was curled around a minute gingery ketling, which was being washed within an inch of its life. As I moved, they both froze, then the ketling leapt down and disappeared into the forecabin. It seemed we had a stowaway. I lay very still, waiting, and gradually a shadow moved forrard, and crept back into the main cabin.

It was the prettiest ketling I'd ever seen. Gingery was an insult; its coat was a blend of cinnamon and ginger, all-spice and nutmeg.

It had a neat amber face with the tabby M in black on its brow, a white bib and paws, and a fluffy tail that ended in a blob of pale apricot. All it needed was a pink ribbon for its photo to go on the front of any chocolate box. I kept still, and gradually it jumped up again, planted a diminutive paw on Cat's forehead, and began washing his ear.

All was now explained. My guess had been right; I didn't need to worry about Cat's appetite or innards. We had a stowaway, and one too young to be eating normal cat food. Tuna was probably too rich for it too. I'd need to lift his plate out of the ketling's way, even though I sympathised with mackerel or tuna being more interesting than dead starlings.

Speaking soothingly and squirming cautiously out of my berth, I went to open the washboards and stick my head out of the main hatch. It was a bonny morning. The sun was veiled by the mist lying on the top of the eastern hill, but it was clear to the west, duck-egg blue at the horizon, shading up to the pale blue of a northern summer. The lush grass by the gravel track was grey with dew, and a breath of wind from the south ruffled my hair.

I left Cat and his ketling to finish their wash, and headed ashore. The tide was almost full out, the shore stretching from the red-brown shingle down through larger stones like chunks of broken rock that twisted your foot as you set it down, to clumps of olive bladder-wrack and neon-green mermaid hair, and finally pebble-sand, licked into bright colours by the translucent water.

Tamar was awake and alert; Felicity trailed in as I began on the toast, sleepy in a green velour dressing gown. After breakfast we went outside, Tamar with her elbow crutches and me with a pair of secateurs and a long wicker basket.

It was easy to see that Tamar had concentrated her efforts on the vegetable and fruit garden. The flower garden, in front of the sit-ootery, was simple: two wide beds of all the sorts of flowers that even I knew grew like weeds in Shetland running down each side of the straight gravel path that led to the seawards gate. There were low trees on the jetty side, still summer-green, and covered with clumps of green berries, and rounded clouds of papery-flowered New Zealand daisy bush. In front of them were the autumn flowers: spikes of yellow stars with red throats, waist-high clumps of the big white daisies, orange montbretia, whisker-faced pansies and a riot of purple-flowered mint. On the Brae side, there was a tangle of honeysuckle with curving red flower hands holding yellow petals like miniature tiger lilies up to the sun. The roses still held a few magenta flowers, three inches across, with gold-stamened centres, but the leaves had begun to turn cadmium yellow. Among them were clumps of dark green, glossy leaves, with tight buds of flower spikes coming up from them: the Shetland delphinium, which wouldn't flower until October. There were violet autumn crocus at their roots.

'Verbascum stems,' Tamar said, after a look round. She came forward, leaning on her stick. 'This one, and the one next to it. Go down the stem as far as you can.' I snipped, and put the long head in my basket. 'Then two along – yes. And, let me see, yes, the second from the end.' I came back to upright. 'Daisies now,' Tamar said. She lowered herself onto the driftwood bench below the sit-ootery. 'The best four you can see, to give one for a spare. You know a daisy when you see it, don't you?'

I indicated them with my secateurs. She nodded, and I stepped through the undergrowth to inspect the daisies. A clear yellow centre, an undamaged ring of petals and a long, straight stem. I found four that I thought would pass, and cut them. 'Next?'

'Montbretia, those orange ones.'

I took another step into the border, and surveyed them. The overall effect was orange, but close to they were splashed with yellow, as if an artist had taken a paint brush to them. 'Do you want blocked orange or streaked with yellow?'

'Can you find me four of each?'

'I can try.' I found the best specimens I could. After that I managed four curved honeysuckle, resisting the childhood impulse to suck the dark red stamens for their honey taste, and a thorny medley of magenta roses and waxen scarlet hips.

100

'That'll do,' Tamar said, eyeing up my basket. 'A pity the monks-hood's so late blooming.'

'Monkshood?'

'Tamar gestured towards the Shetland delphinium. 'Those green clumps there. *Aconitum.* Monkshood. Grows like a weed, lovely blue flowers, gentian blue, and the leaves colour up nicely.' She gave her witch's grin, slyly sideways. 'Very poisonous.' She considered the basket again. 'No, get me three twigs with whitebeam berries too. Give me a reasonable length of stem, and some leaves. That'll do for the structure of the arrangement.' I supposed she knew what she was talking about. 'After that, I'll get you to bring the big vase out here – it's on the top shelf of the pantry. Put only an inch of water in the bottom, and take a bottle for filling up once we get to Skeld.'

I found the vase, set it on the bench beside her, and watched, enjoying the warmth of the sun, as she placed the stems I'd gathered into it. It looked pretty to me, with the ruddy autumn colours, but I had no doubt there would be fierce competition with far more exotic flowers in a variety of containers. Tamar shot me a sideways glance. 'Too simple, you think?'

I shrugged. 'What would I know? I like it.'

'The art of flower arranging is simple.' She put in a last montbretia and nodded to herself. 'Make sure each flower is showing itself off.' She paused, and looked over the shining water. 'Now, that can go to the car. Wedge it as if you were taking it for a sail in a force six.'

As I stood up, a flash of light on a nylon jacket caught my eye, up on the hill. I straightened and turned to look properly. Someone was coming over the crest of the hill and striding down the road to the house, with the occasional pause to inspect the sheep grazing by the fence. I looked down at Tamar. 'We've got company. A walker, making straight for the house.' Another look showed me a dark bulge on his back that looked like a small rucksack, and a flash of brown legs. 'Male, wearing shorts, with a rucksack.'

'I'm not expecting a hitchhiker,' she said, then a startled look flashed across her face, as if she'd remembered something.

'Unless it's . . . ?' I prompted.

101

She gave me a sharp look, but didn't volunteer her thought. 'You'd better go and see what he wants. Put the kettle on as you go through.'

*What he wants.* 'You're not interested in who he is, then?'

She gave a harsh bark of laughter, acknowledging the hit. 'So sharp you'll cut yourself. He's called Bob Irvine. Go on, go and get him.'

By the time I opened the door he'd passed the car and was heading for the house with those long strides. One look told me where he was from; you didn't get that sea-bleached hair, that deep tan, anywhere north of the equator. Antipodean, in his early twenties, out to hitchhike his way round the world. Now hadn't Tamar said something about a brother who'd gone to New Zealand? *Bruce's son was called Bob* . . . Christmas cards . . . there were grandchildren – and here, if I wasn't mistaken, returning so confidently to the house of his ancestors, looking every inch the capable young farmer, was one of them, and by Tamar's invitation too, if I was reading her aright. A possible Irvine heir for her croft?

He greeted me cheerfully from twenty yards back. 'Hello there! Am I at the right house for Tamar Irvine?'

'She's just in the garden,' I said. 'Follow me.'

Seeing him close to, I felt a prick of misgiving. He wasn't as young as I'd thought; looking at his skin, at the slight wrinkles around his eyes and on his brow, I was inclined to put him as slightly older than myself, mid-thirties maybe, and a golden boy who traded on his charm instead of doing a bit of solid work. I thought of Harald, the younger Shetland version, and decided this family seemed to run to charmers. Not that I had any right to look down on drifters, I'd been one myself, but I'd turned respectable at thirty, deciding I needed my own place in the world.

I pushed my prejudices aside and led him through the house to the front garden, where Tamar was sitting as erect as if she was a queen on audience day.

'Hello, Great-Aunt Tamar,' the man said. 'I'm Bob, your brother Willie's grandson. As you see, I've taken you at your word, and come to call while I was in the UK.'

'It's good to meet you, Bob.' Tamar gave him a critical stare. 'Yes, I think I'd have known you for an Irvine. You have a look of my father about the eyes, and the jawline.'

He dropped his rucksack to the ground and sat down on the bench beside her. 'It's good to meet you at last.' He gave the crutches a sympathetic look. 'How's it mending?'

'Slowly.' Tamar gave a snort. 'They wouldn't let me out of Wastview until I had someone looking after me, so this is Cass, who's kindly given up her leave.'

I was to be myself with this one then. I wasn't sure whether that meant Tamar thought he was trustworthy, or whether she didn't think you could pull the wool over a Kiwi's eyes where boats were concerned. Bob looked up at me. 'Leave?'

'I'm second mate aboard the Norwegian tall ship *Sørlandet*. She's in dry dock before we head for America. Coffee?'

'Yes, please. I had a lucky lift right to the end of your track, but it was a thirsty walk over the hill. The view was good, though. Nice flock of little Shetlanders you've got there.' He looked out over the blue water. 'That's Brae up to the right?'

'You came the Aith way then?'

'Yes, I got a lift out to Bixter from folk going to Skeld, then walked into Aith, and got a lift from there. Friendly folk, us Shetlanders. The Skeld ones were some kind of cousins. They sent their best wishes.' His brow wrinkled. 'Ertie and Bella, something like that.'

'My mother's cousin's daughter, Bella, she married a Priest man.' She levered herself to her feet. 'Let me show you around.'

I left them to it, and went into the kitchen to make the coffee, puzzling to myself. I was pretty sure I'd never met this Bob before, but he reminded me of someone – someone I'd disliked, but I just couldn't put my finger on the memory, like one of those annoying moments when you spot an actor in a film but can't remember what you last saw them in. I'd just put the kettle on to boil when Felicity appeared from the shower, head wrapped in a towel. 'Was that a visitor?'

103

'A long-lost cousin.' I quickly ran over the relationship in my mind. 'Your uncle's grandson. First cousin once removed.'

'Long-lost?'

'One of the New Zealand lot.'

Her eyes sparked at that. 'Oh, is he? And what's he doing, turning up so pat? I'd better get dressed.'

By noon it was a perfect sailing day, with the soft wind steady from the east and the clouds thinned from grey to white, child's drawings against the paint-box blue sky. Felicity offered to drive to the show, and I accepted with relief. I didn't really fancy manoeuvring Tamar's car in a packed hall car park. Bob and I squished into the back seat, with the vase of flowers between our feet; the group-of-three flowers had been put in jam jars in a box in the boot, and clinked gently as we headed up the track. The day and the world around us just got bonnier and bonnier as we drove west along single-track roads: the heather hills between us and Aith, just starting to turn from pine-green to purple, the burnt orange of bog asphodel, the first hint of ruby on the spagnum moss. As we came past the battlemented ruin of Park Hall, Tamar turned her head to me. 'I remember when that house was saveable. If I have any say in it, the Ladie's not going to end up a ruin.'

Past Semblister, there was a green meadow below us, notched into Chinese patterns by innumerable burns in the soft turf, and with red and white horses grazing, then a long inlet with the sun dancing on the water. On our left, the north-facing hills were still bronze-green, but on our right the sun-warmed heather was glorious purple tussocks as far as the eye could see. Ahead, thirty miles away, was the dark bulk of Fitful Head, the south of the island.

Beside me, Bob leaned forward with a soft 'Awwwh.' I turned my head. He was staring intently out of the window, a smile touching his mouth. He glanced back at me. 'It's beautiful out this side. I didn't manage to get –' then broke off. He reddened under his tan, and added hurriedly. 'It's like parts of home.'

The parts that didn't have snow-peaked mountain ranges as a

backdrop? 'It's bonny,' I agreed. *I didn't manage to get . . . It's beautiful this side.* How had he meant to finish that sentence? *I didn't manage to get here on my last visit?* I turned and gave him a smile. 'Your first visit to Shetland, then?'

There was a heartbeat pause before he replied. 'It's a long way to come, but I'm glad to see the home of my ancestors.' He nodded forwards. 'Is this Skeld we're coming into now?'

'It is,' I agreed.

He'd slid around the question neatly, but I was pretty sure he'd given himself away. I didn't trust smiling, golden Bob.

It was a bonny place, Skeld, laid out in the traditional way, with a long line of houses on each side of the voe, and a cluster of council houses down by the marina, which was a big one, the size of Brae's, with several masts and a fleet of large motorboats. There were new houses, wooden built in the Norwegian style, with verandas running along the front, and the whitewashed kirk. The school was up to the left, and the hall to the right, both refurbished recently.

When we arrived, Tamar inspected the four flowers in each group, and removed the one which had travelled least well, then I took them into the hall. We'd hit lunchtime for the competitors. The room was filled with people being served plates of mince with mashed tatties and carrots. It was strange to see so many local folk and recognise almost none of them. Although every one of them would have a boat, the Sheepdog Trials called out the crofter folk, focused on the land rather than the sea. I gave the flowers into the keeping of one of the stewards and went back out into the car park. For a moment I couldn't see Tamar's car, and hesitated by the corner, looking round. A voice came right in my ear: 'You'd need to take them away.'

I jumped, and turned, but there was nobody beside me. The speaker was around the corner, behind the hall. I took a couple of steps forward, away from what was obviously a private conversation. When the voice came again, I recognised the sulky tone: it was Harald. 'I'm telling you, I'm no' keeping them. It's no' safe, now Tamar's home.'

'I'm making arrangements,' an English public-school voice said. I glanced over my shoulder, and saw Harald with his back to me, confronting a man in one of those waxed jackets and those green rubber boots with the little buckle at the side. A tweed cap was pulled down over his brow. They were laird-style clothes, highly practical, of course, but they rather stood out against the boiler suits and yellow rubber boots of the natives.

'They need to go,' Harald persisted.

The other man raised his voice to speak over him. 'Another couple of days.' It was an order. 'I've got it in hand.'

Harald managed a sullen, 'No' more as a couple o' days,' and shouldered his way past me, too busy scowling to clock who I was. I glanced over at the other man. He was watching him go, and frowning. If I was Harald I'd modify my tone a bit. He didn't look a good man to cross. *It's no' safe, noo Tamar's hame . . .* I remembered him going into the container, Gary's container it would be, if it was Gary working the mussels, under the pretext of feeding ketlings. *I'm no keeping them . . .* Them? Drugs was the obvious guess, but 'them' was an odd word to use. Several packages of drugs? What else might this laird person be wanting hidden?

I spotted Tamar's car now, drawn forwards by the gate. I clambered in and Tamar directed Felicity up the rough track by the side of the hall. Above us there was a row of pick-ups on the hill, with their tailgates open, each with a dog tethered to the tow-bar, or sitting in the back. Most folk were down in the hall, but some were yarning, or sitting in the sun eating sandwiches. Heads turned as Felicity bumped the car over the rough grass, and parked, under Tamar's instructions, in a good spot for watching goings-on from the car. Bob helped Tamar ease herself out of the front seat, and I brought her crutches forward. She looked around and called a couple of 'Aye ayes', and the greetings were returned. I hovered by her elbow as she walked slowly over to one older man with a litter of whelps in the back of his pick-up, squirming bundles of sleek black-and-white, all sharp teeth, bright eyes and wagging tails. He lifted one out to show us: 'Their grand-dam was old Jet, remember her? And who're this young folk you have wi' you?'

Tamar introduced Felicity, and the old man said he'd known her father.

'And this is Bob. My brother Willie's boy's boy.'

'Aye, aye,' the old man said. 'So you're Willie's grandson. Well, it'll be fine to have an Irvine man back at the Ladie.'

Felicity gave him a startled glance, then looked quickly at Tamar, who smiled, and didn't contradict him. 'And this is Cass Lynch, from Brae.'

There was a moment's pause, then he gave me a sharp glance under lowered brows, and an 'Aye, aye.' I felt oddly rebuffed, as if I'd been judged and found wanting. He turned back to talk to Tamar and Bob, and stepped away to let them admire the puppies. It was only a little comfort that Felicity was equally dismissed, and a relief when Kayleigh came striding up from the hall. 'Tamar! I'm blyde you made it. Aye aye, Cass. Felicity.' Her gaze turned to Bob; her eyes widened in a classic double-take. For a moment her eyes lit up, then grew wary. Her laugh sounded forced. 'Well, well, cousin Bob! What on earth are you doing here?'

'Redding up kin, wasn't that what you called it? Your Aunt Tamar invited me to come and visit, and after all you'd told me about the place, I thought I'd take her up on it.'

Suspicion flared in Kayleigh's eyes. She turned away for a moment, eyes vulnerable in a set-hard face, then came back again, smiling. 'Well, this is a surprise to see you. Welcome to the land of your ancestors.' She turned back to Tamar. 'We're no' been on yet. Practically last in the afternoon.' She made a face. 'I hope you'll be able to wait. Come and see how she's looking.'

She led Tamar on ahead, leaving Bob and I walking together. He was frowning, thoughtful, as if he was working out how to stop Kayleigh being a check to his so-far triumphant progress.

'Of course,' I said casually, 'you and Kayleigh were friendly when she was over there, weren't you?'

He gave a dismissive little wave. 'Oh, I wouldn't call it that,

107

exactly. We took her out a bit, my sisters and I, while she was over. What she told me about her home inspired me to visit.'

I'd have betted it had. What had Kayleigh said about him? *He was interested in farming, but of course their own farm would go down through Allan's family.* And there was Kayleigh, telling him about an old lady and a croft that might be his for the Irvine name and a bit of charm.

No, I didn't trust smiling, golden Bob.

# Chapter Eleven

**park:** a piece of enclosed grazing (Scots, *park*)

We were just following Kayleigh to her pick-up when Felicity gave a surprised exclamation, and stopped to talk to a man who'd just got out of a Land Rover. He was wearing a tweed cap, a waxed brown Barbour and green wellies – the man Harald had been arguing with.

'Eddie Ryland!' Felicity said. 'Well, what on earth are you doing here?'

The name made me focus on him. So this was Felicity's city friend, the grandson of the original Edward that had been ages with Tamar; the one whose father she'd mistaken for her brother. His grey-green eyes were slightly narrowed under brows as immaculate as Felicity's own, and his fair hair was gelled back in a high plume above his forehead. Everything about him oozed privilege: a private school, from there to Varsity, then straight into Daddy's firm. I felt my inner socialist welling up.

Seeing him and Felicity together, I did see a resemblance – not just the colouring, but the shape of eye and set of brow, and the way they held their heads. I could easily take them for *freends*. I summoned up my Shetland upbringing and tried to work it out. Felicity thought her father was the half-brother of this man's father – yes, first cousins.

Eddie's voice matched his looks. 'Felicity, darling,' he drawled. 'I could ask you the same. What on earth are you doing this far from St Paul's?'

Felicity gave a vague gesture. 'Oh, you know. Catching up with family. Getting away from the rat race for a rest.' She added, in a tone so casual that I felt like giving her a round of applause, 'Of course, your people have a place up here, don't they?'

'We usually come up for the dog trials. Daddy's keen on his collies.'

Translated, that meant that Daddy's factor, who ran the croft in his most-of-the-year absence, was interested, and trained them to be entered in Daddy's name in the trials and local shows.

'I didn't realise you had family here,' Eddie said. 'Introduce me, sweetheart.'

I could see Felicity would have liked to get out of that one, but Tamar had paused and was looking expectantly at her, brows raised. 'My aunt,' Felicity said.

'Tamar Irvine.' Tamar leaned her weight on her crutch, and put out her right hand. 'I worked for your great-grandparents, oh, longer ago than I want to remember. When I was a teenager.'

He jerked backwards. His mouth fell open, and there was an awkward, silent moment before the practised charm took over, with the added graciousness of a laird talking to the staff. 'Delighted to meet you, Miss Irvine. I hadn't realised there was any of your gen-eration still going strong.' He looked at her uncertainly for a moment, considering her crutches. His eyes darted from Tamar to Felicity, then back to Tamar. 'Been in the wars?'

'I fell,' Tamar said.

His brow lightened, as if an old lady who kept falling over was good news. 'That's not so good at your age. Don't make a habit of it, eh? Lovely to meet you, Miss Irvine.' He turned back to Felicity. 'Now, tell me all the latest gossip in the world of publishing.' He put his hand through her arm, and drew her back, letting Kayleigh and Tamar go in front, back towards the car, with Bob and me trailing behind them.

The peace had ended when the lunchers began coming up from the hall in a revving and jostling of pick-ups. Kayleigh was keeping Tamar on level ground to the side of the track, and Bob was silent, watching them together, so I let my thoughts stray to what was going on with Eddie Ryland. He obviously knew Felicity from London; what he hadn't known was her connection to Shetland, and the Irvines who'd once worked for his family. *Sorting through a hundred years' worth of papers*, Felicity had said, when she'd been talking about the resemblance to her brother, and then a man who worked for them was found dead near Tamar's cottage, and Felicity had come up to snoop around . . . It all seemed to belong together, but in a nebulous way I couldn't quite make sense of. Maybe in among the papers there had been information about an illegitimate son, school bills, or a lawyer's letter about a Shetland boy using the surname Irvine – except that Eddie hadn't connected him with Felicity Irvine, the gossip merchant, the editor of a glossy magazine that fed on family scandal, and now, it seemed, the niece of someone old enough to remember that scandal. He was putting the two together, and not liking it.

Suddenly there was a crashing of gears and a metallic bang behind us, and a startled shriek. Then there was silence.

I spun around. A Land Rover had come to a halt, slantways across the path, and Felicity was leaning against it, both hands flat against its bonnet, as if she'd slipped and staggered against it. Her face was white; her hands, as she lifted them away, were grimed with dust. There was a smear of blood on one palm, oozing darkly at first, then running scarlet. She looked at it uncomprehendingly for a moment, then fumbled in her bag and brought out a paper tissue to mop at it. Eddie took her arm to lead her away from the Land Rover, and the driver, a burly crofter in a grey all-over jumper, jumped down and came around the bonnet.

'Are you all right, lass?'

Felicity nodded. 'I'm fine,' she managed. 'Sorry.' She achieved a brittle laugh. 'I cross Trafalgar Square every day, then nearly get myself run down in the wilds of Shetland.' She twisted the tissue against her palm. 'No damage done.'

There was a queue of pick-ups backing up behind the Land Rover. The crofter got back in, and moved up into the field, and the others followed. Eddie brought Felicity up to the car, and fished in one of his pockets for a silver hip flask. 'Have a spot of whisky. That'll brace you up.'

'There's a first-aid kit in my car,' Tamar said. 'In the glove compartment, Cass.'

I reached in and fished out a bottle of TCP, a roll of cotton wool and a box of plasters. 'Let me see,' I said. I took Felicity's wrist and uncurled her fingers from the tissue. Her palm was scored by a nasty gash, as if she'd been caught by a sharp corner of the bonnet. 'This'll sting a bit.' I upended the TCP bottle over some cotton wool, and Felicity made a face, took the damp ball from me, and dabbed it around the cut, screwing up her mouth as it stung. I gave her another cotton wool ball to dry it off with, then a plaster.

'That should fix it,' Eddie said. He gave her his smooth smile. 'That'll teach you to wear London boots in the country.'

She gave him a look I couldn't read, calculating, mouth tight, then a sudden smile. 'But really, darling, I couldn't be seen in green wellies. Thanks for the pick-me-up. I'll just sit quietly now, and watch the show.'

Eddie helped her solicitously into the driving seat, then stepped back. 'I must be off – see what Daddy's up to. Maybe catch you later. Miss Irvine –' He sketched a wave at us, and headed into the crowd. I watched him go, thoughtfully. Felicity could have stumbled, of course; the going was rough enough. I just didn't trust Eddie's smooth ways, and it seemed a rather sudden accident just when he'd linked her up with the Irvine family. She was silent now, looking out at the green hill as if she didn't really see it.

Tamar nudged me. 'Wake up, Cass. Here's the first contestant.'

I put my mental red flag away, settled myself down on the grass by Tamar's wing, and looked at the trial area. The first competitor came forward to the post by the pen, and leaned on his staff. The dog lay down at his feet. It was all very leisurely, with the sun warm on my cheek, and a pigeon cooing from the trees below, and yellow coltsfoot among the wiry grass. Far away across the field, a couple of people brought three sheep out. Then, suddenly, the dog shot off

112

like a black arrow, took a wide circuit around the distant sheep and came up behind them.

'He has to bring the sheep through those two gates,' Tamar said, 'up to his handler, then up through those gates there.' She indicated two more hurdles set up on the skyline. 'Then back down the hill to the gates down there.' Bob nodded. He was watching the dog intently, assessing it as if he knew what he was seeing. It seemed a long run, some four hundred metres. 'Back up to the handler, and they pen the sheep, then let them out and separate one of them from the others. They've got ten minutes.'

The sheep came up over the hill towards us, three plump year-olds who looked as if they'd been washed for the occasion, with the dog crouched low as a wolf behind them, ears flattened. It got them through the upper gate, down the hill and wheeled around them to bring them back to the handler. They scampered up towards us and stopped. They were obviously wondering what was going on. For a start, they were used to peaceful grazing, not being herded all over the park at a smart trot. For another thing, you could see them thinking, they'd come up here already. The handler moved over to the pen and swung the gate open, and posted himself by it, staff held out to help guide the sheep in. At this point it all came unstuck. The sheep looked at the pen and decided they weren't going in there. They tried to turn away, and found the dog in front of them. They stopped, thinking, and the dog edged forwards. The sheep edged backwards, then, just as the handler moved forward with the gate, jumped sideways. The dog brought them round again – and then a whistle blew.

Bob shook his head. 'Out of time. Pity. It was a good run till then.'

The dog chased the sheep out of the ring – they headed straight towards the lower part of the park we were in, as if they knew where they were going this time – and charged back to his owner. His red tongue lolled out, twice the length of his mouth.

The time went surprisingly quickly. The dogs were all Border collies, black above, white below, with a white collar and tail tip, and working names like Vic, Tam and Mel, handles that could easily

be shouted out over a hillside, though I suspected the pedigree cer-
tificate would say Viceroy Tamburlane of Merkisayre. The
competitors were all dressed in their best short-sleeved check sarks
and cloth breeks, with black rubber boots instead of yellow, and
those with whiskers had washed them for the occasion. I even saw a
cloth cap in place of the ubiquitous knitted toorie. All the dogs
picked up the sheep quickly, and most managed to get them through
all the gates; it was at the pen that the fun started. None of the sheep
wanted to go into it. For one dog, all three broke away and stam-
peded for their home park; for another, one sheep charged round
and round the outside of the pen, the other two kangaroo faces
watching with interest as the dog tried to gather it up, then, realising
he wasn't watching them, they began to edge away towards home.
The dog and single sheep were still at the far side of the park when
the whistle went.

I was amused to notice that most of the dogs believed they knew
what they were doing better than the owners. Commands like
'stand', 'keep away' and 'lie down' were generally ignored. One dog
kept looking back, obviously puzzled as to why the two dogs which
had helped bring the sheep out from the pen weren't doing any more
work. The final 'That'll do!' was greeted with pricked ears and a
wagging tail, once the dog was satisfied that the sheep really had
gone down to their own park. All in all, it was a pleasant way of
spending a Saturday afternoon, with the sun warm on my face, the
bird-like piping of the whistles augmented by the occasional shout,
the olive-green of the wiry grass overshot by waving gold grass-
heads, the yellow coltsfoot, the purple hills crazed with dark lines of
peat banks, and the cloud shadows moving over the moor.

Kayleigh was the last that we saw. She strode forward with an air of
determination, and you could see that though the dog was only a
youngster, she was just as set on getting this right. She was a pretty
dog, brown and white, with alertly pricked ears and a fine feathered
tail, and the second the sheep were released she was right with them,
rounding them up and steering them to the upper gate, around, down
the hill and round the hurdle, then back up again to Kayleigh, waiting

ready at the pen. Astonishingly, they went in smoothly, Kayleigh isolated the one she wanted, and the dog steered the others out, all before the bell rang. Tamar nodded in satisfaction. 'A good run.'

Kayleigh came over to us, the dog still at her heels.

'Good work,' Tamar said. 'That dog's got potential, though you were lucky with the sheep too.'

Kayleigh nodded. 'Time for a cup of tea now. I'll just put Lady back. See you down there.'

Felicity made a face as she put her hands to the steering wheel, but she drove smoothly enough down to the hall. I helped Tamar out, and we headed in. 'Do you want to look at how your flowers have done first?'

She shook her head. 'My eyes are still good enough for me to spot a red card from the tables. Tea, sandwiches and cake.'

'My own priorities,' I agreed. The hall was filled with people again, and ringing with chatting voices and the chink of cutlery. I looked around, and spotted a group of four just standing up from a table next to where the Cole folk were sitting, Joanie and Gary with a mound of rolls between them. 'Grab that table, Bob, and then Tamar can sit and guard it while I get her food.'

Bob dived for it, and Tamar followed at her own pace, while Kayleigh and Felicity joined the queue at the long table laden with best hall grub: half rolls filled with egg, cheese, ham or corned beef, bannocks with saat flesh, and a display of fancies that made my mouth water. It was £5 for all you could eat, and given that we'd skipped lunch, and I was starving, I reckoned that was a bargain. I collected an assortment of sandwiches for Tamar and I, and took them over to the table, where Bob had organised an extra chair, and Loretta had appeared from the kitchen with a tray to clear the dirty cups. She looked more incongruous than ever, with her gaudy blue earrings glinting under the fair hair, like the real Diana putting on an apron to publicise a children's charity tea party. I noticed she was getting amused glances from the local folk who knew her, and double-takes from visitors. 'Are you all for tea?

I'll be back with it in just a meenit. And who's this smart young man you're got in tow, Tamar?'

'Willie's grandson, Bob, come over from New Zealand. Bob, this is your cousin Loretta.'

Her bonhomie vanished. Those implausibly blue eyes narrowed, the coral pink mouth pursed for a moment, then widened into an unconvincing smile. She held out her hand. 'Pleased to meet you. Are you staying long?'

'Just a visit, while I'm in the UK,' Bob said.

'Weel, we'll maybe meet up later.' Loretta whisked the last dirty cups and plates onto a tray and headed kitchenwards.

'Now then,' Joanie o' Cole said, leaning forwards from the next table. 'That was a good run, lass. That dog's got real potential.'

'Yea, I was pleased wi' her.' Kayleigh jerked her head in Bob's direction. 'We have a new cousin wi' us. Bob from New Zealand, Willie's grandson.'

Gary's head jerked up, and his eyes narrowed. 'Visiting Tamar?'

'Visiting the UK,' Bob said smoothly. 'It's good to see the home we all came from. You'll be Kayleigh's brother Gary?'

So he was up in the family tree, was he? For a moment they were eye to eye, measuring each other up, then Loretta returned with a tray of fresh china, which she dealt out as smoothly as a 500 player dealing cards: Felicity, Kayleigh, me, Bob, Tamar. 'Are you all for tea?'

I suspected that Felicity would have preferred a skinny latte, but she nodded with the rest of us, and Loretta poured out best traditional Shetland tea around the table, Tamar first, then on round with the sun. By the time she got to Felicity it was the rich brown of aged mahogany inside a classic yacht.

'If I wasn't so thirsty,' Felicity said, once Loretta was out of earshot, 'I wouldn't even try to drink this.'

'Here,' Tamar said. 'Mine's not so strong.' She pushed her cup and saucer over to Felicity, and took a swig of Felicity's brew with relish. 'Ah, you can't beat a good cup of tea.'

Felicity rummaged in her handbag, took out a little plastic

container, shook a sweetener pill into her hand and dropped it into the brew, stirring it gloomily.

We were silent for the next few minutes. Felicity took a sip of her tea, grimaced and took another, then started on an egg roll. I polished off my first saat flesh bannock, with the flesh a grand sharp taste, and the bannock most beautifully floury. I was just enjoying a second one when Eddie Ryland came in, looked around, and came over to our table, with an older man behind him. I'd have put him in his late fifties, just short of retirement. His hair grew in the same high plume as Eddie's, but it was dark brown, with eyes to match. Like Eddie, he was wearing laird clothes, and you could tell he'd never had to go waitressing to pay his marina berth fees. He held his hand out to Tamar. 'Edward Ryland. My son told me you worked for my grandfather, back during the war.'

Tamar gave him a long look. 'I've seen you about. You're very like your father.' Then her eyes flashed across at Eddie. 'The war was a good guess, young man.'

Eddie smirked, but I saw his father and Felicity both glance at him. He didn't seem to see what he'd given away: that they knew more about Tamar than they wanted to let on. She hadn't mentioned the war, just that she'd worked for his great-grandparents, *longer ago than I want to remember. When I was a teenager.*

Edward covered up smoothly. 'Glad to see you're keeping up your connection with the family, Miss Irvine.' His gaze turned to me. 'And you're the girl who lives on the boat.'

I was old enough not to have to be patronised by strangers calling me a girl. 'Cass Lynch,' I said, holding out my hand. 'Second mate of the *Sørlandet*.'

'But you have your own boat too, at Brae, don't you?'

'At the moment,' I said clearly, 'she's moored below Tamar's house. While I'm helping Tamar out.'

His gaze darkened, and he frowned, then I saw him assessing my five foot two, and dismissing me. Whatever he was planning, if he was going to have a shot at finding the papers his estate worker hadn't found, this slip of a girl wouldn't hinder him. I gritted my teeth and resolved to hinder as much as possible if he came any-where near the Ladie.

He stepped back and gave us all the charming smile again. 'I won't keep you. Enjoy your tea.'

He and Eddie headed off towards the serving table, leaving me wondering what that was about. Felicity lifted her teacup again and took a sip, screwing up her nose. 'Disgusting.' She added a generous slosh of milk, took a breath and drank it off.

'Have a fancy,' I said, pushing the plateful towards her. 'That'll take the taste away.'

She eyed them with disdain, but condescended to take a piece of best home-baked shortbread. I went for the tiffin, made with bub-bles of green Aero. It was very good, and I was just trying to decide whether to take another piece or to try the millionaire shortbread when Felicity rose abruptly, pushing her chair back so hard that it fell with a crash. She had one hand over her mouth, and her shoul-ders were heaving as if she was going to be sick. She blundered between the tables towards the lavatory, creating a silence around her as she went. The door banged shut behind her.

# Chapter Twelve

**the Gilbert Bain:** the common local name for Shetland's main hospital, which was first sponsored by the sisters of Gilbert Bain in his memory; the original GBH is now an undertaker, on the corner of King Harald Street.

There was a long stillness, then slowly the talk began again, in soft whispers gradually rising to normal volume. Heads turned towards our table, and I felt I was getting that same lowered-brow look that the old man up in the park had given me, as if it was my fault that Felicity was ill.

'Well!' Kayleigh said. 'I ken soothmoothers aren't used to our tea, but that's a bit overly.'

Tamar and I exchanged glances. I couldn't read what Tamar was thinking: surprise, concern, suspicion. 'If she doesn't come back soon,' I said, 'I'll go see what's up.'

She didn't come back. We waited, and made desultory conversation, always with one eye on the lavatory door, but when five minutes had passed, there was still no sign of her. Another woman went in, then came out again rapidly, looking around, then scurried to the nearest tea-server. I saw her gesture towards the lavatory. I rose and hurried over, feeling a hundred pairs of eyes on my back as I went in.

Felicity had collapsed on the floor of one cubicle. The pan was filled with vomit, and there was a trail of it on the lino beside her head. I drew her backwards away from it, out into the space before the basins. She was surprisingly heavy for someone so bird-thin. Her pulse fluttered under my fingers, and she was breathing in whistling gasps. I checked her airway was clear, and turned her into the recovery position, mouth open. Just as I'd done that, the door opened, and two women in hall committee pinnies came in, followed by a confident woman in her thirties that I took to be the local doctor. I got up to let her at Felicity. She checked the pulse, as I'd done, and listened to her breathing. 'Know anything about her? Name? Medical history?'

I shook my head. 'She's Felicity.'

The doctor gave her shoulder a shake. 'Felicity – Felicity, can you hear me?'

There was a half-groan response. She wasn't quite unconscious yet.

'It came on suddenly,' I said. 'She left the table to be sick, and didn't return.'

The doctor checked Felicity's other wrist and felt round her neck. 'Any history of epilepsy?'

'I'll ask her aunt.'

I hurried out to Tamar, who shook her head. 'Not that I've ever heard. Nobody else in our family has it.' She didn't detain me with questions, but by the time I returned to Felicity the doctor was already on the phone.

'Not that she knows,' I told her.

'No known history of epilepsy,' the doctor said. 'Yes, Skeld Hall.' Her hand was on Felicity's wrist, her face was grave. 'As quickly as you can. I'll put the patient in my car and meet you at Bixter, at the hall.'

I waited in silence until she'd put her phone away. 'What's wrong with her?'

The doctor gave me a steady look, assessing me. 'Vomiting, difficulty breathing, unconsciousness. What's she had to eat today, or have you seen her taking any pills?'

'For breakfast, she had toast. Nothing else until just now, here. No, I haven't seen her taking any pills, except for a sweetener in her tea. What I took to be a sweetener.' I understood why she was asking; if it was poison, they needed to know what. 'I'll check her handbag.'

'What's happening?' Kayleigh demanded when I got out again. 'Any help needed?'

'Yes, to get her into the doctor's car.' Bob stood up, nodding. 'The ambulance is on its way. They'll meet up at Bixter. The doctor thinks it may be poison of some sort.' I tipped Felicity's bag out onto her chair, and sifted through its contents. Handkerchief, make-up, assorted pens, diary, a box of paracetamol, mobile, hairbrush, the little green container of sweeteners, assorted debris. No pills or pill bottle. Out of the corner of my eye, I saw the doctor leave the toilet and stride towards the door. Kayleigh and Bob rose and followed her. I shovelled Felicity's stuff back into her bag, and returned to her. One of the hall women was crouched beside her now, smoothing the tumbled hair from her brow with a damp cloth. She had worsened just in these five minutes, her chest fighting for every breath, her stomach heaving to bring up a thin trickle of green bile.

'Felicity?' I said. 'Can you hear me, Felicity?'

She didn't respond. It seemed an age before the doctor returned, with Bob and Kayleigh carrying a makeshift stretcher of a blanket rolled around two fence posts.

'There was nothing in her handbag,' I said.

'Right. Let's get her into the car.' With four of us it was easy enough to lift her, and by the time we came out into the hall, the committee woman had shifted the tables to give us a clear run out. The doctor's car turned out to be an estate car, parked right in front of the hall doors, with the back seats laid flat. We slid Felicity into the back of it.

'You go with her,' Kayleigh said, 'and I'll make sure Tamar gets home.' Her voice hardened. 'I'll clear that Bob character too, you're no' wanting him camping on you when you have everything else to worry about. Phone from the hospital and we'll find some way of fetching you.'

'One minute,' I said. I ran back into the hall. Another old woman was speaking to Tamar, low and urgent. I caught only the last phrase: '– folk that carried the typhus, when we were bairns.' She broke off when I came over, and stepped back, with a bitter glance at me, then a nod at Tamar. 'You mind what I was saying, now.'

'A lock o' nonsense!' Tamar said.

121

I grabbed my jacket from the back of the chair, and Felicity's handbag. 'Tamar, I've to go with her to the hospital. Kayleigh'll take you home. I'll see you later.'

It felt like chairs were being drawn away from me as I made our way through the hall, children snatched back at my approach. It was just the natural courtesy of the country folk, I told myself, making room for someone in a hurry. I had no connection with Skeld; there was no reason they should dislike me. *Folk that carried the typhus, when we were bairns* . . . I was glad to get out of there, and have the door swing to behind me.

The doctor had turned her car. I scrambled into the passenger seat, and she set off while I was still buckling up. We turned onto the main road, went around the head of the voe, accelerated up past the kirk and graveyard, curved onto the road leading across the hills and accelerated again. Fifteen minutes to Bixter, and the ambulance would be there about that time too, if it had come with blue lights flashing. Twenty minutes back to Lerwick, to stomach pumps and respiratory machines and antidotes. Thirty-five minutes. I hoped Felicity could keep breathing for that long. The doctor's face was set, intent on taking the road as fast as she could. I didn't interrupt her.

The Red Ayre, a white house set by a beach of red sand. Lambsholm, a rock of an island crowned with green grass, where I could just see the ruins of an ancient monastery, from Shetland's Catholic days. Garderhouse Voe. I watched the long shore slip past, and brooded. *Folk that carried the typhus* . . . The look Tamar's friend had given me made it clear that she meant me, but it didn't make sense. I was as healthy as anyone could be, and I was there to help Tamar, not to make her ill. I *was* helping her.

We came around the corner at Garderhouse, a bit further, and now Bixter was in sight. There was no blue flashing light. Behind us, Felicity groaned, and retched again.

The houses of Effirth slipped past us; the ruined white bulk of Park Hall; the harled wall of the graveyard. Below, the water of Bixter Voe lay still as polished steel, and ahead we could see the road leading down from the top of Weisdale Hill. At last there was the ambulance moving down it, blue lights going. I heard the doctor's sigh of relief. 'Good timing.'

She slowed to come into Bixter, parked and leapt out, opened the tailgate and took Felicity's pulse again. 'Felicity, can you hear me? Felicity? We're transferring you to the ambulance. You're going to be fine now. Hang on in there. You're going to be fine.'

I could see shadows at the house windows as the ambulance pulled in beside us. The news would have spread; no doubt it was on Facebook already, maybe even on the *Shetland News* website. Then, quicker than it takes to tell it, the ambulance doors were opened, the trolley wheeled out, Felicity loaded in and strapped up to the monitors, and all I had to do was sit on the dickey seat opposite her, and keep out of the way. The doctor was on the phone, giving the hospital an update. I caught the words 'suspected poisoning . . . still retching . . . lost consciousness 16.10 . . .' as the door closed on her, and we were off.

I could see nothing from inside the ambulance. I just had to guess at where we were: going up Weisdale Hill and down it again, flung against the metal wall of the ambulance by the curve before the Swedish houses, along the straight piece past the shop. Down to the Whiteness shop, and up again, up; we must be at the Westings. Ten minutes to Lerwick. I didn't know anything about the monitors above Felicity, but the green blips were moving more slowly across the screen. Around the corner onto the main road from the north. Tingwall valley, up towards the wind turbines on the hill, down past the golf course, around the Brig o' Fitch corner, and up the hill again towards Lerwick. Felicity moaned again. Her face was deathly white, and her hair dark with sweat.

'Keep fighting it, Felicity,' the paramedic said. 'Nearly there. You're going to be fine.'

His voice was too hearty. Now we were slowing down with the sound of traffic around us, turning and turning again. The van halted, backed and stopped. The doors were flung open, and green-overalled porters hurried forwards to whiz Felicity out of the ambulance and into the hospital. I unbelted myself and ran after them until they went through swing doors marked, 'No unauthorised entrance.'

The doors snicked behind them with a hollow sound, leaving me standing alone in the corridor.

I was there only a moment, gazing blankly at the grey metal, when a nurse with a clipboard came out.

'Are you with the patient?'

I nodded, and she set the clipboard horizontal, pen poised. 'I need you to give me information about her.'

'I'll phone her aunt,' I said, and managed to get Tamar, on the way home from Skeld. I listened as the nurse asked for full name, age, address, medical history and details of everything she'd eaten in the last two hours. Once she'd scribbled them onto her form, she disappeared back behind the closed doors, leaving me with nothing to do but sit on the other side of them, looking blankly at the posters telling you to wash your hands.

'Why don't you go down to the canteen?' the nurse suggested, popping out again. 'We'll know you're there if we need you.'

At least the canteen had a window, looking out across Sound bay, with the sea stretching on and on to reach the clouds. Next stop, Norway. My ship was on the other side of that sea; my colleagues. I glanced at my watch. It was six o'clock in Norway. In their scattered homes, they would be settling down to an evening meal: fish, or maybe a reindeer steak with cloudberries. Chatting to their families; bathing their children. Agnetha, our First Officer, would be with her parents; Petter, my second-in-command, would be at home with Frederik. Alain would be working on his own boat in far-off Boston, toolbox open on the chart table, starting to unravel the tangle of electrics. I shook the thought of him away, and drank my cup of tea. This was no time to be mooning about, with Felicity fighting for her life upstairs. Then I realised I ought to phone Sergeant Peterson. If this was poison, she'd need to know.

I dialled 101 and got through to Lerwick station right away, and, after a wait, to Sergeant Peterson herself. 'Well, Cass?'

'I'm at the hospital. Felicity Irvine collapsed suddenly. She's really ill. The doctor seemed to be thinking it was poisoning of some kind.'

'When, where, what with?'

'I don't know what with. She was fine in the morning, but we were at Skeld Hall for afternoon tea, and she suddenly began being sick, then went unconscious.'

'She's still alive?'

'Yes.' I hoped it was true.

'Where are you, at reception?'

'In the canteen.'

'Right. I'll meet you there in ten minutes.'

It was nine minutes exactly when she walked in, not a hair out of place as usual, black suit immaculate, and her laptop bag under one arm. She installed herself opposite me, and said, 'Tell me all about it.'

I was used to her interviewing ways now. I did my best to lead her through the afternoon, glancing at the door every time someone came in, and at the end of my recital, she nodded. 'Until we know what the poison was we can't be certain, but the speed it acted at on her suggests it was something in the hall, not breakfast. You're sure the only thing she took herself was hall food and the sweetener from her handbag?'

'Unless she took something while we were watching the trials, but why should she?'

'Quite. So, the rolls were from the sales table. Individually wrapped?'

I nodded. 'A plastic bag for each half roll. I can't see how she could have been poisoned in that, unless someone at our table substituted a poisoned one for the one she took, and to do that you'd have to know in advance what filling she was going to take.'

'I agree it's unlikely, so let's eliminate it as much as we can. Who was by her when she chose her roll, and who could have substituted another one?'

I tried to think. 'I couldn't.' Being free of suspicion was a nice change. 'They went straight to the serving hatch while I was spotting a free table, so I was way behind her in the queue, too far to see what she took. Bob was several people behind her; he might have, I suppose, and Kayleigh was immediately behind her.'

Sergeant Peterson considered that. 'This Kayleigh – she's the other niece?'

'Great-niece. The son of Tamar's nephew, you know, Joanie o' Cole, who found the body in the Skro. He was there too, with his son Gary, at the next table, but they were at their table when we arrived, so unless it just happened that one of their rolls was the right sort, they're out of it.'

'Great-niece. If we're talking inheritance, might she see Felicity as a rival?'

I shook my head. 'No. What Kayleigh wants is the croft to be assigned to her. Felicity wouldn't want that.' I wondered if I should try to explain the family situation, and thought I had better. 'But Bob might. It's complicated.'

Her eyes flashed green as she looked up. 'Explain.' Then she held up a hand. 'No, let's deal with Kayleigh first. Motive uncertain. Did she know you were going to Skeld?'

'Yes, definitely, for Tamar and I, and she could have expected Felicity too.'

'Was she there when Felicity bought the roll?'

I nodded. 'They went together.'

'So she would have seen what Felicity chose, and could have chosen the same.'

'Yes.'

'And from the sound of it, it was natural that you should all come down to tea together, after Kayleigh's run.'

I nodded again.

'So Kayleigh could have brought something prepared to slip into the roll she bought.'

'She could,' I agreed, 'but where do you get hold of poison? Something so effective, yet something that Felicity wouldn't taste in the roll?'

We both thought about that one, and shook our heads. 'It just isn't possible,' I said. 'They came over to the table, they sat down. Kayleigh launched straight into her roll, as if she'd been too nervous about the trial to eat earlier. She didn't open another one, or sprinkle anything on one. She couldn't have done that and then swapped it for Felicity's without us noticing. Bob neither.'

She tapped a fusillade of words into her laptop, then lifted her head. 'Okay. The roll, unlikely. Let's keep working through. Were the fancies wrapped individually as well?'

'No. There was a plateful already on the table, and Felicity didn't eat any of them – no, hang on, she took a shortbread, and got a bite at it before she keeled over. It would have to be an awfully fast-acting poison.'

'That's the point, isn't it? We need to know what poison it was. The tea then. That's the most obvious, because from the sound of it, Felicity complained about the taste.' She checked her notes. 'Loretta, that's the niece? The Princess Di lookalike. She brought the cups over on a tray, and set them on the table, then poured the tea, starting with Tamar and going round.'

'Round with the sun. Tamar, Bob, me, Kayleigh, Felicity.'

'Then Tamar swapped her cup with Felicity. How soon after it was poured?'

'Straight away. Felicity was making a face at how strong hers was, and Tamar's had been first poured, so it was weaker. She hadn't even put the milk in yet – Felicity did that, just before she drank it.'

Sergeant Peterson's green eyes narrowed. 'Wouldn't it have been more natural for Loretta to pour the tea on the tray, then pass the cups out?'

I shook my head. 'There wasn't really room for her to balance the tray on the table while she poured. The cups were standing ready in their saucers, and she dished them out as if she was dealing at 500, then tucked the tray under her arm, and leaned across to pour. I don't see how she could have done any jiggery-pokery with it. It all came straight from the same pot, and we were all looking at her as she poured it.'

'But if someone had carried poison in a little container it could

127

have been poured into the cup, on the table. Kayleigh's father and brother. Could either of them have reached over to poison Felicity's tea?'

I made a face. 'I'm not sure. Joanie was back-on to Tamar, and Gary was beside him. No, I don't see how they could have reached over to Felicity without being noticed.'

'But it was actually Tamar's cup that Felicity drank from. Could they have reached that?'

I visualised them. 'Not so easily for Joanie, but Gary half-turned to talk to us; I think he even had a hand on our table, to steady himself.'

She made a couple of notes then looked up again. 'And there were no classic detective-story diversions, someone dropping a loaded tray in the middle of the hall that made everyone look around?'

'Not until Felicity got up. They looked then, all right.'

'How about the two men who came over to talk to Tamar? Edward and Eddie Ryland.' She rolled her eyes. 'Confusing. There's a lot to be said for sticking "Peerie" in front of a son who has the same name as his father.'

'Edward and Peerie Eddie,' I agreed. This seemed to be where I should explain. 'The Rylands . . . there's a family connection. They're the Sand lairds, and Tamar's mother came from Sand. Felicity was asking about her own father, Tamar's youngest brother. He was a posthumous child, and she thought he might be the laird's son. Edward's half-brother. No, this Edward's half-uncle. Old Edward, that's the laird now, his half-brother.' I was beginning to feel confused myself. Sergeant Peterson pulled out her notebook.

'Draw it for me.'

I did my best to reproduce Leeza's family tree, and added the Rylands level with the generations. 'Old Edward, he's ages with Tamar, she remembered him as a boy when she worked there. So it would be his father who had the affair with Tamar's mother, and was Felicity's father's father.'

'Inheritance,' Sergeant Peterson said. 'An illegitimate child would get equal shares with a legitimate.' She frowned. 'He's a generation down, though. It should have been this old Edward's father he claimed from. I'll need to look it all up. There'll be a statute of limitations.'

'Felicity's father didn't seem pleased she was here in Shetland.' I couldn't believe I was sitting here, cosily sharing information with Sergeant Peterson. 'You likely know who he is, the Solicitor General.'

'Oh, yes, I know all about him. Well-enough off to prefer reputation to riches. He wouldn't want her stirring up the family scandal.' She tapped in a few words, then paused, pursing her mouth. 'But there'd be money in it. Do you know anything about Felicity's financial affairs?'

I remembered the phone call I'd heard. *Keep staving them off.* 'In trouble, I think.'

'I'll need to talk to these Rylands. Do you think they knew about the illegitimate child, if that's what he was?'

I tried to sort out the impressions I'd got. 'I think they knew about them separately, if that makes sense. Peerie Eddie knew Felicity in London, but he didn't know she had family here, and when he connected her with the Irvines here, he didn't like it. Then Edward came over to do the gracious laird bit to Tamar.' I paused and thought again. 'I got the impression that they knew from family papers about the illegitimate Irvine child, but they thought it was all old history, until it connected up with Felicity in the present with a much older relative who might know all about it. Eddie gave away that they knew about Tamar, anyway, that she'd worked for them. "During the war" he said, but she hadn't said that.' Suddenly I remembered the Land Rover incident. 'There was an odd thing earlier on. Felicity slipped in front of one of the Land Rovers coming back up to watch the trials. She was walking behind us, with Peerie Eddie, and I heard the brakes screech, and her scream. Her hand was cut, as if she'd caught at its bonnet. It was a queue of cars, not going fast, so she'd only have been seriously hurt if she'd fallen flat and a wheel had gone over her.'

'She slipped?'

'She didn't say anything other. Peerie Eddie made some remark about her town boots in the country, and she gave him a funny look, then said something about rubber boots not suiting her.'

DS Peterson made another note. 'There would have been people all around. Somebody might have seen something. Where were these Rylands when Felicity was choosing her roll?'

I shook my head, then remembered that I'd been enjoying my bannock as they'd come in. 'They came into the hall as we were eating. Too late to substitute a roll, and I don't see how they could have slipped a piece of shortbread stuffed with fast-acting poison on the plate.'

'Or why,' she agreed. 'There was no guarantee Felicity would eat it – they could have poisoned any of you.'

Young Eddie might have taken that gamble, I thought.

'And there was the change of cup. Was it Tamar or Felicity who was aimed at?'

'Tamar's the one with the knowledge, and maybe the papers, to prove that Felicity's father is old Edward's half brother. Without her help, Felicity couldn't prove it.'

'Don't forget DNA.'

I made a face. 'Of course. Felicity, then. She was the one who was up here rocking the boat, trying to get information out of Tamar. If Edward and Peerie Eddie wanted to stop any investigation, she was the one to stop . . . but how could they have know she'd be there? Peerie Eddie definitely hadn't connected her up with Shetland.'

'They might just be the types to carry poison. Landowners have a nasty habit of leaving poisoned meat out for birds of prey.'

'I suppose there might be birds of prey around Sand Haa. There're the trees at Da Gairdins for nesting in.'

'Merlins,' Sergeant Peterson said. 'Peregrines. What else? There was that osprey that visited, and hung about on the west side for a while.' I gave her a surprised look, and she smiled. 'No, I'm not a birder. We get information from south about people coming up. There's a lucrative trade in raptor chicks.' Her face changed suddenly, as if a piece of puzzle had clicked into place. 'The body on the beach. Mr Luncarty.'

I waited.

She hesitated for a moment, then made up her mind to tell me. 'He was involved in the bird trade. He had a special suitcase in the back of his car. It looked like an ordinary cabin flight case from outside, but it had concealed air holes, and inside it was divided into four small cages.'

'So he was up here collecting birds? Raptor chicks?'

'That's what it looks like. And he worked for the Rylands.' She shook her head. 'But I don't see how that connects up with this attempt on Felicity.'

I didn't either. It wasn't likely that Felicity would be involved in smuggling or selling wild birds. 'I don't suppose she found out about it, and was threatening to tell the authorities?'

'Exposure, or our old friend blackmail, in the best crime novel tradition?' She considered it for a moment. 'You can see the headlines, can't you? *Laird's family in wildlife scandal.*' She tapped another few words. 'Court photographs of people under blankets, or hiding their faces. *My family connection with the bird-smugglers.* That would sell a few more copies of Felicity's gossip-rag.'

'Peerie Eddie had gone to tell Edward about Felicity being connected to the Irvines, so they had time to get poison from the car, or the house, even. Sand's only ten minutes drive from Skeld, and we were there all afternoon.'

'I can check that. If they went home during the afternoon, and if anyone saw what they did there.'

There was a hurrying of footsteps outside the canteen door. We both looked up. A tall man in green surgical pyjamas came in, glanced around, and came over to me. I knew as soon as I saw his face.

Felicity was dead.

# IV

## The sausage

After the first triangle, the yachts do a sausage, zig-zagging back up to the weather mark, then returning to the starting line goose-winged, that is with the wind coming from dead astern, and the jib poled out on the opposite side from the mainsail.

# Chapter Thirteen

**klett:** an isolated rock [Old Norse, *klatt*, a lump or mass]

I felt deadly tired. Sergeant Peterson had organised a police car to run me home to the Ladie. Cat was waiting for me on *Khalida's* curved coach roof, his little ginger friend at his side. When he saw me get out of the police car, he rose, stretched, leapt the gangplank and came trotting over to meet me, plumed tail high. I made a fuss of him, and the ketling crept closer as I stroked him, but backed away when I held a hand out. Being thrown the occasional dead starling obviously hadn't given her a high opinion of the human race, and if the only representative of it she'd met was Harald, I didn't blame her. I would back away from him too. *I want them moved . . .* and the dead man had been coming to collect raptor chicks. I needed to get a look inside that container.

I gave Cat his supper. The ketling was straight in there, purring like an engine in idle, shoving its head beside his, the pale end of its tail waggling. Half of me was saying I'd have to get ketling food for it, but the other half reminded me we'd be here only a couple of days longer. Unless I could persuade Tamar to adopt it, there was no kindness in letting it get used to a better life. I watched the little ginger head butting against Cat's grey side, and was sorry. It'd miss us when we went. I left the pair of them washing each other's faces on the couch, and headed up to the house.

I called out a hello as I went in. Tamar was in the sit-ootery, spy-glasses idle in her lap. There was no sign of Bob, so I supposed

Kayleigh had indeed cleared him. Tamar turned her head as I came in, and gave me a long look. 'The doctor did everything she could. You all did.'

I nodded, and sat down. Knowing that everyone had done their best didn't make Felicity's death any easier to bear. Framed in the window, the sun shone out for a moment behind the Vementry hill, then the colour faded to rose, cream, grey. The last rays of the sun turned the browned flowering tips of the rugosa bushes to glowing amber.

'I've phoned Archie,' Tamar said. 'Her father. He's coming up tomorrow. He'll hire a car at the airport. But I don't know if he'll be able to do anything, about a funeral, I mean. Your policewoman phoned too. They're not going to release Felicity's body.'

I was expecting that, but I still felt a cold clutch at my chest. 'They think it wasn't a natural death.'

'Murder,' Tamar said. She was silent for a moment, then continued, 'Archie'll talk to Goudie's, the undertakers, then come on to us. I don't know whether he'll want to bury her here and have a service south, or have her taken south to do it all there. He'll need to go in the spare room.'

'I'll clear it out for him, first thing tomorrow.'

She nodded. Her voice had been matter-of-fact, and her face was calm. Only the still binoculars in her lap suggested that she felt Felicity's death. She turned her head to me and echoed my thought. 'Am I being too practical?'

I shook my head. 'It all has to be organised.' I looked her straight in the eyes. 'But who do you think killed her, and why?'

The sly witch's expression transformed her face again. 'You've been here, listening, watching us all with your outsider's eyes. What do you make of it?'

'That she wanted to dig up things best left buried.'

Tamar's eyes narrowed. 'That my mother had an affair with Edward Ryland. A slander on a good woman.'

The anger in her tone stung. Her hands rose from the spyglasses, emphatic. 'And if she'd known the old laird the way I did, she'd never even have thought of it. Him and Madam Monikie, a pair of . . .' She paused, her mouth working, hands clenching on air. 'Smug, self-righteous, class-ridden. As if he'd even have considered having an affair with a crofter's wife. No, it was all a nonsense.'

I wasn't sure whether it was true, or whether she just didn't want to believe it. The upper classes might look down on the peasants, but it didn't stop them expecting *droit de seigneur*. She was so angry about it too . . . I remembered the way she'd pushed her cup across to Felicity. As Loretta had handed them out, we'd each been focused on receiving our own cup. Tamar could easily have put something in hers before passing it across. She was alert, Tamar, she knew all about DNA and what it could prove. If Felicity was determined to prove her father's descent from the Rylands, she could do it. Tamar was old, she took death more calmly than we younger folk did . . . there were no doubt boxes of ancient poisons in that cluttered shed. *Monkshood. Poisonous.*

I looked at Tamar's face again, the hawk profile turned away to gaze towards the sunset. She'd defied convention all her life. Old age gave you a value for life as well as acceptance of the inevitability of death. Old age put things in perspective. Her mother was long beyond being harmed by scandal. Besides, I thought more practically, she couldn't have counted on Felicity making a fuss about the taste of the tea. She might have had to drink it herself.

'Sergeant Peterson was talking about wildlife crime. That man who died on the beach. He had a suitcase specially fitted out to transport birds.'

'Merlins and peregrines,' Tamar said. She laughed at my startled look. 'Come on, Cass, you know the Shetland grapevine. We wildlife folk talk to each other, and the police give us warning if anyone suspected of wildlife crime gets on the boat.' She frowned. 'So that was what he was doing here. There are merlins breeding on the hill here, at the foot of the Klett.' She nodded southwards. 'That lump of rock on the skyline, just about straight up from Quiensetter. Three weeks ago was just the time the chicks would be almost fledged. But I thought most of the nests were watched. I haven't heard of any being robbed.'

'Were you watching the one on the hill here, the merlins?'

She nodded. 'Four chicks. They nest on the ground, in the heather, and as soon as the chicks are old enough, they scatter away from the nest. Until they're fledged, though, they're vulnerable.' She nodded over her shoulder. 'It's the hill you see from the kitchen, and the back skylight in my bedroom. There's been no sign of any strangers snooping around.'

'You've been in Wastview these last weeks,' I reminded her.

'I think I'd still have heard. Joanie or the South Voxter folk would have noticed someone about. No, unless he was hoping to get lucky, and they don't usually work that way, it was a nest nobody knew about.'

I gave her a sceptical look. 'In Shetland?'

'In the roof of a byre, say.' She was thinking it through. 'A byre belonging to an isolated house that doesn't have many visitors.'

'Sand Haa?'

'I've heard mention of peregrines there. He worked for the Rylands, didn't he? The man who died?'

I nodded.

'He could have been collecting raptors from their estate here, thinking that it would be less well policed than Monikie.' She made a face. 'That young Eddie, Edward's grandson, he might be a City slicker who wouldn't know a hawk from a handsaw, but I wouldn't be in the least surprised at him making a bit of fly money on the side anywhere he could get it.'

It wouldn't surprise me either. 'How much would they be worth, these young birds?'

'On the black market? Well, there was a case a few years back, where a man was caught smuggling peregrine eggs. Fourteen eggs, value seventy thousand. And that was eggs, not live birds.'

*Seventy thousand?* My jaw dropped. I did the arithmetic. Nearly five grand per egg. 'So if he got a nest of four chicks . . .'

'Yes,' Tamar agreed. 'Probably forty thousand, maybe more. Falconry's very popular in Saudi Arabia.'

There was a pause while I assimilated this; though of course what sounded a fortune to me might be peanuts to city-slicker Eddie. 'But if the dead man, Luncarty, was taking young birds from the nests at Sand, what was he doing here at the Ladie? And how does that link with Felicity's death? That was three weeks before she came.'

'Yes,' Tamar agreed. 'I don't suppose Felicity knew one bird from another. He was after something else here, then heading over to pick up his birds and leave with them.'

I looked her straight in the eye. 'If you don't know what he was after, then nobody does.'

For a moment, she looked confused, her face suddenly aging, then she shook herself alert again. 'I thought I knew what he was after, but I didn't know then that he was connected with the Rylands.' Abruptly, she began to struggle to her feet. 'I need a breath of sea air before an early night. How about letting me have a look at your boat?'

I rose with her, and walked slowly beside her, along the track to the car, then down between the metal containers on one side, the bins of mussel lines on the other, to the pier. The sun had set behind the Ward o' Vementry now, but it was still daylight on land.

Walking beside her brought the old lady at the table in Skeld back into my head. *Folk that carried the typhus, when we were bairns.* The look she'd given me, and the brusqueness of the old man with the puppies. *You pay heed, now.* There was no point beating around the bush with Tamar. I asked her straight out. 'What's a typhus carrier, and why should I be one?'

She was startled for a moment, then smiled, and stopped walking. 'Direct.' Her tone approved. 'A typhoid carrier is someone who doesn't get the disease, but can spread it around others. There was a Typhoid Mary in New York in the last century. She died when I was a child. She'd been a cook, and had the typhoid baccillae in her. Every family she worked for got ill, and in the end they put her in permanent isolation in a hospital. My aunt was one, poor soul, my mother's sister – she lost several babies, and one of my cousins got it too, and died.'

'Died? But you were young in the thirties, forties . . . I thought the awful infant mortality rate was from Victorian times.'

139

Tamar shook her head. 'Almost every one of the families I knew lost a child. Measles, whooping cough, mumps, diptheria, TB, typhoid fever, they could all kill. Poor Aunt Elsie. She was the first adult I'd ever seen cry, sitting in the kitchen with my mother, but then she had a lot to cry about. It wasn't her fault. She felt her own babies so badly, and then cousin Annie was the straw that broke the camel's back.' Her eyes went to the hill that masked the Skro. 'She threw herself over the banks, poor soul, rather than infect any more.'

I felt my heart contract with pity for that poor woman. How awful, to know that you were a danger to others, responsible without having done anything wrong for the deaths of several children. I had felt the weight of murder on my conscience for eleven long years, thinking I'd killed Alain in the middle of the Atlantic, and been released when he'd turned up again. To have killed your brother's or sister's child – how dreadful.

'You've got a reputation,' Tamar said. 'Not here, in Brae, where they know you, but in Skeld. You're the girl that murder follows.'

The accusation cut the breath from my throat. It was true that I'd been involved in several cases of murder, but my presence hadn't caused any of them. I'd got enmeshed in events just because I was there. I thought back through them, the Longship case, the Trowie Mound, the witches in Scalloway, the njuggle case, the events at Belmont House with Maman's opera company, and the cases on board ship, on the way to Ireland and then only a month ago in Fetlar. I could acquit myself of having caused any of those deaths, not the first death, nor the subsequent ones by my meddling. I'd just been there. All the same, I could see that for someone not professionally involved with murder it was an unusually large number of coincidences.

'And now Felicity,' Tamar said.

'A murder carrier,' I said bleakly. 'That's what your friend thinks I am.' Now I understood the look the old man with the puppies had given me, the way he'd drawn back. My face felt stiff.

Tamar gave me a long look. 'It's superstitious nonsense. There was a medical explanation for poor Aunt Elsie. There's none for you – you've just been unlucky. Felicity brought her death on herself, meddling with things better left alone.'

I shook my head at that. 'No. Murder's too strong a reaction to meddling.'

'Murderers have no sense of proportion,' Tamar said, and began to walk forward again, in silence until we reached the gravel back-fill of the pier. 'Will you invite me onto your yacht? I'd like to see your home.'

I looked at Tamar's crutches, then at my makeshift gangplank. It was strong, but not wide enough. 'I'm not sure I can get you on board. I can't bring *Khalida* in any closer. There's a ledge of rocks sticking out underwater.'

'Never mind. I'll just stand here a moment and enjoy the sea air.' She looked over towards the Quiensetter point, and nodded. 'That's the dog otter having a dusk foray.'

I could just see him, among the rocks; then he launched himself into the water and began hunting, dipping down and coming back up for air at the same spot, as if there was a crab or an eel under a rock that was refusing to come out. We watched until he came up at last with something pale in his mouth, and legs waving on each side of it, a substantial crab. He brought it ashore and crunched it down, then dived back into the water. Tamar sighed and turned away. 'Bedtime.'

Going up was harder for her than coming down. I hovered at her elbow, ready to support her if need be, as she made her painful way up the slope then, with a sigh of relief, reached the downward slope to the house.

'This day,' she conceded, 'has tired me out. I'll head up now.'

'Would you like a last cup of tea?'

She shook her head. 'No, just see me up the stairs, and wait till I'm horizontal, in case I stumble, then you can go home too.'

I saw her up the stairs, and checked that everything was ready for her – bedside light on, pyjamas laid out, covers turned back, electric blanket warming away. 'Radio?'

'Yes.' She steadied herself on the bedstead. 'Right, that's me. That breath of air did me good. Thanks, Cass.'

'I was wondering if I could sail over to Mass tomorrow morning.'

'Sail over?'

'They have a mass in Voe every second Sunday. Just round the corner, far handier than Lerwick.'

'Why not? What time is it?'

'Half past eight.'

'So you'd need to leave, oh, half past seven. If you could be bothered to boil me an egg before you go, I can have breakfast in bed, then get up when you get back.'

'No bother.'

She gave me a long look. 'And Cass, the typhoid thing, it is just superstitious nonsense, you know.'

'I know,' I agreed.

'Good night, sleep well.'

I waited downstairs until I heard the creak of the bed as she got into it, called up a last goodnight, and headed out into the darkness. The sky was still clear, with the stars white points in the cloudy ribbon of the Milky Way. The Plough hung over the Wart of Papa Little, and the W of Cassiopea in the east. A blinking light was a satellite, or a flight of sleeping people heading from Holland to New York. The burn tumbled over its rocks, louder in the silence than the waves that shushed halfway down the shore. A night bird called, and another answered; far off on Muckle Roe a dog barked, the sound carrying over the still water. Under the seaweed smell of the ebb was a chill land smell of grass that was starting to brown, and frost to come. There could be rain tomorrow.

I gave myself a few minutes to let my eyes adjust, then set off over the grass to the dark bulk of the container. The ketlings mewed within it as I passed, then were silent again as I scrunched my way down the gravel to my gangplank. *Home.* I clambered aboard and shut the washboards behind me. I didn't have an electric blanket – I suppressed a pang of envy – but as soon as I lit the lamp it was welcoming, with the flame sparking on the gold flecks in the woodwork, and five minutes of the gas ring would warm it up. Cat raised his

142

head to greet me. His little friend was curled up within his paws, head pillowed on his grey shoulder, at ease enough now to stay fast asleep, miniature paws padding at his belly as if it was dreaming of milk. I frowned. If it was here, then who was mewing? Its siblings, I supposed, or another feral litter, there could be a dozen of them in a nest under the container.

I'd just got my hot-water bottle into my bunk when Gavin phoned. 'Late Saturday was an awkward time for another murder.'

*Murder carrier* . . . 'I didn't plan it,' I said tartly. 'Why is it awkward?'

'I got the word too late for me to get on the boat, and there are no planes from Inverness on a Sunday, so I'm having to drive over to Aberdeen. I'll be with you tomorrow afternoon.'

'They're sending you up?' My heart lightened.

'Leaving 13.15, arriving 14.15. My boss said something along the lines of I'd know the flight times by now. Keep yourself safe till then, will you?'

'I'll try.'

'DS Peterson's told me the story so far. She's hoping toxicology will rush the poison through.'

'This is a wild guess,' I said, 'but I don't suppose the symptoms might fit monkshood? I've been too busy to look.'

'Monkshood?'

'Shetland delphinium. It's a vivid blue flower, with glossy leaves in a rather sinister shade of dark green.' I held the phone with my shoulder while I shoved my pyjama thermals on the hot-water bottle, then sat down on the couch beside Cat.

'Rather a medieval way of poisoning someone.' I heard a faint tapping noise. 'Nausea, vomiting, burning mouth, breathing difficulties.'

'Yes, all of those. She was sick first, and then really labouring to breathe.'

'It's quick acting. Bitter taste.'

My throat felt tight. 'She complained about the taste of the tea. We just thought she was being soothmootherish.'

143

'I'll suggest it to them as worth trying. Why did you ask?'

'It's in the garden here.' Had it only been this morning? 'Tamar was picking flowers for the show, and she mentioned what it was, and said it was poisonous.'

'Does you calling it "Shetland delphimiun" mean that it's in everyone's garden?'

'Magnie certainly has a border of it, and there's some in our garden too, I'm pretty sure.'

'How's your old lady taking the death?'

'Hard to say. A mixture of upset, resigned and she brought it on herself, meddling.'

'I know you've gone through it all with Freya, but tell me again about your tea party in the hall.'

I did my best to describe it for him: Loretta dishing out the cups and pouring the tea, Tamar changing cups with Felicity, Edward and Eddie Ryland coming over.

'If it was monkshood,' Gavin said, 'from the looks of this website, you wouldn't need much of it. A couple of teaspoonfuls. If Felicity wasn't used to strong tea, she wouldn't know that the bitterness was odd.'

'She wasn't. She made a face and drank it straight down. Then, oh, ten minutes later, she began to be ill. But how would you poison someone with monkshood? Would it be two teaspoonsfuls of grated root, or could you, say, grate the root and boil it up and make a liquid poison?'

'I haven't a clue,' Gavin said. 'Toxicology will know. But we're just speculating – it may have been best patent weedkiller, though I'd have thought from the smell of the stuff that the taste of it would have been so obviously chemical that she wouldn't have drunk the tea.'

'And country water is proper water too,' I agreed. 'Not like Lerwick, where you can smell the chlorine as you raise the cup to your nose.'

'If it's any comfort,' Gavin said, 'there's no antidote. Even if you'd known what it was, that wouldn't have helped.'

It was a small comfort. 'Did DS Peterson mention the wildbird suitcase?'

'Of the man you found in the Skro?'

'I didn't find him!' I said, rather too sharply.

There was a silence. Gavin said, gently, 'Something's wrong.'

'Something really stupid,' I said. 'Just superstition . . . I seem to have a new reputation as someone who brings murder in her wake.' To my horror, I could feel I was about to cry. I blinked hard. 'It is stupid. It's just, you know, this is *home*. This is where people know me. And this old man, the minute he heard my name, he kind of backed off, and then one of Tamar's friends, an old wifie, warned her against me. She compared me to a typhoid carrier.' My voice was rising. I stopped, and took a deep breath. 'I shouldn't let it hurt. You must get it all the time, being set apart as a policeman.'

'Aye.' It was a single word, but in it I heard a hundred little instances of the shop, the cafe, the pub falling silent as the policeman walked in. His world was harder, never being able to leave the job behind. I shoved my self-pity away.

'It's just silly gossip. I didn't cause any of the murders I've been involved with. I was just there.'

'Try not to mind it. I ken that's easy to say, and no easy to do.' His voice was soothing as warmed honey. 'You've had a long upsetting day too. That makes things worse.'

'I know,' I said. 'I'm glad you're coming.'

'I won't be able to stay on *Khalida* though. I'll be too official.'

'But you'll be here. Maybe we'll manage a takeaway together. I could even join you in your hotel.'

'I'll hold you to that. The wild birds of prey thing's interesting. That kind of money's a motive, and a possible jail sentence is even better. Is there any way, do you think, that Felicity could have found out about the birds?'

'I don't see how. Unless she'd somehow picked up something at the London end. A gossipy word that meant something to her because of the Shetland connection.'

'That's an idea. So she perhaps overheard someone telling

145

someone else that Ryland was the person to go to for falcons, realised there was something shady about it, and looked up what breeds in Shetland?'

'She might,' I conceded, 'but I think it was the inheritance thing she was going for.'

'Either way we could be talking blackmail.' His voice was grave. 'It's dangerous to blackmail a murderer.'

# Chapter Fourteen

**lambie hoose:** a small stone-built outhouse, generally with only a door and no window; often used to stable young or premature lambs in bad weather

It was the ketling that woke me. It was up on the chart table, paws on the windowsill, and a steady, low growl came from its throat. Under the growl I thought for a moment that I heard the sound of a car engine, then the ketling jumped down and there was silence. I wriggled forwards so that my shoulders were clear of the bulkhead, and raised myself up on my elbows, just in time to see a flash of car headlights. One long beam travelled along the boat, then it cut out. I got out of bed and eased the hatch open. It was too dark to see anything moving on the road, but I thought I could hear a faint rumbling, as if a car was rolling down the road with its engine off. We had visitors.

My jeans and jumper were lying on the couch, ready to put on. I pulled them over my pyjama thermals and thrust my feet into my seaboots, straining my eyes against the darkness outside the window all the while. The flash didn't come again, but I heard the snick of a car door being closed, then I saw a light moving in the darkness between the road and Tamar's house. Someone was walking down the path to the house, the bright pinprick bobbing with each step. I looked at my watch. Half past one. I remembered the man who had come here dressed for burglary, who had died at the Skro. Now here was another. What in the name of goodness had Tamar been keeping in the cottage that was worth so determined an effort? I thought of the tub tucked down in my bilges, and decided I'd insist on her putting it to the bank, and telling the whole family that that was where it was.

My phone was on the table, where I'd left it after talking to Gavin. Tamar picked up on the second ring, as alert as if it was day. 'Cass?'

'We have a visitor,' I breathed.

'Where?'

'Walking down your path. You won't have time to lock the back door. Do you want to phone the police?'

'By the time they arrive, he'll be long gone.' She sounded amused. 'He won't find what he's looking for.'

'I'll come after him.'

'Don't put yourself in danger. Just watch. See who it is.'

I hauled my black jacket on over my jumper, shoved my phone in my pocket, and slid cautiously out into the night, across the gangplank and along the edge of the pier, on the rocks, to avoid the crunching gravel. I could just see the paler gravel of the track, and make out the shapes of the assorted bruck on the grass. I slid into the darkness by the black rectangle of the Portakabin, and felt my way to the hurdle beyond it. From this angle, the light had gone again, hidden by the low lambie hoose between Tamar's cottage and the pier. I quickened my pace, and came a cropper in the first sunken burn, saving myself only by grabbing at the tussocked grass on the other side of it. I extricated myself quietly, went uphill to the dark bulk of the lambie hoose, slid around it, and flattened myself against its dark walls for a moment. The light was in the house now, moving round the living room. Upstairs, Tamar's room was still in darkness.

Suddenly a blanket was flung over my head. My mouth filled with the smell of dog. Before I had time to even try and fling it off, I was grabbed and shoved forward into the lambie house. The blanket was snatched off, and another shove had me sprawling on the earth floor, my hands just managing to break my fall. I was rolling

148

over onto my feet just in time to hear the wooden thud of the latch falling into place.

Swearing, I flung myself at the door. Naturally, it held; it was designed to withstand Shetland weather from the outside or an annoyed ram from the inside. *Bastards.* They'd tricked me good and proper, flashing their light into my cabin, to make sure I'd wake up, then sending one of them out as a decoy while the other waited to grab me.

I had my phone. I shone its light at the door, then round my prison. It was a rectangular, stone-built shed with an earth floor and no windows. A shelf ran along in the angle between walls and roof, stacked with sheep-related spray cans and dusty boxes. The door was my only way out. Right. The police . . . but even as my finger hovered over the first 1, I knew they'd take at least half an hour to get here, even if they sent a car straight away. I needed someone sooner than that. Whatever these people were planning, I wasn't going to leave Tamar alone with them. Joanie o' Cole was nearest, but I didn't have his number. Magnie. I dialled quickly and waited while it rang and rang. Come *on*, Magnie . . .

I was just about to cut off and re-dial when he answered at last, voice thick with sleep. 'Yea?'

'It's Cass.' I compressed it into the fewest words I could. 'There's trouble over here. Two people at least. They've locked me in the lambie hoose, so there's nobody with Tamar. Can you phone Joanie o' Cole, or the South Voxter folk?'

'I'm on my way,' he said, and rang off.

I put my phone back in my pocket, and calculated. If he phoned Joanie straight away, help could be here in . . . five minutes to dress, another seven, ten, on the road. Fifteen minutes. It was too long. I needed to get out of here.

I went forward to the door and ran my fingers over it. It was typical shed construction, planks held together with a Z on the back. I gave the diagonal an experimental tug, but there was no sign of give, and I couldn't feel any nails in it; they must be on the front. Outside, unless the person who'd shoved me in here had done something clever with a stone, or wedges, it was held with the normal wooden latch. I felt in my pocket for my penknife, and opened the blade. I might be able to open the door just enough to slip the blade between it and the jamb, and shove the latch upwards.

A couple of tries showed me it was no go. Pushing the door out just jammed the latch against its wooden holder. *Right.* My anger against my assailant was rising. I'd get out of here by myself if I had to dismantle the door plank by plank. If I couldn't get at the latch, I'd go for the hinges. There was a screwdriver on my knife. I felt down the other side, and gave a grin of triumph. The hinges were those long byre ones, put on the inside to slow the rusting process. I flashed the torch briefly to see how old they were and was pleased to see that they looked in reasonable nick.

There was a noise outside, a metallic thumping, then a rattling. Someone was trying to get into the container, and not caring how much noise they made about it, now I was corralled in here. Well, I wouldn't be shut in for long. I wedged my phone on the shelf to give me some light, and set to, blessing the crofter who'd taken the trouble to dip his screws in Vaseline before putting them in. They came out sweetly, dropping into my hand one by one. I stowed them in my pocket for putting back tomorrow, then switched my light off again, felt down the freed edge of the door and shoved it gently with my shoulder. It gave six inches, then stuck, held by the latch. I shoved harder, pressing my body against it. One leg out, one arm, my body, a good push to get my head through, and the rest of me followed. I eased the door back into position, and stood against it, listening intently. The rattling had stopped; he, they, must have given up the container as a bad job. There was no sound of anyone about. I slid out into the darkness and crouched down in the shadow of the wall.

There was a light in my *Khalida*. I felt a wave of fury wash through me. For a moment I was actually trembling with it. Whatever they were after, they'd thought of Tamar giving it to me. I wanted to storm down there like Boudicca in her scythe-wheeled chariot, sword

150

in hand. I clenched my fists, and took a deep breath. There were at least two of them, and the one who'd grabbed me had been tall and strong. Surprise might help me, but uncontrolled rage wouldn't, especially when I had neither sword nor scythe-wheeled chariot. I took three deep breaths and set myself to think.

Help would be here soon. I turned away from *Khalida* to look towards the house. The light was still there, moving about in the downstairs room. They were hedging their bets: one in the house, the other searching my boat. They didn't know that I'd phoned Tamar, that she was awake above them. If they'd thought of me having my phone on me, they'd expect me to call the police. They weren't wanting confrontation; they'd lured me out to disable me. The one in the house might have tied Tamar into her bedroom with the old trick of a rope across the landing, but he wouldn't have harmed her. I hoped.

I scowled a curse towards the one in *Khalida*, and began to walk cautiously towards the house. Tamar had to be my priority, however much my rage wanted me to charge down to my boat. They wouldn't do her any damage, just searching, and Cat would have got himself safely out of the way the minute he heard a strange foot on the gangplank.

There were several boulders in the grass, shining grey-white in the dark, and it was bad luck that the one I walked straight into turned out to be a sleeping sheep. It leapt up with a startled beeeeh. The light in the room snicked off; there was a long silence. I edged to the corner of the porch, and wondered what I should do. It would be stupid to tackle an unknown thug. 'Just watch,' Tamar had said.

I waited there in the dark for what seemed like an age before the light snicked back on. It was a phone; I could see the square shape, the dark silhouette of hand holding it. The light moved around the room: the china cabinet, the mantelpiece, the bookcase, the desk, and stayed there. Now I could see the shape of the person, outlined by the light: short-haired, broad-shouldered in a bulky jacket. Eddie Ryland? He leaned forward to pull a drawer open, and set the light within it, tilting his head upwards as if he was listening. I slid closer to the window, keeping my face in the shadow still. His hands were sifting among the papers.

There was the rumble of an engine now, distant. The cavalry was on its way. I looked up at the hill for the first flash of headlight, then realised help was coming by sea. I knew that engine note; our largest RIB was pounding at full throttle over Cole Deep towards us. I turned my head, and saw a floodlight switch on, sweeping the hill. Good for Magnie! Rather than bring his own boat, he'd gone for speed, and rigged up some kind of light. A gunshot, two, cracked out into the dark.

Upstairs, Tamar's light snicked on, flooding the dark grass with a square of brightness. The silhouetted head went up. The square hands withdrew, and closed the drawer. Then, quicker than it takes to tell it, the phone light moved through the house, and came out of the back door. I dived around the sit-ootery, hand fishing in my pocket, and caught him square in the light of my phone, but before I could even get a look at him he came charging at me like a bull, head down, and knocked me over with a shoulder-thrust. I landed flat on my back, and by the time I was up onto my feet his engine was running. His headlights flared out to show another man running up from the pier. His hands were empty. I hoped that meant he hadn't had time to find the box. The car leapt forward, skidded in a circle at the pier and paused. A door slammed, audible even over the roar of the approaching RIB. The lights dazzled as the car sped up the road towards me, passed me and disappeared over the hill.

I ran into the house, calling out, 'Tamar, it's Cass. Are you okay?'

'Fine. Come up.' Tamar's hair was standing on end, and there were tired lines at the corners of her mouth, but her eyes were bright and sharp. 'Who's the boat to the rescue?'

'Magnie. If you're fine, I'll go and take his lines.'

'Say thanks from me.'

'They got away.'

'Did you see who they were?'

I shook my head. 'I tried to shine my torch on the face of the one who'd been in here, but he knocked me over and legged it. The other one was on board *Khalida*.' I paused, swallowing my fury. 'I don't think he found the box.'

She gave me an amused look. 'Maybe it's as well you didn't have a weapon on you. Well, we should have peace for the rest of the night, surely. Take that back-door key, and lock up as you go. If the house goes on fire, I'll phone you to let me out.'

I nodded. 'You don't want to tell me what's going on?'

She gave her witch's grin. 'Family business. See you in the morning.'

I could see that was all the information I was going to get. I locked up behind me and headed down to the pier, where Magnie had brought the RIB in alongside *Khalida*. 'Well done,' I said. 'Tamar said to say thanks.'

Magnie made the RIB fast and clambered aboard. 'I got no answer from Joanie o' Cole, so I figured I'd come mesel.'

'You did it beautifully,' I assured him. 'All very official. All you needed was a megaphone to shout "Police" with.'

'I had that aboard, the een we use for the regatta. I saw them making a run for it before I got close enough to use it.' He chuckled. 'Besides, we'd a looked a bit red-faced if I'd shouted "Police! Stay where you are!" and they'd taken me at me word, and found only an old man in a gansey ahint the light. So, what were they up to?'

'Searching,' I said. I jerked one shoulder towards my cabin. The man had begun in the main cabin. All the starboard couch cushions were flung forwards into the heads, and the plyboard locker tops shoved aside. He'd found the bottles of drinking water, the butter and cheese, my tins collection and my larger tools and bits-and-pieces store. The next locker would have given him Tamar's box.

Magnie looked down at the chaos and shook his head. 'Aye, aye.' He shot me a sudden look from under drawn-down brows. 'Something o' Tamar's, no doubt. And did he find it?'

I'd trust Magnie with Tamar's secrets. I swung down into the cabin and opened the next plyboard lid. My engine spares were there, undisturbed, with the box underneath them. 'No. Turn the gas on, will you? I think we need a cuppa.'

I tidied up while the kettle boiled, sending black thoughts in the direction of the perpetrator, then sat down. Cat slipped out of the shadows, fur ruffled, and slid onto my lap.

'Well,' Magnie said, 'who was it?'

I shook my head. 'I didn't see. Two of them, both male, I think. The one in the house certainly was, and the one who bundled me into the lambie hoose was strong, and looked male in the car headlights.'

'Yea. The one on the pier here was a man.'

'Two men. Edward and Eddie Ryland?'

Magnie's brows drew together. 'The laird o' Sand? Why would he be searching here in the dead o' the night?'

'Felicity was investigating a link with their family, that her father's an illegitimate son of the old laird.'

Magnie's brow cleared. 'Oh, that old story. Her father'd no' have been best pleased if she'd resurrected that one, and him a high-up solicitor in Edinburgh.'

'She was asking Tamar about papers, and Tamar said there were none. But the Rylands wouldn't know that.'

'If Tamar's no' willing to wash that dirty linen, then the lass'd have got nowhere wi' it.'

'But the Rylands knew Felicity from London, and weren't pleased to find her up here, connected to Tamar. They came over to talk to us at Skeld. It could have been them who poisoned her, and then came to make sure there was no proof of her claims.'

'Aye,' Magnie said, considering it. 'There're other pairs o' men in the family, though. Joanie o' Cole and Gary. It was queer I couldn't raise him on the phone. There's Loretta's man, Brian, and her boy Harald. I didna try them. She's one as is keen on money. She wouldna want to lose her inheritance from Tamar.'

'Whoever it was has dogs,' I said, remembering. 'The blanket he flung over my head stank of dog, and it felt muddy, as if it was the one kept in the car for the dog to lie on.'

154

'They all have dogs. Well, Joanie has the working dogs, and the lairds would have a Labrador, I've no doubt, and Loretta, well, Brian has no sheep, but she has one o' these peerie yapping things.'

'Bob doesn't have a dog.' Magnie lifted his brows, and I explained. 'But we don't know who he's staying with in Shetland. He was strong enough to be the one that grabbed me.'

'I doubt,' Magnie said seriously, 'that Tamar had better give up playing with fire, and make up her mind about the croft.'

'I've tried telling her that. I'll let you have a go.'

He gave a half-laugh, then yawned, stretched and rose. 'Well, lass, I'd better be going, since the excitement's over. Me bed's calling me.'

I gestured towards the forepeak. 'You're welcome to the forrard berth.'

'Na, na, me own bed's just ten minutes away across the water. What's the tide doing?' He glanced out of the window. 'Pretty well full. I might just beach the RIB on the shore at the hoose, and put it back to the marina in the afternoon.'

'Nobody'll be needing it before then,' I agreed.

He paused in the act of clambering over the guardrail. 'You'll mebbe be wanting to win to the kirk in the morning?'

Tomorrow, *today*, was Sunday. I rubbed a hand over my face. 'Yeah, normally – there's a mass at Voe at half past eight, so I was thinking just to sail over, but with all this I don't want to leave Tamar on her own.'

'When'll you be setting out, the back side o' seven? I'll come over at eight, and keep a watching brief. I can take her up a cup o' tea, and if she's feeling up to getting up by herself, I'll have breakfast wi' her.'

'I said I'd give her a boiled egg in bed before I left, and help her up once I got back.'

'I'll come over anyway. I dinna like what's going on in here.' He swung down into the RIB, agile as a man half his age. 'You sleep well now. They'll no' be back this night.'

'I hope not.' I passed his ropes down to him, and gave him a shove off. 'Sleep well yourself. Thanks.'

He spun the RIB away and raised a hand, then shoved the throttle forward, and roared off towards Brae. I waved and headed back to my own berth. Cat curled up in the curve between my shoulder and my neck. Just as I was dozing off, I heard a soft movement in the forepeak, and felt a light weight jump up on the couch. There was a bit of licking and purring as Cat greeted his little friend, and then we all slept.

# Chapter Fifteen

Sunday 24th August

*HW 03.17 (1.4); LW 09.39 (0.6); HW 16.06 (1.3); LW 22.11 (0.6)*

*Sunrise 04.41, sunset 19.32; moonrise 18.10, moonset 00.54.*

*Waning quarter moon.*

**kirk:** church [Old Norse, *kirkja*]

I woke up feeling stiff and sore. Yesterday's bright colours were gone; the sky was a uniform fleece grey, the sea glinting leaden. A cold northerly breeze pushed at the back of my neck as I brushed my teeth. I fed Cat and the ketling, then went up the jetty, across the wet grass of the park and into the house. There was no sound of life above me when I went in. I had a quick shower, then, as the kettle boiled, I heard Tamar rise and go to the toilet, moving slowly on her crutches. I boiled an egg, and set a tray while the toast browned: butter, marmalade, plate, knife, egg cup, teaspoon.

Tamar was back in bed when I took it to her room. Her face looked drawn. 'Good morning, Cass. Thank you.'

'You're welcome.' I shifted the radio from the table by the bed, and set the tray down. 'Boiled egg and buttered toast. And Magnie's coming over at eight, to keep watch in case there's any more excitement.'

'That's good of him. I'll be glad to see him. Enjoy your Mass.' She gave me a sudden sideways look, almost shy. 'Say a prayer for us all.'

'I will,' I promised, and headed back out into the morning. Cat was on the jetty, investigating beneath the container, but he came bounding on board the minute he saw me come out of the cabin with my scarlet jacket on. His little shadow followed him. I put it firmly back on land, and pulled the gangplank on board. It had a comic expression of disbelief as we pulled away, and its little gingery curve was still crouched on the end of the pier watching as we turned around and headed out of the sound. Cat settled himself on the thwart, in the corner of the cockpit. I put the throttle to full. A proper run would do the engine good.

I knew where the various lines and buoys were now, and took a straight course between the house on the lake and the point o' Grobsness. Once I'd passed that and come round into Olna Firth, the wind was side on to me; I unrolled the jib, and our speed rose from five knots to six. Clear water ahead, apart from the lines of mussels, grey buoys against the grey sea. The pier on the north side had been a coaling station in World War I, when Britain's navy moored up in Swarback's Minn and St Magnus Bay, under the protection of the Vementry guns. After that it had been Shetland's last whaling station. Now, it had the traditional jumble of old cars and cranes and *stuff* that no true Shetlander would throw out, because you never knew when it might come in handy, and you could be sure that the day after you balled it oot would be the day you needed it. I had a feeling the owner was some kind of cousin of Magnie's.

Coming between the narrows at the Point of Mulla, I could see the Voe pier, and the laird's haa that had been taken over by Sullom Voe in the oil days as accommodation and entertaining space for their executives. There were trees around it, leaves browned. Below it was the Pierhead restaurant, and the old weaving and knitting sheds of Adie and Co. The jumpers worn by Hillary and Tenzing when they climbed Everest in the fifties had come from here.

Quarter past eight. My quickest way was along the shore, rather than climbing up to the road and walking round it. I moored up at the end of the pontoons, and strode briskly along the road to the new houses, across the soft, sheep-grazed turf to the ruins of the old kirk, where the Giffords of Busta House had worshipped, then diagonally across the field to the white Church of Scotland. I rattled the door open, shut it firmly behind me, and joined the half-dozen folk in the pews. It was a bonny little kirk, plain in the Scottish style, painted in grey and white. There was a scroll-carved harmonium at the front, and an elegant pulpit. Just behind the pulpit was a memorial stone headed by a skull and bones.

The readings were as apposite as scripture often is: our Lord rebuking the Pharisees. 'Nothing that enters one from outside can defile a person, but the things that come from within their hearts: evil thoughts, unchastity, theft, murder, adultery, greed, malice, deceit, licentiousness, envy, blasphemy, arrogance, folly.' We had murder here, and a long-gone adultery, and theft, envy, greed. *Say a prayer for us all . . .*

There was no tea and chat afterwards, as there was in Lerwick, because Father Mikhail had to get back there for the 10.30 Mass. 'Cass!' he greeted me on the way out. 'I'm glad to see you, to say goodbye.'

My stomach somersaulted. 'Goodbye?'

'I'm being moved. A seminary year, and then the Bishop is to give me a new parish.'

'Moved? But you like it here!'

'I'll be sorry to go, but that's the decision.'

'I'm sorry to hear that,' I said, and meant it. The parish would miss him, particularly the Polish community, who'd been able to have Mass in their own language. I'd miss him — his mixture of faith and common sense.

He shook his head at me. 'You cannot expect everything to stay the same at home while you globetrot round the world. There are always changes.'

I made a face, mouth turned down, and got a serious look. 'Cass, change is part of the growing process. If we stay always in our old habits, where we are safe and familiar, we will never progress towards God.'

I thought about that for a moment, and nodded, reluctantly. He shook his head at me. 'No, you need to be more positive than that.

Embrace it as an opportunity. Of course I am sorry to leave you all, but I will be going to new places and using the skills I have to help new people, differently from the way I hope I have been of use here.'

I couldn't manage that much enthusiasm, but I tried to be positive. 'When do you go?'

'They don't drag these things out. In four weeks.'

'Four weeks!' An awful thought struck me. 'But we will get another priest, won't we? They won't try and make us share with Orkney?'

Father Mikhail shook his head. 'No. The Bishop understands how impossible that is. He's promised that while he can achieve it, Shetland will have its own priest.' He abandoned that topic and gave me a grave look. 'What's this I'm hearing about a death in Skeld?'

*Murder carrier.* 'The niece of the old lady I'm helping out.'

'Her name?'

'Felicity Irvine.'

He fished underneath his vestments, pulled out a notebook and jotted it down. 'I'll say a mass for her, and put her on the prayer list in the newsletter, if you think the family wouldn't object.'

I thought of her father, the Solicitor General. I supposed he'd be a pillar of the Kirk, with official attendances at St Giles, in the heart of Edinburgh. 'They might object to the newsletter, but say a mass, please.'

'I'll do that.' He looked past me to greet another parishioner, and I murmured a 'good luck' and headed back out into the sunlight.

I headed off down through the fields towards the old kirk, uneasy. Changes, changes. *You cannot expect everything to stay the same at home.* I knew all about the shortage of priests; Britain was missionary territory now. We had four African priests in the diocese, and Father Mikhail himself had come through the previous bishop forging links between Aberdeen and Warsaw. I was glad our present Bishop seemed to have vetoed the idea of sharing a priest with Orkney; the only way that could work was if he spent a week in each place, travelling mid-week to make sure he was in one or the other for Sunday. Mass one week, Eucharistic Service the next.

*Embrace it as an opportunity*. I'd do my best, I promised; when I was here. *You cannot expect everything to stay the same at home while you globetrot round the world*. Gavin had said he'd wait for me while I enjoyed these two years with *Sørlandet* as a floating academy, but things might change with him too. I was asking a lot, expecting him to wait.

I scrambled over the last fence, and scrunched along the shore road to the marina, collecting Cat from an investigation of the Pierhead's black bags en route.

It was a bonny run home. It was barely half past nine, and Tamar would be fine with Magnie, so there was no need for me to hurry. I hoisted the main and soon we were reaching along Olna Firth with the wind warm on my face, and the water trickling along *Khalida*'s sides. The wind was light enough to let me hoist the spinnaker, so I stayed in Olna Firth until past Linga, then turned for Houbansetter, hooked up the tiller and scrambled forward to attach the pole to the guy. I adjusted it until it was level with the boom and continuing its line, then hoisted the rainbow-striped sail. It rose and flapped, making Cat crouch down in his corner until I had it under control, a glorious half-balloon lifting *Khalida*'s nose and pulling us forward. The helm lightened, and we surged across the dancing water. I stood with the helm between my legs and played the sheet to keep the spinnaker filling, and felt the world lighten around me. Father Mikhail was right; it was no good glooming over what couldn't be helped. His successor would bring new skills to the parish, new ideas, experience gained elsewhere. As for Gavin, we'd talk about it. I wouldn't keep trying to have my butter and the money for it, as Maman used to say. I'd make the decision myself, so that I'd never blame him for taking me from the sea.

He would be here today.

We skimmed across Cole Deep and into the Sound o' Houbansetter, where I unrolled the jib and dropped the kite behind it. We bobbed about for a bit while I dealt with the sails, keeping a wary eye on the Blade as we drifted towards it, then I motored in and moored up.

The ketling had stayed on watch; it oozed out from between the boulders as soon as we came level with the jetty, and trotted across the gangplank the minute I set it up. It gave me a miaow, rubbed against Cat in greeting, then headed for his food bowl and tucked in. I shook my head at it, and reminded myself that I needed to ask Tamar if she'd consider taking in a ketling. I suspected not; people who liked cats usually had one, and people who liked birds took a dim view of animals who also liked them, but for different reasons. I feared a cat who'd been reared on dead starlings might see everything with feathers as legitimate prey.

There was the savoury smell of meat cooking in the kitchen. Magnie's doing, I'd be bound. Tamar had got herself dressed, and she and Magnie were installed in the sit-ootery. Bob had arrived too, long legs stretched out across the width of the room. He caught my glance at him. 'I thought I'd come and see if I could be any help this morning.'

'Lucky to get a lift out, this early on a Sunday.'

He reddened, but didn't answer. Someone had driven him out; I was right about him having a friend in the isles.

'You were having fun,' Tamar said.

'I was. All quiet here?'

'Peaceable as a hen on her nest,' Magnie said. 'No strange callers, no police.'

'Something smells good.'

'I put a pot roast wi' carrots and onions in the oven, and twartree tatties from the garden. It's on slow, so it'll be ready for you when you're ready for it. You just need to add some greens.' He rose. 'Well, I'd better be getting back. Will you be able for another practice wi' the bairns on Tuesday, Cass? The forecast's good.'

I nodded. 'No bother.' He raised a hand, picked up a long parcel rolled in newspaper, and stumped out. I looked at the tea mugs on the table. 'Shall I make some toast?'

Tamar wrinkled her nose. 'A bit late for toast. It's more like cake time. Can you do a microwave cake?'

Her asking reminded me that I'd forgotten to pick that particular

162

bone with Magnie. *Going to marry a policeman.* 'If I went to live with my policeman, it would be in a cottage without electricity.'

'No oven either?'

'He's installed a Rayburn,' I conceded.

'Then this morning's lesson can be cake-baking. It's very easy; the same amount of butter, flour and sugar, and half that of eggs.'

I gave her a blank look.

'In ounces,' she added. 'Handily, that's a tablespoonful.'

'I think you're making it sound more complicated than it is.'

She laughed and levered herself to her feet. We left Bob flipping through a magazine in the sit-ootery and went through to the kitchen. I measured out tablespoonfuls and beat the ingredients under her instruction. She was right, it was dead easy. We were just taking the fragrant cake out of the microwave when we heard a car coming down the road. Tamar grimaced. 'Loretta. Full of sympathy and avid for the latest news. Or no, she'll be at the kirk. She always gets her best hat out on a Sunday. Kayleigh, maybe, or Joanie.'

It turned out to be Joanie and Gary, for a formal visit of condolence. Joanie had put on his funeral suit and black tie. His fair hair shone in the grease it was slicked back with, his cheeks were red with shaving, and his aftershave hit you at three paces. Gary wasn't in a suit, but he had black cloth breeks on, rather than jeans, and a dark grey jumper under his black blouson jacket. He nodded, and sniffed appreciatively, leaning towards the cake on its wire stand. 'We're come at a good time. You're been baking.' He flashed the smile at me. 'A woman o' parts.'

'It's only just out of the oven.'

'That's fine,' he said peaceably. 'It'll be cooled by the time the tea's brewed.'

'Slice through it with the bread knife, Cass,' Tamar said, 'and put a layer of jam in the middle.' She nodded towards the fridge. 'There's the last of the raspberry, that'll do. Remind me tomorrow that we need to pick the fruit and make more.'

She took the men through, and I put the kettle on to boil while I cut a rather uneven line through the cake and slathered the bottom

163

half generously with jam, then slapped the upper half on top. It looked amateur compared to the perfection of the Skeld women's piped icing and irridescent sprinkles, but it smelled good.

By the time I'd brewed the tea, set out mugs, milk and sugar and sliced the cake, they'd got the awkward spoken condolences bit over with, and relaxed into silence. Joanie's folded arms suggested a lack of enthusiasm for Bob's presence, but Gary was asking him if he was planning to bide long, and offering him a run out to the salmon cages, if he'd be interested. 'You'll maybe no' have that in New Zealand.'

'We have aquaculture, sure,' Bob said. 'It's one of our big industries.'

From Gary's scowl at his ignorance being shown up, I hoped Bob wouldn't be going swimming in any boat run.

'Nowhere near us, but I worked on a mussels farm one summer. I'd be interested to see how it's managed here,' Bob said smoothly. 'I can see it's a key part of a croft income. Diversity.'

Now Joanie's expression mirrored Gary's. 'Aye, well,' he said. 'It's no use having just the one croft to work wi'. You need several to make a go o' it. The Ladie here, for example, you couldna do anything wi' it on its own, even wi' the mussels and salmon.'

'Kayleigh reckons she could make a croft trail of it, like that one down in Burra,' Tamar said. 'Native animals and a petting corner for the tourists.'

Kayleigh hadn't said anything of the sort, I reflected, as I dealt out mugs and offered sugar, though it sounded not a bad idea, if you could improve the access road. Joanie didn't like it though, and Gary's mouth set in a grim line.

'We had a bit of excitement last night,' Tamar said, once I'd served everyone with cake. All three heads went up. 'Intruders. No, sit down, Cass –' she added, as I made a move to retreat, this being family time, 'you need to try your cake.'

'Intruders? Here?' Bob asked. I couldn't tell how genuine the surprise in his voice was. Bob and the friend who'd run him over this morning . . .

'In the middle of the night,' Tamar continued. 'Half past one, they arrived, rolled down the hill with the engine off. Luckily Cass saw their lights, and phoned Magnie to come over.'

'You shoulda phoned me,' Joanie said. 'I'd a been here quicker as Magnie.'

'He brought the club RIB over,' I said. I raised my eyes to Joanie's face. 'He said he'd phoned you, and got no answer.'

Joanie reddened, but he said nothing. Tamar gave me a sharp look, and took up the tale. 'Blazing with lights, and if he'd had a police siren he'd have used it. They got into their car sharpish and were off.'

'I'm sorry I didna hear the phone,' Joanie said. 'I dinna aye sleep that well, so I took a dram afore I went to bed. I musta been sound out.'

Spent the evening with crofting cronies at Skeld, more like, come home just able to drive, though nowhere near legal, and crashed straight out.

Gary gave me a sly, wind-up smile. 'No' like you to be asking for help, Cass. I'd a thought you'd a cleared them on your own.'

I felt a stab of suspicion. Gary hadn't answered the phone either, and he was well capable of the strength my adversary had shown. He leaned forward, still smiling, as if he was just waiting for me to say that I'd been grabbed and shoved into the lambie hoose. I wasn't going to give him the satisfaction. 'I've got sensible in my old age.'

'But who was it?' Joanie asked. 'Could you see?'

It was a natural enough question to ask, and I could be imagining the tension in his shoulders as he leaned forward for my answer.

'No. It was two men, that's all I know.'

Gary spread his hands. 'And what were they after?'

'That's unknown too.' Tamar had had time to think that one out. 'But I'll be giving all of Felicity's belongings to her father. I'm not keeping them in the house.'

Joanie leaned back, but his shoulders were still braced under the dark cloth. 'You think they were after something o' Felicity's?'

'It was Felicity that someone killed,' Tamar said, and the words left a silence like a loch after a stone had been thrown into it. She let it hang, then added, 'Why should they burgle me? I don't have anything worth stealing in the house. And I'm sure Cass doesn't own anything worth stealing either.' She shot me a bright, malicious glance. 'Unless you've got a king's ransom of jewels or a lockerful of cocaine hidden aboard.'

I thought of the ice-cream tub under my tools. 'Not that I know of.'

'No,' Joanie said slowly, 'no. That's right enough. It's just, well, I was minding about that man in the Skro. It was a bit o' a coincidence, him being found dead just after you went into the hospital. What had he been doing, lurking around when there was nobody in the house? Felicity wasna here then.'

Tamar swept a hand around the shabby, comfortable room. 'Joanie, just look around you. You ken this house as well as I do. Do you see an undiscovered Rembrandt? You wouldn't get £100 for the lot at a Harry Hay's sale.'

'Harry Hay closed down years ago,' Gary said.

Tamar gave him a withering glance. 'I'm not in my dotage yet. I know the sales are gone, and a great pity too – but then, your generation need everything new, and never mind the earth's resources. The point I'm making is that there's nothing here to steal.'

Gary relapsed into sulky silence, brows drawn down and lower lip jutting. Bob shot him an assessing glance, then went for cheerful, by contrast. 'Well, whatever they were after, between Cass and Magnie I'm sure they'll think twice about coming back.'

There was silence for a moment, then I saw Gary give his father a jab with his elbow, and a 'Go on' nod. Joanie cleared his throat. 'Tamar, I don't suppose you're given any more thought to what we were speaking about the other day? Well, the last time I was over, afore you broke your hip. About reassigning the croft? I ken you like Kayleigh's idea that you mentioned, but it's no' realistic. She'd need to plough far more money into it than she'd ever get out. A new access road, for a start, and tarmac paths, an' all this Health and

Safety. Whereas wi' Gary it'd still be part o' a working croft, joined up wi' mine.'

'I agree that it needs to be worked,' Tamar said, 'and that's as far as I've got. I'll keep thinking.' She gave Gary a hard look. 'So long as I'm not hassled about it. Now, if you don't mind, I'm feeling a bit tired after the night's excitement.'

'The boss is thinking to harvest these mussels,' Gary said. 'I'll be about for the next twartree days.' He gave me the smile again. 'That'll maybe make you feel safer.'

I glared at him. 'I don't feel unsafe.'

He turned to Bob, eyes going down him and up again. 'Can we give you a lift anywhere?'

'Bob's staying for Sunday lunch,' Tamar said. She added, looking at me, 'D'you want to try a redcurrant crumble?'

'I likely could.'

'Sounds good,' Bob said. 'I'll go and stretch my legs while you have a rest, Tamar.'

He and I went with Joanie and Gary to the door. Joanie and Gary got into their car and drove off. Bob strode down the gravel track to the pier. I watched him for a moment to make sure he didn't go near *Khalida*. He headed along the shoreline, fumbling in his pocket, and took out his phone.

I wondered who he was calling.

# Chapter Sixteen

**rönnie:** a heap of stones [presumed Old Norse]

I collected a bowl and went out into the garden. Redcurrants. The sky had lightened now, the clouds pearl grey; as I came into the garden, the sun dipped out for a moment, and the currants shone translucent as balls of red glass in the sun.

Suddenly, just as I'd filled my bowl, the light darkened. I felt a large drop on my head, another on my hand, and then the rain was falling in great lumps, straight down, heavy as pebbles. I ran for the house, feeling the cold drops already soaking through my jumper to my t-shirt.

I paused in the doorway, looking out. The rain drummed on the roof and slanted in the air. The far hills and sea horizon dissolved into greyness; the gentle ripples on the water gave way to rings centred round a splash. Bob had made it as far as Quiensetter and was sheltering against the wall, red jacket bright against the grey stones, head tilted, one hand still up at his ear, shoulders squared aggressively. Even as I watched, he straightened up, whole body bristling. I couldn't hear his words, but the tone drifted across to me: an alpha male defending his patch.

Tamar approved my bowlful, and came into the kitchen to supervise me making the crumble. I twisted the tails off the currents and put them in a sieve to be washed. 'If you were to die without re-assigning the croft, who would it go to?'

She gave me a dry look. 'In the absence of a son and heir? It would go to the Grazings Committee, who'd decide the best family member to take it over.'

'Gary, Kayleigh, Harald. Who would your money be on for them assigning it to?'

'Gary. He's male, and the land's adjacent to Cole, so it would make a more viable income for him. Kayleigh would never be able to live off it, though she'd be a more traditional crofter, with a cow and ponies as well as sheep.'

'I liked your idea of the croft trail.' I chopped the butter into the bowl, added the flour and allspice and began crumbling. 'I think she'd be really good at that.'

'Joanie was right about the cost though. She'd need to spend a lot on it.'

'She wants it.' I thought of those long evenings waitressing that had paid for my RYA qualifications. 'If you want something enough, you'll achieve it, whatever it costs.'

'Hmmm.' She gave me a sly look. 'Or Bob was speaking about coming to spend time in Shetland. Don't you think he would make a good crofter? An Irvine.'

I added the sugar. Mix, mix. 'I've told you what I think about that.' Pour it over the currants, put the result in the oven. 'Magnie obviously didn't get the chance to give you a stern warning about playing Jarndyce and Jarndyce.'

She raised her brows. '*Bleak House*.'

'Sailors read too, you know. So,' I said, thinking it through, 'the only reason Gary or Joanie might have had for murdering you yesterday would be if they thought you were going to assign it to Kayleigh, after you saw the way her dog ran. Unless they saw Bob charming his way in, the obvious successor, and decided not to let you have time to leave it to him.'

She gave me a sharp look. 'It was Felicity who died.'

'It was your tea she drank.' I looked her straight in the eye. 'And don't try to pretend you hadn't thought of that.'

169

She didn't try to pretend. 'It would depend on how long I keep living, of course – Harald's too young right now. If I can manage another half dozen years, he'd be in the running too.'

'So Loretta wouldn't have that motive for poisoning you.'

Tamar gave her witch's grin. 'You don't think my tongue's enough for her to want to see me off?'

'You weren't exactly polite,' I agreed.

'I'm old enough to call a spade a bloody shovel if I want to. She's paid by the social work department to come and do my housework. I'm sure she put in her hours and took the money for the time I was in Wastview without once having been near the place.'

I suspected she probably had. Nobody counted fiddling the system as fraud. 'She maybe reckoned she was entitled, for the times she'd done more than her hours.'

Tamar snorted. 'And what times were those? No, don't try to tell me she has any more affection for me than I have for her. Her husband should have shaken that Lady Di nonsense out of her years ago.'

'Yes, what's with that? I mean, why?'

'I blame her mother. Joyce.' Her tone would have peeled varnish. 'There was the resemblance already, when Loretta was a peerie lass, and the world had gone Diana mad.' She gave me an assessing look. 'Do you remember Lady Di at all, or are you too young?'

'I remember her dying in that car crash in Paris. I was still in primary school.'

'Ah, well. Back in the early eighties, when Loretta was in her primary school, Lady Di was a shy Sloane with blue eyes and flicked back blonde hair, and you couldn't move without seeing a photo of her. Not just in London. Everywhere. It was a cult that swept the country. The fairytale bride. Loretta had a doll of her in her wedding dress, I remember. Paper cut-out dolls of her in every conceivable outfit. The way little girls have Disney princesses now. Anyway, people commented on how like her Loretta looked, and that started Joyce off dressing her like her too, and insisting she had her hair cut the same way – well, along with all the other girls in her class. They grew out of it, Loretta never did.' She gave an exasperated sigh. 'I don't know whether she thinks that she's living on the life Lady Di never had, or feels she's channelling her in some strange way, or whether she's just an older woman who's never grown out of doing what the teenagers do, trying to look like their favourite celebrity.' Her eyes shifted to the window, looking at the ruined house of Houbansetter further up on the hill. 'We were much more contented in the days when we weren't being bombarded with images of the celebrity lifestyle.'

'People bought postcards of Queen Victoria,' I reminded her. 'Lily Langtry, Clara Bow. The forties stars like Lauren Bacall.'

'Oh, yes, and copied their hair and dresses. I favoured Kate Hepburn myself. What's that hideous modern word, feisty? She had more go to her. But I never tried to *be* her. I never thought I'd get a movie-star lifestyle. I bought what was fashionable at my own price range.' She grimaced. 'When the shops had it, and I had coupons for it. Post-war London, you've no idea.' As if reminded, she reached over, cut herself a sliver of cake and ate it slowly, then dusted the crumbs from her fingers. 'Not bad. You use as much of the brain you've got on cooking as you do on sailing and you won't starve.' She put her plate back on the table, and shot me a sharp glance. 'Those sapphires are real, you know.'

I gave her a blank look.

'Loretta's earrings,' Tamar said impatiently. 'The Lady Di ones she was wearing yesterday at Skeld. Like a figure of eight, two sapphires ringed by diamonds. God knows what they cost. Loretta's got a thing about real jewellery – well, you heard her, going on about the Romanovs. Designer dresses. Brian may be a rich fisherman, but the money to wear diamond necklaces and Chanel dresses, that's a different league. She'll never achieve that.' Her mouth turned down. 'Unless she's lucky on the lottery. She does that too. Lady Di's birthday and her own. A tenner every week.' She tilted her head, listening. 'Well, speak of the devil. I'll go and sit down again, if you can put the kettle on.'

Another car was coming down the road. I followed Tamar through to the sit-ootery, fetched Joanie and Harald's mugs and plates, dumped them in the sink, and fetched clean mugs from the cupboard. While I was in the kitchen, I took a quick look out of the door, and saw Bob striding away along the shore. He'd almost reached the point when he turned as if he'd heard something, looked up at the car, and began to walk back towards the house.

I'd just put the tealeaves in the pot when Loretta came in, with a broad-shouldered man I took to be her husband, Brian. Loretta was Princess Di in mourning, in a dark grey wool dress, long and slim, almost to her ankles. I couldn't help a quick glance at the earrings, a rönnie of stones dangling below the broad-brimmed hat. If those were real sapphires, four of them, each one almost the size of my pinky-nail, they must be worth . . . *a king's ransom in jewels* aboard my boat, Tamar had said, with that twisted grin. Had she somehow substituted fakes for Loretta's earrings? It was a joke I could see her enjoying, watching Loretta preening herself in the real thing when it was best quality paste. I remembered last night's search. Tamar was getting that tub from my bilges back the first chance I got.

'Aye aye, Cass. How's Tamar doing, after such a shock yesterday?' Loretta asked.

'Fine.' I indicated towards the sit-ootery. 'She's through-by.'

She went by me without another word, her husband behind her. Harald and Leeza trailed behind them, Harald in sulky-teenager mode with his hoodie pulled up, Leeza plugged into her phone. The choonk, choonk of music sounded briefly. I put the new mugs on a tray and took them through. There wasn't room for me to stay this time, but it was obviously only a brief visit of condolence as they passed on their way to somewhere else. All the same, I couldn't help eyeing up the husband as I served him his tea. A Whalsay fisherman, Tamar had said. He was broad-built, easily strong enough to have grabbed me, while Harald went in to do the searching. He'd know where to look for things in a boat too. Whoever had searched my *Khalida* had gone methodically for the obvious places, the lockers hidden by the couch cushions. But then Gary was used to boats, I suspected Bob would be, and no doubt the Rylands would have friends with yachts. I couldn't rule any of them out on those grounds.

'. . . just wanted to make sure you were okay,' Loretta was saying. 'It's an awful thing, this. Do the police have any idea o' what killed her, and who?'

Tamar shrugged. 'You were the one who poured the tea.'

Loretta gave her a suddenly panicked look. 'But it couldna have been in the tay! You all drank it.' Her voice rose to un-princesslike shrillness. 'You're no saying it was me poisoned her!'

'Who mentioned poison?' Tamar's voice was harsh.

She flushed and calmed down. 'Weel, but I thought – it came on that sudden – are you saying it wasna poison after all? That she had a stroke or something? A bad heart?'

'Nobody knows yet,' Tamar said. 'Unless she visited her own doctor before she came, there'll have to be an autopsy.'

Loretta's mouth fell open. 'An autopsy! We're never had one o' them in our family.' It was, I took it, a personal insult. 'You'd better just say no to it.'

'It'll be Archie whose permission they'll ask.' She shot Loretta a malicious look. 'I don't think the Solicitor General'll be saying no to a police request, do you? What would the papers say?'

'If the police ask for it, they'll likely insist on having it,' the husband rumbled.

Loretta gave him an irritated look. 'No doubt you'd let them walk all over you.'

'You could have poisoned her,' Tamar cut in calmly. 'If you'd been trying to poison me . . . if there'd been something in the bottom of my cup before you poured my tea into it. A clear liquid, I'd never have noticed that, and you poured mine before anyone else's, so I had no time to look.'

It was startlingly plausible. I remembered myself how I'd thought it awkward the way Loretta'd dished the cups out, and then poured the tea, rather than pouring and passing to the nearest person to be passed on. She had given Tamar her cup last, too, and then poured it first.

Loretta turned white first, then scarlet. Her mouth opened, but she made no sound. Her husband put his hand on hers, but spoke directly to Tamar. 'Now, Tamar, there's no call for firing accusations like that about. Loretta's looked after you all these years and put up with your tongue an' all, but you're going over far now.'

'I didn't say she'd done it,' Tamar said calmly. 'Just that she could have.'

Brian's face darkened. 'Well, I'll trouble you no' to say that kind o' thing again. I'm no' having my wife accused o' poisoning someone.'

Loretta laid a hand on his arm. She'd recovered her colour again, though her chest was still rising and falling quickly. 'Now, Brian, it's fine. I understand Tamar. She's no' really accusing me. She's just seeing if I'll rise to her teasing.'

Brian's brows were still lowered. 'I like jokes to be funny. I think we'll be going now.' He rose, and the family rose with him, surprisingly obedient. 'See you later, Tamar.'

'I'll be in the morn,' Loretta added.

Brian humphed, but said no more, and they trooped out. Tamar let them leave the house before bursting into her witch's cackle. 'Well, that put the wind up them.'

'You went a bit far.'

She shook her head. 'You be careful of that, lass. There's nothing wrong with speaking the truth, bold and clear. Felicity's dead, and someone killed her. Are you going to be too mealy-mouthed to wonder who, and how, and why?'

I remembered Felicity lying on the toilet floor, fighting for breath in a pool of vomit. 'It's not a game,' I said.

Tamar's eyes flashed. 'No, it's not.' Suddenly, sitting very upright, she was a Viking warrior, sword drawn. 'Felicity was my kin, and she's been murdered. I'm not going to let the person responsible get away with it. And right now this is my land, to pass on as I want, and it's not going to Felicity's killer.'

'You think that's why? But then what were the two men searching for last night?'

She gave me a curious look, half approving, half defensive. 'Let's hear your theory, then.'

'I don't have one. That's the police's job.'

'Oh, the police!' She snorted. 'You think that blonde woman's any good?'

I managed not to make my usual face at the thought of DS Peterson. That was a weakness I wasn't showing Tamar. 'Gavin thinks well of her. Anyway, he's coming up – Gavin. He'll be here this afternoon.'

'And he'll wave a magic wand and say, "This murder was done by Miss Scarlet in the conservatory with a candlestick." No, you leave me to investigate in my own way. Maybe I'll share my conclusions with the police, and maybe not. This is my family. I'll deal with them.'

There was no point in arguing with her. 'I want to give you your box back,' I said. 'Whether it's a king's ransom or cocaine, it's to go somewhere safer than *Khalida*. The bank, your solicitor. We can drive into town tomorrow.'

She gave me a sharp look. 'What do you think's in it? Have I taken to smuggling cocaine in my old age?'

'No,' I said, watching her, 'but I had a sudden notion it might just be a king's ransom in jewels. A little thing in a big box, to put me off the scent. Easy enough to swap Loretta's earrings for best-quality paste, one day when you were visiting.'

She looked startled for a moment, then flung her head back and cackled with laughter.

'Well?' I said.

'My solicitor,' she replied. 'Put it in the shed for now, shoved under a load of other boxes, and tomorrow we'll take it to him.'

# V

# The second triangle

After the yachts have come downwind to the start line again, they do another triangle: zig-zagging back up to the weather mark, out to the wing mark, than back to the starting line again.

# Chapter Seventeen

**soond:** a narrow stretch of water between two coasts, often where there is a stronger current [English, *sound*]

It poured all through lunchtime, in a white mist that blotted out hills and sea. The shore, the Blade, Papa Little, were all lost. I cleared the but-end table of the assorted land bruck, papers, letters, pens, a laptop in a festoon of wires and a little blue china pill box, and we ate around it, Tamar, Bob and I. Magnie's pot roast was very good, and my crumble went down a treat.

'I was thinking,' Bob said, once we'd moved out to the sit-ootery for the cup of tea stage. 'Listen, I'm not sure I'm happy about leaving you two girls alone in the house here. I don't want to intrude, after Felicity's death, but I didn't like the sound of your visitors last night. I could easy bunk down on the sofa through there.'

My suspicions of him sprang up again. He was just too tanned, too smiling, too pat, and Tamar and I were about as far from being *girls* as you could get. He could have been one of last night's intruders. On the other hand, if he hadn't been one of them, he could be handy to have about.

Tamar was already shaking her head. 'Good of you, of course, but my brother will be arriving this afternoon, and he'll be staying with us.' She turned her head to me. 'That was what I was going to ask you to do next, Cass, get the guest room ready. Just put everything of Felicity's back into her suitcase, and make the beds.'

'Sure.'

I was busy collecting Felicity's cosmetics when I heard the rumble and crunch of a heavier vehicle approaching. A look out of the skylight showed me Kayleigh's Land Rover sploshing through the puddles. Piccadilly Circus, I thought. I wasn't sure whether this flood of visitors was condolence or curiosity. Well, I wasn't going to indulge my own nosiness. I finished repacking Felicity's suitcase, made both beds and refilled the water jug before going down.

Kayleigh had made more tea. My stomach was beginning to curl at the mere thought of the stuff, and this was strong too, the colour of stained teak darkened by rain. 'Here, Cass,' she said, passing me a mug. 'Milk's on the table. This is an awful thing, this. Do you really think she was poisoned?'

I shrugged.

'It's what the police think that'll count,' Bob said. 'Strange that they haven't been here.'

'I talked to DS Peterson in the hospital,' I said, 'and I suppose she'll be interviewing Felicity's father too.'

'They came to Cole this morning,' Kayleigh said. 'DS Peterson. Just after Dad and Gary left for here.' So they did still live at Cole, both of them. I wondered even more why that phone ringing in the middle of the night had been ignored. 'She wanted to know all about yesterday afternoon in Skeld, who sat where, and what Felicity ate. Whether anyone could have reached her cup to put something in it. All that. Well, I told her. I'd seen nobody putting anything in her cup, other as Felicity herself putting a sweetener in, and I didna think Dad or Gary coulda reached it, they were at the other table. Tamar and I coulda, one on each side o' her, but why would we? I only met her the day afore yesterday. You couldna reach her, Cass, you were right the other side o' the table, and Bob, you'd a had to reach across Tamar.'

'He didn't,' Tamar said.

'And same as me, you'd only just met her. Why should you want to kill her? You're travelling too. I told her that. "Why on earth," I told her, "would he carry poison round with him in his backpack when he's just coming to redd up kin? It's a bit overly for a first meeting."'

Bob laughed at her, and Kayleigh reddened. 'There's no need to spring to my defence, Kay. I don't even begin to be on the list of suspects.' He looked at her flushed face and turned the charm on. 'Mean of you though, thanks.' She gave him a half-smile, her eyes lighting up, and continued her tale.

'And then the policewoman headed off towards Voe. I kept an eye out, and saw the car going north through Gonfirth. Loretta, I thought, or of course if Uncle Archie's coming up, she was maybe meeting him in Lerwick.'

'He'd booked on the first flight,' Tamar said. 'Ten thirty from Edinburgh, arriving at midday.'

'That would fit,' Kayleigh said. 'It woulda been just before eleven when she left me. She'd be meeting him at the airport maybe.'

Maybe. I'd have guessed myself that she'd be taking statements before memories faded, or were improved by discussion. A talk with Loretta was more likely, but she'd have been in church, airing her Lady Di mourning. I didn't say anything; ideas from *the policeman's girlfriend* would be taken as gospel and spread accordingly. Outside, as abruptly as it had begun, the rain stopped, and the sun dazzled down on the new-washed colours: the blue sea, the orange buoys bobbing on it.

'Isn't that cool?' Bob said, looking out. 'I could get used to this landscape.'

'Kayleigh,' Tamar said, 'why don't you take Bob up to the top of the hill while it's dry, and show him the territory? There's a good view from up there, Bob – all the croft, of course, and then the lie of the whole land, down to Aith, up to Brae and out past Papa Little to sea. Don't forget to show him the Vementry guns and Papa Stour.'

Kayleigh's eyes brightened, but her face showed only polite willingness, and her voice was casual. 'If you'd like that, Bob. We can give Tamar a bit of a rest before her brother arrives.'

'That'd be mean,' Bob said. This time it was Tamar who got the smile. 'I'd like to see your world.' He rose, and he and Kayleigh headed out. He hadn't offered to do the dishes, I noticed, though these days everyone took it for granted there would be a dishwasher, so it wasn't necessarily a black mark against his character. I didn't see why I wanted to give him black marks, he'd been charming to me – and then the way Kayleigh's eyes had brightened as he'd smiled at her made that teasing resemblance that had been nagging me fall into place at last. Adam King, third mate aboard *Sørlandet* when I'd been an AB, oh, six, seven years ago. Well, well. He'd been a Kiwi too – no, an Australian. I shook the memory away. 'Shall I give you a hand upwards?'

Tamar shook her head. 'I'll just rest in my chair here. I want to think. What do you make of that pair?'

'Kayleigh and Bob? As a pair, you mean?'

She looked out of the window. Bob and Kayleigh had gone down towards the shore, and were heading for the point o' Houbansetter. They were walking quickly, long strides matching, but there was a couple of metres width of grass between them. 'She was startled to see him at Skeld, but there's something there.'

I'd got that sense too. Adam King. It was all flooding back now. My fellow AB on the white watch had been Maria, and she'd had the qualifications for that third-mate post. 'It's their own business if there is. They're both free adults.'

She hadn't been pretty, Maria, but a good practical seaman. She'd known the post was coming up, and she'd wanted it. Then, two days after it had been advertised, she'd met Adam in one of the Tall Ship post-crew parade shindigs. He'd singled her out from among us and turned on the charm.

'Come back,' Tamar said. 'You're thinking about something. Are they in league?'

Now she had startled me. I pulled my thoughts away from Maria's radiant look as Adam had courted her, taken such an interest in her everyday life and the people around her. 'In league over killing Felicity? Why on earth . . . ?'

'Not killing Felicity. The croft.'

'I think you're obsessive about the croft.'

She gave me a long look. 'Of course, you're not a Shetlander.'

I'd heard that at school, when I'd disagreed with the majority view in the playground, the clincher argument. 'I grew up here. If this isn't my home, I don't have one.'

'Land. It's in our bones. How much you could get of it and which bits were the difference between survival and dying of starvation. More land meant fuller bellies, healthier children.' She nodded towards Kayleigh and Bob, just disappearing upwards above the headland. 'Did she bring him here to give me an Irvine for the croft?'

'No.' I paused and thought it through. 'She wasn't expecting him at Skeld. She was pleased to see him, he'd shown her round in New Zealand. But she didn't know he was in Shetland – well, unless she's a better actress than I'd have expected.' Maria hadn't known Adam was going to turn up at the interviews, primed with all the knowledge about the ship that she'd given him. I could still see her shocked face, the bitter hurt in her eyes, as she'd realised it had all been a lie.

'She's not a regular on the Drama Festival stage,' Tamar said drily.

'Anyway, why should she, they, hide it if they're an item? I'd have thought you'd have fallen on their necks and signed the croft over straight away – double Irvines, the grandchildren of your parents, great-grandchildren, whatever, there are just too many of your family for me to keep track of them. Double descendants, come home to make the croft live again – and they could, between them, except that I don't feel like that's happening.'

I tried to remember what Kayleigh had said about Bob. *He was interested in farming, but of course their own farm would go down through Allan's family.* Kayleigh would have told him about her own dreams, told him about Tamar and what she longed to do with the Ladie. A croft up for grabs on the other side of the world, and all he had to do was charm an old lady. I rose abruptly. 'If you're no' needing me, I'll go down to the boat.'

'You don't like what you're thinking.'

He'd come to Shetland without even a casual 'Maybe we can meet up' postcard. That was a pretty obvious brush-off to someone who was maybe still dreaming of a golden lad on the other side of the world. I shook my head. 'I don't know these people. I can't read their thoughts. I could be completely wrong.'

Tamar looked at my face for what felt like a long time. 'Well. You go down and talk to your boat. I'll keep thinking.'

I didn't look up at the hill, just strode to the pier with my head down. I didn't want to see them together again. I could see Kayleigh's flush as Bob had laughed at her for defending him; her carefully masked eagerness to be alone with him, in the hope that she was wrong, that his interest in her life, her dreams, her world, hadn't just been to give him the information to take the Ladie away from her. I felt a stab of pity at my heart for her – plain, practical Kayleigh, who everyone assumed would never get a husband, trusting a golden boy who was out to rob her.

Adam had got the third-officer post. Maria had transferred to another ship, away from all of us who'd seen her face lit up with happiness. As I crossed my gangplank I glanced up at the two figures silhouetted on the brow of the hill and felt a sickness in the pit of my stomach.

Cat's little friend had got used to me now. It rose and stretched as I opened the hatch, tiny paws white against the blue cushions, then jumped down, headed for the food bowl and sat by it, looking up expectantly.

'Chancer,' I said, and doled out the last of the tuna. The smell in the cabin, I was pleased to notice, had subsided; this was obviously what its stomach needed. Cat followed in his own time, giving his own long, lazy stretch and coming onto my lap for a moment before going to join the ketling. I sat back on the couch and watched the pair of them lick the bowl clean, the ketling's little head shoving in under Cat's nose. Then they washed their whiskers for five minutes, Cat checking on the ketling's, before heading out for a foray on shore. The ketling was only just big enough to climb the cabin steps but it tackled the catflap with confidence, the pale-tipped tail waggling last through the gap. I stood up in the hatchway to watch them go: Cat first across the gangplank, the ketling following. They crossed the pier, wriggled under the Portakabin, came out again and disappeared among the long grass behind it. Hunting, no doubt. I hoped there would be no more mice aboard.

I'd left my phone on board. Gavin was in the air now, but I checked it anyway and found a text: *Made it to airport no reported delays see you when I can xxx*

I spent the next hour messing about with the engine. It hadn't been starting well recently, and as the batteries were relatively new I suspected either the starter motor or the alternator belt. I fitted a new belt and changed the oil while I was at it, a messy job which left me with a milk carton of black goo to be disposed of the next time I was at Brae. I was just getting the oil off my hands when I heard voices floating down from the road: Kayleigh and Bob, still with that wary distance between them, heading towards Kayleigh's Land Rover. Bob had his rucksack swinging from one hand. Tamar must have told him firmly that there was no room for him at the Ladie this night, and Kayleigh had presumably offered him a lift to the main road, at least. I let them get out of sight then headed up to the house. 'You cleared him, then.'

'No room for him with Archie staying. No need for him either.' She shot me a sharp glance. 'I've arranged an appointment with the solicitor for half past one tomorrow.'

'How did you manage that, on a Sunday?'

'Phoned him at home, of course. I've known him since he was a toddler. His grandfather was my parents' solicitor, in so far as they needed one.'

'The box is still in my bilges,' I said. 'I suppose it can stay there till then.'

Tamar lifted her head. Her face shone, expectant. 'A car at last. That'll be Archie.'

# Chapter Eighteen

**waar ebb:** the ebb is the area of shore exposed by the tide, and a *waar ebb* is generally a lower tide, exposing the *waar*, or kelp, which grows in deeper water as well as normally hidden rocks [Scots, *wair*, seaweed]

By the time he was at the door Tamar was on her feet ready to greet him. 'Archie!' They didn't hug, but she put a hand on his arm, and he gave her shoulder a clap. 'This is an awful blow.'

'It's an awful business altogether.' He came in and took his cap off, hanging it up on the peg without needing to look, and came through into the living room. 'And this'll be Cass.' He held out his hand, and we shook, formally.

I nodded. I couldn't think of the right words for Felicity's death, and managed only, 'I'm very sorry.'

His face was heavy with grief. My first thought, looking at him, was of his presence: elder statesman, king-in-waiting. You knew he was somebody. I could imagine him dominating a court, playing to the jury, quick to pounce on the least contradiction in a witness's statement. There wasn't any resemblance to Tamar in him, nor to Felicity: his brown eyes, dark brows and drooping moustache gave him a French look. Only a second look showed the firm jaw and Irvine beaked nose. His hair was hovering between grey and white, brushed smoothly back from his brow. He was dressed like a countryman in black trousers and a grey gansey of Icelandic wool. I was just closing the door when I realised another man was picking his way down the path: black suited, shiny shoed. Archie indicated him with a tilt of his head. 'My son Lachlan, Cass.'

He was in his fifties, older than Felicity, and nothing like her. Like his father, he was dark haired, dark eyed. I took one look at his face, and felt I'd had the breath knocked out of me. I'd only had that short chance yesterday to study Edward Ryland, and I wasn't good at faces, but here Edward was, standing in front of me. The likeness was uncanny, and I could see why Felicity had been so struck by it. Tamar had been vehement that her mother hadn't had an affair with Edward's grandfather, which made me wonder if there was something more unpleasant behind the resemblance: a rape in the days when the serving girls were considered fair game for the gentry, and turned off without a character when a pregnancy resulted. But Tamar's mother hadn't been a serving girl, I reminded myself; she'd been a women in her forties by Archie's birth. The laird could still have taken advantage of her, his tenant, a woman on her own while her husband was at sea.

I pulled myself together, and shook the hand he held out. 'Cass Lynch. I'm Tamar's home help.'

'She's selling herself short,' Tamar said from behind me. 'Cass is second mate on board the Norwegian sail-training vessel *Sørlandet* and she's kindly giving up her leave to give me a hand these first few days home.'

'Very good of you,' Lachlan said, moving his expression several social notches upwards. 'That must be an interesting job. Whereabouts do you sail?'

I did my best to answer that one as I ushered him through to the sit-ootery, and escaped to make more tea. I sliced what was left of the cake into three, set the tray again, and carried it all through.

They were discussing Felicity's death. 'A DS Peterson came and spoke to me at the undertaker's,' Archie said. His voice was steady, but his eyes showed the bleak disbelief within. 'Very civil, preliminary enquiries, but we can't begin to think of a funeral just yet. They'll be taking her to Aberdeen, so we'll arrange a memorial service in London, where her friends are.'

187

'I don't understand it,' Lachlan said. 'How it came about . . . Felicity, of all people! I mean, I know her mag annoyed the people she exposed, but it was all just tittle-tattle, nothing to take seriously.'

Tamar looked at him. 'You think her murder was to do with her paper?'

Archie winced. 'Tamar, please. We don't know yet that it was murder.'

Her gaze softened, but her voice was acerbic. 'Archie, it's no use hiding your head in the sand. The papers will be blazing "Solicitor General's daughter in murder mystery" by tomorrow, and speculating as hard as they can.' She gave Lachlan a hard glance. 'Someone her magazine had annoyed is a good line. I'll pass it on to the rest of the family.'

Archie turned to me. 'You were with her when she died, weren't you?'

'Soon after she took ill,' I amended, 'and at the hospital when she died, but not actually with her.'

He spread his hands. 'Did she say anything?'

I shook my head. 'She was unconscious pretty quickly.' He was her father. I wanted to add something about her not suffering, but I remembered her clenched face in the toilets, the long drive to Lerwick, and couldn't frame the words.

I was saved from trying by the sound of another car coming down the hill, heavier, a pick-up or Land Rover. Tamar and I looked at each other. 'What is this,' Tamar said, 'Piccadilly Circus?'

I went to the kitchen door. It was Edward Ryland, dressed this time in dark trousers and a black jacket. He shut the door on a couple of barks from inside the Land Rover. A dog, no doubt with a blanket to shake off the wet on.

He paused for a moment, looking around, then came striding down the path towards me. 'It's Edward Ryland,' I called through, and put the kettle on again.

I hadn't realised, sitting down in Skeld hall, how big he was – a good head above me, with shoulders that seemed to stretch across the kitchen. I'd take a bet that he was a gym man. 'Hello,' I said. 'Tamar's just through by.'

I ushered him into the sit-ootery. Lachlan rose as they came in, and for a long moment he and Edward confronted each other: height for height, the same dark eyes, hair of the same dark brown, though Edward's was drawn up from his brow, and Lachlan's flopped over his forehead. Beside me, Archie drew his breath in sharply, then rose, and broke the silence. 'Edward Ryland?' He held out his hand. 'Archie Irvine. I'm Felicity's father.'

'I'm sorry for your loss.' Edward shook his hand, and went smoothly into formal words of condolence. When he turned to Lachlan there was a look of shock in his eyes, as if he couldn't believe what he was seeing, as if he was meeting his own ghost. 'You're Felicity's brother?'

Lachlan looked at him with mild surprise. There was no sign that he recognised the resemblance. 'Yes, I'm her brother. Thank you for calling.'

Edward let his hand go, and turned to Tamar, who was watching them all, bright eyed, like a bird of prey surveying pigeons. 'My condolences, Tamar. This is an awful shock for you all.'

He sat down unasked, smoothing out his perfectly creased trousers, and turned to me. 'And you were with her, Cass?'

It was smoothly done, but not quite smoothly enough. Something snagged in his tone, like a rope catching on a rock as you hauled it up the beach, and he was looking at me a bit too hard, as if he wanted to keep my attention on him. All my suspicions of him flared. 'Not when she died,' I said. 'Will you take a cup of tea?'

'That's very kind, if I'm not intruding on you all.' He looked round at Tamar, Archie, Lachlan, his face contracting with that same shock again. 'I have to go on up north, so a pit-stop's welcome.'

I took the teapot away and came back with a refill and an extra cup and saucer. He took his tea, but he was still on edge. Something wasn't right . . . As I bent over him, I got a choking headful of aftershave. Tamar caught my expression.

'It's a bit close in here, Cass, open the door.'

I'd just taken one breath of fresh air when he was calling for my attention again: 'Thank you, Cass. This is what Shetlanders call a right cup of tea.'

I turned. He was smiling at me, best charm initiative, but there was still something not right – and then the penny dropped. I spun around and stepped outside. *Khalida*'s hatch was open, and the washboards; I could see the dark square in the white fibreglass. He hadn't come alone. There was someone on board my boat.

I was out of the door faster than a gannet diving, charging down the park towards the pier, jumping each of the burns as I came to it, and vaulting over the metal gate. I crunched loudly on the gravel of the pier, and shouted, 'Hey!' then stopped at the end of the pier, chest heaving, and called again. 'Hey!'

There was no response. I moved to where I could see into the cabin. Eddie Ryland was straightening up and rearranging his face into elaborate, unconvincing bonhomie. 'Cass!' he said. 'I was just looking for you.'

I didn't say anything to that. Eddie came up the steps and out into the cockpit. His hands were empty, and from what I could see he'd only just had time to lift the cushion from the locker he hadn't got to last time.

'Nice little boat,' he said.

I glared at him. 'It's my home,' I said, 'and I don't appreciate you going aboard when I'm not in.'

He spread his hands, and turned the charm on. 'Hey, sorry! This is Shetland, you know, people just walk in, and call, Is there anybody home? That's what I did.'

'Another time,' I said, 'just call from shore, and if I'm in I'll hear you.'

I moved to the end of the gangplank, and waited. There was a long pause then, reluctantly, he came up onto the side decks and walked across it. I let him pass me, then went on board, closed the washboards, fished out the padlock from the binoculars case on the bulkhead, and ostentatiously secured them. 'There's a cup of tea for you up at the house.' My voice would have iced the sound over. 'This is the quickest way.'

I gestured him over the metal gate, and enjoyed watching as he tried to cross both burns without getting his shining town shoes wet. He gave a glance at the lambie hoose as we passed it, and I saw him register the door open at the hinged side. His eyes came to my face, and dodged away again.

I wondered what excuse Edward had made for my abrupt departure. Tamar gave her sardonic smile as I ushered Eddie in. 'You perhaps didn't realise, Eddie, that Cass is mostly up at the house at the moment, keeping an eye on me.'

'I didn't,' he agreed, and laughed at me over his shoulder. 'I thought these sailor types couldn't be prised from their boats.'

I was sure my expression made it clear that I didn't wash that one. 'It's usual,' I said, almost civilly, 'to wait to be invited before going aboard.'

He smiled round the company at that. 'But I thought you were on board, just not hearing me.' Then his eyes registered Lachlan, and widened with the same expression of shock that his father had had. He looked from Lachlan to Edward, then back to Lachlan, gave that fake smile again, and held his hand out. 'You're Felicity's brother? I'm so sorry. We were good friends in London.' They shook hands, and he turned to Archie. 'My condolences, Mr Irvine.'

Edward rose. 'Well, we must keep driving. I just wanted to call in.' He gave a nod of his head at Archie. 'Good to meet you, Mr Irvine.'

He gave Lachlan one last, incredulous glance, and then gathered up Eddie and swept him out.

I left them alone then. I washed the tea things, checked there were enough eggs for an omelette for tea (just, but I had a boxful on board *Khalida* as well), braved the midges in the garden to pick a cauliflower for veg and a bowlful of strawberries for pudding, then called out a goodbye and headed down to *Khalida*. I needed peace and quiet to think it all through.

We'd all been assuming that Felicity's killer had had to be there

191

in Skeld, but Kayleigh had reminded me of the sweetener she'd taken. I wondered what the active ingredient of monkshood was. Suppose you could get pills of it, similar to the size of a sweetener tablet. Anyone who knew Felicity, like her father, would know what she took in her coffee. In that case, it could have been doctored in London or Edinburgh. If she was determined to dig up the skeletons that Archie wanted to keep hidden – I stopped at that one. His own daughter – surely not. It hadn't been a spur-of-the moment loss of control, whether someone had picked the monkshood, grated the root, or ground it down and boiled it to make a liquid, I supposed, boiling it off until it was concentrated enough to make a lethal dose in a few drops, or whether they'd just ordered something off the internet. You could get anything off that if you knew where to look. I couldn't imagine a father killing his own daughter, not just for respectability, but then I'd never been respectable. I'd been a scruffy, salt-stained sailing vagabond. I tried to imagine how I might feel if someone was all set to overturn something I really valued – my reputation for honesty, for example. If I'd told a huge lie, and someone was set to expose it . . . Suppose I'd cheated on Gavin, and DS Peterson, say, was all set to tell him. I still couldn't imagine killing her. If I'd cheated on him, I couldn't care enough to kill.

It wasn't a fair analogy. This wasn't something Archie'd done, it was something he was, through no fault of his own. The laird's son. He'd inherited his father's colouring in an Irvine face, but he'd passed face shape and colouring and carriage on to his son. It hadn't mattered, because he was in Edinburgh, and the Rylands were up past Dundee for their country house, and in London for their town life. Nobody was linking the two, until Felicity saw her friend Eddie's father. I wasn't surprised she'd wanted to find where the likeness had come from. It was her own ancestry, her grandfather, but there was a difference between wanting to find out and taking advantage of the knowledge to put in for a share of the estate when the old laird died.

If that had been her intention, it would cause a stink, unless the Rylands were willing to share. I considered Edward's face. He didn't look like a sharer, and Eddie certainly wasn't. If she'd been prepared to go to the length of a court order for DNA proof, there would be a fuss. Newspapers. Even if it was Felicity making the claim, Archie would be drawn in whether he liked it or not, the old laird's unacknowledged half-brother. I wished I knew more about inheritance law. Illegitimate children inherited equally with legitimate, Gavin had said, but I didn't suppose a brother would have equal shares with a son, and if Archie refused to have anything to do with it, shares for a niece and nephew would be even less.

I was interrupted in my thinking by the scrunch of feet on the gravel of the pier. The ketling dived forward into the space under the forepeak berths; Cat slid down onto the floor. There was a call from outside: 'Hello? Anyone aboard?'

A glance through the window showed me a pair of cloth breeks above black town shoes. I came up through the companionway, and found Lachlan hovering at the pier end of the gangplank. 'I thought I'd leave the old folk on their own for a bit. Can I come aboard?'

'Sure.' I came forward to hold the gangplank steady for him. 'Watch your step, it's a bit slippery.'

He came across and stood on the foredeck a moment, looking up the mast. 'You sail this boat all on your own?'

The incredulity in his voice told me he wasn't a sailor. My eight-metre *Khalida* was a very nice size for single-handing, and these days people went solo all over the world in carefully set-up forty and fifty footers. I nodded. 'More tea?'

He shook his head. 'I'm awash with it.' His face lightened suddenly. 'That's a good nautical metaphor.'

'Oh, there are loads of them.' I indicated forwards. 'I don't like the cut of my jib, so I'm busy measuring up for new sails. That's the jib, the foresail.' I gave him a sideways glance. 'Do you take a professional interest in words?'

'I'm a lecturer at St Andrews. English literature.'

I looked at him with more interest. I'd taken it he'd be a solicitor, like his father. An academic . . . yes, he had that unworldy air of eyes fixed on a horizon far in the past. 'Which era do you specialise in?'

'Medieval Scots.' He laughed. 'I think it was my Shetland ancestry that started that off. There are words in the Shetland dialect that came up with the Scots settlers that haven't been used on the mainland since the seventeenth century. "Spell", for example.'

I looked blankly at him.

'As in relieving someone of their charge.'

'Oh, I'll spell you at the helm for a bit. Yes, that's still going strong.'

'You grew up here?'

I nodded, and indicated over my left shoulder. 'The second last house on Muckle Roe. Have a seat.'

He sat in on the slatted cockpit seat, but his eyes were going down into the cabin, looking at the chart table, the cooker, the fiddled shelf with containers, my row of books. 'This is bonny. It's wee, but it's like a real home down there.'

'It is my home,' I said. 'Well, at the moment I've got my cabin on board *Sørlandet* as well. She's in dry dock so we have leave.'

I'd run out of conversation now. I sat down opposite him, and looked him over. He was shocked, yes, and grieving, but under those surface emotions was a kind of calm, an acceptance of death as an inevitable part of life. The medieval world was steeped in death: battles, the plague, childbirth. It was hard to guess his age; close to, he looked younger than Felicity, in spite of her bright clothes and expert make-up. There was a smoothness in his skin, an eager look in his eyes which were childlike against her weary town expertise. I thought he'd be a good lecturer, keen on his subject and able to inspire others with his enthusiasm. He turned his head away from the cabin, and looked up at Tamar's house.

'We used to come here, when I was a bairn,' he said. 'When Granny was alive. We'd spend part of the summer here. Our parents hated it, they only stayed for a couple of days, and Felicity went back to Edinburgh with them as soon as she was old enough to throw a tantrum about being left, but I'd stay for a fortnight, and spend it running wild. I know every inch of this beach – yes, even now. I could lead you along it blindfolded.' He looked at the assorted fishing gear along the shore, and amended that. 'Well, I could have, before all this arrived.' He sighed. 'Everything has to change. I know.'

'It's a good change,' I said. I nodded up at the empty shell of Houbansetter. 'No more people having to leave for New Zealand. Those salmon cages and mussel lines are work. Your cousin Gary, this is what lets him keep living here.'

He nodded. 'I know. I know. But part of me doesn't like it. We all want everything to stay the same, always.'

'It can't,' I said, harshly.

He gave me a shrewd look. 'You sound like you're trying to convince yourself.'

'I am,' I admitted. 'Not about this though. Just life.'

We sat for a moment in silence, listening to the waves tapping *Khalida*'s sides with soft fingers.

'Tamar asked me,' he said, looking out over the soft green hills, 'if I might think of retiring here, if she was to leave the house to me. Not the land, just the house.' He gave a wry grin. 'She didn't bother asking Dad, but she did ask me.'

'What did you say?'

He shook his head. 'I'd have liked it as a holiday home, for old times' sake, but it's not practical. You can't leave a house empty for nine months up here, and if you let it for that time it's not your house any more. I said that to Tamar. She looked disappointed, but she agreed that it was no good.'

Yes, she would have been disappointed. Here was her obvious Irvine heir, her little brother's son, who was too settled south to want his heritage.

'This is an awful thing,' he said abruptly. 'Felicity. You really think somebody assassinated her?'

That was a good medieval word. 'The police think so.'

'That's what DS Peterson told Dad. But not because of her magazine.' He was watching my face. 'What, then?'

I was a lousy liar, Gavin had told me. My voice gave me away. I shook my head. 'It's maybe related to family stuff . . . look, I really don't know anything about it.' I rose before he could ask any more. 'Did you have any lunch?'

He shook his head. 'We had to go to the undertakers – to identify –' He stopped and swallowed. 'I've never seen a dead person before. If I hadn't known it was Felicity I wouldn't have recognised her. She was so still – she was just gone – she looked like a waxwork.' He turned his face away from me, throat working. I sat down again and waited until he mastered himself, and rose, still keeping his face away from me.

We walked slowly up to the house together. Archie was still in the sit-ootery, leaning back in his chair, his face greyed, the lines in it pulled downwards. It had been a long, hard day for him. I presumed Tamar had gone upstairs for a rest; I'd leave her there for the moment. Lachlan sat in the living room with his phone and I worked around him: cutting up the cauliflower, beating the eggs, grating the cheese, setting the plates to warm above the Rayburn. I'd make the omelette when Tamar felt ready for it.

My phone lay silent in my back pocket. Still no word from Gavin. He'd be in Lerwick now, discussing the interviews with DS Peterson, inputting what had been said into the computer. Statements, actions, when they were to be done by, who was to do them. He wouldn't come out to Tamar in the evening, I thought; he'd wait until tomorrow. But he might come to me.

The thud of her stick on the floor told me that Tamar was awake now, and getting up. I went upstairs and knocked on her door. 'Can I help?'

'Oh, Cass, come in. I've got one foot tangled up in this cover.'

She was lying on her bed, back propped up with pillows. I freed the bedcover from her foot, and she swung her left leg down, swivelled her torso round, and placed the other leg after it. 'There. I heard you doing preparations in the kitchen. An omelette?'

I nodded. 'With cauliflower and cheese. Strawberries for pudding. The men haven't eaten today, but I didn't think they'd want anything heavy.'

It was a silent meal. Archie took a small cup of coffee after it, but waved away a refill. 'That was enough to keep me awake for driving back to Lerwick.'

'Lerwick?' Tamar said. 'Your bed's made, upstairs, in your own old room.'

Archie shook his head. 'Thanks, Tamar, but I booked us into the Shetland Hotel.' He paused, throat working, then finished bleakly, 'It's nearer Felicity.'

There was nothing to reply to that, though I saw the disappointment in Tamar's face. She came to the kitchen door to wave them off. Her face was grey and strained, the lines pulled downwards.

'I need to sit in quiet for a bit,' she said. 'It's been too long a day.'

I followed her through to the sit-ootery and draped a rug round her legs.

'Cass?' she said, as I hovered in the door.

I waited.

'What did you make of the Rylands?'

'I'm pretty sure they were our visitors from last night. Eddie was all set to look in the lockers he hadn't got to.'

Tamar shook her head. 'He's not after what's in that tub.' She sighed. 'I thought I had it all worked out, and now it seems quite different.'

'Tell the police.' I leaned forward to her. 'Please. If you have information which might help find Felicity's killer, tell them.' I paused, then added, 'I've learned over this last year that once the taboo is broken, not to murder, then the killer's likely to commit another murder. You don't want that on your conscience.'

'You worry about your own conscience,' she said, with a flash of her old spirit, and reached for her spyglasses. 'I'm just going to rest.'

'Can I work on your computer for a bit?' She gave me a surprised look. 'There's no signal down at the boat,' I explained.

'Of course not. Go ahead.'

I opened up her laptop, and looked up 'inheritance scotland'. English law would be different, of course, but as the estate was in Scotland, I'd start here. There'd been a new law in 2017, and there was a helpful guide to it. Divorced spouses . . . I scrolled down.

Bequests to a group of close relatives . . . I read it through twice, frowning. If you left your estate to be divided between your three children, say, and one died before you did, their children could inherit that child's share, but the new Act meant this only worked with direct descendants. If, as I understood it, you left your estate to be shared by, say, three nieces, and one died, her children got nothing. The other two got half each. I tried to apply that to the situation we had here, scribbling a family tree on a bit of scrap paper.

| | | |
|---|---|---|
| Old old laird (deceased) | (affair with) | Tamar's mother |
| father of | | parents of |
| | | |
| Old laird (dying) | (half brother to) | Archie |
| father of | | father of |
| | | |
| Edward | (half cousin to) | Lachlan and Felicity |

That made Lachlan and Felicity the dying old laird's nephew and niece. Pre-deceasing him meant Felicity couldn't claim inheritance, but then I didn't see how she could have anyway, if his property was willed, as it surely was, to his son, Edward.

I tried illegitimate child inheritance, and found a useful site on 'Legal rights in Scotland'. Yes, here it was: all children, whether legitimate or illegitimate, were legally entitled to a third of the deceased's estate between them, or a half if there was no living spouse. Archie could, if he'd known about it or wanted to, have claimed a son's share of the estate on the death of the old old laird.

I rubbed a hand over my brow and looked at my scribbles. This was all too complicated, but I thought I had got it. Archie could have claimed on the old old laird's death. If the old old laird had died less than twenty years ago, Archie could still make that claim, and if that claim extended to children, then Felicity could still make it. Scrolling down, I found that it did. As far as I could see though, Archie had no claim on his half-brother, the dying old laird, so

198

Felicity definitely wouldn't have. It was spouses and legitimate or illegitimate children only.

So: if the old old laird had died in the last twenty years, Felicity could have made a claim, and the Rylands had a good motive for silencing her. Presumably the old old laird had been called Edward too. I tried Googling him, without success, though there were mentions and pictures of both Edward and Eddie – Edward in sporting-style shoots, Eddie in City deals. Okay. He might, just might, be on Bayanne, the geneaology website of Shetland folk. I found it and tried him in the search engine.

He was there. He'd died just six months short of twenty years ago.

# Chapter Nineteen

**corbie hadd:** a high rock or crag where ravens are nesting [Scots, *corbie*, from Old French *corb*; Scots, *hald*, a dwelling]

Eight o'clock, and still no word from Gavin. I checked my phone, in case a text had sneaked in unheard, then went to the back door for a better signal. *Naething, rien, ingenting.* I made a face at it and put it back in my pocket.

The wind had fallen, and the evening was warm. The tide was halfway down the beach, exposing the first of the seaweed. I thought I saw a movement down in the ebb, one of Tamar's otters, its red-brown coat so exactly the colour of seaweed that it was only the movement that made me see it. I went through to the sit-ootery to see if she'd spotted it.

She was sitting upright now, spyglasses to her eyes, and a better colour in her face. 'There!' she said with satisfaction, and handed me the spyglasses. 'Just along the shore.'

I swung them up and followed the tideline until I found it, sharp in the glass circle. It was sleek and sinuous, the brown fur glistening. The cat face turned towards us, tiny eyes suspicious, whiskers bristling, then, just like a cat, it began to groom, bending into circles to smooth its back, its tail, then rolling over to show his white throat, just as Cat did.

'The dog otter,' Tamar said.

He brushed himself up for a bit longer, then sat up again, face turning so that we saw the long profile and tiny, flattened ears.

Then he dropped to all fours, back arched, the thin tail curved up, and slid smoothly into the water. The brown back surfaced, sank again, then we saw his head in the water. Looking up at the shore, he began making a sharp cheet, cheet noise that I'd have taken for a seabird's call.

'That's odd,' Tamar said. She leaned forward, scanning the shore-line. 'They don't usually – ah!'

'What is it?'

'Another otter, curled up asleep on the shore. Directly up from him, by that lone greenish rock – see it?'

She gave me the glasses again, and I saw: a much smaller beast, dried to a light golden brown. The dog otter came to the water's edge, slid up between the rocks, chittered again at the sleeper, and waited. The sleeper raised its head.

'That's last year's female cub,' Tamar said. 'Sixteen months old now. Maybe she's coming into season.'

The dog otter chittered at her again, then retreated to the sea. We watched him make his way along the shore, dark head, a rolling curve of back, a spike of tail. Then there was a scuffling in the water, and he came out with a fish in his mouth. 'A courting present?' I asked.

Tamar shook her head, smiling. The female otter uncoiled and stretched, then loped over to the male, back arched, paws delicate on the pebbles. She was within ten yards of him when he noticed her. His back arched, and he gave an intense, indignant chittering. I didn't need to speak otter to know he wasn't sharing his fish. The female watched as he ate it, but when he tried coming forward to her, once the fish was gone, there was a brief rolling in the sand, more of the indignant chittering and the dog otter was bowled over backwards. The female bolted for her hole above the beach, lithe and fast as a whitteret. The dog otter shook himself with the otter equivalent of a shrug, and headed back into the water.

'He should have shared that fish,' I said. 'Cat's found a little friend among the ketlings down at the pier, and he's giving it free access to his Whiskas, which it's far too young for. They're on tuna right now, but I'll need to go fishing.'

'There's some whitefish in the freezer,' Tamar said. 'Help yourself.'

'Thanks. Harald's feeding them on dead stirlings, but I draw the line at dead birds on my cabin floor.'

Tamar's head jerked around. 'Harald's doing what?'

I explained, and even as I was talking it sounded implausible. He wasn't the type to be fussing over feral ketlings; he was more likely to drown them. Tamar levered herself up and reached for one crutch. 'Let's take a walk down there.'

We took the easiest path, across from the kitchen door to the gravel track, and on down to the metal container. 'In here,' I said. 'At least, that's where the mewing was coming from.' I gave the wall a knock, raising a chorus of ketling mews from inside. Tamar's head jerked up.

'That's not ketlings, Cass.' Her mouth set in a thin line, and her eyes snapped. There would be trouble for somebody. 'Those are raptor chicks.' She took a firm hold of her zimmer, steadied herself, and gave the padlock of the container a shake. 'Have a look and see if he's left the key anywhere obvious.'

I looked, but there was no sign of it under any of the stones by the door. 'They were trying to get in here, the other night.' The pieces were coming together, click, click, click. Derek Luncarty, with his suitcase adapted for smuggling birds. Harald, confronting Eddie Ryland in the shadow behind Skeld hall. *I'm no keeping them. It's no safe, noo Tamar's home.*

'Do you have bolt cutters on board?'

I nodded. Any ocean-going yacht carried bolt cutters, or a hacksaw, in case the worst happened and the mast came down, so that it could be cut away quickly before it holed the hull. I had a closer look at the padlock. 'I could probably saw through it.'

'No, don't bother.' Her voice was still tight with anger, the tension of Felicity's death being released in righteous fury. 'Do you have your phone?' I nodded and passed it over. Tamar jabbed in the number. 'Loretta . . . yes . . . I want your Harald here, right now. *Now.* He's got several wild bird chicks in this container . . . I don't care. You just bring him over here, and tell him to bring the key to his padlock with him.' She snicked the phone off without saying goodbye, and dialled again. 'Andrea . . . hello. It's Tamar Irvine, from the Ladie. I've discovered an attempt to smuggle raptor chicks. They're locked in a container, so I haven't seen them yet, but I don't think it'll be as simple as just releasing them. They may not be able to hunt for themselves yet.' She listened, nodding, then repeated the address, and gave road instructions. 'Okay, we'll see you in about three-quarters of an hour.' She put the phone away and added, to me, 'The SSPCA. She's on her way. Now we'll just wait here for Harald.' She looked around. 'We can sit on those tyres there. He shouldn't be long.' She paused, frowned, then said, 'Loretta is one of these "my bairns are always right" women. You could go to your boat, if you want to avoid the fireworks. No need for you to be involved.'

I was tempted, but I thought I should be there. I didn't trust Harald not to resort to violence if thwarted. 'I'll stick with you.'

We sat on the pile of tyres and gazed over the dimming water. Cat came to sit on my lap, with the ketling waiting in the shadows, then gradually coming forward until it was almost at our feet.

'Is that the one you were talking about?' Tamar said. 'Are you going to adopt it?'

I shook my head. 'One's bad enough to get through Customs. I don't suppose you'd think of looking after it, after we go? It can use a litter tray.'

'I've discouraged them from coming up to the house so far, but I suppose it might be company for me of an evening.' She turned to look me straight in the face. 'But it'll live longer than I will, so it might have to go back to being feral. Would it be kinder to leave it that way from the start?'

I thought about it, and supposed that it would.

'I'd never abandon a cat that had been domesticated,' Tamar said. 'But one that grew up feral, well, of course it won't be as sleek and spoiled as a house cat, but it won't starve either.' She looked at the ketling. 'This one's mother will still be looking after it. Or we could trap it. I'm sure the Cat Protection League would soon find a home for it.'

'That might be best.' I watched, feeling mean, as the ketling crept up to nestle beside Cat. He bent his head to sniff its whiskers and give its ear a lick, and the ketling sat up on its back legs, slightly wobbly, and washed his face for him. I tried to shove down the feeling of guilt. One travelling pet was complicated enough.

It seemed an age before the first far-off rumble of an engine came to us from over the hill. The headlights flashed into the darkening sky as it came up, then sparked the dimness into dark coming down the hill. Cat stood up and scampered for *Khalida*, the ketling following. The catflap snicked twice. Tamar rose, stiffly, and stood erect, waiting by the container.

Loretta had brought Harald over. Her face was flushed, her fair hair ruffled. She dived out of the car door and swooped on Tamar like the wrath of God. 'As if your talk this afternoon wasn't enough. You're lucky Brian was out when you phoned. What's all this nonsense you're accusing Harald o'?'

Tamar ignored her, and spoke directly to Harald, following Loretta reluctantly from the car. His handsome face was set in sullen lines. 'Open this door, Harald. I know you have the key.'

He shrugged, mouth turned down, and fished the key out of his pocket. The padlock clicked, and he pushed the door open. The mewing cheeps intensified. Tamar reached in and snicked the light on. The interior of the container sprang up before us: metal walls, wooden boards on the floor, bags of feed, dusty sacks, and, at the back, a large birdcage with three birds in it. They were odd-looking creatures, with the rounded beaks and sharp eyes of adult birds, brown spotted breast feathers and sharp-clawed feet, yet their heads and backs hazed with fluffy grey baby-feathers.

'Peregrines,' Tamar said. She rounded on Harald. 'Do you have any idea of how much trouble you're in? These are a protected species.'

'They're just birds!' Loretta protested. Tamar ignored her, gaze hard on Harald.

Harald shrugged again. 'Eddie Ryland said I was to take them. I was just keeping them for him. You were in hospital, so naebody would ken they were here.'

'And what were you going to do with them next?'

His lower lip pouted. 'I was to give them to this man that Eddie sent, only he never showed up. Twartree weeks ago, that was. I went over to Sand and the birds were still there, and still there the day after. Well, I couldna keep driving over to Sand, no' every day, so since you were in the hospital, well, I thought I'd bring them here, where they'd be easier to get at. I tried to phone him, but there was no answer.' Suddenly he turned into an uncertain teenager. 'Well, I didna ken what to do. I didna want to be landed with the things, what would I do with them? I shot stirlings to feed them wi, Eddie'd made a big thing o' how valuable they were, but I didna hae a phone number for him, except the Sand Haa one, and he wasn't there until the end o' last week. So I managed to speak to him then. He said the arrangements had fallen through, and I was to keep them for a bit longer. They're been a right pain, and I'll be glad to be rid o' them, but I don't see how they can get me into trouble. All I did was look after them for Eddie.'

'And take them from the nest.'

'Yea, well, he said I was to. I was to take them as soon as the fluffy feathers started shedding, and put them in the cage. It was in the roof o' the old byre on his land. He had the right to tell me to. I was just doing what I was told.' There was no whine in his voice, just truculence. He'd never had to suffer for his actions.

'Robbing the nest,' Tamar said. 'That's an offence in itself.'

'If Mr Ryland told him to,' Loretta burst in, 'then o' course he did what he was told. He was working for him, wasn't he? Nobody'll blame him. How could he know the birds were protected or whatever?' She gave them an angry glance. 'They just look like a set o' young seagulls.'

Tamar turned her set face towards her. 'He's old enough to be held responsible for his actions. He kent fine well it was illegal.' She glanced up at the hill as a second set of lights breasted it and came down towards us. 'That'll be the SSPCA.'

205

Loretta swelled with anger. 'You've never reported my boy to the authorities!'

'The birds need taken care of and taught to hunt,' Tamar said. 'It's up to them if they pursue it further.'

'Right,' Loretta said. 'That's that. I ken you're family but this is going too far.' She turned on Harald. 'You get back in the car.' Harald scurried for the car door, and Loretta gave Tamar a last glare. 'I'll let the social work know they'll need to find you another home help.'

She swung down into the car seat and slammed the door behind her, but she hadn't been quick enough. She'd only just started reversing the car up towards the turning place when the SSPCA van came down to block her exit, and she was forced to stop and wait, fuming, while the uniformed inspector got out. The inspector came in to look at the chicks, and noted that they were indeed peregrines, and not yet fledged. After that it got properly nasty, with shouting from Loretta over whether the SSPCA woman had the right to take Harald's name, and general threats of solicitors and court cases.

In the middle of that another set of headlights came down the track, with the caution of someone who didn't know it. My heart gave a jump, and began to beat faster. It was a red hire car which stopped above the turning place, effectively blocking everyone. The door opened, and Gavin got out.

The cavalry to the rescue. He strolled down in the light of Loretta's headlights, head held high, kilt swinging, exactly as if he was walking along his own street, and introduced himself to the SSPCA inspector. Then he turned to Loretta and held his hand out. 'DI Macrae. We haven't met yet, but DS Peterson showed me your statement about what happened yesterday in Skeld. Now, what's the trouble here?'

Astonishingly, Loretta calmed down. It wasn't that her boy had meant any harm, she insisted; he'd been told what to do by his employer, and he'd done it. How could he be blamed for that?

'How indeed?' Gavin agreed smoothly, and turned to the SSPCA inspector. 'And you're taking the birds into your charge? Well, I think that's fine then. If you can bring your boy into Lerwick tomorrow, Mrs Williamson, we'll get a statement from him, in your presence if you want. Thanks for your help over this. Now, I'll just get my car out of your way.'

He backed as far into the turning place as he could go; the SSPCA van followed, and Gavin got out to have a word with the inspector while Loretta turned and drove off in a revving of wheels and a spurt of gravel. I hoped Harald would catch it when she got him home. Once they were safely gone, Gavin and the SSPCA inspector came walking down towards us.

'Well,' Tamar said, 'I didn't expect that to end without bloodshed.' She was smiling in the light spilling out from the Portakabin. 'So you're Cass's policeman.'

Gavin held out his hand. 'Gavin Macrae.'

'Pleased to meet you.' She turned to the inspector. 'Thanks for coming out, Andrea. So what next?'

'It'll be up to the police, of course, what charges they press.' She glanced at Gavin, then looked back at Tamar. 'But I'd encourage them to take a hard line. Even if Eddie Ryland gave the orders, your nephew's sixteen, and old enough to take responsibility for his actions.' She drew on a pair of thick gloves and lifted the cage from the table it stood on. The chicks mewed shrilly. 'He's kept them in good condition for the last fortnight. I'll take them home, feed them, and get one of the local falconers to take a look at them. He'll know how we can go about releasing them back into the wild.'

'Let me know how they get on.'

'Sure.' Gavin made a movement to carry the cage for her, but she waved him away. 'Thanks, but these chicks draw blood. I'll put a report into the station tomorrow.'

She headed off up the road, and Tamar turned, slightly unsteady on her crutch. 'I'll maybe have your arm, Gavin, for the road to the house. I was standing longer than I meant to, and it's been a long day.'

She leaned on him as we headed back up to the house, and, once we got there, made straight for the stairs. 'That's me done for now. Bedtime.' She turned to give Gavin a long, approving look. 'I hope to meet you again, Cass's policeman.'

I was feeling wrung-out myself. I got Tamar's hot-water bottle, and waited for her to brush her teeth, get her pyjamas on and settle into bed before I went back downstairs to where Gavin was sitting peacefully flicking through the latest *Shetland Times*. 'I can't stay as long as I'd like,' he said, laying it aside. 'My B&B gave me a key, but it'll do Police Scotland's reputation no good if I come in with the milk. They're not to know I have a legitimate girlfriend on Shetland.'

'Don't you bet on it,' I said darkly. He stood up, and I hugged him, and was reassured at once. I felt diffident about kissing where Tamar could hear every move we made, so I drew him towards the back door. 'Let's go down to *Khalida*.' We paused on the grass to kiss properly then followed the track in the moonlight to the boat. I shone my mobile phone to guide him across the gangplank, closed the cabin washboards behind us, and walked into his arms.

# Chapter Twenty

**stack:** an upright rock in the sea, separated from the land by cliff erosion [Old Norse, *stakkr*, a stack or pile]

I was woken in the dark by my phone ringing. I fumbled for it and put it to my ear. There was silence, then a choking sound, and Tamar's voice stuttering my name. I leapt out of bed, shoved my feet into my seaboots and ran for the cottage.

She was vomiting, just as Felicity had been. She hadn't tried to get up; she was bent over the side of the bed, with a pool of sick below her on the carpet, and the sour smell of bile filling the room. The phone dangled from its cord by her hand.

She was barely conscious. I checked her airway and eased her into the recovery position, thinking furiously about what would be the fastest way to get her to Lerwick. I couldn't get her to the car on my own, or I'd have risked being done for driving without a licence. Magnie would take twenty-five minutes to get here at the very fastest. Joanie o' Cole, though, he could be here in ten, which would have us in Lerwick half an hour later, whereas the ambulance would take forty minutes to get here, assuming it was sitting by the hospital ready to go, then forty minutes back. 'Tamar,' I said urgently. 'What's Joanie's phone number?'

For a moment I thought she was too far gone to hear me, then she muttered, '574.'

I leapt for the phone and dialled. This time Joanie answered. 'Who's this?'

'It's Cass. Tamar's been taken ill. She needs to get to the hospital, as fast as we can take her. Can you run us?'

'I'm on my way,' he said, and rang off. I got back on the phone, to the hospital.

'I'm bringing in an emergency. An old lady. I think she's been poisoned.' They gave me the doctor on duty, and I explained. He'd been one of the team that had treated Felicity, which made it easier. Keep her warm, keep her airways open, and bring her as fast as we could. They'd be ready for us. I put an extra blanket over Tamar, and checked her pulse. It was fast and jerky.

The police. I'd left my own phone on the boat, but Gavin's number was stored in my head. I called him. He sounded as alert as if he'd slept since ten, not left me a bare hour before. 'Cass?'

'Tamar's taken ill. I'm just waiting for Joanie to come and run us to the hospital.'

'What sort of taken ill?'

'Like Felicity. Vomiting, and her pulse is racing. She's an awful colour.'

'Stay with her. I'll meet you at the hospital. Good luck, *mo chridhe*.' He rang off, and I was left to concentrate on Tamar. I grabbed a bag and threw things for her into it, trying to remember what I'd unpacked only three days before. Pyjamas, slippers, toothbrush. The little brass egg wasn't on the mantelpiece where I'd put it, but she wouldn't be worrying about nail clippers and the like right now. Dressing gown. The book she was reading, and her glasses. I took the blankets from the chest of drawers, to wrap her in for the journey, and both downies from the spare beds.

I heard the Land Rover at last, then footsteps, and Joanie's voice calling. He came straight upstairs, lifted Tamar as if she weighed nothing, and carried her to the car. I scurried behind with the downies, blanket and hospital bag, and grabbed towels from the kitchen on the way. We wrapped her up as best we could and laid her on one of the back benches, with the towels pillowing her head. She roused briefly with the cold, then relapsed into unconsciousness. I clambered in beside her, and Joanie set off.

We'd just turned south onto the main road from Voe when a police car came up behind us, blue lights flashing. Joanie pulled over, and Sergeant Peterson came to the window. 'I was in Brae. We'll give you an escort into town.'

They set off ahead of us. I knelt on the floor in the back, clinging on to the bench seat of the Land Rover with one hand, and steadying Tamar with the other. She was still retching, but it seemed like an automatic reaction, because nothing was coming up, and as far as I could see in the glow from the windscreen instruments, there were no signs otherwise of her being conscious. 'Hang on in there, Tamar,' I said to her, hoping the urgency in my voice would get through to her. I took her hand, fragile in mine, delicate bones under the papery skin. 'Twenty minutes, Tamar, and we'll be in Lerwick. Hang on, Tamar. Keep fighting. Tamar, we're on our way.' *There's no antidote*, Gavin had said. 'Tamar, hang on.'

Her name must have penetrated, for her hand moved in mine. 'Edward,' she said.

'You've been poisoned, Tamar,' I said. 'We're taking you to Lerwick.'

'Box. *Solicitor.*' She said something more, in a thread of a voice that I could barely catch over the rattle of the Land Rover, but I thought it was 'Edward' again.

'Edward Ryland?' I asked. 'Tamar, Edward Ryland? Did you see him do something suspicious? Tamar, was it him who poisoned you?'

It was no good. Her breathing changed to a horrid rattling, harsh in her throat. I'd never heard anything like it, but I knew what it was. We would arrive at the hospital too late. I felt the Land Rover swoop down the last hill, go around the long curve and begin the climb up to the golf course hill. Down again to the Brig o' Fitch. The hoarse, harsh noise stopped as we began climbing again. Tamar's hand was already chilling in mine.

Gavin brought me home an hour later. There was nothing to stay for. I sat silent beside him, brow leaning against the cold glass of the car window, looking drearily out into the darkness, and only roused myself when we got to Tamar's track, and I had to get out to open the gate. There was a police car in the turning place at the house, with two dark heads in the front seats. Gavin got out and went over for a brief word, then returned. 'Given what's been going on, I want the house guarded until we can search it properly.' He eased the handbrake off, and we rolled down the last hundred metres to the end of the road. Below, at the jetty, *Khalida*'s mast rose black against the silver water. I fumbled in my pocket and found my little torch. The ring of light fumbled over the stones of the jetty and slid onto the rounded white fibreglass of the cabin roof. I should have been tired, but I was shaken awake. 'Cup of something?'

'That'd be good.' He followed me on board, waiting in the cockpit until I'd lit the oil lamp, then came down into the cabin. There was a scuffle as the ketling disappeared into the foredeck. 'Was that your stowaway? *Halo*, Cat.' He sat down in his usual place, head tilted back against the bulkhead and smiled at me. 'This feels like coming home. Tea, please, then I may make it back to Lerwick in one piece.' He glanced at his watch. 'Half past two. I might even manage four hours' sleep.'

I made us a mug of tea each and sat down opposite him, hands curled round the warming china. 'What next?'

'Is the house locked?'

I nodded.

'And you have the keys?'

'Yes.'

'But you're using the shower and suchlike.'

I shook my head. 'I don't need to. I'll go back to Brae in the morning. My job here's done.' I felt a bleak pang shudder through me. I had failed to keep Tamar safe.

Gavin's hand crossed the table to close over mine, warm and comforting. 'If someone is determined to kill, it's very hard to stop them.'

'I know.'

'Is there anything you're needing to fetch from the house?'

I tried to think. Towel, washbag, clothes in the washing machine.

'No.' The thought reminded me. 'But I have this, and I want it out of here.'

Cat growled as I shifted him over. 'Sorry,' I said. I lifted the cushion he'd been lying on, then the board under it. I set them on the engine box and fished under the other boxes for Tamar's ice-cream tub. 'Tamar gave me this to keep.'

Gavin's mouth quirked in a smile as he looked at my label. 'Fuses and engine spares? Is that the box you told me about? What's in it?'

'I don't know. But that was what they were looking for, I think – the Rylands.' I hefted the box in my hands. 'Papers, or a book, though what could be in a book that could be dangerous, I don't know. An inscription, maybe? Archie, from Dad, in the old old laird's writing?' I remembered my guess about Loretta's earrings. 'Or jewellery, something little in a big box. But just before she died, Tamar said "Edward" then "Box. Solicitor." I think she meant I was to give the box to her solicitor. We were going to do that tomorrow afternoon. She made an appointment.' I put it on the table in front of him. 'There. You take it.'

'We'll be talking to her solicitor.' His hands hovered over my parcel tape. I could see he was restraining his natural curiosity. He lifted it and tested the weight. 'No, it's not just papers. I'll open it in his presence. And if you give me the keys, I can pass them on to Forensics.'

I fumbled in my pocket and gave them to him. 'The Chubb is the back-door key.'

'And you'll head off for Brae in the morning?' He frowned. 'Except that you might be safer here, being guarded with the house.'

I bristled, and he held a hand up. 'Sorry, sorry. The police can guard any wrongdoers from you.'

'Brae Marina's locked.'

'So it is, with a handy key reachable inside the gate for people who've forgotten theirs.'

I conceded that one. 'I'll hide myself in among the yachts instead of being out on the visitors' pontoon. There's aye a berth free. Someone'll have their boat out for painting, or be away in Faroe. Those Rylands wouldn't know mine from the others.'

'Do you have any ideas about how she was poisoned?'

I'd been thinking about this too, in that hour at the hospital. 'She had a glass of water by the bed, for waking in the night drinking, but I gave it to her myself, fresh from the tap, just before we left her. Nobody could have sneaked in and poisoned it without waking her.'

He took out his black notebook and scribbled a few words. 'She'd have tasted monkshood in water.'

'It acted so fast on Felicity.' I tried to think of a scenario in which Tamar would be snacking on poisoned biscuits at midnight, and couldn't. 'She was in bed. She didn't keep a tin of biscuits at her bedside, or anything like that. Just the glass of water.'

'Did she take any capsules?'

'The painkillers from the hospital. They were all pressed pills, in foil. I don't see how you could doctor those.'

'How about cod liver oil, vitamin supplements, that kind of thing?'

I jerked my head up. 'Oh, yes! She did. I think it was something like cod liver oil. Those gelatin capsules.'

'Aha. Promising.'

'That would slow it down, wouldn't it? If the poison was in one of those, she wouldn't taste it, and it wouldn't start acting until the capsule dissolved.'

'When did she take them, and where did she keep them?'

'On the table. They were in a little china box, dark blue with a gold picture on it. She took one at breakfast and one at dinner.'

He was scribbling hard. 'Does the box live on the table?'

I nodded. 'I suppose you could suck the cod liver oil out with a syringe, then fill it with monkshood. A dab of glue to keep it in.'

'It's all very domestic,' Gavin said. 'Home-grown poison, capsules, syringes. I don't often see poisoning cases.' He took a new page in his notebook. 'You said you'd had a day of visitors. Who, exactly?'

I sighed. 'The whole caboodle of them. There was Bob, from New Zealand, he arrived while I was at Mass, while Magnie was with Tamar. Then Joanie and Gary o' Cole, and then Kayleigh came over after them. Then after lunch we had Loretta and her husband and the two children, and Archie, Felicity's father, and her brother, Lachlan. The Rylands came while they were there, and oh, Gavin, Edward really is a dead ringer for Lachlan. Oh, okay, not twins dead ringer, but there's no question of them not being related. It's no wonder Felicity started asking questions. *And . . .*' I paused dramatically. 'I looked up the old old laird's death. It was nineteen years and six months ago, and their chance to claim runs out after twenty years.'

'I've been looking him up too,' Gavin said. 'My ship, Cass.'

His case, he meant. 'Feel free to put young Eddie straight in clink over the peregrines. I'm pretty certain he was the one ransacking *Khalida* the other night. He tried to finish the job today, while his father kept me talking.'

'Where did you put all your visitors? Did they sit around the table the box was on?'

'They all came through to the sit-ootery. I don't see that Joanie or Gary had any opportunity to tamper with the pill box, but Bob had been about all morning, and he and Kayleigh had lunch with us, at the table – except that I'd cleared all the stuff on it, including the pill box, over to the dresser. Loretta and her lot didn't stay long, and they were only in the sit-ootery.' I smiled at the memory. 'Tamar was on good form, needling Loretta about how she could have poisoned her, and her husband took offence and bristled them all out.'

Gavin's head lifted. 'Oh? What was her theory?'

'That Loretta had put a clear poison in the bottom of her cup, and poured the tea quickly over it.'

'Did that sound plausible to you?'

'It did, actually. It explained the odd way Loretta doled out the cups, though it could have been lack of room on the table too. But it was an easier way of poisoning that cup of tea than someone leaning over and putting something in it. Only I don't see why she should have. She's not involved in the Ryland thing, and if she wants Harald to inherit the croft, Tamar needed to live till he's old enough – and, of course, to assign it to him. He's not likely to get it now.'

215

Gavin made more notes. 'Then Felicity's father and brother came?'

I nodded. 'And the Rylands.' I tried to envisage taking them through. 'I escorted them both to the sit-ootery, and escorted them out again. I don't think either of them could have slipped a doctored pill into the box, and they only met Tamar at the sheepdog trials, so they wouldn't know what she took.'

'Archie and Lachlan?'

'They stayed for the rest of the afternoon, and they were at the table later. I made us all an omelette.'

'So in theory, Bob, Kayleigh, Archie or Lachlan could have slipped an extra pill into that box, but you don't think the others could have.'

'Bob was here on Saturday morning, and in the house. I suppose he could have opened the box out of curiosity, and seen the pills.' I frowned. 'But he's here backpacking. Why would he be carrying poison around with him? Archie and Lachlan might have known she took capsules, and likely Kayleigh as well.'

'If it was in the pill box,' Gavin reminded me, 'it needn't have been done yesterday. It could have been in the box for days, just waiting for Tamar to get round to eating it.'

I looked at him in dismay. 'So it could. But then, Felicity's death –'

'Don't forget the swapping of the tea. That may have been someone getting impatient for Tamar to go.'

I felt a cold shudder down my spine. 'Horrid.'

'Yes.' He put his notebook away. 'I should be going.'

We sat in silence for a moment. The ketling's little face peered round the forecabin doorway, then gradually it crept forward, whiskers twitching. It sniffed at Gavin's sock, then slid past him and jumped up beside Cat again and snuggled into his belly. Its ginger fur glowed in the lamplight. He put one paw over it, gave its head a perfunctory lick and went back to sleep. 'Pretty little thing,' Gavin said. 'Are you going to keep her?'

I looked at him in alarm. 'Her?'

'Colour is sex-linked in cats. Gingers are almost always male, tortoiseshells are almost always female.' He laughed at me, eyes dancing. 'Besides, look at them! If ever I saw a man who's enjoying being smarmed up to by a pretty girl, Cat is that man.'

I looked at the ketling, and she looked back from her pillow of grey fur, smugness written across her whiskers. None so blind as those who don't want to see. Now I looked properly there was no way she could be a boy: the delicate pointed face, the neat snub nose, the snowy bib and paws, the graceful way she moved. The first time I'd seen her I'd thought of pink ribbons. I felt even meaner about spoiling Cat's romance, but one set of vet appointments and injections and passports really was plenty.

'The Cat Protection League can find her a nice home,' I said firmly. 'Ashore. Dealing with the rules and regulations for one travelling cat is quite enough. Oh for the days when ships just came with a ship's cat, or several, including ship's ketlings, and nobody turned a hair about it.'

Gavin rose so smoothly that the ketling only lifted its head, and stayed put. 'I'd better go.' He gave a huge yawn, then put his arms around me and laid his cheek against my temple. I breathed in the smell of him, a hint of hospital overlaying that old-fashioned soap with the red label stuck to it.

'Tomorrow, I'll get a bus into town and join you in your B&B, if it won't destroy the police's reputation.'

He laughed. 'A gallant offer, to stay ashore for a night. If you can.'

'If it's safe to leave *Khalida* unguarded.'

'Once the solicitor's opened this box, I'll tell whoever's affected by what's inside that we've got it. That'll take the heat off you.' We kissed, then he moved to the steps, I leaned past him to take the washboards out, and came out with him into the night. The wind had eased, and the clouds cleared. A faint light up at the turning place showed where the police car was. Otherwise, it was velvety dark, with no moon to light the water, only the soft silver of the stars. Gavin's head turned towards Brae. 'Look. The aurora's out.'

I followed his gaze. Curving across the sky to the north was a ragged curtain like a sky arch of luminous paint. 'The mirrie dancers.' As we stood and watched, patches of brighter green glowed and faded against the dark sky.

'The first I've seen this year.' He turned his head to kiss my brow. 'You'll get cold, *mo chridhe*. Go and get some sleep.'

'Can I come with you to the solicitor?'

'No. But I'll report back, as soon as I can, to let you know what dynamite you've been harbouring aboard.' He gave me a last kiss, reached into his sporran for a torch and headed across the gangplank. I watched the white circle waver its way to the car, and heard the door snick, the engine start. The lights curved up the hill, dazzled for a moment as they went over the crest, then disappeared, letting the darkness flow back.

I brushed my teeth out on deck, and went back to bed.

# VI
## The final beat

The final leg of the race is a last zig-zag up to the weather mark, where the finish line is laid.

# Chapter Twenty-one

Monday 25th August

*HW 04.23 (1.3); LW 10.55 (0.6); HW 17.15 (1.3); LW 23.38 (0.6)*

*Sunrise 04.44, sunset 19.29; moonrise 18.32, moonset 02.02.*

*Waning quarter moon.*

**bister:** a farm or several farms; now generally found in place names, e.g. Fladdabister [Old Norse, *bølstradr*, a farm or farms]

I awoke with a start, and the events of the night rushed back at me. Tamar's call in the night, finding her in her bedroom, the drive to the hospital. Her death as the Land Rover drove up the hill towards Lerwick.

Cat and his little friend were curled into my neck. I turned over onto my front, trying not to disturb them, and pillowed my chin on my arms. I felt drained. I'd become a part of this family's concerns, but now I had nothing more to do here. I'd leave them all behind and head up to Brae, where I'd focus on getting our sailors ready for the coming Interclub. Gavin was in charge of the investigation, and he'd tell me anything he was allowed to.

The sense of failure was still with me, even though I knew that there was nothing more I could have done to protect Tamar. She'd been determined to play a lone hand, as she'd done all her life. Someone had killed her to protect the secrets she wouldn't share. Or for an inheritance, I reminded myself. Land was important in Shetland.

The warmth had gone from my bed. I shifted the cats and slid out into the cold of the cabin, feet shuddering as I thrust them into my boots. I boiled the kettle and had a basin wash, dressed with an extra jumper, then went out into the cockpit and did a few stretches to warm me up.

The cold night had changed the colours of the land. It was hairst now, with the auburn grass on the hills darkened to brick red, and highlighted by the bright orange of the bog asphodel. By Tamar's cottage, the rugosa bushes were bronze in the early sun. The berries of the whitebeam were scarlet among the crisped brown leaves. The cottage looked forlorn with no smoke from the chimneys, or maybe I was just feeling it forlorn, knowing Tamar had gone.

Gavin's police guard were still there, the white and neon stripes standing out stark against the amber hill. I wondered when Forensics would get here. This afternoon, perhaps, flying up on the plane, or not till tomorrow, coming on tonight's boat, to arrive in the morning. It would be a long, boring day for two members of Police Scotland.

Breakfast. I poured museli into a bowl, chopped up an apple to go with it, and fished in the locker behind the sink for a new carton of long-life milk. There wasn't one. It would have to be Carnation. I found the tin, pierced it, and poured it cautiously over. Cat jumped up, looking hopeful. He liked the milk from the red tin. I poured some into a saucer, and wasn't surprised to see the little ginger head butting him away from it. 'It's not good for you,' I told the ketling. Once she was safely washing her face I gave Cat his portion.

Suddenly the smell brought back memories. Magnie's mother had always used Carnation milk in her tea. I had a sudden picture of myself as a teenager waiting at the garden gate. 'Magnie's just shaving, lass, are you wanting a cup o' tea?' It had been May, a bonny summer's day, and I'd been waiting for Magnie to come and get the RIB out. 'I'm just spraying the gooseberry bushes, against the saw fly.'

I'd stared at the spray in her hand. 'Wi' Windolene?'

'Na, na, lass, wi' boiled up rhubarb leaves, an' a peerie grain o' baking soda, an' a drop o' Fairy Liquid. It kills the caterpillars off a

222

treat.' She gave a final skoosh, and I saw several caterpillars writhing and dropping.

Boiled rhubarb leaves. I was reaching for my computer when I remembered I didn't have wifi here. If Magnie's mother had had it, then it was one of those good old-fashioned remedies to be found on every croft. Boiled rhubarb leaves, baking soda and a drop of fairy liquid. We'd exonerated Bob on the grounds that he wouldn't be carrying poison, and I couldn't envisage Archie or Lachlan grating and boiling up monkshood root, but it could well be that there was poison more easily to hand than we'd thought of. The garden shed where all the tools were, that would be the place to keep such a thing, and now I was remembering Magnie's mother I had a feeling I'd seen a spray bottle in there. I tried Gavin's phone, but it went straight to voicemail. The policemen up in the car would have smartphones, I'd bet.

I finished my museli and headed upwards to the police car. The older man was reading the paper; the younger one was tapping away on a tablet. 'Hi,' I said. 'A quiet night.'

The younger of the two yawned. 'Quiet's how we like it.' He looked at his watch. 'We'll be off home soon. You ken you're no' allowed in?'

I nodded. 'Nobody till Forensics has been. Can I go into the garden, though?'

'Don't see why not.'

'I had this idea,' I said. 'Could you look something up for me? I don't have Wifi down at the boat, and the computer's in the house.'

'Yea, yea. What're you wanting looked up?'

'Rhubarb poisoning.'

The older one gave me a suspicious look.

'I remembered Magnie's mam,' I explained. 'Magnie o' Strom. She used to kill greenfly with rhubarb. I wondered what effect it would have on a body.'

The older man folded up his *Shetland Times* and showed signs of interest. 'You're fairly right. Me own mother uses that on her greenfly. Boils it up in a special pot that she only ever uses for that, and makes a fresh batch every year. We were aye warned no' to touch it as bairns.'

The younger one tapped away into his tablet. 'There's no much here.' There was a pause, while he read it. 'They poisoned folk in World War I when the leaves were recommended as a vegetable.' He scrolled down. 'A 140-pound person would need to eat ten pounds of rhubarb leaves to die.'

'That's an awful lock o' leaves,' the older man commented.

'A small amount can still mak' you sick. Symptoms, symptoms . . .' He scrolled down. 'Boiling it up wi' baking soda makes it more poisonous.'

Just as Magnie's mother had done. Tamar would have known that too.

'Yea, here we are. This one's more sense. A burning sensation in the mouth and throat, nausea and vomiting, stomach pains, breathing difficulties, seizures and coma.'

The same symptoms as for monkshood; the way Felicity and Tamar had died.

'Are you thinking then,' the older one asked, 'that the old lady died o' rhubarb poisoning?'

'They're talking about leaves,' I said, 'and that's a lot of leaves, but once you'd boiled it up the poison would be concentrated. It maybe wouldn't take very much. And an old lady, well, surely she'd need less than a healthy adult. Can I go and have a look in the garden shed?'

The older officer shook his head. 'Forensics.'

'I'll stand in the doorway and look. You can come with me and make sure I don't touch anything.'

'Well, I suppose.' He got out of the car and followed me to the shed. There would be no prints on the paving stones leading to it, so I walked straight up to it, and used my penknife to press down the latch and hook open the door. The light flooded in on the dusty boxes, the battered biscuit tins. One shelf had what looked like a pharmacy's worth of poisonous concoctions in brightly coloured plastic containers. Among them was the window-spray bottle I'd half-remembered, with sticky label written in felt-tip pen: 'Rhubarb'. Even from here I could see there wasn't as much dust on it as there should have been if it hadn't been touched since May.

The officer was peering in over my shoulder. 'That's a careless place to be keeping shotgun cartridges. They should be locked up with the gun.'

I followed his gaze to a couple of boxes on the top shelf. You could just guess through the dust that they'd been faded yellow on a navy base, with 'Super' written in a cartouche over a red X. 'Those yellow boxes? They're for a shotgun?'

'Careless. We'll take them away once Forensics are done here.'

'Sergeant Peterson said that there wasn't a shotgun licensed to this house.'

'Well, there may no' have been. You didn't need a shotgun licence until 1967, and plenty o' crofters had one long before then, and just didn't bother.' He looked at the boxes again. 'Those could date back to the fifties, even. The gun may be long gone. Seen enough?'

I'd seen more than enough. Not only a handy bottle of poison, but shotgun cartridges too. Derek Luncarty had been peppered with a shotgun.

Tamar had been odd about that, when Sergeant Peterson had questioned her. I hadn't known her well enough then, but looking back now I felt uneasy. She'd led an exciting life, travelling round the wild places of the world. I bet she'd have learned to shoot. If the places she'd been in had been wild enough, she might even have got into the habit of keeping a gun under her pillow, or at least to hand. If Tamar had surprised an intruder in the house, might she have picked up her late father's shotgun and let fly at him as he ran towards his car, to make sure he didn't come back again? I could just see her doing it.

Suddenly I remembered. '*That*,' she'd retorted to Loretta, over stopping Harald shooting, '*was before someone apparently took to shooting at people.*' I hadn't picked up on it at the time, because I'd known Luncarty had been shot, but DS Peterson hadn't mentioned that to Tamar. She shouldn't have known – unless she'd shot him herself.

'You're having ideas,' the officer commented.

'If you were an old lady,' I said, 'and you'd been surprised by an intruder in the house.'

He gave me a sharp look.

'Some sneak thief, you thought, or a druggie after money in an isolated house with only an old lady. So you'd make a noise so he knew you were awake, hoping that'd clear him. And you had your late father's shotgun to hand.' I gestured, thinking it through. 'And you wanted word to go round that this old lady was best left alone. You could shoot at him out of the skylight as he ran for his car.'

We both turned and looked up at the rectangle of window in the roof above us. It looked old, but it opened easily enough, I remembered; I'd opened it to let air in, that first time that Magnie and I had come here. The officer looked from the window towards the top of the hill, where the red hire car had been left. 'You'd pepper him nicely.'

'No real damage, but enough pain to make him lose his way in the hills and go over the cliff. Joanie's dog followed a blood trail.'

'Hmmm,' the officer said, considering this. 'It's a good theory.'

'Maybe, even, he sat down for a bit, wi' the pain, then ran in panic when he saw blue flashing lights,' I continued, working my way through it. 'Because in the excitement of it all, you, the old lady, fell and broke your hip.' The mattress had been dragged sideways, as if she'd caught at it as she'd fallen. 'He didn't know it was an ambulance, of course, he just saw blue lights and ran in the dark, and that was why he went over the cliff. But that leaves the old lady with a dilemma. She can't walk to put the gun away, and the ambulance men are coming, and the law takes a dim view of people blasting off with shotguns, especially shotguns they don't have a licence for.'

'It fairly does,' the law agreed. 'Minimum twelve-month prison sentence.'

'And someone got three years, not so long ago. An older woman who hadn't given in her father's gun. She'd no intention of using it, just wanted to keep it. So what might happen to a woman who'd actually shot someone with an illegal gun?'

226

The officer shook his head, with an air of a man considering the black cap. 'The sherriff widna like it.'

'So you'd shove it either right under your bed, at the back, though your home help might find it there when she hoovers, or, safer, under your mattress.' I hadn't lifted that dragged-sideways mattress, just shoved it back into position, then pulled the fitted sheets around the corners. 'Just till the hospital lets you out again and you can hide it safely. After all, it's not likely the man you shot at is going to complain, is it?'

'No' if he was burgling your house.'

'In fact, nobody would have known if he'd not fallen from the hill and died in the Skro.' I turned to look at him. 'When Forensics arrives, you could maybe suggest they look in the bedroom for a shotgun.'

'I'll do that.' He nodded at the rhubarb poison bottle. 'And this an' all. Any more detecting ideas?'

'I think that'll do for one day,' I said.

I headed back to *Khalida* and sat in the cockpit, thinking. Edward and Eddie Ryland had found something among the dying laird's papers that had told them about Archie. Eddie Ryland had Luncarty organised anyway to collect the young peregrines from Sand, which was one piece of illegal work. Make it two; check that the last surviving Irvine at the Ladie, Archie's sister Tamar, had no evidence of who her brother really was. Luncarty'd been told to go to the Ladie and snoop among Tamar's papers. She'd heard him and got out of bed; he'd heard movement above him, scarpered, and she'd grabbed the shotgun and fired a charge after him.

I paused there, frowning. If I was right, if she'd had a gun, she'd kept it well hidden. Even if you'd lived in the wildest of places for a good long time, you wouldn't be toting an illegal gun obviously here in Shetland, and if you did, your gossipy home help, Loretta, would have told all her cronies about it. She'd certainly have retaliated when Tamar was telling DS Peterson about Harald's gun. I envisaged Tamar's bedroom from the point of view of hiding a rifle. The chest of drawers was a likely place, under a layer of clothes. No;

I'd looked for pyjamas, and all the clothes seemed undisturbed, not rumpled as they would have been if someone had grabbed a shotgun out from under them. Lower down was more likely, under the blankets in the bottom drawer. There'd be no reason for Loretta to be ferreting around in there. Tamar might have been able to put it back in its place before she called the ambulance; it wouldn't have been easy, given the pain she must have been in, but she'd been determined, Tamar. Pain or a prison sentence.

It hadn't been there when I'd hidden the tub. I bit my lip, thinking. She'd suggested that hiding place right away. But then – and then I had a sudden memory of Magnie leaving the house that Sunday morning. Only yesterday. He'd risen, and paused to pick up a long roll of newspaper, picked it up as if it was heavy, I remembered now. Tamar had asked me if I'd hide something, and I'd said no explosives or guns. *No,* Tamar had said, *I won't give you a gun to hide aboard.* She'd wrapped it in newspaper and put it under the bed ready for Magnie to take away, and now I'd better forget I'd even thought that, otherwise he'd be getting into trouble too. I hoped that with Tamar gone he'd have the sense to drop the thing overboard the next time he took his boat out.

But why did she have it there at all? I snorted out loud at the idea of Tamar being a nervous type. No, she'd had it because she had something valuable to protect. I remembered her scathing tone: *A Leonardo or a Ming vase that I'd picked up for pennies in Europe in the chaos after the war . . .* She'd said it again to Joanie o' Cole: *Do you see an undiscovered Rembrandt?* She'd been one to enjoy telling the truth in a way that made nobody believe her. Then she'd covered up quickly when I'd mentioned papers in her desk, and focused the conversation on that. She'd fired at Derek Luncarty because she wanted word to go back to whoever'd sent him that trying to rob her was too much bother. She'd been surprised, I thought, looking back, to find that the police knew about him, but not so surprised as to lose her presence of mind. It was Felicity who'd shown shock, knowing that someone employed by Edward Ryland was searching Tamar's house. How had Tamar reacted to that? I remembered her look of surprise, followed by relief. He'd been sent by the Rylands, after papers to do with that long-over affair. He wasn't looking for what she'd first thought he'd be after.

Then when Loretta had told us Luncarty was dead, the next day, that was when she'd reacted. She'd gone very quiet. I remembered the look on her face: thoughtful, angry. She hadn't looked guilty, and I was sure she hadn't felt guilty either. She reckoned he'd got his just desserts for breaking into her house, and if they'd turned out to be more severe than she'd intended, well, that wasn't her fault.

I was just washing up my mug when I heard a car engine. I looked out through *Khalida*'s window to see a Land Rover coming down the hill. It stopped at the police car. I saw Kayleigh lean out of the window and exchange a few words, then she came on down the road and right to the pier. I came out into my cockpit, and made a 'come aboard' gesture. 'Tea?'

She nodded. 'It's an awful shock, this.'

She looked as if it had been. Her face was pale under the weathered tan, her round cheeks deflated. Her hands gripped the mug as if she was cold. She raised her eyes directly to mine. 'Who did it, Cass? Who killed them both?'

I shook my head. 'I don't know.'

'Felicity, well, if that poison was in her tea, it coulda been any one of us at that table, or the Ryland men that came to speak. Her tea, or Tamar's.' She'd been thinking it out too. She drank a couple of gulps of her tea, then looked at me again, dark eyes clouded. 'You're the one who's had experience o' this. Why would someone kill Tamar? Why noo? We're put up wi' her tongue all these years.' She gave a short laugh. 'We're even a bit proud of her being that cantankerous. So it's no' that. No' personal. Is it the Rylands, then, and something to do with the old laird dying? That old story?'

'Tamar told me that any papers to do with Archie's birth, he had himself. She didn't actually say so, but it was pretty clear that any claim he wanted to make against the Rylands, it was up to him.'

She gave me a long look. 'And would papers count for more in court than an old woman's testimony?'

'I'd have thought so. A DNA test would count for even more.'

'Then there was no point in the Rylands killing Tamar to stop her talking.'

I shook my head. It seemed a sensible conclusion. 'But Felicity was wanting to open it all up. She was asking about her father's birth, and how come he was educated in Edinburgh.'

'So she coulda asked for a DNA test.'

'It wouldn't do her any good, though. I looked it all up. Archie could still put in a claim, but she couldn't.'

'She coulda made a fuss, though, especially with her having that newspaper. The Rylands wouldna a liked that kind o' publicity. So they mighta come and looked for any papers that might prove it.'

'Except that they couldn't find the papers to destroy,' I said. 'That seems pretty clear. They sent the Luncarty man who died in the Skro to burgle her house, but he didn't get anything. Tamar cleared him.'

'Oh?'

I explained my shotgun theory, without mentioning Magnie or Leonardos, and she gave a full, ringing laugh. 'Oh, yea, she would hae. I can joost see her, and good on her too. So that Rylands couldna get their hands on the papers they thought she had.'

'Felicity was stirring up about it,' I said. 'Archie was no' best pleased, I don't think, but if she was determined she coulda gone over his head. Blood from a generation down would be just as good for DNA.'

'So you think it was Felicity they meant to kill?'

'If it was them.' I shook my head. 'It just doesna feel right. Why would they go on and kill Tamar? She wasn't claiming anything. It didn't matter what knowledge she had, if she wasn't going to use it.'

'But she might have done, as revenge, if she'd thought they'd killed Felicity to stop her. That would be like Tamar.'

It was like her. 'So they had to kill her too. Maybe.'

'Ah, weel.' Kayleigh stretched her legs out and gave a long sigh.

230

'She was a character, right enough. There're no, many like her about now.' She gazed up at the house for a moment, then turned her head to me. 'Did she tell you she'd made up her mind about the croft?'

I shook my head.

'She phoned me, yesterday evening. She said she'd thought it over, and she'd phoned Geordie, and told him she wanted the croft made over to me. The house too. I don't ken what'll happen about that now, the house, I mean. Unless she's written that down somewhere as an alteration to her will, I don't know if I'll get that, but she told Geordie about the land. That's what matters.'

It also gave her a good reason both to keep Tamar living, and to kill her before she could change her mind again. I didn't say so. 'What will you do with it?'

Her eyes lit up. She leaned forward over her mug. 'A mixed croft. A real old-fashioned croft, like the one at Burland, open to visitors and schoolbairns, so they can see how life used to be lived here. We spoke about it, Tamar and I. It's to be called the Irvine Croft Trail. I'll have a couple o' Shetland kye, to milk by hand, and ponies, right traditional ponies that can do a day o' work, and I'll keep her herd o' coloured sheep going, and give demonstrations of dogs working, maybe even host the trials in a few years' time. Shetland hens and ducks too, and eggs for sale. It'll be work, but I'm no' afraid o' that.'

There was silence for a moment, then she turned her head away from me. 'It was Gary brought Bob over.'

I felt the breath knocked out of me. 'Gary?'

'I tackled him this morning, and he admitted it. Bob wasn't going to move here. He was to come and charm Tamar into leaving him the croft, then he'd sell to Gary.' There was a thread of pain running through her voice. 'A nasty piece of work. Both of them. I widna a thought my own brother would go behind my back like that either.'

'No,' I agreed, and we fell silent again, until she gave me a sideways glance, almost shy. 'I think I have you to thank. For the croft, I mean. Tamar admitted she was thinking o' Bob as her heir, but you said to her I wanted it enough to make it happen.'

I waved her thanks away, but I was glad it had worked out in the

231

best way, with the croft as compensation for dreams of a golden boy. She'd make it work, and find a better man too, I hoped. 'And the house, if you get that? Would you move in?'

'No' till I get started. I'll need to see what I can get by way o' grants. I can start planning now, and saving, and looking out for beasts. I could maybe get a grain o' money letting it.' She gave it a critical stare. 'But it might cost as much as I'd make, to get it up to standard for a let. Folk expect things.' She gave a look around the jetty. 'I'll need to do something about all these cats, too. I'll get a trap from the Cat Protection League. They'll soon find homes for the ketlings, and the adults can be homed or neutered and re-released.'

I was glad to hear it. Cat's little friend would be looked after. 'Can you make sure you get the ginger one, with a white front and white feet?'

Kayleigh nodded. 'I'll look out for her. You wouldn't be interested in the cottage? Live ashore for the winter?'

I shook my head. 'I'm going back to my ship.'

'Pity. Well, thanks to you for all you did for Tamar.' She turned away, paused, then turned back again, and gave me a straight look. 'And dinna feel you failed her. If we in the family couldna protect her, how could you have?' She nodded, then headed for her car, raising her hand for a final wave before she got in.

# Chapter Twenty-two

**ayre:** a low promontory, beach, sometimes a double beach between the shore and an island, as at St Ninian's isle [Old Norse, *eyrr*, a bank of gravel or sand]

I watched her drive up the gravel path, then turned my attention to my own departure. There was no point in lingering. Cat watched as I put on my jacket and bustled round taking the sail cover off, lifting the fenders, starting the engine, taking all but one of the shore lines off. I fed the ketling the last of Tamar's fish, then lifted her, wriggling, and put her back on land. Cat gave me a reproachful look. 'No,' I said to him. 'I'm sorry.' I reached over and hauled the gangplank in before the ketling could get back on to it. 'The Cat Protection league will find her a nice home, with a fire, and people who'll love her.'

I hauled the last rope in and put the engine into gear. *Khalida* began to slide backwards from the jetty just as the ketling prepared to jump. I saw her tense her back paws and launch herself into the air, across the gap, and knew she couldn't make it. It seemed to happen in slow motion; the ginger ball was in mid air as I was frantically putting the engine out of gear and pressing the stop button, and then, with a splash, she hit the water and went under. Cat was leaning over the side of the boat as if he was ready to go in too. I hauled him back with one hand, grabbed my bucket on lanyard with the other and leapt for the guard rail. She had gone down just there . . . she was struggling to the surface, little paws paddling frantically, but

233

she wouldn't last long. I dipped the bucket in and she panicked first, and tried to swim away from it, but on the second shot I managed to scoop her up and haul her aboard.

The fluffiness was gone. The little thing was a damp bundle of fur, smaller than my hand, sneezing water out and shivering. I set her on my fleece and wrapped the sleeves around her. Cat came up and began licking her, sneezing too at the salt taste. On the third lick, the ketling began to purr. 'You win,' I told him. 'But she's strictly your responsibility. You'll need to teach her to stay below at sea.'

I didn't dare think about what Captain Sigurd was going to say.

I set the engine going again, and putted out into the bay to the north of the Blade, then went forrard to put the mainsail up. I unrolled the jib, and was just tacking around to head for Brae when I heard the noise of another boat, a motorboat, roaring into Busta voe from the Røna, then cutting its engine abruptly to roll gently around the corner. It wasn't the aluminium workhorse I'd expected, but a sleek pleasure craft, gleaming white against the grey sea. I didn't recognise it, and couldn't see how many people were on board; one at the wheel and another head behind, but there could be more below. As I watched, the driver opened the throttle, and the purr became a roar. Two white plumes of water spurted from the bows. The motorboat came straight towards me.

It took an astonished second before I realised he was intending to ram me. I was a sitting duck under sail here, broadside on to him, and he was hurtling straight at me, bows aimed at the middle of *Khalida*'s hull. I had no chance of out-running him, and precious little chance of dodging him. I glanced swiftly at the shore. We were coming away from the pier, thirty metres away. My engine was still running. I could spin her around so that if he rammed us, *Khalida* might make it close enough to get me and the cats safely ashore. If I turned stern on to him as he approached, that might damage *Khalida* less than a hit amidships, but it would be best if he didn't hit us at all. My hand was on the engine gearstick. If I pulled my sails in as if I was making all speed to get away, and waited until the last minute then gunned the engine for an unexpected spurt forwards when it was too late for him to turn . . .

I hauled mainsheet and jib in then lifted Cat and the ketling from their corner and put them below. If there was a collison, I'd get them out of there. My heart was thumping, my throat tight, as I watched the approaching pointed bow between its two curves of water coming closer, closer. Now I could see that it was Edward Ryland at the helm, and Eddie standing beside him. They'd given up searching; they were out to destroy. I waited until the last moment I dared, with their engine roaring in my ears, then shoved my engine into forward gear. *Khalida* leapt forward and was flung further by their wash as they skimmed past, an inch from her stern. They bounced over the waves past us, heading straight over the Blade as if it wasn't there . . . My heart gave a leap of hope. They didn't know about the Blade, sticking out under the surface much further than you'd think from the visible promontory. We had a chance after all.

I heard Edward swearing, then the motorboat began to curve round in a large circle. Up on the hill, I saw a black–clad figure come out of the police car, and stand for a moment in binoculars pose. There was the distant crackle of a radio, and a shout, but Edward gave no signs of having heard it. The white motorboat paused for a moment, then jumped forward.

I was almost at the opposite shore now, just short of the rocks we'd christened the Hippopotami. They were barely breaking the surface at this state of tide, and only someone who knew where they were would see them. They would be my second line of defence. I let the jib go so that the sail was flapping, and loosened the mainsheet, dodging as the boom jerked up and down above my head, then eased her around behind them, doing my best to look like a boat in trouble. Dear God in Heaven, let this work. A sitting duck, a peewit trailing her wing to lure hunters from her nest. Both officers were out of the car now, with one of them running down to the pier.

Edward hadn't noticed them. He'd got his bows facing me again.

235

The engine roared, the two white plumes of water spurted. He came directly for me and hit the crooked part of the Blade at full speed with a most beautiful crunching sound of fibreglass on pebbles. The motorboat stopped dead. Eddie went flying over the windscreen and landed in the water with a splash like a whale jumping. The propeller threw up a spurt of stones which splurted in the water around them; the engine gave a horrible juddering noise and choked into silence.

I was trembling with relief, my heart thumping double time, my breathing shaky. I sank onto the cockpit seat, and closed my eyes for a moment, giving thanks. When I lifted one hand to haul the mainsheet in again, it was shaking as if I had the palsy. Jib next. I edged cautiously out from behind the Hippopotami and into the sound, still watching them. Eddie stood up in a wallow of water, swearing, and tried to push the motorboat off the Blade. It didn't shift, partly because he was trying to push it along the underwater portion instead of trying to get it sideways off. The two men shouted at each other, then Edward clambered overboard. He had a look at the terrain, then they both set their shoulders to the white bows and shoved, with absolutely no result.

I wanted to cheer. They were firmly stuck, and judging by the sound it had made, the engine wouldn't be starting again even if they did manage to get her off before a police boat got to them. I was almost in the middle of the sound when they spotted I was leaving them. Eddie waved frantically, and Edward shouted. I smiled sweetly at them and indicated the neon-striped car, and the two police officers watching their every move. 'They'll come and get you,' I called.

Both heads swivelled; both jaws dropped. It was a beautiful moment.

I turned *Khalida*'s nose towards Brae. There didn't seem any need to go back to Tamar's pier. Gavin knew where I'd be, when he wanted a statement, and I couldn't get the men off Papa Stour anyway, had I felt inclined to, which at the moment I didn't; my keel kept me offshore. If I felt duty-bound towards shipwrecked

236

mariners I'd send Magnie with the RIB. The wind was behind me now and *Khalida* lay flat in the water – a much more suitable point of sail for the ketling's first excursion. I glanced below and saw she was pressed hard against Cat, eyes wide and alarmed, and he was washing her in a reassuring way. Boats do this, he seemed to be saying. You'll get used to it. My fingers were still trembling. I nipped below to put the kettle on. A mug of white drinking chocolate would see me to rights.

I was just drinking it, hand on the tiller, and thinking about the Rylands' urgent determination to get whatever papers they thought I had, when my radio crackled. It was Magnie's voice: 'Yacht *Khalida*, yacht *Khalida*, channel 8.'

I reached for the handheld and re-tuned. 'Yacht *Khalida* here. Over.'

'Cass, are you okay? The police called me wi' some tale o' a motorboat trying to ram a yacht in the Sound o' Houbansetter. I'm to come and take them off, so they can arrest them.'

I couldn't help laughing. 'They missed me. The motorboat's stuck fast on the Blade with the two Rylands trying to shove it off.' My worse nature kicked in. 'Don't hurry about getting them. Being marooned for a start in wet claes will do them no harm.'

'Aye aye.'

'I'm on my way to Brae now.'

'Then I'll bide here to take your lines and hear the story before I head down.'

I'd glided only a hundred metres further when my phone rang. Gavin. 'Cass, are you okay?'

'Fine,' I assured him. 'Did the police on duty tell you all about it?'

'They thought you were a goner. James said you seemed to get stuck with your sails flapping right in their path, but luckily the motorboat got stuck on a sandbank between them and you.'

There was a slight stress on *luckily*. My conscience was clear about luring pirates trying to sink me onto a handy ayre, but an official report might look at it differently. I suppressed a Mae West-style 'Luck had nothing to do with it, dearie', and substituted, 'They obviously weren't familiar with the area. Everyone knows the Blade is there. It's on the charts too.'

'They phoned Magnie to see if he could go and get them. He's on his way – you'll probably see him soon.'

'There's no point in him coming now. It's an ebbing tide. He'll need to wait until the motorboat floats to tow it off. If it will float, of course. It hit the Blade at full speed, so it may be holed.'

'What about the two men? The Rylands, I'm thinking?'

'The Rylands,' I agreed. 'After the contents of Tamar's tub, I suppose. It's an island. They can't get away. Being marooned will do them good.'

'That must have been a very narrow shave. You sound light-headed.'

'It was scarily close,' I conceded.

'I'd need to speak to them. I want a look at your discoveries too – the men on duty told me all about them. Rhubarb poison, and a possible shotgun.' I could hear the smile in his voice. 'I can just see your Tamar letting fly at a burglar with a gun.' Then his voice sobered. 'But that made her responsible for his death.'

'Yes,' I agreed. 'She knew that.'

'Ah, that's my car. I'm just leaving Lerwick now. I'll meet you at Brae in half an hour?'

'See you there,' I agreed, and went back to brooding as we glided past the Burgastoo, past Busta House. There was too much hurry and worry about this for a chance of Felicity putting in a claim against a death nearly twenty years ago. I'd got something wrong somewhere, and I was beginning to have an inkling what. Magnie was the man I needed.

The rock wall of the marina was only a hundred metres away now. I turned my concentration to getting my sails put away and put-putting in. Since the Rylands would be talking to the police for a while, and no doubt in the course of that conversation Gavin would inform them that Tamar's tin was now in police custody, I berthed myself on my usual visitor's pontoon. Magnie reached over to take my shore ropes, and Cat came up from below, obviously recognising home.

'So,' Magnie said, 'how did it come about that they ended up on the Blade?'

'Oh,' I replied airily, 'folk that can't use a chart shouldn't be out on the water.'

Magnie gave me an appraising look. 'You're high wi' reaction. A narrow escape then.'

'The closest I've been to being sunk,' I agreed. 'They were out to ram me. Tea?'

'You tie the boat,' he said. 'I'll put the kettle on.'

By the time I'd got *Khalida* attached to my satisfaction, there were two mugs of tea and two chocolate biscuits lined up on the cockpit step. 'You're got a ketling,' Magnie commented, nodding to where Cat and the ketling were sitting together on the forward deck, looking around at the marina. From the slant of his whiskers, I could imagine Cat was conveying information about the best burn ends to chase eels.

'Cat likes her.'

'Another one to get through Customs.'

'I'll manage somehow.' I looked at the little ginger lump at Cat's side. 'She saved us. If it hadn't been for her jumping in after us, and needing to be rescued, I'd have been in the middle of Cole Deep when they came at us, with nowhere to run. We'd have been beyond all help by the time rescue came, even if I'd managed to get out a Mayday. I reckon that's earned her a place aboard.'

We sat down together in the cockpit. 'Now,' Magnie said, 'let's have the whole story.'

I explained, and Magnie chuckled at the thought of the city Eddie flying heels over head into the water. 'But why were they after you?'

'I think you maybe know,' I said.

Magnie gave me a blank look.

'You're heard that Tamar's dead?'

239

He nodded. 'Yea, I heard that this morning.'

'So it doesn't matter any more, old stories.' I looked out across the glinting water. 'I was trying to work out why they were so set on getting those papers. It didn't make sense. The old old laird died nearly twenty years ago, so it wasn't too late to claim a share of his estate, but even so it seemed a lot of panic for something that Felicity couldn't claim from.'

'The old old laird? This Edward's grandfather, you mean? What has he to do wi' it?'

'Nothing,' I said.

I let the word fall into the silence. That was my thought of this morning, remembering the way the motorboat had roared at me. There was too much violence for a small share of the inheritance; and then I'd remembered the age gap between Tamar and Archie. *Our tail-end Archie.* 'At least, I don't think so. It's the one who's dying now that matters. Edward's father.' I remembered Tamar's voice, and the softness in her eyes. *That high-couraged boy who thought the world was there for the taking.* Her venom when she'd spoken of Madam Monikie. *Until his mother taught him better.* 'Archie wasn't Tamar's brother at all, was he? He was her son.'

'Yea, yea,' Magnie said. 'Everybody knew that. Well, everybody o' my generation. I doubt the younger ones widna know. Yea, she had him to the Ryland boy when the pair o' them were just teenagers. He wanted to marry her, but his mother wouldn't hear o' it. Tamar's mother declared the baby as her own, and Tamar left for London.'

'And in Scotland there's no inheritance difference between legitimate and illegitimate children. Archie was this dying laird's oldest son. Tamar's Edward's son.' *Edward*, she'd said as she was dying. 'He and this Edward —' I jerked my shoulder in the direction of the Blade — 'are half-brothers, so they would get equal shares ... or maybe, even, Archie would get the whole estate, as the older brother, if it couldn't be divided. No wonder they were after any papers that might prove it. They searched Tamar's house, and found nothing, and then we interrupted them searching *Khalida*. They were

240

determined to get rid of the evidence, even if it meant sinking me in the process.' I paused to think about it. 'They must have known who Archie was. Sorting through old papers, Felicity said, when Tamar's Edward went into a nursing home. They found something, I bet, like a lawyer's letter about his school fees. That would have mentioned his name, likely. And they must have known about Tamar, because they sent that Luncarty to search her house.'

'But Tamar widna be stirring up trouble for her boy, not after so long,' Magnie said. His eyes danced. 'And I'd like to hear what that snooty wife o' Archie's wid ha said about finding out he was the illegitimate son of a crofter's daughter. My heavens, she'd die o' the shock o' it. No, Archie'd no' be wanting that to come out.'

'There'd be a bit of money to inherit.'

Magnie shook his head. 'Archie's no' short o' a bob or two. Na, na, he'd keep quiet and keep his reputation. Our Solicitor General go stirring up long dead scandal? Na, na.'

'But Felicity would have.' I was sure of it. 'Her magazine was in trouble and she wanted money. She could have used DNA to prove the connection. That gave them a motive for killing Felicity. She was the one rocking the boat.'

'Killing you,' Magnie said, 'if you'd gone down in Cole Deep.'

I nodded, and shuddered, thinking of my *Khalida* going down in a rush of turbulent water, Cat and the ketling and I being flung overboard, the cold, the struggle for breath, and the black waters closing.

'Aye, aye,' Magnie said, considering it. 'But did you have these papers?'

'I had something – an ice-cream tub Tamar gave me to keep safe. She said it was papers, though it feels heavier, more like a book. But she said . . .' I frowned, trying to remember. *Destroying it's the last thing she . . . they would want.* I repeated it slowly. 'Destroying it's the last thing she would want. *She.* I took it she meant Felicity, and the *they* was just to be less specific. So either the tin contains papers, the ones Felicity was after, and the they was just to be less specific, or . . .' I paused, trying to make sense of my thoughts. 'Or the tub contains something else entirely.' *A Leonardo or a Ming vase . . . a king's ransom of jewels or a lockerful of cocaine . . .* 'Something valuable.' I leaned forward into the cockpit, brain working. 'Suppose she was telling the truth when she said Archie had all the papers?'

'Truth's aye easiest,' Magnie agreed.

'And she didn't know before Felicity told her that the laird, her Edward, was dying. She didn't know the inheritance thing was going to come up.'

'They were both well on in years,' Magnie pointed out. 'It wouldna a been a surprise that he was dying.'

I thought for a moment about her expecting trouble at the laird's death, and shook my head. 'No. It's what you said. Archie wasn't going to rock that boat. Reveal the family scandal when he was as high up in his profession as he was, and with a gong in the offing to boot? No' he. No, it was Felicity meeting Eddie Ryland's father and seeing the resemblance to her brother that started her asking questions – and it really was an extraordinary resemblance. I can see why it startled her.'

Magnie nodded.

'So when Tamar woke in the night, the night she broke her hip, and there was a burglar, she thought he was after . . . something she knew she did have.' I remembered her dismissive glance around the room. *What was he after, the Chippendale?* 'Something she was hiding in plain sight, but that she thought someone had recognised, or heard about, and come to steal.' *A Leonardo or a Ming vase . . .*

Suddenly I remembered that lovely drawing of the horse above her mantelpiece. Suppose it was real, that heraldic charger with his arched neck, in his old-fashioned gold frame. Hadn't Leonardo done sketches of horses as designs for statue commissions? The Nazis had looted works of art from the Jews, everyone knew that. Suppose this was one of them, that somehow Tamar had acquired *in the chaos of Europe after World War II*. If it really was a Leonardo, then it would be worth stealing.

'She's never mentioned anything like that to me,' Magnie said.

'But she had a shotgun.' I flushed. 'I had this idea . . . I'm sorry, I

242

told the police about it, that she might have hidden it in her bed-room. Then I remembered that long roll of newspaper you took away on Sunday morning.'

'They'll find nothing in her bedroom,' Magnie said. His rare smile creased his face. 'Cole Deep, she said, for a gun that had killed someone, and that's where it went.' He turned his head as a car turned in above the boating club, and the gravel on the drive crunched. 'That'll be your man now. Maybe he'll have some answers for you.'

# Chapter Twenty-three

**gaet:** a footpath or a direction for a journey (Old Norse, *gata*, a road or path)

It was Gavin. I greeted him with suitable nonchalance under the eyes of Magnie and his police driver. 'Noo dan.'

'*Halo leat.*' His hand touched mine and withdrew. 'Tamar's solicitor's giving me her appointment, if Magnie would go and rescue those men from Papa Little and put them over to the officers at the Ladie.'

'You're not going to arrest them?'

'Driving a speedboat in a manner conducive to the public danger. The men who saw them do it can have that fun, if Magnie'll be the Rylands' transport into the arms of the law.'

He and Magnie greeted each other, and Gavin explained. Magnie roared off in our RIB. 'D'you want to come and see what was in your box?'

'Can I?'

'It might save you getting into trouble on your own here. Besides, they had a shot at killing you for it. I think that gives you the right to be curious.' He considered a moment. 'You can be there to inspect the box and testify that it's just as you gave it to me. If it gets sensitive, though, I'll have to ask you to leave.'

'Okay,' I agreed.

I shut *Khalida* up, and fastened the washboards with a padlock. The Rylands might be marooned now and in custody soon, but better safe than sorry. I climbed into the back of the police car (no doubt there would be rumours that I'd been arrested) and brooded in silence as we drove through Brae. I felt exhausted.

Voe. The Kames. Sandwater Lodge. By the time we'd reached Girlsta Loch I was beginning to revive. I leaned forward so that my chin was almost on Gavin's shoulder, my cheek a hand's width from his, and told him the latest developments: Tamar having made up her mind about the croft, and the story of Archie's birth.

'I wondered about that,' he said. 'I was going to talk to Magnie about it, the first chance I got. It struck me that Tamar was the age to be his mother. They did that in the Highlands too, a servant girl coming back pregnant, and the child being brought up as her brother or sister. It gave the Rylands a much better motive for silencing Felicity, if Archie was equal heir with Edward.'

'Tamar was keeping quiet, though.'

'Would she have stayed quiet after Felicity's murder?'

I remembered her sitting upright with the light of battle in her eyes. *Felicity was my kin, and she's been murdered. I'm not going to let the person responsible get away with it.* 'No. But Tamar thought it was to do with inheriting the croft – or at least, that's what she said. "I'm not letting it go to her murderer."'

Gavin shook his head. 'You described Felicity as a right city girl. None of the possible inheritors would see her as a threat.'

'That's true. But then –' I sat back in my seat again and considered that one. Maybe Tamar thought she'd been the intended victim after all, poisoned by someone who was after the croft, who was afraid that if she lived she'd assign it to someone else. That pointed to Joanie and Gary. She'd said they were the obvious heirs, from the Grazings Committee point of view. Harald was too young, so Loretta would have wanted her to live until he was older, and Tamar's final decision suggested she'd exonerated Kayleigh of causing Felicity's death. The croft motive exonerated the Rylands too. I remembered her amused tone as she'd spoken about them. She hadn't been worried about them.

'I had another idea,' I said, leaning forward again. 'She made a joke to Sergeant Peterson about there being nothing worth burglars

245

coming to steal. "A Leonardo or a Ming vase," she said, "that I picked up for pennies in Europe in the chaos after the war?" Well, I wouldn't know a Ming vase if I saw one, but there's this drawing on her bedroom wall, reddish chalk on old paper, of a horse. An old-fashioned charger, pawing the air. It doesn't look old, but it's in one of those heavy gold frames. Suppose that really was a Leonardo, hidden in plain sight? It would be like Tamar's sense of humour, to trail the idea in front of our noses like that. Didn't Leonardo draw horses? Suppose it was that she thought Luncarty was after? She fell, remember. She heard him in the house, and cleared him. She didn't get the chance to see he was rummaging among her papers; she only knew that when I told her.' I remembered her expression, that sly smile. 'She pretended she'd thought they were damp, and she was airing them.'

'A painting, no, a sketch, of a horse in her bedroom.'

'Above the mantelpiece. It's the only one in there.'

He made a note of it. 'I'll get Forensics to photograph it. A possible Leonardo sketch of a horse. That'll get our art expert excited.'

'Do you have an art expert?'

'We have experts for everything.' His mouth curved. 'Some of them are more like geeks. Shoe prints, matchers of car paint, you name it. Look, we're here.'

The solicitor's office turned out to be in the re-designed kirk at the top of Church Road. The police driver dropped us off in front of the modern glass entrance. The solicitor himself was called Mr Sayers, of Sayers, Mathieson and Clark. He was young and energetic, with dark, rumpled hair, glasses with thick black rims, and the wiry build of someone who ran for fun. Gavin produced the box, and I agreed that it was as I'd received it from Tamar, parcel tape untouched, and confirmed that I didn't know what was in it. Mr Sayers produced a silver-dagger paperknife worthy of the best Agatha Christie novels to cut round the taped lid and open it up.

There was a layer of folded newspaper first, then a letter with the solicitor's name on it underneath, and then more newspaper, crumpled. Mr Sayers picked up the letter, and left us wriggling with impatience while he slit it open – at least, I was wriggling inside. Gavin looked as calm as if he was on the first hour of a foredeck watch. There was a single sheet of paper inside; Mr Sayers drew it out and read it, brows drawing together. He shot a look at me, then read it through again. Then, with maddening slowness (I was beginning to wonder if he was normally a defence solicitor with a grudge against the police) he put the letter to one side and began to lift the scrumpled balls of newspaper. I caught a flash of white material: not papers or a book, as I'd thought, but a handkie wrapped round something. He exposed it: a palm-sized ball, nestling among the paper. I recognised it then: Tamar's brass egg that she'd taken to hospital in that same way, wrapped in a handkie. The solicitor lifted it out, spread the handkie and exposed it in all its garish splendour.

'Tamar's manicure set egg,' I said. 'It lived on her mantelpiece. I wondered where it had gone to.'

Mr Sayers made a throat-clearing noise, and read the letter. 'Dear Cass, Thank you for giving up your leave to take care of me. This egg went round the world with me, and I'd like to think of it continuing its travels with you. Tamar.'

I gave him a blank look, then lowered my eyes to the egg. It was totally unsuitable for living on board a ship, and far too gaudy for my workmanlike *Khalida*, but it was a kind thought of Tamar's, and I supposed it could be kept in its handkie in my washbag. 'But why would anyone be so keen to get hold of this?'

'May I?' Gavin reached forward and picked it up, turning it over, then unscrewed it, and let the little clippers and file fall out onto the handkie. 'Unusual. There's nothing new inside it, Cass, do you know?'

*Diamonds worth a king's ransom* . . . I laid the items out in a line, and shook my head. 'Not that I remember. I only had a brief look at it before – she showed me when she came out of hospital, as I was unpacking her stuff and putting it away.'

'It was important enough to her to take to hospital?'

'She said it had been given to her by someone she loved.' *Edward.*

Gavin picked up the egg again. 'It's well made. The little tools look as if they might work too.'

'She wouldn't have carried it round the world if they didn't.' I spread my hands. 'Well, I suppose – am I just to take it, then?'

The solicitor lifted the letter again, took up another paper to compare it with and laid them both down. 'This is certainly her handwriting, and it seems clear she wanted you to have it.'

'I don't get the hiding it like this, though.'

'Did she tell anyone she'd given you something to keep?' Gavin asked.

I shook my head. 'The other way round. I had to sneak the tin up to her, and the paper and parcel tape, and then sneak the tin out and down to *Khalida* while nobody was looking. It wasn't a red herring. She genuinely wanted it hidden.' I turned it over in my hands. 'I wonder if it might have been a present from Edward. Her Edward, the old laird, who's dying. Something that came from Monikie House, that the Rylands might have recognised.'

The solicitor was keeping his face impassive, but I thought I saw a flash of recognition at the name Ryland. Tamar had told him, I thought, that Archie was her son.

'Had Miss Irvine made a will?' Gavin asked.

The solicitor glanced at me, then decided that if Gavin allowed me to be there, I must be approved. 'Two. Most irregular, but there were unusual circumstances. I don't feel at liberty to disclose them.'

'At a guess,' Gavin said, 'one will allowing for her son Archie declaring himself as her son, and the other going along with the fiction that he was her younger brother.' The solicitor didn't comment, but I could see that Gavin had guessed right. 'When was it made?'

The solicitor consulted some sort of inner ethics and conceded reluctantly, 'After her accident. I went out to her at the Care Home. We got the wills signed there. She kept one and gave me the other.'

It made sense now. I remembered that first phone call, and Tamar saying, *'No, I'm not going to. I'm leaving the choice to you.'* Then she'd asked me, *'Have you made a will, Cass?'* She'd made the two wills and posted one to Archie, the one leaving him everything. He could produce it or not at her death.

Gavin was still speaking. 'Can you tell me, at least, what she had to leave?'

'Her main asset was the house at the Ladie. When I drew up an older will for her, oh, some ten years ago, she said she hadn't yet decided who to leave it to, so, as a temporary measure, she left it to her nephew, John Irvine.'

Joanie o' Cole. I wondered if he knew about the more recent wills, or if he thought that Tamar's death would have given him the croft.

'A moderate income from her wildlife books, which has always been left to Archie, outright, as a personal bequest.' He rustled his papers again. 'She telephoned me yesterday. She wanted the house to be left to her great-niece, Kayleigh, to go with the croft. She said she'd decided to re-assign it, as she was no longer able to work the land properly, and that she'd conveyed this decision to the Grazings Committee. I actually have the codicil drawn up, for her to sign at this appointment today. However, her intention was clear, and I hope the family will abide by it.' He didn't like it, you could see that. 'I'll do my best to persuade them.'

Good luck with that, I thought. Maybe Archie would weigh in on Kayleigh's behalf and call in the will which left him everything, then make it over to her. I hoped he would.

I looked at the brass egg again. 'It's the sort of Victorian thing you might find in an old house like Monikie.'

Gavin picked it up and looked at it again, frowning. 'Victorian Indian brassware, I suppose, or late eighteenth century, if you're lucky.' He picked it up, weighing it in his hand. 'It's heavy, that's a good sign with brass. Can I take a photo? I suppose we should let our expert look at it too.'

I shrugged, and made a 'be my guest' gesture. 'Hang on to the actual thing, if you like. There's no hurry for it to begin its travels again.'

Gavin nodded and rose. 'Thank you for your time, Mr Sayers. It's given me a few ideas to think about, anyway.'

We hand-shook our way out into the fresh air. Gavin made an apologetic face. 'Cass, I need to stay in town, but I'll get a driver to run you back to Brae.'

'Don't worry,' I said. 'I'm sure it's not a good use of police time. There are plenty of buses. I'll maybe see you later?'

'I'll do my best.' He touched my hand briefly and strode off in the direction of the police station.

We had several quiet days. I managed to get into Lerwick on Wednesday, taking the 18.40 bus from Brae back into town, and met Gavin for a meal at the Golden Coach, followed by a night together in his lodgings.

'All stalled,' he said, when I asked him about the case. 'Nobody in Skeld saw anything by way of someone adding poison to either Tamar's tea or Felicity's. Your guess about it being rhubarb poisoning was right. The poison spray was rhubarb, as the label said, but the last person to use it sensibly wore gloves, and that could have been a week ago or a month. If the poison that killed Tamar was in a capsule, and the pathologist thinks that likely, then any of the family could have substituted one at any time. They were all familiar enough with the household to know she took the capsules, and where she kept them. None of your visitors saw anyone touching the box. As for a syringe to extract the cod liver oil and put in the poison, well, easy enough to get one of these, between human use and animal.'

'But the capsule idea would rule the Rylands out, for Tamar's death anyway.'

He nodded. 'Probably, though as we said it was a reasonable guess that an old person might take some sort of supplement capsules. They were both down south when Luncarty was up here – I've had that checked up on.'

'And they hadn't linked Felicity with the Tamar of their family scandal then,' I pointed out.

'No, but he was looking for papers in the house, as well as collecting the birds from Harald, so they knew about Tamar.'

'True.'

Gavin sighed. 'But we can't make it them just because they tried to sink you. They did know all about Tamar and Archie, though. Your guesses were right there. Young Eddie went for the tight-lipped act, no comment without my lawyer – he's got the makings of a criminal, that one, and I hope the sheriff comes down hard on him for instigating the bird-smuggling. Edward was more forthcoming, in a "let's all be reasonable about this" man-to-man way. When they were sorting out the old laird's papers, they found old school bills which gave Archie's name, and a lawyer's letter which mentioned Tamar. They'd heard nothing about it before, so it was a severe shock to them to find that Edward wasn't his father's only son and heir, and an even worse one to find out Tamar was still alive and living at the Ladie. Archie was easy to trace, but since he'd never had any contact with the Ryland family, they reckoned he either didn't know or wanted to keep it unknown. Sending Luncarty after any papers Tamar might have was just insurance, as you might say. Otherwise, Edward assured me, they never meant to stir up any trouble about it. It was connecting Felicity up with the family, and knowing through London gossip that her magazine was in financial trouble, that got them really worried. There'd been rumours, he said, that she was as happy to be paid not to publish scandal as she was to publish it.'

'Blackmail.'

Gavin nodded. 'They didn't want her to have anything on them – hence the attempt to search your boat as well as the house. They both assured me, solo and chorus, that of course they hadn't attempted to ram you, they just wanted to scare you a bit so that you'd hand over anything Tamar had given you to keep.'

'I trust you're taking your own officers' word of how it looked from the shore.'

'Naturally. Don't worry, they'll be up before the sheriff soon, and we've definitely got Eddie for the birds – I don't think Edward knew anything about that. But –' he sighed. 'Much as I'd like to clear the case up that way, I don't think they're our murderers. So you pays your money and you takes your choice for the person who killed

Felicity and then Tamar. Joanie and Gary, for the croft. Kayleigh, ditto. Archie, to stop the secret of his birth coming out, except that he wasn't here for Felicity's death.'

'Unless the sweetener wasn't.'

Gavin shook his head. 'He didn't know she was coming here. He told me that, and I've no reason to disbelieve him. He only found out when Lachlan told him – hence the phone call with the row that you told me about. Why would he pre-poison her when he didn't know she was meddling with things he'd rather keep hidden? No, I think he's out of it, which I'm glad of. I hate these high-profile cases. The papers would have a field day with the arrest of the Solicitor General.'

'Loretta, for the croft too, for Harald. Except that she needed to keep Tamar living until he was old enough to take it on.'

'Land. People used to kill for it in the Highlands. Now, when a croft brings in so little for such a lot of work, I don't know if they still would.'

'It's not just the land, though,' I reminded him. 'It's the place, the heritage. "Wir folk are aye bidden here." Tamar was delaying over the re-assignment because she wanted the Irvine name to stay at the Ladie. That's why she sent for Bob. He was a far-out Kiwi cousin, but he was an Irvine.'

'We'll have to stand down the main investigation soon. I'm getting nowhere. Till Friday, the boss told me.'

I hated the look of defeat on his face.

252

# VII

## The finish line

The finish line is between the weather mark and another buoy, or a feature like the point of the pier. The first yacht to cross the line gets a gunshot, and line honours.

# Chapter Twenty-four

Saturday 30th August

LW 03.34 (0.5); HW 09.56 (1.7); LW 15.52 (0.5); HW 22.09 (1.8)

Sunrise 04.56, sunset 19.14; moonrise 19.38, moonset 08.22.

New Moon.

**banks gaet:** the *banks* are the cut-away piece of grass above a shore-line, which can be anything from a couple of metres to a steep cliff. The *banks gaet* is the path along the edge of the grass by the shore, or, figuratively, a tricky enterprise [Old Norse, *bakki*, edge and *gata*, road or path]

I was back to where I'd begun, the starting line. Magnie had his motorboat moored up at one end, with the flags ready to be run up the short mast on his cabin roof and the gun for the actual start; Gavin and I were at the other end of the line in the small RIB, with the hooter. The big RIB was waiting up by the windward mark, to show them where to go. We'd talked through the course on shore after the flapping-sails flurry of getting ready; now sixteen pairs of red sails jostled for position downwind of the start.

'Five, four . . .' Magnie counted on the intercom.

I joined him. 'Three, two, one . . .' I honked the hooter. The sound was less than impressive, so I followed it with a shout, 'Five-minute gun!' and tried to remember when any of us had last taken it to the garage to have its air pumped up again.

'A bit poor-amos,' Magnie commented in my ear.

'Run out of air?' Gavin asked.

'I've got one on board *Khalida*. We can go and get it once we've got this race under way.'

We did the four-minute hoot and shout, two minutes, one minute, then Magnie fired, and they were off, the keenest and best getting their boats' noses over the line within seconds of the gun, and the rest straggling behind. I waited for the last of them to make their way across, then called, 'Won't be a minute' across the starting line, thrust the throttle forward, wheeled the boat around, and headed for the marina.

It was Cat and the ketling that warned me. Instead of being asleep on my berth, as I'd left them, Cat was on the pontoon with the ketling beside him, both looking ruffled. Cat had his grumpy expression; the ketling's apricot tailtip was swishing, and her face looked as if she was growling in the direction of *Khalida*. I put the RIB out of gear and it stopped instantly.

'What's wrong?' Gavin said.

I nodded at the tell-tale ripples coming from *Khalida*'s stern. 'There's someone on board.' A surge of rage swept through me. I forgot about being cautious. I'd had enough of this. I jumped the RIB forward, leapt onto the pontoon, leaving Gavin to tether the RIB, and swung on board my boat. 'Who's there?'

I'd left the washboards open, to air the cabin. Someone, a dark shape, was moving about in the forrard cabin.

'Hey!' I said. 'Come out of there!'

There was a long pause, then the dark shape turned, and came forward into the light of the main cabin. I looked in disbelief at the blonde Lady Di hair, the blue eyes, the perfect lipstick. 'Loretta?'

'Cass.' She came forward as if she had every right to be ransacking my cabin, graceful as if she was inspecting a line of Girl Guides, and spoke to me from the foot of the steps. 'I was hoping to see you.'

I glared at her. 'You knew perfectly well I was out on the water. What were you looking for?'

She blushed delicately under her English-rose make-up. 'Well . . . it's a bit awkward.' She came up the steps and out into the cockpit.

256

'I noticed something missing from Tamar's house, and I thought, well, if you'd taken a fancy to it, after she died, and wanted to keep it, well, maybe the easiest thing to do was just to take it back, no questions asked.'

I hadn't thought it was possible for me to get any angrier. I could actually feel myself trembling with rage. 'You're accusing me of stealing from Tamar's house?'

She took a step backwards. 'Nothing like that. For all I know Tamar may have given it to you.'

'Given me *what*?' I thrust my hands into my pockets to suppress the impulse to grab her and shake her till her china-white teeth rattled.

She gave an unconvincing laugh. 'Nothing valuable. It was just that little brass manicure egg, that lived on her mantelpiece. Our Leeza was aye fascinated by it, and I thought she'd like it as a memory of Tamar. It's no' there now, so I thought maybe . . .' Then she raised her head, and looked straight into my eyes, and I felt a chill down my spine. Her eyes were cold and hard and hungry, although her voice continued in the most reasonable tone. 'After all, Leeza was a blood relative, and right close to Tamar, while you only knew her for a few days. So if you could just let me have the egg, now, and I'll give it to Leeza.'

Behind me, I heard Gavin speaking softly, asking for backup. The pieces of the puzzle dropped together at last . . . *this programme about the Romanovs . . . they used to gie each other Easter eggs . . . sold for sixteen million pounds . . .* I heard Tamar's voice: *Something I picked up in the chaos after the end of the war . . .* Whether it really was one, or whether her royalty mania had just tipped her over the edge, Loretta believed Tamar's manicure egg was Fabergé, one of the ill-fated Czar's presents to his wife. She'd gone up to look at it after we'd spoken, after she'd heard the radio programme; I remembered now, the hoover stopping, the silence from above. Tamar had been listening to the radio too, the evening before. She'd sent me up to fetch Loretta down before she could look at the egg too closely, and then she'd given it to me to hide. It had been a present from Edward, and she didn't want Loretta pawing it over.

There was a stir at my shoulder as Gavin came out of the motorboat behind me, and swung over into the cockpit. Loretta's mad eyes turned to him. 'She has no right to it, you know. Nor that Felicity either, for all her smarming in and talking of London, and trying to get Tamar to leave everything to her. Leeza was Tamar's favourite relative.'

I took a deep breath, and spoke in my calmest, most reasonable tone. 'I don't have it,' I said. 'Tamar gave me a tub to keep on board, the second night I was there, and the egg was inside it. When she died I gave the box to the police, since she obviously wanted it kept safe.'

Her eyes flared and fastened on Gavin. She drew her breath in with a hiss. 'The police have it?'

'Yes,' he said. 'If you come with me I'll let you see it. A car's just coming for us.' He stepped back over the rail, onto the pontoon, and held out his hand to help her over. 'Come with me.'

She jerked back from him. 'I don't believe you.' Her mouth drew back in a grimace, showing her incisors. 'She's taken it. She's hidden it somewhere on board.' She whirled away from us, and clattered down into my cabin again. Gavin caught my arm as I moved to go after her. 'Cass, don't. Don't try to tackle her.' He drew me towards him. 'Your boat's tough. Tougher than you.'

She was pulling the books out of the shelves now, throwing each down on the floor, and muttering to herself. Gavin's hand was insistent on my arm. 'You have knives down there, bottles, china, far too many weapons.'

I wanted to charge in there and grab her. Gavin's voice soothed in my ear. 'Help's on its way. You're safe, and Cat's safe.'

Reluctantly, I took a step backwards. Gavin's hand slid up to my shoulder, and gripped it. 'I'll go down and stop her.'

A surge of fear filled me. I turned away from the noise, the destruction, and put both hands on his chest. 'No. *No*. We'll both wait for your backup.' I swung off my boat onto the pontoon and held my hand out to him. He looked down at me and smiled, a tender, gentle smile I'd never seen before.

'Cass, *mo chridhe*, I'm trained for this. I may have to help her look if she won't come out, but I won't let her wreck your boat. Trust me. You get back to your sailors.'

*Trust me.* I nodded. Turning away felt the hardest thing I'd ever done, as if the very air was a force I had to push against to swing myself over the guard rail. My legs felt stiff. I could hear his voice behind me as I walked the few steps to the end of the pontoon, matter-of-fact, soothing. The crashes stopped. I crouched down beside Cat, legs tense, ready to spring up again, and waited. Magnie's voice crackled at my chest: 'Cass, if you canna find it, never bother.'

I took a deep breath. 'All fine out there, no capsizes?'

'No' yet.' He'd picked up on the tension in my voice. 'Are you okay?'

'Trouble. Can you send the big RIB in?'

John's voice answered. 'On my way.' I heard the engine roar from the other side of the rocky marina wall, and listened to the soothing voice from my boat, and the engine getting closer. *Knives, bottles, china, far too many weapons.* My throat was dry and my chest hurt. I clenched my hands hard on each other, and waited. Then there was a crunch of gravel from above the boating club, and I looked up to see the neon and white of a police car rolling down. I leapt up and waved both arms, then ran along the pontoon to let them in. The car made it to the marina gate just as the big RIB came through the marina entrance, and stopped in a swirl of water beside the pontoon. John and Neil leapt out of it. I held up one hand in a 'wait' gesture, and flung the gate open to let the uniformed officers in. 'They're in *Khalida*, the yacht at the end of the pontoon.'

I thought they'd go straight for her, but they halted in the gateway. The leader was an older man I hadn't seen before. 'Now, it's Cass, isn't it?' His voice was Scottish, smooth and reassuring. 'What's going on here?'

'Gavin's in there,' I said. I took a deep breath and kept my voice level. 'DI Macrae. He's with Loretta Williamson. She's trying to search the boat. I think she's gone mad. He's got her soothed down now, but I don't know how long she'll stay that way.'

He turned slightly away from me to speak into his intercom.

'We're at the marina now. DI Macrae's dealing with a suspect. We might need a doctor, can you see if one's available?' He nodded down at the big RIB. 'That part of your team?'

I nodded.

'Okay, we can let them get back to your racing. You too. We'll deal with it.' He waved to John and made an 'off you go' gesture. A moment, then the big RIB turned around and went out of the marina. 'The small RIB right beside the yacht, is that yours?'

'Yes.' I wanted to jump with impatience. Why didn't they just get in there and get Gavin out? He read my thought and gave a half-smile.

'It's when people rush in that tragedies happen. Now, we're going to go down quietly and see how your man's doing. Is seeing you likely to set her off again?'

'It might,' I admitted. 'She thinks I stole something from Tamar's house.'

'You keep well out of sight then. If you won't go back to your dinghies, go onto one of the other boats.'

I knew about taking orders from the man in charge. I went quietly aboard the first big motorboat on the pontoon, and sat out of sight in its wheelhouse, leaving the door open so that I could hear. The officers went past me, and there was a long pause while they arranged themselves into a rectangle around *Khalida*. Silence, except for the waves lapping against the motorboat's stern, and the distant throb of the RIB's engine. My radio crackled. Magnie's voice came out at me. 'Cass, are you okay?'

'Yes. I'll speak soon. Out for now.'

Nobody was moving at the end of the pontoon. The men just stood there. I clenched my hands so hard that I felt my nails dig into my palm. *You have knives down there.* My chest hurt. *Lord, let him be safe.*

Then, at last, there was movement. I saw *Khalida* rock in the water. Gavin came up the steps, head bent courteously, lips moving, although I couldn't hear what he was saying. He extended his hand into the cabin. The leader of the officers made a back-away gesture.

Silently, the others moved back along the pontoon arm to the central walkway, and further back, along an opposite arm, to the cover of a navy fishing boat.

I waited. I could scarcely breathe, and my heart was thudding. It seemed an eternity before Loretta's blonde head came up into the cockpit. Gavin stepped back and gestured her forwards, then he swung over *Khalida*'s rail and held his hand out again, for all the world as if he was a Highland gentleman escorting his lady to her carriage after a ball. He helped her over the rail, and offered his arm on the pontoon.

He'd seen his backup. A little nod kept them out of sight as he brought Loretta forwards, along the central walkway. It was only when he had her safely into the wire cage at the gate that they came swiftly forward, surrounding her. I heard a metallic click, and then she began to scream and struggle with them. I gritted my teeth and turned my head away until a closed car door cut off the shouting.

Gavin straightened up and looked around. The older man indicated the motorboat I was hiding in, and he nodded and came down the pontoon. I ran out from the boat and flung myself into his arms, closing my own jealously around him, feeling the warm muscles move under his shirt. I couldn't speak. I just wanted to hold him, to be sure he was safe. His hand came up to stroke my hair, and he kissed my cheek, then put me from him. 'I'll have to go with them. Interviews. Statements.' His hand slid to my chin, and tilted it up. 'Hey, hey. Dealing with disturbed people's all in a day's work for Superplod.'

'A disturbed murderer.'

His smile smoothed to gravity. He nodded. 'But now we know who, and why. I'll come back as soon as I can.'

I nodded, and let go of him.

'So,' I said, 'it was the egg. Loretta heard the radio programme about the Romanovs, and thought it was Fabergé. And Tamar heard it too, and when Loretta went upstairs and it all went quiet she knew she was looking at it, and didn't want her to. It was a present from her Edward, that she'd loved, and she wasn't having Loretta tinkering

261

with it. She gave it to me to keep safe.' I thought about the way older Shetland folk left one door unlocked at night, just in case, and the note she'd put with the egg. 'To keep it travelling, if she died before I gave it back.'

Gavin nodded. 'Loretta couldn't steal it, because Tamar would have noticed, and she was worried that Felicity might get it, smarming round Tamar with her London ways and her talk of jewellery. She thought Tamar didn't know what it was. She said she'd talked about the Romanov programme in front of her, and Tamar didn't react at all. So she decided the only way she'd get it was by killing Tamar. Only Felicity made a fuss about her tea being too strong, and she had to try again.'

It was evening, dark outside, with the wind blowing cold around the marina. *Khalida*'s lantern swung on its hook, sending shadows and points of light dancing around the wooden cabin. Gavin looked up from his plate of special rice. 'I've been wondering how to break it to you.'

I gave him a questioning look.

He laid his fork down and reached in his sporran for the egg, still wrapped in its handkerchief. He put it on the table between us, and slid the cotton away to reveal the gold and stones.

'Your Leonardo horse was just a red herring. It is an actual drawing, but a copy of a Leonardo, well done, but not the real thing. An art student's practice, signed on the back. This is what Tamar was protecting, what she thought the burglar was after.'

I looked at the brass egg shining in the lamplight. 'This?'

Gavin took a deep breath. 'It is Fabergé. The real, genuine article. Remember I said we'd get it valued? I sent photos to one of our police experts on antiques, and he came back practically incoherent with excitement. He'd need to see the actual thing, of course, but from the photos I sent him he's pretty sure. It's not just Fabergé, it's one of the Imperial eggs. Fifty were made, and seven of those are still missing. This one's called the Necessaire Egg. It was given by Alexander III to his wife – that's the parents of the Czar who died in the Revolution – and sold by Stalin to a London jeweller, who sold it on to "A Stranger" for £1,250. It's never been seen since. There wasn't even a photo of it till one turned up a year ago.'

A present from Edward. His parents wouldn't let him marry her, but he wanted her to know, always, that he'd loved her. 'It was travelling round the world with Tamar. But –' I waved my hands helplessly, searching for the words.

'I listened to the programme. Tamar kept it in her bedroom, didn't she?'

I nodded. 'On the mantelpiece. It wasn't in public view, it was where only she would see it.'

'And Loretta. Her home help. The programme gave the description they had, and Loretta reckoned it sounded just like Tamar's one. When she looked at it the day Tamar came back from hospital she was sure, and she'd just have waited till Tamar died to take it, and nobody any the wiser, but then she saw Felicity smarming up to her, and talking about jewellery, and she was afraid Tamar might give it to her. Her granddaughter.'

'Town mouse and country mouse,' I murmured.

Gavin dug out a piece of paper and read from it. 'Commissioned for Easter 1889. A fine gold egg, richly set with diamonds, cabochon rubies, emeralds, a large coloured diamond at top, and a cabochon sapphire at point. The interior is designed as an Etui with thirteen diamond-set implements.'

We looked at it together, gleaming in the candlelight against the white cotton handkie. 'I thought it was brass,' I said. 'And what's cabochon?'

'Those oval red stones.'

'They're rubies?'

Gavin unscrewed it, and tipped the little implements into his palm. 'Eleven, twelve, thirteen. She managed not to lose any.'

'Knowing they were set with diamonds likely focuses your attention.'

Gavin put the implements back and looked across at me. 'I found out on Thursday, but I wasn't sure if I should tell you. Tamar didn't want you to know.'

'It's like her sense of humour.' I could hear her witch's cackle. 'She teased me about having a simple life, not much money and no possessions. So she engineered it that I'd be sailing round all unawares with a Fabergé egg worth goodness knows what in my spongebag.'

'About thirty million.' I gaped at him. He turned it over with one finger, and shook his head. 'Too many zeroes for me to compute.'

'Too many for me too.'

'Christie's, Sotheby's, any of them will sell it for you. My expert says that not knowing the full pedigree doesn't matter. The workmanship is what proves it a Fabergé. His thirty million was just a guess. It's unique, and there's no chance of another one coming up for sale – they're mostly in museums.'

I shook my head. 'Tamar didn't give it to me to sell. She wanted it to keep on travelling.' I leaned forward and wrapped it up again. 'If your expert's police, will he keep quiet about it?'

Gavin quoted my own words back at me. 'You're seriously planning to sail round with a Fabergé egg worth goodness knows what wrapped in a handkerchief in your spongebag?'

'So long as nobody knows I've got it, I'll do what Tamar wanted.' I set my jaw stubbornly. 'Besides –' I swept a hand round the boat. 'It'll be hidden in plain sight, just like it was on Tamar's mantelpiece. Who'd ever think it would be the real thing, here?'

Gavin began to laugh. He stretched his hand out and curled it round mine. 'Cass, I do love you.'

I returned the pressure of his fingers, then rose, took the egg to the heads and stowed it in my washbag, sitting ready beside my packed kitbag for going back to Norway tomorrow. 'Then that's settled. If anyone asks, it's Victorian brass, and I was given it by an old lady I was fond of.' I looked straight at him. 'I was, you know. She was . . .' I stopped, and swallowed. 'We won't see her like again.'

I took a deep breath, sat back down beside Gavin, and slid my hand into his. 'Mid October till we meet again. Six weeks.'

'Before I went off on that last course, I had a long chat with my boss.'

'And?'

'I'm coming out of the serious crimes team. I won't be demoted, I'll keep my DI rank, and I can still use my detective skills. There's no' a vacancy in Inverness, but he said that in about three months the DI post in Shetland would be coming up.'

'Here?' I felt the breath had been taken away from me.

'Aye. If I'd be interested.'

My brain suddenly felt it was ticking over at double speed. He'd be here, not just for individual cases, but all the time. If ever we were being offered a chance together, this was it, now.

'I have time to think about it.' His voice turned non-committal, which I knew meant that this mattered. 'I'll still be with the special crimes squad meantime, and I could wait till a vacancy in Inverness came up. But I'd take Shetland, Cass, if you'd be part of that . . . if you'd consider being with me here. We could set up house together. I'd have to live ashore . . . do you think you could get used to that?'

I looked at Tamar's house, and thought of the view over the sound, and the otters on the shoreline, and the jetty, though I wouldn't want to leave *Khalida* there if I wasn't about. I thought of us waking together as the first sun came in the upstairs windows, and looking out at the stars before we went to sleep. 'Yes,' I said, slowly. 'Yes, I think I could, if it was the right house. But would you need to live in Lerwick?'

'No. Out in the country would do me fine. Half an hour to an hour's drive would be a treat after the two hours it takes to get home to the loch.' He paused, then asked, 'You're sure?'

'I'm sure,' I said.

# Acknowledgements

Writing a book is just the first part of it. Thank you, first and always, to my husband, Philip, for his constant support and encouragment. Thank you, my fellow Westside Writers, for your monthly encouragement, in person and currently on Zoom – ah, when will there be shared cake again? Thank you to Bertha and Raymond Brown, for letting me commit imaginary murder and mayhem on your land, moor Cass up at your salmon pier (please don't try it, fellow sailors) and refurbish the deserted crofthouse at the Ladie. Thank you, Ina Henry and John Tait, for naming the geo round the corner from Houbansetter. Thank you, Brydon Thomason of Shetland Nature for a wonderful afternoon watching otters, and Robert Tonkinson, for telling me about peregrines and the illegal bird trade during a panto rehearsal when we were both off-stage. Thank you to the BBC, for a fascinating programme on the jewels of the Romanovs broadcast just as I was driving home from a sailing session with bairns at Brae. There really is a missing Nécessaire egg, sold to A Stranger in the UK, and looking just as it's described in the book. Actually, I'd originally described it using the inventory Gavin quotes and a photo of an existing Nécessaire egg I found on the internet – then the only known photo of the actual egg turned up, and I had to redo my description. These coincidences happen regularly to authors.

After the book is written, there are many people who make it happen. Thank you to Teresa, my wonderful agent who took me on for my first detective story, and whose support and comments on each new MS are always invaluable. Thank you to Celine Kelly, my new copy editor, who homed in unerringly on every place where I hadn't thought my plot through properly; thank you to Toby Jones, my new editor at Headline, for his encouragement and welcome.

Finally, thank you to all you readers who write, post or message to tell me that you're enjoying Cass's adventures. Your enthusiasm keeps me going on bleak days when ideas seem to have migrated elsewhere; your praise keeps me at my desk when the sun outside is calling me to my boat at the marina – well, usually, unless it's too good a day to miss. Thank you!

# A note on Shetlan

Shetland has its own very distinctive language, *Shetlan* or *Shetlandic*, which derives from old Norse and old Scots. In *Death on a Longship*, Magnie's first words to Cass are:

'Cass, well, for the love of mercy. Norroway, at this season? Yea, yea, we'll find you a berth. Where are you?'

Written in west-side Shetlan (each district is slightly different), it would have looked like this:

'Cass, weel, fir da love o mercy. Norroway, at dis saeson? Yea, yea, we'll fin dee a bert. Quaur is du?'

*Th* becomes a *d* sound in *dis* (this), *da* (the), *dee* and *du* (originally thee and thou, now you), *wh* becomes *qu* (*quaur*, where), the vowel sounds are altered (well to *weel*, season to *saeson*, find *to fin*), the verbs are slightly different (quaur <u>is</u> du?) and the whole looks unintelligible to most folk from outwith Shetland, and *twartree* (a few) within it too.

So, rather than writing in the way my characters would speak, I've tried to catch the rhythm and some of the distinctive usages of Shetlan while keeping it intelligible to *soothmoothers*, or people who've come in by boat through the South Mouth of Bressay Sound into Lerwick, and by extension, anyone living south of Fair Isle.

There are also many Shetlan words that my characters would naturally use, and here, to help you, are *some o' dem*. No Shetland person would ever use the Scots *wee*; to them, something small would be *peerie*, or, if it was very small, *peerie mootie*. They'd *caa* sheep in a *park*, that is, herd them up in a field – *moorit* sheep, coloured black, brown, fawn. They'd take a *skiff* (a small rowing boat) out along the *banks* (cliffs) or on the *voe* (sea inlet), with the *tirricks* (Arctic terns) crying above them, and the *selkies* (seals) watching. Hungry folk are *black fanted* (because they've forgotten their *faerdie maet*, the snack that would have kept them going) and upset folk *greet* (cry). An older housewife would have her *makkin* (knitting) *belt* buckled around her waist, and her *reestit* (smoke-dried) *mutton* hanging above the Rayburn. And finally . . . my favourite Shetland verb, which I didn't manage to work in this novel, though the related noun maybe puzzled you on the first reading, but which is too good not to share: *to kettle*. As in: *Wir cat's just kettled. Four ketlings, twa strippet and twa black and quite.* I'll leave you to work that one out on your own . . . or, of course, you could consult Joanie Graham's *Shetland Dictionary*, if your local bookshop hasn't *joost selt* their last copy *dastreen*.

Diminutives like Magnie (Magnus), Gibbie (Gilbert) and Ertie (Arthur) may also seem strange to non-Shetland ears. In a traditional country family (I can't speak for *toonie* Lerwick habits) the oldest son would often be called after his father or grandfather, and be distinguished from that father and grandfather and probably a cousin or two as well, by his own version of their shared name. Or, of course, by a *Peerie* in front of it, which would stick for life, like the *eart kyent* (well-known) guitarist Peerie Willie Johnson, who reached his eightieth birthday. There was also a patronymic system, which meant that a Peter's four sons, Peter, Andrew, John and Matthew, would all have the surname Peterson, and so would his son Peter's children. Andrew's children, however, would have the surname Anderson, John's would be Johnson, and Matthew's would be Matthewson. The Scots ministers stamped this out in the nineteenth century, but in one district you can have a lot of *folk* with the same surname, and so they're distinguished by their house name: *Magnie o' Strom, Peter o' da Knowe.*

# Glossary

For those who like to look up unfamiliar words as they go, here's a glossary of Scots and Shetlan words.

**500:** a popular card game in Shetland, a cross between bridge and whist.
**aa:** all
**aabody:** everybody
**aawye:** everywhere
**ahint:** behind
**ain:** own
**all-over jumper:** a jumper which has stripes of Fair Isle pattern alternated with bands of plain.
**amang:** among
**an aa:** as well
**anyroad:** anyway
**apportionment:** not a Shetland word, but perhaps an unfamiliar term. Each crofter is entitled to graze a number of sheep on the shared rough hill ground.
**ashet:** large serving dish
**auld:** old
**aye:** always
**bairn:** child
**ball (verb):** throw out
**banks:** sea cliffs, or peatbanks, the slice of moor where peats are cast

**bannock:** flat triangular scone
**birl, birling:** paired spinning round in a dance
**blinkie:** torch
**blootered:** very drunk
**blyde:** pleased
**boanie:** pretty, good looking
**breeks:** trousers
**brigstanes:** flagged stones at the door of a crofthouse
**bruck:** rubbish
**caa:** round up
**canna:** can't
**clarted:** thickly covered
**cludgie:** toilet
**cowp:** capsize
**cratur:** creature
**crofthouse:** the long, low traditional house set in its own land
**croog:** to huddle down, sheltering
**daander:** to travel uncertainly or in a leisurely fashion
**darrow:** a hand fishing line
**dastreen:** yesterday evening
**de-crofted:** land that has been taken out of agricultural use, e.g. for a house site
**dee:** you; *du* is also you, depending on the grammar of the sentence – they're equivalent to thee and thou. Like French, you would only use dee or du to one friend; several people, or an adult if you're a younger person, would be you.
**denner:** midday meal
**didna:** didn't
**dinna:** don't
**dip dee doon:** sit yourself down
**dis:** this
**doesna:** doesn't
**doon:** down
**drewie lines:** a type of seaweed made of long strands
**duke:** duck

**dukey-hole:** pond for ducks

**du kens:** you know

**dyck, dyke:** a wall, generally drystane, i.e. built without cement

**eart:** direction, *the eart o' wind*

**ee now:** right now

**eela:** fishing, generally these days a competition

**everywye:** everywhere

**faersome:** frightening

**faither, usually faider:** father

**fancy:** a sweet cake or biscuit

**fanted:** hungry, often *black fanted*, absolutely starving

**fjaarmin:** making up to someone to get something out of them

**folk:** people

**frae:** from

**freends:** relatives

**gansey:** a knitted jumper

**gant:** to yawn

**geen:** gone

**geo:** a cleft going into a sea-cliff

**gluff:** fright

**greff:** the area in front of a peat bank

**gret:** cried

**guid:** good

**guid kens:** God knows

**hadna:** hadn't

**hae:** have

**harled:** exterior plaster using small stones

**heid:** head

**hoosie:** little house, usually for bairns

**howk:** to search among: I *howked* ida box o' auld claes.

**isna:** isn't

**kale-casting:** a children's Halloween prank, where kale (cabbage) is taken from a householder's garden and thrown in their door

**keek:** peep at

**ken, kent:** know, knew

**ketling:** kitten

**kirk:** church

**kirkyard:** graveyard

**kishie:** wicker basket carried on the back, supported by a *kishie baand* around the forehead

**knowe:** hillock

**lem:** china

**Lerook:** Lerwick

**likit:** liked

**lintie:** skylark

**lipper:** a cheeky or harum-scarum child, generally affectionate

**mad:** annoyed

**mair:** more

**makkin belt:** a knitting belt with a padded oval, perforated for holding the 'wires' or knitting needles

**mam:** mum

**mareel:** sea phosphorescence, caused by plankton, which makes every wave break in a curl of gold sparks

**meids:** shore features to line up against each other to pinpoint a spot on the water

**midder:** mother

**mind:** remember

**moorit:** coloured brown or black, usually used of sheep

**mooritoog:** earwig

**muckle:** big – as in Muckle Roe, the big red island. Vikings were very literal in their names, and almost all Shetland names come from the Norse.

**muckle biscuit:** large water biscuit, for putting cheese on

**myrd:** a good number and variety – a *myrd* o' peerie things

**na:** no, or more emphatically, *nall*

**needna:** needn't

**Norroway:** the old Shetland pronunciation of Norway

**o':** of

**oot:** out

**overly:** over the top, exaggerated

**ower:** over

**park:** fenced field

**peat:** brick-like lump of dried peat earth, used as fuel

**peerie:** small

**peerie biscuit:** small sweet biscuit

**Peeriebreeks:** affectionate name for a small thing, person or animal

**piltick:** a sea fish common in Shetland waters

**pinnie:** apron

**postie:** postman

**quen:** when

**redding up:** tidying

**redd up kin:** get in touch with family – for example, a five-generations New Zealander might come to meet Shetland cousins still staying in the house his or her forebears had left

**reestit mutton:** wind-dried shanks of mutton

**riggit:** dressed, sometimes with the sense dressed up

**roadymen:** men working on the roads

**rönnie:** a heap of stones

**roog:** a pile of peats

**rummle:** untidy scattering

**Santy:** Santa Claus

**sark:** man's shirt

**scaddiman's heids:** sea urchins

**scattald:** common grazing land

**scoit:** to look around

**scuppered:** put paid to, done for

**selkie:** seal, or seal person who came ashore at night, cast his/her skin and became human

**Setturday:** Saturday

**shalder:** oystercatcher

**sheeksing:** chatting

**sho:** she

**shoulda:** should have, usually said shoulda

**shouldna:** shouldn't have

**SIBC:** Shetland Islands Broadcasting Company, the independent radio station

**skafe:** squint

**skerry:** a rock in the sea

**smoorikins:** kisses

**snicked:** move a switch that makes a clicking noise

**snyirked:** made a squeaking or rattling noise

**solan:** gannet

**somewye:** somewhere

**sooking up:** sucking up

**soothified:** behaving like someone from outwith Shetland

**spew:** be sick

**spewings:** piles of sick

**splatched:** walked in a splashy way with wet feet, or in water

**steekit mist:** thick mist

**sun-gaits:** with the sun – it's bad luck to go against the sun, particularly walking around a church

**swack:** smart, fine

**swee:** to sting (of injury)

**tak:** take

**tatties:** potatoes

**tay:** tea, or meal eaten in the evening

**tink:** think

**tirricks:** Arctic terns

**trows:** trolls

**tulley:** pocket knife

**tushker:** L-shaped spade for cutting peat

**twa:** two

**twartree:** a small number, several

**unken:** unknown

**vee-lined:** lined with wood planking

**vexed:** sorry or sympathetic – 'I was that vexed to hear that.'

**voe:** sea inlet

**voehead:** the landwards end of a sea inlet

**waander:** wander

**waar:** seaweed
**wasna:** wasn't
**whatna:** what
**wha's:** who is
**whit:** what
**whitteret:** weasel
**wi:** with
**wife:** woman, not necessarily married
**wir:** we've – in Shetlan grammar, we are is sometimes we have
**wir:** our
**wouldna:** would not
**yaird:** enclosed area around or near the crofthouse
**yoal:** a traditional clinker-built six-oared rowing boat